THE CURSE

He smiled. Desmond Mershan *smiled!* And oh, what a smile. It was one of those feline smiles to turn a woman's knees weak. Smug, he unbuckled his pants.

She gulped. "Can you not push the leg up?"

"It'd be awkward."

"Not as awkward as you dropping your bloody breeks!"

She strangled when he did precisely that. The man was perfect—everywhere. Well, maybe not his toes—men rarely had pretty toes—but she barely paid them interest as the rest of him made up for standard-issue male feet. And wow, nothing typical in the underwear department. No sexless Jockey whites women abhor, but black silk. Black silk covering a blatant erection!

No, Sir, she won't catalog the perfection there, the devil on her shoulder chortled.

Her vision jerked up, colliding with his feline eyes.

Then it hit her. He had green eyes. *Green* eyes. No wonder her lads had dropped him into her bed.

Och, she ...

The Invasion of Falgannon Isle

DEBORAH MACGILLIVRAY

LOVE SPELL NEW YORK CITY

LOVE SPELL®

December 2006

Published by

Dorchester Publishing Co., Inc.
200 Madison Avenue
New York, NY 10016

ISBN 0-505-52691-3

Printed in the United States of America.

Visit us on the web at www.dorchesterpub.com.

For:

Dawn Thompson & Mizz Fuzz

Monika Wolmarans & Ballou

Carol Ann Applegate, Kelly & Brandy

Leanne Burroughs & Tigger

Sandra Heath, Ollie & Jazz

Robin D. Owens, Samba & Fam kitties on pods

and last but never least

The Cat Foutchie

and Sandi.

The Invasion of Falgannon Isle

Chapter 1

Falgannon Isle, Hebrides of Scotland, present day

"So much is riding on this venture." B.A. Montgomerie spoke her concern to the empty room.

She blinked, her eyes strained from staring for hours at the Web site for *Isle of Love.co.uk*. Not satisfied with the results, she sat tinkering with the new homepage. She needed glasses. Another entry on her endless to-do list. Like most of those items, it'd have to wait until her next trip to the mainland. She shouldn't keep pushing; she'd end up with a headache. Only, she so wanted the Web site perfect—the future of Falgannon rode on its success. Changing the html to narrow the width of the gold border, she stared at the results.

> *Ladies, tired of the stress of big city living? Fed up with men who only want one-night stands and leave you with "the fuzzy end of the lollipop and a tube of toothpaste all squished out?" Hate traffic jams, telemarketers calling at 8:00 A.M. and long queues at the grocery store? Sick of noise pollution?*

Do you dream of romance—that special man wishing for matrimony?

Consider a vacation to Falgannon Isle—a wee bit of heaven in the Hebrides of Scotland where magic exists. Our pace is relaxed, the scenery majestic. The climate is mild since the isle is in the Gulf Stream. Summer twilight lasts forever—ideal for romantic walks. White beaches with tidal pools for swimming. Green hillocks to wander and explore. A medieval castle, a stone ring and ancient Pictish ruins dot the hillsides. I cannot imagine a more romantic place, one as breathtakingly beautiful, that stirs the soul and spellbinds the heart!

Ladies, listen up!

Falgannon Isle has 213 braw Scots lads eager to find a bride. You see, there's a shortage of marriageable women on the isle. Yes, over two hundred males, ages eighteen to forty-seven, and all anxious to make your acquaintance!

Fill out this application. If chosen, you'll receive airfare and expenses to our remote isle. You'll have two weeks to explore the ruins, walk on the sands in the gloaming . . . maybe find that special man waiting for you to fill his heart.

If you decide this life isn't for you—well, you've had a free vacation. However, I'm betting there's a handsome Islander who can convince you to stay . . . forever.

Come for the vacation of a lifetime, remain for love . . .

Click on our BACHELOR REGISTRY *and see dozens of braw Scots lads impatient to welcome you to Falgannon.*

Address queries to BAMontgomerie@Isle_of_Love. co.uk

B.A. smiled at the laptop screen, hope in her heart. Satisfied, she hit the FTP button to upload the page. The monitor suddenly switched to *Page Not Found.*

"Bloody hell! Not again!" Used to the Net being slow on Falgannon, she reached for the telephone to check. "Dead. Grrrr . . . I'd sell my soul for the rare beastie broadband."

"Any word yet, lass?" a voice called from the front of the store.

B.A. considered ignoring Callum since he'd already asked the same question five times in the past hour. In an irritating fashion, he began to beat a tattoo on the counter, saying he wasn't going away until she answered. Shutting down the computer as she arose from the desk chair, she went out into the storefront.

Redheaded Callum Mackenzie's gray eyes blazed with anticipation similar to that of a four-year-old peeking at presents on Christmas morn. Willing to stoop to a little mental torture just to break the ennui of the afternoon, B.A. pretended she had no idea what he wanted.

"What can I be helping you with, Callum the Bicycle?"

The odd appellation linked to Callum's name stemmed from his running the bicycle shop. B.A. smiled at the island quirkiness: On Falgannon, it wasn't the village oddball or black sheep whose name was coupled with a descriptive tag, but the whole bloody isle! Gravestones in the ancient churchyard illustrated this wasn't passing eccentricity, but tradition born from necessity—or stubbornness. Currently residing on Falgannon—and driving her batty—were five Michaels, six Callums and eight Anguses, all with the last name of Mackenzie, Grant or Fraser. Adding in those generations going back before King Kenneth I, it was hard to keep them separated, so ages ago Falgannonians had began tagging each other with a label to set them apart.

Callum's face pruned with dismay. "B.A., one might infer you hate men the way you torment the male folk of the isle."

Michael the Fiddle ambled up behind his cousin. Of course, on Falgannon—population 297—family lines were so tangled, islanders joked it was possible to end up being a fifth-cousin to yourself! Michael was of the sandy-haired Mackenzies. Beautiful males, each reminded B.A. of a Byronic poet; their soulful gray eyes could lure a lass to stare at them for hours.

Only, that was the problem, as B.A. knew too well. Two hundred and thirteen unmarried males lived on her isle. The quandary arose because the only unwed ladies were

Oonanne and Morag—but they didn't count since they were lesbians—and the Marys—Mary Annis and Mary Agnes, sixty-seven-year-old twins. And herself: BarbaraAnne Montgomerie-Deshaunt—thirty-seven, widowed seven years, owner of Falgannon Isle.

The one woman none of the males could court.

B.A. knew if an outlander asked any of the men why with such a dearth of women the lone eligible one wasn't wooed, he'd get that prune face and a sharp retort, "Are you daft in the head, man?"

She sighed. She was the Lady of the Isle, a title passed to her at seventeen upon the death of her grandmother, Maeve. The eldest female of her line had always ruled this tiny speck of an island, going back to Pictish times, and *none* trifled with their Lady. All manner of catastrophes befell the feckless lad who tried. Hadn't Michael the Story warned of The Curse and its ghastly repercussions, a fate dire enough to ensure no male dared more than cast an admiring eye in her direction?

"What did B.A. say, Callum?" Michael shifted in his Reeboks as if ants infested his knickers.

B.A. slid her soft shawl about her shoulders. Autumn's chill embraced the isle, the sun setting earlier each day. "Afternoon, Michael the Fiddle. Enjoy walking in *the soft* last night?"

"Aye. I spotted you near Maulkin Tower in the gloaming." Michael smiled at her with lovesick, puppy eyes.

Not vain; she knew men looked. But then The Curse never struck down a lad for admiring.

Callum gave him the point of his elbow. "Eegit, *Herself* is yanking our chains, are you not, B.A.? 'Tis them Yank ways you acquired going to school in the colonies corrupting you. Ashamed you should be."

"Here now, our B.A. would do no such thing," Janet Grant chided, breezing through the side door to B.A.'s left.

Toting a basket of gourds, the gorgeous redhead paused to flash a smile at both men. The cousins rushed to lift the counter's trap to let Janet pass, bonking noggins with a crack.

B.A. shook her head, thinking the three visitors due

shortly—the ones Callum inquired about every ten minutes—couldn't arrive soon enough. Springtime these past six years was rough when a young man's fancy turned to romance and there were no lasses to serenade by the light of the moon. And, come autumn when nights grew longer, Falgannon males got quite cranky as they envisioned spending those winter months alone.

Janet Grant—called Janet the Red, though island males sniggered bawdier nicknames behind her back—sashayed between the hormone-riddled Mackenzies. B.A. knew Janet was a born flirt. What woman wouldn't relish being the center of attention on an island of love-starved men?

Well, other than me, she thought.

"Our B.A. is too serious to pull a kitty's tail," Janet teased, arranging the gourds inside the glass case. A blast from the ferry horn caused her to jerk up and hit her head. "Och, Angus, you sad excuse for a husband, I may take a knife to you in your sleep." Rubbing her scalp, she rushed to the window, observing the ferryboat pulling into the harbor.

"Best up his insurance first," Michael howled.

On Falgannon, ferry-docking passed as high entertainment, right up with watching Friday nights as Wee Dougie chased the old men lovingly called the "Morn, B.A." Club around with his scooter after the *cèilidh*.

Janet gasped. "Look at that."

On tiptoes, Janet leaned into the casement, her heart-shaped derriere wiggling in Marilyn Monroe fashion. B.A. knew that undulating pulchritude generally held the Mackenzies transfixed as vipers before a snake charmer, so to speak. However, with the promise of the arrival of "wild females" muddling their brains, they nearly toppled Janet from her perch.

"Have the lasses come, Janet?" both males asked.

"Not unless you fancy them near giants and on the masculine side." Janet practically purred, "Verra masculine."

"What we dinna need on this bloody rock is more men," Michael grumbled.

Janet's hip swishing—similar to a cat in heat—tweaked B.A.'s curiosity. Obviously, they were getting visitors, just not the ones expected. Once in a blue moon, tourists found their way to her hidden isle.

B.A. leaned on the counter to glimpse the unloading ferry. She observed three men disembark and start up the steep hill. One was of medium height with blue-black hair; the others were near giants and bright blond.

"Are the Vikings invading, Janet?" Michael bumped his hip against hers.

"Sure and all, you'd expect to see those two in hats with horns." She giggled.

B.A. smirked, knowing Janet probably pictured herself ravished by the barbarian horde, horns on hats not the ones on her mind! Untying her apron, B.A. stepped to the other side of the counter, almost hearing the redhead's thoughts—*wonder if he's that big all over?*

Near her own age, B.A. adored Janet, the bride Angus had fetched from Ireland six years ago, but she pondered if their marriage would last. She doubted it, not with The Curse having the isle in its grip. Down at the pub, the duffers comprising the "Morn, B.A." Club ran a pool on how long she'd stick it out on their bucolic island. Janet had surprised everyone by staying this long. But B.A. feared her fun loving friend would one day grow bored and run off with some lad tired of island life.

"St. Columba," Callum exclaimed. "They're reversing a Range Rover off the ferry."

"Where do the Vikings think to drive that juggernaut?" Michael pushed his cousin aside to look. "They'd make a circle of the isle in three shakes of a stick, then what? 'Tis daft."

Janet winked at B.A. "Typical males—if they cannot have a lass to ogle, a car will do."

"I thank you not to insult me, Janet the Red." Michael sniffed, though his eyes remained glued on the car.

B.A. spied Wee Gordie Grant—so-called because he was eleven and had no trade with which to link his name—dash up the hill toward the general store, carrying the alarm of the Viking invasion. Brass bells over the door chimed, heralding the lad's arrival. He knocked into Callum, panted, "Pardon me, Janet the Red," then continued on to crash into the counter.

He blurted, "You see, B.A.? Angus the Ferry unloaded a machine! Did you order one, B.A.? Can I go driving in it with you?" and thirty other questions.

Callum rapped the top of the child's head. "That's for calling me Janet, eegit."

B.A. watched the racket outside escalate. The "Morn, B.A." Club piled out of the Hanged Man to witness Falgannon under siege from Viking raiders for the first time in 743 years. The Escape Artists—five foxhounds, fugitive from the kennels—got into the act, yapping and jumping in the air for attention. This drew the Marys and their tubby tabby, The Cat Dudley.

Willie the Writer, Robbie the Butcher and Innis the Thatcher brought up the rear of the impromptu parade. Wee Dougie Mackenzie puttered up on his scooter, riding ovals about the procession, the two-cycle engine's irritating noise the perfect touch to the three-ring circus. The hullabaloo caused the cat to slap the hounds as if the whole affair was their fault.

B.A. chuckled at the antics of her islanders and their delightful ability to turn the mundane into high camp. A Viking invasion was doomed facing that formidable welcome!

Walking behind the counter, B.A. reached for the aspirin bottle by the register, shook out two, hesitated, and added a third. Sometimes being the owner of an isle where the inhabitants reveled in their madcap Brigadoon ways really called for that third aspirin. She twisted the top on a Pepsi and washed down the tablets. Keeping an eye on the hubbub cresting the steep hill, she strangled when she spotted the black-haired man at the center of the group.

For a suspended heartbeat, she thought she saw Evian.

Hope rose as a vision played through her mind that Evian had somehow survived the plane crash: picked up at sea by Norwegian fishermen, he'd been unable to recall who he was and it'd taken all this time to regain his memory. As her heart swelled with longing, the crowd drew closer and parted. She saw the man full in the face—the face of a stranger.

In that breath she lost her husband a second time.

Too much to absorb, she slammed down the Pepsi and fled to the back room. Leaning against the wall, she tilted her head back and closed her eyes against waves of emotion so strong it was crippling. The pain hadn't been this bad for a long time. In the early days after the crash, she'd been gutted. Over time, she survived by wrapping her heart in cotton and getting through one day at a time. Only sometimes she was *so* lonely.

Minutes passed before the droning in her head receded enough to hear the crowd making the welkin ring on the store's porch. Naturally, the Outlanders would stop here. A private isle, no one landed on Falgannon without registering with the harbormaster. Foolishly defying The Curse, Davey the Harbor had abandoned his job to go wife hunting in Edinburgh, and so the task had temporarily fallen to B.A.

Swallowing raw emotions, B.A. gathered the tattered ribbons of her composure and strode to the storefront as the bells chimed, ballyhooing the Vikings' arrival.

With The Cat Dudley in the lead, three men came through the door, dodging The Escape Artists as the yapping foxhounds circled through their legs and tugged at their pant cuffs. B.A. sniggered, surprised no one tripped due to the animal brigade's antics.

Ah yes, it seemed the Vikings had landed. The two taller men were stereotypical Norsemen. With long white-blond hair and a rugged face that'd see women fall at his feet, the first towered over everyone. A ruddy cast touched the complexion of the second, with waves of straw-blond hair framing his handsome face. His blue eyes flashed in mirth as he spotted Janet staring at them in the same manner The Escape Artists would a steak.

Their virile perfection left B.A. unmoved. She judged both as healthy males, but no more emotionally involving than Campbell Grant's blue-ribbon bull.

It was the third man—the one with the raven-black hair—who drew her eyes. If a Viking, he had Black-Irish blood in him coming through a female stolen in a long-ago raid. Both blonds stepped to either side of the aisle to let him pass, a gesture of deference. Almost a head taller, they were physically dominating, but *he* was the power. B.A. sensed this clearly as if both men had gone down on one knee in obeisance. With a panther's grace he strode to the counter, then bent to set a Louis Vuitton duffle on the floor. B.A.'s breathing clutched, and she girded herself to confront the invader. Dizziness buzzed in her blood.

Then he rose up, meeting her stare . . . and everything stilled.

Not a blue of any shade, his eyes were pale green—warlock eyes capable of freezing a person with the arch of one black brow. Lifting her chin, B.A. fought a frisson as his gaze locked on her. Aware of the moggie pussyfooting on the countertop, the newcomer ran his hand along its spine.

The gesture triggered images within B.A. of that hand upon her body, stroking with the same sensual magic. A premonition? She blinked, loath to recognize the prospect.

She was right—he was a bloody warlock!

The Cat Dudley arched under the man's hand, turned and head-butted his elbow for more pets. *Turncoat*, B.A. thought.

Security came in the fact the stranger looked nothing like Evian, B.A. assured herself as she appraised him. Quite healthy, no middle-age paunch hid under the expensive silk shirt and black leather jacket. Though probably in his early forties, most would judge him a decade younger. The lines bracketing his mouth gave him away, hinting at someone who'd lived longer and seen disappointments that had hardened him.

Long black lashes were unblinking over penetrating eyes. A feral stillness about him re-conjured the image of a panther—so beautiful, so compelling. B.A. itched to reach out and stroke him as he did the cat. Self-preservation stayed her hand, fearful he'd strike in a wink.

Outside of his wavy blue-black hair, little about the invader evoked the memory of Evian. Her tension should ease, seeing this man didn't resemble her dead husband; once more she was safe, buffeted by the cocoon the island provided. She didn't have to feel, wouldn't risk her soul. How could any man reach through the wall she'd built for protection?

Yet, inexplicably, alarmingly, this man did. He unnerved her, put her on the defensive. An air of mystery, and calculation, swirled in those jade eyes. B.A.'s fae sense whispered a warning that his coming to the isle had something to do with her—he'd change her world if she permitted it.

Din from the crowd abated as they watched the invader and "their B.A." locked in a staring contest. It bordered on droll for neither of them to break the ice and speak first, but strangely, she held back, waiting . . . watching.

His right brow arched, conceding this round. "I'm searching for B.A. Montgomerie. Is he about?" Lilt of the Irish touched that deep melodic voice, sending shivers up her spine.

Twitters rippled through the crowd over his error. A tattle-tale, Wee Gordie opened his mouth to correct the man, but Callum grabbed the child's shoulder and placed a hand over his gub to silence the jabber-box.

The Viking leader turned to each side, looking at the grinning villagers—again, that cold air of assessment. Returning to B.A., his gaze narrowed on her, shocking her to discover those ice-green eyes were capable of heat. They raked slowly over her face, the gold hair fanning about her shoulders, down to her breasts and then lower in a scorching fire before traveling back to lock stares with her. His appraisal finished, he watched her as if he knew things about her, secrets, things she loathed to admit, that he *dared* her to admit. Those well-formed lips parted in feline appreciation, pantherlike arrogance, as if he'd put his mark on her.

The impact of this man hit her senses hard. Her traitorous body roared to life. Her breasts heavy, their tips sensitive—without glancing down she knew the thin silk of her gold blouse outlined the crowns of her betraying nipples. Lifting her chin, she tugged her shawl about her as a blanket of armor.

"What might you wish with B.A. Montgomerie?" she inquired.

"Business. My commitment was originally with Sean Montgomerie, but my solicitor wired of his passing in May. I must instead deal with his heir, B.A. Montgomerie. Wonder if you'd give me his directions?"

Go out the door, turn right and keep walking in a straight line is what she chafed to reply, meaning he'd walk into the bay. Then she wouldn't have to deal with the panic he provoked within her. Forcing a smile, she struggled to ignore those challenging eyes.

"I'm B.A. Montgomerie."

He arched a brow. "B.A. Montgomerie is a woman?"

Wee Gordie escaped Callum's constraint and blurted from a safe distance, "Aye, she's the Lady of the Isle like her *seanamhair* Maeve was."

"Lady of the Isle? Is that similar to Lady of the Lake?" A smile twitched at the corner of his made-for-sin mouth. "Then you and I have matters to sort out."

"And you are?" she queried.

He tilted his head, vouchsafing her another point. "Desmond Mershan. You're expecting me?" He held out his hand.

B.A. stared at those long, magician's fingers as if they were cobras. His polished manner triggered warning bells within her, cautioning that Desmond Mershan lied through those pearly white teeth—predator's teeth. He'd known precisely who she was. This man wasn't stupid. Incisive, shrewd intelligence radiated from those pale eyes. He wouldn't have come to Falgannon without knowing every detail about the isle, and about B.A. Montgomerie. He'd strangely played out this charade. Lying. Why?

B.A. attempted to shake that impression, but it lingered.

"You presumed wrong."

Impatience flared in his expression, yet even that struck B.A. as having a thespian air. "Details were fixed at the first of the year with Sean Montgomerie, owner of the isle—"

"I'm owner," she interrupted. "Have been for twenty years."

The golden moggie Dudley stood and put his paws on Mershan's chest, meowing for attention. The man shifted to evade the pesky feline, then finally gave in and scratched its chin. "Affectionate animal."

That drew guffaws from the crowd, prompting Callum to grumble, "Despite the wee beastie from hell greeting you as a long-lost friend, look up 'cantankerous' in a dictionary, you'll see a picture of The Cat Dudley for illustration."

Blinking innocently, the cat bumped the invader, reminding him to keep his fingers moving. B.A. rolled her eyes in disbelief when he then rumbled as though Mershan were 100 percent catnip.

"As I was saying, my arrangements were with—"

"I own Falgannon, not my grandfather. I've never heard of you or any arrangements."

Gently pushing away the persistent cat, Desmond smiled. "I'm exhausted. So are my companions. If you'd point us to lodgings, we'll sort this out—say, over supper?"

The piercing gaze traced over her with blistering sexual fire. Confident of acquiescence, he reclaimed the expensive duffle.

So, the warlock was being charming? B.A. almost huffed. Supper? Those soporific eyes promised a meal, a bedtime story and breakfast! "No one lands on my isle without written permission. I've no idea what you—"

Reaching inside his jacket, he pulled out an envelope and sighed. "Permission to land, Lady of the Isle. While you get up to speed, I'd appreciate a meal and a bath."

"Read it, B.A.," Wee Gordie urged, only to be hushed by several islanders.

B.A. no more wished to accept it than she had to shake his hand. Her grandmother Maeve had taught her to be wary of a warlock, distrustful of accepting anything from him. More important, never to pass him any object he requested—especially salt. You'd give away a part of yourself, empowering his control over you. B.A. had never met anyone who qualified as a warlock, but she'd bet Maeve's silver torque she was staring one in the face now.

Watching the envelope dropped to the counter, it took all her concentration to maintain her calm facade. Nerves raw after years of maintaining a buffer between herself and the world, this man broke down her barriers and sent her emotions careening like balls in a pinball machine. The pale eyes were mocking; he was aware of her fear. Worse, B.A. saw that it pleased him.

"If you'll point my companions and me in the right direction?"

"It's directions you need?" Devilment twitched at the corner of her mouth. "Start up Harbour Hill, turn right and follow the cobbled road. It takes you where you need to go."

He tilted his head in thanks, and a sexy smile tugged at his mouth. That mouth conjured images of long, deep kisses. "I'll see you later?"

Sooner than you think, B.A. vowed silently, ignoring what that smile did to her heart.

If he attached significance to the snickers when he passed, he gave no indication. The three Vikings started up the hill road, the silly Escape Artists falling in, barking and bounding after them, followed by the *putt-putt-putt* of Wee Dougie's scooter.

B.A. rushed to the porch to watch. With athletic strides, the three men passed the postcard-perfect businesses and homes. The cobbled road circled the isle's southern tip, with a neat row of two-story stone buildings lining the inner curve. Doors kept opening as Falgannonians came to eyeball the Vikings and their bizarre entourage. The group vanished around the bend.

Hurrying inside, B.A. went to see what the envelope held. Closest, Michael peered as if it'd pop open and a jack-in-the-box would spring forth. B.A. joined him in glaring at the envelope. She needed a long stick to touch it, to make certain it was safe, maybe just to whack it a few times in order to be sure.

Sharing her sentiment, Michael snagged a pencil and poked it.

B.A.'s mouth flattened in a frown as she snatched it away and lifted the flap. While her eyes scanned the photocopies inside, her shawl snaked down one shoulder.

Eyes alight, Callum leaned on the counter. "Interesting bloke, eh, B.A.?"

"As interesting as a panther on a leash. I should count my fingers to see if any are missing."

"Oh aye, it's easy to discern how *uninteresting* you found this Desmond feller." Seeing the silk-clad breast proclaiming her arousal, Callum and Michael exchanged knowing male glances then burst into laughter.

Adjusting her shawl, B.A. stuck her tongue out at them. She couldn't even summon a scathing retort, too distracted by studying the copies of letters between her grandfather and Desmond Mershan.

Robbie the Butcher rushed in. "A wicked lass you are, B.A., sending them to trod the town circle. Another five minutes they'll be returning. Quick, what's it say?"

"Arrangements Sean set up last winter. The Vikings are to survey the land on the eastern slope." She rattled the pages in the air. "Nothing was in the investment portfolio given to me upon Sean's death. While I gave leave to invest the island's money, I dunna believe he'd undertake anything of this magnitude without my permission."

The shop bells *ting-a-ling*ed, causing B.A. to glance up as Willie the Writer hurried inside. A beloved islander, he churned out best-selling cowboy romances set in the U.S. West under the penname Willa Macgregor. A hoot, since the farthest west he'd ever been was Belfast.

"A naughty lass you are, B.A. Villagers are rushing to see the excitement. Expect tempers when they discover it's only a wee Viking invasion and not the Yank lasses come," he cautioned.

The racket of Wee Dougie's scooter grew audible in the distance as the crowd rounded the far bend, giving B.A. little time to gather her wits. She needed to ring her brother, the family solicitor; he'd know if this was legit or Desmond Mershan was a snake-oil salesman.

She reached for the wall phone, only Callum, Michael and Willie cried in unison, "Blower's down."

"Fuuu . . . dge." She questioned, "Where's Jock the Repair, MacGyver of the East? With the matchmaking project, we need to be online 24/7, not seven hours out of twenty-four."

"He's fixing Davey the Weaver's washer-machine," Callum answered. "B.A., since we're discussing our sorry state of communications—the Yank lasses won't believe we only have five phones on the whole bloody isle. Any chance of dragging the island into this millennium? Poor sweet things will probably faint when you say no cell phones."

"B.A., this Desmond feller won't appreciate being sent on a tour of our downtown business district." Robbie asked, "Who were you going to ring, lass?"

"My brother the solicitor. Moot now. These papers appear to be a contract between Mershan and The Montgomerie."

"Contract?" several echoed.

"If it's not a scam, my grandfather sought to turn us into an exclusive tourist spot. Mershan's here to judge if it's feasible to place a hotel on the isle's eastern tip."

The irksome *putt-putt-putt* of Wee Dougie's scooter increased.

"Look, it's like a bloody May Day parade," Robbie called from the porch.

B.A. came over to the window, watching Mershan and his Viking bodyguards stalk back down Harbour Road in determined strides, The Escape Artists rollicking about them. In the lead, strutting proudly, was The Cat Dudley, and yes, a large portion of the isle's populace was now in tow. Eleven were on bicycles, while Ian and Brian Fraser rode horses. Wee Dougie, on that blasted scooter, trailed after the islanders afoot, staying out of reach of everyone.

"The invaders approach," B.A muttered drolly. She stood tapping the envelope against her chin while the din outside increased.

Cane clicking on the wood floor, Angus the Ancient tottered in, leaving the door open. "You've done it, B.A. That black-headed feller dunna appear thrilled a'tall being butt of your joke, lass."

Silence descended, causing B.A. to turn. Abruptly, the storefront shook with the force of a small blast. For a fleeting second B.A. wondered if they'd suffered an earthquake. But no, someone had slammed the door shut with such violence everything on the shelves rattled. Not seismic activity. Another force of nature.

He stood there.

Her stomach dropped. Maybe she had been a *little* abrupt

in handling him. Well, it was his own bloody fault, setting off such frantic emotions within her!

"Och, now you're in for it, B.A." Angus waved a shaky finger at her.

Mershan's jacket was off, draped in the crook of his arm. Lasers of fury, his ice-green eyes targeted her, and despite the tension crackling in the air, she was positive it wasn't sexual. Though his chest rose and fell, she noted it was in effort to control his anger and not from the walk. He hadn't broken a sweat from the tour of the tiny village, showing his peak physical condition.

All the better to throttle you, B.A., her mind whispered as she battled the instinct to run.

"He's right," Mershan growled, "I'm not happy." He dropped his bag and coat on the floor as if needing both hands free.

All the better to wrap around your neck, B.A., echoed her brain.

Desmond took a step toward her. B.A. took one back. She feared no man, but for the first time in her life one rattled her.

Frozen in a fight-or-flight response, it took seconds for her to recognize an odd creaking from overhead. Jerking her gaze to the ceiling, it locked on the old shark jaw suspended by a wooden peg from the rafter. Hung before she was born, it suddenly dropped, hurtling straight at them. She stood too stunned to move. With feline reflexes Mershan yanked her aside, shielding her with his body. Razor sharp teeth just missed them. Chunks of the brittle bone ricocheted into the pyramid display of soup cans, sending them dodging again.

Twining around Mershan's ankles, Dudley squalled when his tail was stepped on. Reverting to his nasty little self, he protested by sinking claws into Desmond's right calf, then followed with his patented vampire bite.

The man howled. The cat yowled. Cat dangling from his leg, Desmond danced over bone chunks and rolling cans.

B.A. knew that Dudley had earlier fixed in his brain the source of all evils in kittydom originated with Callum. Thus, she wasn't surprised when he released Mershan and launched that fat tabby body at the thigh of his nemesis, glomming on as Callum's foot landed on a rolling can.

No time to regain footing, Desmond ducked to avoid Callum's flailing. Callum, with the tabby hanging on, went flying backward. He collided into the off-balance Desmond; both men and cat crashed into the five-tiered rack of jars of sweets.

Dozens of glass containers shattered, flinging shards, jawbreakers and gumballs across the wooden floor. Everyone hopped to dodge the confections and glass. Hard candies acted like ball bearings, while cream-filled treats squished to a slippery goop. B.A. gaped in horror as Mershan skated on the jawbreakers, his feet flying into the air. Going down, he cracked his head against the floor.

To escape chaos, Dudley leapt to the countertop. He flopped down and stuck his hind leg in the air. With a sneeze of disdain, he started giving it a tongue bath.

For several heartbeats, B.A.'s mind reeled, waiting for the invader to get up. He didn't move. No rise and fall of his chest was visible. Step-by-step, everyone made their way over to him and peered at his still form.

B.A. glanced up to see her villagers crammed against the shop windows and door; noses pressed to the glass, they resembled creatures from the *X-Files*. With unabashed glee, they howled at the Marx Brothers antics inside.

Robbie shook his head in disbelief. "You have to admit, B.A., this is the most excitement we've had on the isle since the Floating of the Sheep last June, when we prepared them for shearing by tossing them into the creek to wash them."

"B.A.," Angus muttered, "you've gotten yourself in a pretty pickle. Gone and murdered the Viking leader. Ashamed you should be."

Panic setting in, she knelt beside the almost too beautiful man—the man alarmingly still. "He isn't dead," she pronounced. Her hands hovered just above Mershan, afraid to touch him. "I . . . dunna think."

With a thespian wink, Angus shook his cane, a touch of farce to reinforce his idiotic statement. "Told Sean Montgomerie he should've beaten her regularly. He dinna listen.

Now she's gone and kilt this feller. 'Tis a sad day. Our Lady of the Isle is a murderess."

"Oh, Angus, put a sock in it," B.A. snapped. Her life was suddenly spiraling out of control.

Chapter 2

When Desmond opened his eyes, the first thing—two things actually— they focused on were breasts. They were firm, round and about the size of grapefruits, perfect to his way of thinking, and encased in iridescent gold silk.

And just above his face.

If he raised up, he could latch his lips around one silk-clad breast. First, he'd graze it with the edge of his teeth, then suck it into his mouth, drawing to the point of pleasure-pain. He craved to make this fantasy real. For some strange reason he could only lie there and allow the erotic vision to play through his mind.

Ethereal forms floated within his peripheral vision. The oddball thought flittered through his brain—his aching brain—that they might be angels. If men knew angels had such breasts, morgues would see queues of mass suicides. Then the ghostly forms took on definition and he started hearing words.

"Is Doc coming?" a sexy voice asked.

Did angels speak with a burr?

The breasts jiggled with the firmness of overchilled Jell-O as vibrations of her words surrounded him. *Lucky me:* His head was in the angel's lap. Desmond had no idea what he'd done in his sad, sorry life to rate heaven, but hell, he wasn't one to look gift breasts . . . hmm . . . a gift horse in the mouth.

Disoriented, he fought two rising sensations, mild nausea being first. Superceding the queasiness was a blaze of lust that nearly crippled his body.

The angel's scent enveloped him. It was earthy, unlike anything he'd ever encountered, affecting his senses on an animalistic level. Never had a woman's body heat, her scent affected him so.

But it was more. So much more.

More than *a* woman—this was *the* woman—one who'd haunted his fantasies for more nights than he cared to admit. This was the woman he'd watched from afar, and like some lovesick puppy had carried her picture in his wallet these past fifteen years. This woman had become the standard by which he measured all others, and none ever reached her level of class, beauty or intelligence. As a man long denied that which he most cherished, Desmond hungered for her with a soul-deep yearning that paralyzed him. Only *this* woman could break his control, could have him willing to go down on his knees ready to beg for her touch.

And it was the one woman in the whole bloody world he couldn't have.

Allowing the fantasy, for a brief moment he willingly relinquished his iron control. He envisioned taking her wrists and pushing them over her head; bowing her body to his, he'd slowly lick his way down her stomach and lower—drink in her hot female essence, lose himself in the sweet bliss of madness.

His angel spoke again. "You're sure he's not dead, Robbie?"

Robbie Mackenzie closely monitored Mershan's pulse. He glanced up to see the man's green eyes were wide open, though B.A. didn't see. Feeling the heartbeat jump from comatose to that of a marathon runner, he noticed the stranger staring up at B.A. like a man possessed. Placing his arm across Mershan's stomach, Robbie noted the rock-hard erection defined against the black slacks. He checked to see if B.A. noticed. Nope. At times their lass tended to wear blinders where men were concerned.

A seed taking root, he stifled a smile before answering. "Aye, lass, he lives."

Stroking Desmond's forehead, B.A. asked, a quaver threading her words, "Did you find a pulse?"

The men sitting on the long bench glanced at Mershan's groin and then to each other.

Staring at the lad's healthy response to being in their B.A.'s lap, Robbie arched a brow and nodded to them. *Oh aye, he's got a pulse. Dead men don't get erections.* In male sympathy, he figured it was to the point of painful, the sort of lust that makes a man silly-buggers to all around him.

He'd seen one of those police shows about forensic evidence on telly. In it, they discussed how a poor blighter had been murdered, strangled to death, and he'd died with a hard-on. Tap a woman on the head and she'll sit and whine about the pain. Cosh a man, put his head in a female lap, and when he opens his eyes the first thing he sees is a pair of world-class breasts, all the blood travels south so there's less pain. It's one of those women-are-Venusians-and-men-are-lower-than-slugs things, Robbie figured. A man could be quite dangerous in that state, a cocked pistol with the safety off.

"Stop fashing, B.A, he has a fine steady pulse." To Robbie's way of thinking, their lass seemed quite concerned. A heartening sign, though he doubted she'd appreciate his logic.

Never far from the minds of all Falgannon's lonely lads, The Curse dated so far back in ancient history it was now lore. It was placed on Falgannon by Sgathach Buanand, Skye's Warrior Queen. In a jealous fit of vengeance, she decreed the males of the isle wouldn't find true and lasting love unless the Lady of the Isle mated with an Outlander— one who had black hair and green eyes and was of Irish descent. If those conditions remained unmet, the females of the island would bear only boy babes, leaving Falgannon with a perpetual shortage of marriageable-aged women.

Much to the consternation of Falgannonian males, they'd discovered it wasn't a simple matter of moving away either. The Curse had far-reaching effects. Robbie was aware men who tried leaving found all manner of dilemmas befell them and wouldn't cease until they returned to the wee rock in the Atlantic Ocean.

When B.A. announced her impending marriage nine years before, all the males had muttered no good would come of it. They'd held their tongues around B.A about grave doubts. The aristocratic half-Irisher Deshaunt wasn't one the islanders considered good enough for B.A. Still, when dealing with The Curse they'd clutched at straws. A sticking point, though Irish and he had black hair, Deshaunt lacked green eyes, so the men of Falgannon had rubbed their rabbit feet and prayed for the best. And when Deshaunt's plane went down in the North Atlantic seven years ago, Robbie knew the hopes of every Falgannonian male went with it. As long as B.A. lacked a mate who met the terms of The Curse, the men of the isle were doomed.

Robbie studied the green eyes fixed on their B.A., then skimmed over the Outlander's body. A fit man, a hard man. Of course, it'd take one with grit in his craw and a will of iron to deal with their lass. He had a feeling this Desmond might be the feller. B.A. and he were certainly getting buzzes off each other.

More importantly—he had green eyes! Robbie glanced skyward and whispered a paean for this godsend. So maybe . . . with a nudge here and there? Of course, with their B.A. it'd probably require something more subtle—like a broom over the head. However, needs must when the devil drives.

Michael the Story returned with a dustpan and two brooms, elbowed Callum and handed him one. Wiggling his brows, Michael jerked his head in the direction of the couple on the floor. When Callum made his prune face and said a silent *huh?*, Michael mouthed the words, *our B.A., the Outlander . . . black hair, green eyes . . . The Curse.*

Robbie saw the lightbulb come on over Callum's head, though he deemed the wattage a wee bit dim.

"How come Doc isn't here yet?" B.A. wailed.

"He has to pump up the tire on his bicycle." Michael suggested. "Maybe one of the Vikings could fetch him around in that machine?"

B.A.'s face brightened. "Oh aye, hurry."

B.A. watched Michael go out the door, jostling through the throng of villagers still pressed there. Suddenly, Mershan flexed those cat muscles, and in a move that'd bring a smile to Hulk Hogan, she was on her back with Desmond the Panther on his knees looming over her.

It certainly put to rest the question of him being dead, B.A. marveled. She opened her mouth to . . . what—ask how his head felt? To scream? Only, warm soft lips covered hers. They moved, kissing her slowly, thoroughly, and with such surprising sweetness that tears welled in her eyes.

Her hand lifted to his face in a caress of wonderment. She shook, forgot all about herself. There was only him. Tasting hot as cinnamon and intoxicating as Highland whisky, his velvet tongue slid in, stroking, proclaiming a male intent that ignited a yearning in her. A heat hit at the base of her belly and exploded outward, causing her to tremble with longing.

You don't know this man, ranted the logical part of her brain—the part she always referred to as Angel B.A. Her Devil B.A side laughed and said, *I don't bloody care, as long as he's kissing me like there's no tomorrow.*

Prodded by her angel side, B.A. scooted to sit up, but there wasn't room to maneuver with him hovering over her. Worse, she had to be careful of the broken glass. Hands in the air, she glanced about in frustration, then back to the grinning, sexy man.

Sensing her uncertainty, he took advantage, leaning forward to kiss her again. She drank in the fire, the male pheromones, drowned in his blatant masculinity. Unprepared for her physical response, the sensations were agonizing! He kissed her, cherished her as though he were the last man on earth and she the last woman.

Of course . . . they weren't.

Angus shuffled over, peering at them. "Lads, our B.A. dinna kilt the Viking after all. He's comin' around."

"Aye, not dead a'tall, Angus. Not sure about the around part, but I'd say he'll be comin' if he keeps that up." Callum began sweeping up the glass shards and candies near them. "Mind, B.A., wouldn't want this muck to get in your long hair."

Angus remained in an awkward position, his head tilted sideways, watching. The Cat Dudley padded over and rubbed against the old man's legs. "Think our B.A. is giving the lad mouth-to-mouth reassesses—that breathing thing—to keep him going 'til Doc gets fetched?" he asked.

Leave it to her nutty islanders to turn the whole thing into a joke at her expense. B.A. pushed against the stranger's shoulders, breaking the embrace. A tear formed in her eye from the shock of how this man reached through her barriers and had touched her—and not physically, but her soul. She glared at him, resenting how he'd upset her well-ordered world.

He leaned and kissed the furrow of her brow, almost as if he understood her confusion, shared it. B.A. tilted her head to study this beautiful, black-headed man. Her trembling fingers traced over her lips, befuddled by the mix of emotions he provoked within her.

He kissed the tip of her nose. Once more, a simple gesture of reassurance. Then their eyes locked and B.A. felt the world about her revolve. She drowned in those jade depths. Moved, she almost reached out to touch him, the wonder of this bizarre moment shaking her to where she couldn't think. Typically male, he recognized his power, that his scent fogged her brain. Taking advantage, he brushed his lips against hers again.

"Guess he needed a second dose to rise from the dead—you think, Angus?" Callum sniggered.

Snapped back to awareness of the others around her, B.A. decided to kill them. First Callum, next Angus, then The Bloody Cat Dudley. Finally, she would skin a green-eyed panther. As soon as he stopped kissing her—as soon as she stopped kissing him back.

Dormant for years, her body clamored with a hunger so strong it was incapacitating. She'd forgotten the heat that radiated off a man's body, how hard muscles compared to a woman's softness, how male scent clouded your brain. How a man could make you blind with need.

The bells clattered as Innis shuffled in. "Shoo, devil's

spawn," he addressed Dudley. The feline sniffed at him disdainfully. Innis leaned over in a fashion mirroring Angus. "What's our B.A. doing to the Outlander?"

"That PCV stuff," Angus informed him.

Robbie burst into gales of laughter, which infected Callum. "I . . . think . . . you . . . mean . . . C . . . P . . . R, Angus." He barely got out the sentence before the boffos exploded again.

"Och, I see it!" He nudged B.A.'s shoulder. "Should you not be a huffin' 'n, puffin' 'n knockin' the lad in the chest? Seen it on telly once. Dunna seem, B.A, as if you have the hang of it."

B.A. drew back, feeling much like Alice after tumbling down the rabbit hole.

"Her heart's in it, give our lass that." Innis dragged over another bench, the racket as distressing as fingernails on a chalkboard. "Angus, take a load off. And thought you'd want to ken, B.A., one of them Vikings drove Michael over in the juggernaut to fetch Doc. Janet the Red, poor thing, is sacrificing herself by taking the big braw one down to the Hanged Man."

"Considerate of our Janet, her being an Outlander and all. I ken how much a sacrifice that be for the lass," Angus commiserated, tongue in cheek. He nudged Innis with his cane and looked at B.A. and Mershan. "A bonnie pair they make, eh?"

"That they do. It's good, B.A., to see you showing interest in a man again," Innis teased.

B.A. floated on a cloud of sensations, tingling from head to toe with those strange achy prickles one gets when you sit on your foot too long. This man singed her, branded her with an ardor she found devastating. Even so, it didn't stop the notion of purchasing a gross of voodoo dolls and putting them to use from fleeting through the back of her head.

Rushing in, Gordie the Piper announced, "Juggernaut's returning. You can see headlights half across the isle." Wee Gordie, trailing three steps behind his da, almost stepped on his father's heels. "Gor, look at that! Them bloody Vikings have started their rapine ways. Next they'll want to pillage something."

Wee Gordie scrunched up his forehead. "Da, what's pillage mean?"

Enough! If permitted, these eegits would make a whole evening's entertainment out of this. Gathering her wits, B.A. pushed away from Desmond. Blasted man followed as if he intended to kiss her again—the damn panther wasn't letting go of his prey.

She wagged her index finger in front of his face. "Now, stop that!"

His pale eyes narrowed on her finger and, before she knew what he intended, he sucked it into his mouth. His tongue swirled around it, sending deep shudders down her spine.

The bells sounded again as Michael dashed in with Cedric in tow. "Found him," he declared.

Cedric the Doc strolled in, the fabric of his kilt swinging as he walked. "Evening, Innis, Ian, Callum, Robbie, Angus, Gordon, Wee Gordie."

"Evening, Cedric," all on the benches chorused.

"Missed the landing of the Vikings, did I? Must've been a thrill to see! What's this mess?" He raised his shoes in turn, looking at the sticky soles.

"Da says the Viking is pillaging," Wee Gordie offered.

"Did he now?" Doc set his bag on the counter and glanced down. "Och—evening, B.A. Dinna see you sitting there. So, what's wrong with your feller? Was led to believe he's at death's door. Seems healthy to me. Back, Dudley, or I'll talk the Marys into neutering you next time they bring you for shots."

"Make him stop." B.A. blushed as she fought arousal, legions of goosebumps and rising anger.

"Our B.A. gave him PVC." Angus shook his finger. "Dunna ken what she's doing to him with the finger. They never showed that part on telly."

"Silly woman ain't doing it right," Innis huffed.

"Dinna tell *Herself* that—she's a Montgomerie." Doc pulled his stethoscope out of his kit. "You ken Montgomeries never listen to anyone."

"Oh aye," the chorus agreed, with Innis adding, "Might also be that our lass went to school in the colonies. Them Yank ways corrupted her."

All heads bobbed in solemn reflection. " 'Tis true, 'tis true."

"The tap on his noggin knocked the invader silly buggers, eh?" Michael commented.

"Not too scrambled, I'd say. He's certainly taken to our lass—at least to her finger," Doc said, winking at the bench.

Frowning, B.A. yanked it from Desmond's mouth with a loud pop. "Bloody panther," she grumbled. "I *told* them I needed to count my fingers."

"Come on, B.A., let's have a peek at your lad. A bump to the noggin can be a sticky wicket. I need to look into his eyes, make sure they're normal. You dunna want the other Vikings to go berserker if this one expires 'cause you had him down on the floor wallowing him around and poking him with your finger."

At the edge of his vision, Desmond noticed a man in a skirt—or a woman with big feet and seriously ugly legs—reaching for him. His mind struggled to focus. Over the years, he'd experienced intense dreams about B.A. Montgomerie, but never one this bizarre: slightly wacky, a near-death experience, a cross between *Braveheart* and *Cold Comfort Farm*.

Gazing at B.A., Desmond tried to differentiate nightmarish fantasy from reality. She was so stunning. Petulantly looking at her finger, those whisky-colored eyes were unfocused, dreamy. Her mouth was wet from his kisses.

His vision swirled. Some nonsense was said about looking into his eyes. Silly nonsense. He brushed the intruder's comments from his mind. If he could touch B.A. in his dream, he damn well didn't want a woman with big feet intruding.

His eyes targeted the woman so heartbreakingly beautiful before him. He wanted to hold her, to feel her heart beat against his, to caress her golden hair. Leaning forward to kiss that lush mouth, he saw her long black lashes go wide.

As if shaking free of a trance, she let forth with an ear-piercing scream that pierced his brain like a thousand red-hot needles.

The high-pitched note summoned utter catastrophe.

B.A.'s howl provoked The Cat Dudley to join her, creating an off-key harmony. The silly beast jumped onto the middle of Desmond's back, claws sinking into his flesh. Mershan's head snapped up, colliding hard with Doc's pointy chin at the same time Doc stepped on a stray jawbreaker. The older man's foot went high above his shoulders, his kilt swirling about his hips.

"That answers the question of what a Scotsman wears under there," Willie sniggered.

Callum, Willie, Innis, Ian, Angus, Michael, Gordon, Wee Gordie and Robbie gawked, poking each other with their elbows, as they eyed the two men sprawled over B.A. she fought the inclination to take the broom to them.

Flexing his paws at the small of the insensate Desmond's back, Dudley settled down to take a nap.

Angus admonished, "B.A., you shameless hussy, look what you did! If Sean had listened to me and beaten you regularly, none of this'd be happening. Being a Montgomerie, did he listen?"

"Angus, you ken Montgomeries never listen to anyone," Innis reiterated, with a twinkle in his brown eyes. " 'Ashamed you should be, B.A. Not enough to kill the Outlander again, you go and murder poor Doc as well. What are we supposed to do come time to worm the sheep?"

Scathing retorts ran through B.A.'s mind. But, tongue-tied from being kissed senseless, she'd futz up delivery, giving the eegits another giggle at her expense. That annoyance paled compared to how furious she was at Mershan for making her feel things she'd kept locked away all these years. Her body vibrated—one aching keen of need—and if she wasn't pinned beneath two deadweights, she'd have kicked him for it!

"Blethering pelicans! Get . . . them . . . off . . . me!" B.A. shoved at Mershan's shoulders. He was limp. With Doc draped over his legs, she was unable to extricate herself, though Dudley seemed content with the situation.

Robbie continued the teasing. "Let's consider, lass. With Doc cold-cocked, we blethering pelicans hesitate to do anything to make this mess you created worse. Doc might not be much—being a critter doctor and all—but he's the only medical-type person we have on the isle. Any of you ken what to do for a concussion?"

All eyes swept to the others, then back to her, followed by murmurs of, "No."

Innis leaned forward. "What's that you're muttering, B.A.? Speak up, my hearing ain't what it used to be."

Callum mimed a straight face. "Best you not hear our B.A. behaving unladylike. Ashamed The Montgomerie'd be, lass, you murdering people and cussing a blue streak."

Angus clucked his tongue and shook his finger. "What our lass needs is a braw lad to take her in hand, to stop these ball-ups."

"Aye," echoed the glee club. "That's what she needs."

B.A.'s eyes locked on Michael, being the nearest. "If you dunna get them off me—"

"You'll what?" he taunted. "A lass in your position should be more polite. Like, saying *please*. It's them bloody Yank ways coming out in you."

"Michael, if I get my hands on you—"

He waggled a finger, imitating Angus. "Careful, lass."

Innis chimed, "You're wasting breath, cautioning *Herself*. Montgomeries never listen."

A feral growl began deep within B.A. as she shoved with all her might. Her snarl shifted into a stream of Gaelic curses when she couldn't budge either man.

Eyes wide, Wee Gordie gasped, "What she said! Mum'd wash your mouth out with soap, B.A.!"

Michael grinned. "Lass, you're not going anywhere unless we hear the secret word." He put his hand to his ear, waiting for her to beg.

B.A. grabbed at the long strands of his hair with her free hand. Michael jerked back. "No male on this isle is daft enough to get close when you've a mad on. You're a Montgomerie after all. What's that you say, lass? By chance did I hear . . . ?"

B.A. closed her eyes, and the word came out on another big cat growl: "Please!"

Chapter 3

"Here?" B.A. gasped, hurriedly tying the sash on her robe.

She'd barely peeled off her sticky clothes when a car had pulled up in her driveway. Never would she have expected *this*.

She stared them down—or tried to—but the worms avoided eye contact. In the lead was Callum, next stood Wulfgar, the tallest Viking, with Desmond the Panther flung over one shoulder. Behind them came Michael carrying Mershan's flight bag and jacket with the reverence Sméagol would The One Ring. Callum muscled past B.A. and into the empty living room, Wulfgar the Moving Mountain trailing in his wake.

B.A. tried to stare him down, too. It was hard when she had to look up at him. Did one stare a person up? *Sheesh*, B.A. grumbled to herself, she'd get a crick in her neck maintaining eye contact with the Norseman.

"I dunna have a place for him." She stomped her foot. Michael filed past, ignoring her, then Robbie, Angus, Innis and Ian the Horseman's brother, all heading with uncanny accuracy upstairs and straight to her bedroom—the only bedroom currently with a bed.

She went to close the door, but The Cat Dudley—their caboose—bounded up the stairs. Accidentally getting hairs of his tail caught in the door, he squalled and hissed as if she'd crippled him for life. Bouncing sideways, he threatened to bite her. In defense she picked up an umbrella from the stand, opening and closing it rapidly to shoo him. The feline

wasn't impressed. She adored moggies, but Dudley wasn't re-
motely like a cat, was closer to Freddy Krueger in a fur suit.

" 'Tis unlucky to open a brolly inside, lass." Angus and his
cane joined the procession up the stairs. "You've caused
trouble enough for one day, trying to kill poor Doc and this
Viking feller. Now you want to murder the moggie, too? The
Marys won't like you tormenting their kitty."

"Me tormenting *him?* Out, kitty. I won't have you shred another duvet with your tiny daggers. You ruined my last one."
Too late, she thought. Dudley had bounded up the stairs to
follow his new pal.

Rushing after the cat, she forced her way to the bedroom.

Unlike the rest of the two-story thatched house, this room
was furnished. Panes of pink-veined glass covered the walk-
in closet doors, reflecting the perfection of B.A.'s design.
White carpet ran wall to wall, showcasing the George III
platform bed with wooden tester refinished in antique
white. No hint of plaid anywhere.

She loved tartan, but had enough up at the castle. Pulled
back to the bedposts, the curtains along the canopy
matched the blush-pink duvet. A sensual room designed for
a woman's taste, B.A. intended Rose Cottage to be Falgannon's honeymoon lodge. She'd live here only until renovations were completed to Lady Cottage in the castle.

"Stand aside, lass." Michael yanked back the comforter as
they placed Desmond down.

"Eegit, you can't dump him here," she fumed.

"Stand aside, lass." Callum pulled off Desmond's short
boots. "You half kill the man, you can bloody well tend him
for the night."

"Ever suffer nosebleeds, B.A., from the high altitude of
this parade ground you call a bed?" Michael bounced on it,
testing its firmness. "All this pink gives me insulin problems,
like I've overdosed on candy floss. The mattress is verra bonnie though—I like the pillow-tuft top."

"Why can't Doc care for him?" She edged toward the window, reluctant to be nearer The Panther Desmond.

"Some daft lass went and coldcocked Doc. We took him

to the Marys and propped him up on the rollaway bed with an ice pack on his pointy chin." Ian, one of the Fraser twins, took her hand and placed an aspirin bottle in it. "No alcohol or pain pills—just these. Cold compresses for the goose egg. Wake him every two hours and look into his eyes, lass. If his pupils get squirrelly or he gets a pain in the tum like he might blaw, give a ring."

"On *what?* MacGyver of the East dinna fix the blower." B.A. stood helpless while the group filed out—fled, the cowards—leaving The Panther dozing on her satin sheets.

The room felt smaller, stifling because of his presence.

She started after Ian, but a mountain of flesh blocked her path. Her eyes at nipple level, they traveled up his frame to a chiseled face and ice blue eyes. She wondered what Wulfgar thought of her nutty islanders.

"This is his," he rumbled, shoving a leather laptop case at her. "I'll bring the rest in the morning."

"Rest? What rest? He'll be leaving come morn."

Wulfgar shook his head. "Desmond isn't going anywhere until he finishes what he came to do."

Over my dead body, B.A. vowed. The Viking horde and their shape-shifting panther leader could decamp from her island come morning. Oh gor, this was Monday; the ferry wouldn't run again until Thursday. She was stuck with the Vikings until then.

Putting the laptop on the dresser, she followed, determined to have it out with them. "Why not leave him at The Hanged Man?" she called to their retreating backs.

"No can do, lass." Robbie leaned on the newel post, waiting for her. "A call came from Hamish the Lighthouse on the radio. A cruiser is fetching the three Yank lasses over. They'd detoured to Iona to sightsee. That's why they missed the ferry. The Hanged Man will be full shortly, leaving only the garret designed for Hobbits. I took in Dennis, the other Viking, and Wulfgar's bunking with Callum."

"Surely, one of you can stay here then?"

Ian smiled. " 'Tis a chaperone you'd be wanting? The Cat Dudley volunteered."

"A chaperone's needed for this Desmond feller," Angus chortled, "the way our B.A. had him on the floor wallowing him."

" 'Tis true," several of them agreed.

Black-headed, blue-eyed Ian tweaked the faint cleft in her chin, jerking back as she slapped at his hand. "Mind, B.A., no wallowing your Viking until he wakes up."

"You're wasting breath, laddie. She's a Montgomerie. You ken they never listen," Angus reminded from the front walkway.

"Pelicans," she snarled to Ian's and Michael's backs. "Where am I going to sleep? I dunna have furniture for the house yet, just the bedroom and kitchen—as you bloody well ken."

Ian turned around on the porch. Fog swirled about him, so thick it swallowed up the other traitors. She heard car doors slamming as they piled into the silver Range Rover.

"There's room enough on your bloody parade ground, Florence Nightingale. He'd have to be a sprinter to catch you. If he gets frisky, sic the cat on him." He winked and then vanished.

Speechless, B.A. watched the Rover's lights show up in the mist, slightly disembodied since the silver car blended with the gray fog. Something brushed against her. She glanced down to see Dudley weaving around her legs. "Some chaperone. You *like* The Bloody Panther! Go home to the Marys, I'm sure they wonder where you are."

Dudley sniffed at her, then loped back up the stairs.

Oh, great! She had two un-neutered males upstairs.

Carrying the tray into the bedroom, B.A. set it on the nightstand. The Panther Desmond hadn't moved. She seethed over their foisting him off on her, but anger shifted to concern. Surely, this was too long for him to be unconscious.

She hesitated before sitting on the edge of the bed, female skittishness pulsing in her blood. Taking a deep breath, she steeled herself to touch him, then fought the instinct to jerk back due to the heat his body radiated. Not fever—high-metabolism men came blessed with it, while women shivered, counted calories and struggled not to turn into Goodyear Blimps.

Her hands trembled. It'd been so long since she touched any man outside her brothers and a few islanders—who were one extended pack of siblings. So long since she'd wanted to.

She checked his clothes for glass shards, finding none. His raven-black hair lay in waves and ringlets so thick it was hard to tell if the skin was broken where he'd hit his skull. She ran her fingers through the curls. *Only to check the lump*, she told herself. The knot felt soft, but no blood. Leaning back, she spotted streaks on the back of his white silk shirt.

"Maniac cat." She glanced around for the wee beastie.

As if conjured, Dudley popped up on the bed and began kneading the duvet beside Desmond. She glared at the stupid feline. Glared at the man. No way around it. The shirt would have to come off so the scratches could be cleansed.

For a sweet second she considered taking pinking-shears up the middle of that Armani silk, as payback for those devastating kisses. For awakening that grinding hunger within her. Conscience whispered it was the coward's way. Well, she was no bloody chicken—she'd rather not touch him any more than necessary.

"Who knows, Vikings might have cooties," she told the cat.

Rolling him over, B.A.'s fingers shook as she undid the studs and tugged the shirttails from his slacks. Barely able to draw breath, she stared at his chest. The man was beautiful. His muscles were sleekly defined in a well-maintained pantherlike way; the conformation of his shoulders, arms and upper torso was, to her taste, perfect.

Another plus—he wasn't hairy. Men with chests that looked as if someone Crazy-glued a French Poodle there gave her the willies. He had a dusting of hair on his breastbone, then the dark line traveled down to his insy bellybutton and thickened into an arrow below.

"Mercy," she said on a sigh.

She placed a hand on his stomach and trailed it up to his heart. *Checking his pulse,* she lied to herself. B.A. *wanted* to touch him. For the first time in years she yearned to stroke warm male flesh, to savor unyielding muscles under her hand. Heat roared through her as she recalled how he tasted—that slow sensual slide of his tongue in her mouth. Desire more than she could bear, she bit back a groan.

Get a grip, Angel B.A. screamed, *you'll have a bloody orgasm just touching the man!* Ignoring her tiny guiding conscience, she flexed her fingers, indulging in the tactile sensuality. After all, The Panther was out cold and had no idea how she enjoyed petting him.

The heartbeat jolted, startling B.A. Strong and rapid, it pounded under her hand.

Desmond blinked, then glanced about the room. The one Scot had been right. Pink! Not bad like Pepto, still enough to give him the heebie-jeebies. The only hue worse was yellow. Something about pink and yellow were nails on a blackboard to men. Find one wearing either color by choice and you could bet he wasn't straight!

Focusing on the lovely B.A., he saw guilt flood her face. B.A. Montgomerie had her wicked way with him while she believed him unconscious.

Talk about Providence! Suppressing a grin, Desmond wondered why the Scots dropped him in the middle of B.A.'s bed. Since it furthered his plans, he wouldn't look the proverbial gift horse in the mouth.

Aware of the Scots' scheming, he'd been conscious as Wulf hauled him inside her house. Seeing her chin tilted in that lady of the manor mien—even from the upside-down position—Desmond had figured she'd put up resistance if he were awake, so he'd played possum.

His head throbbed, but the pain was a small price. He'd plot his next move soon. For the present, he was content to play patient to B.A.'s angel of mercy. He enjoyed her rolling him over onto his back and was tempted to return the favor.

Sitting up set fireworks off inside his skull. "My head—"

Desmond considered his memories. Some made no sense, a mishmash of pain, angels, Viking raiders, giant gumball machines attacking him—and a wild sexual fantasy about Sean Montgomerie's granddaughter. *The woman who'd haunted his dreams for years.* Then, men in skirts waltzed through his mind. He closed his eyes against rising nausea.

"Och, dunna go to sleep. I need to look into your eyes."

Look into his eyes was part of the Benny Hill nightmare buzzing inside his skull. She scooted closer in a small bounce, intensifying his agony. He bit back a groan.

Desmond felt sandpaper scraping his face. Fearing what could be on the end of that tongue, he risked peeking. Two sets of amber eyes blinked at him—B.A.'s and, oh yeah, that nutty cat.

"Your cat has eyes like you." Reaching up, he patted the kitty on the head. Never much of a cat person, he found this one oddly charming. "What's her name?"

"*His* name's The Cat Dudley," she corrected, "and he's not my cat."

"Hi, Dudley." The puss pushed against his fingers, demanding attention. "So affectionate, I thought it a female."

She sniggered. "His name isn't Dudley. It's *The Cat* Dudley. Scotland's other monster. Not as well kenned as Nessie, but Nessie had a head start."

"Maybe she's not a cat person, eh, Dudley?"

The silly feline meowed, his purr kicking into overdrive. Flopping over, he curled into the curve of Desmond's arm, then turned his head backward in one of those only-cats-can-do moves, and looked at him upside down. MY HERO was in the kitty's amber eyes.

"Shoo, Dudley, I need to get him to take off that shirt."

Desmond's mouth quirked up at one corner. "*You* called him Dudley. Why did you name your kitty *The Cat* Dudley?"

"He's not my cat. The Marys own the demon spawn, named for a beau the twins had in their teens." B.A. pushed the limp moggie away and took Desmond's upper arms to help him up.

Instead of being shaky and weak, he sprang at her, invaded her space. Nose-to-nose with her, his warm breath fanned her face.

"You mentioned looking into my eyes?" he asked. His voice was husky.

Clearly lightheaded, unable to draw air, B.A. jerked back before leaning into him. "Aye, they said look into them, watch for changes."

"You fear a concussion." He put a hand on either side of her lap and leaned closer. "Stare into my pupils. They should be the same. If one's dilated, it's a warning sign."

Desmond saw B.A.'s dazed reaction to his nearness, to the heat off his body. In the same measure, her female scent clouded his brain. Her small mouth was full and faintly parted—a punch to his gut. He resisted the temptation to close the last inch between them and cover her mouth with his, kiss her long and hard just to see the stunned look on her face.

Familiar with a concussion, Desmond knew he didn't have one. On the other hand, he wouldn't tell her that. Thanks to a bizarre accident, the Scots had plunked him down in her bed and forced her to play nurse. Lady Fate had smiled on him!

Memories were muddled following the knock on his head, but he recalled kissing B.A. Oh, boy, had he kissed her—as he'd dreamt of doing for longer than he cared to admit. Perhaps kissing B.A. hadn't been the smartest thing he'd ever done. He'd intended to ingratiate himself, win her over to his plans. On the other hand, in the deepest of night B.A. had played a part of his most sensual fantasies more times than he could count. For too long, she'd haunted him. Being knocked loopy, he'd been unable to resist. The taste of Pepsi had made him want to kiss her forever. And by her stunned reaction, he inferred that though surrounded by men, she wasn't kissed often enough.

"They all right?" he prompted when she kept staring with that perplexed expression.

She batted her lashes as if coming out of a trance. "Aye, um . . . they're normal. You need to remove your shirt so I can treat the scratches. 'Tis ruined, I fear."

"Plenty more where that came from." Unbuttoning the shirt, he tossed it onto the floor.

Desmond glanced at the ruined Armani shirt. Costing more than his mother had earned in a month, the price would've been a godsend on many an occasion when he was growing up. Now he discarded it without thought. He suspected that spoke volumes about his character—and not anything he liked. Pushing down inner demons, he summoned the control that came second nature to him.

B.A. jumped to her feet. "If you'd . . . turn . . ."

Raising his brow, Desmond silently marked her stammer and blush, but did as she asked.

B.A. wanted to kick the man for his drop-dead, sexy grin.

She picked up the cloth to clean his scratches, working in utter silence, though the kitty's purr rivaled a badly tuned diesel engine as he rubbed against Desmond's elbow. Toweling the scratches dry, B.A. saturated a cotton ball with tea tree oil. When the pungent fluid touched the raw skin, he jumped.

"Sorry, they're cat tracks. They need disinfecting."

"No problem."

B.A. couldn't contain her sigh. The man's back was as gorgeous as his chest. The shoulders were strong, square, and with the right amount of muscular contours. Two intriguing moles lay above the small of the spine, fortunately missed by Dudley in his attack.

Maybe you ought to kiss them and make it better. Devil B.A.'s suggestion dripped with enticement.

Having Mershan in her bedroom conjured a surreal *Twilight Zone* quality. Pulse pounding, B.A. disliked the out-of-body sensation, which sucked all the air from the room. Desmond the Panther upset her nerves, awakening that part of her she'd carefully packed away after Evian's death.

Heaving a sigh, B.A. set aside the cotton ball, desperate to flee the room. She picked up the tray, escape within reach.

He stopped her with four words. "What about my leg?"

Tray rattling in her hands, she squeaked, "Your leg?"

He rotated on his hips and got to his feet, fixing her with those warlock eyes. "Your cat bit me on the leg."

"He's *not* my cat."

She recalled the scatty feline had sunk his claws into Desmond's leg and bit him. Mesmerized by the piercing eyes and the wonderful expanse of naked chest, her gaze traveled down his body to the tailored black slacks.

"Uh. . . . oh!" she spluttered, the walls of the oxygen-deprived room closing in on her.

He smiled. And oh, what a smile. It was one of those smiles to turn a woman's knees weak. Smug, he unbuckled his pants.

She gulped. "Can you not push the pant leg up?"

"It'd be awkward."

"Not as awkward as you dropping your bloody breeks!"

She strangled when he did precisely that, then kicked out of them. The man was perfect—everywhere. Well, maybe not his toes—men rarely had pretty toes—but she barely paid them attention. The rest of him made up for standard-issue male feet. And wow, nothing typical in the underwear department. No sexless jockey whites women abhor, but black silk. Black silk covering a blatant erection!

No, sir. She won't catalog the perfection there, Devil B.A. chortled.

Her vision jerked up, colliding with his feline eyes.

Then it hit her. He had green eyes. *Green* eyes. No wonder her lads had dropped him into her bed.

Och, she was doomed!

Desmond watched the door close on B.A.'s shapely rear as she beat a hasty retreat. He'd rattled the walls of her safe life on this tiny island in the Hebrides. *Good.* His mouth tugged at the corners. Male dominance surged in his blood, urging him to fling aside the duvet and run B.A. down like prey. He let her flee.

All good things to those who wait. He'd waited a damn long time. For now, he could go slowly, relish the victory almost within his grasp.

He lay back on the silk sheets, feeling out of place in the pale pink bedroom—yet loving every minute. His masculine presence was a stark contrast to the room. He was alien, dark . . . the invader. He recalled the Scots calling him a Viking. Well, he didn't have a drop of Norse blood in him, but the aura of a Viking raider suited. Like a conquering war-lord of old, he'd come to this island to claim it, and if he ad-mitted it to himself, he'd come as much to face B.A.

BarbaraAnne Montgomerie Deshaunt was his riddle of the Sphinx. She was unique to his world, a prize he'd denied himself for a very long time. Ever since he'd clawed his way out of grinding poverty and to the pinnacle of his high-powered world, all else he wanted he'd taken and kept until he lost interest.

B.A. was different in a way he could never define. He'd watched her from afar for years. Wanted her. Maybe he'd made a mistake keeping his distance, turning her into a shimmering chimera forever out of reach.

No more. He'd touch her. When he wanted. As often as he wanted.

He'd touched her tonight. His body bucked as he closed his eyes, thinking back on her soft mouth, her taste, how she responded to him.

With her looks and family connections, it made no sense that B.A. buried herself on this isle straight from some quirky Alec Guinness movie. She had money to live any-where, to go first class without asking the price. Why hide here? From profiles his friend and employee Julian Starkad-der had supplied about the Montgomeries over the years, Desmond knew all the details of B.A.'s life, such as her mother's death when she was in her teens, and how she was raised in Falgannon by her grandmother, away from her sib-lings. Dry facts that failed to prepare him for the woman. Could she have cared for Evian Deshaunt so much that his death had affected her so?

Desmond mistrusted the word *love*. It was a means to bind people to your will. Another form of a price tag.

Oddly, he'd feared the real B.A. would somehow be less than the B.A. who lived in his mind, that he'd find disap-pointment in their confrontation. There'd been no letdown in facing her. In fact, he hadn't felt this alive . . . well, for longer than he could recall.

The fat cat hopped up beside him. Not used to four-legged creatures crawling into bed with him, Desmond jerked. The feline purred and flexed his claws on the fluffy duvet. A soft chuckle rattled through Desmond's body as he considered how Ms. B.A. Montgomerie wouldn't like that.

Groggily, he petted the puss. "Falgannon's ice princess better get used to a man mucking up her world."

B.A lifted her head and glanced around. Gor, she'd fallen asleep on her laptop—again. Focusing on the keyboard, she checked if she'd drooled on it. Bad enough when you drooled on your pillow. Only, when you ended up sleeping on your computer three nights out of five, the specter of shorting out the system was no joke.

She listened to the house, sensing a difference. Then it hit her. *The invader.* Mershan's male presence seemed to permeate the air.

Rolling her neck to ease the kink, she fretted. She needed sleep desperately, since she hadn't slept well these past two weeks.

An edginess crawled under her skin, but she couldn't put a finger on why. Or more to the point, she didn't want to face why.

Damn her meddling islanders. There wasn't anyplace to lie down except the bed upstairs. New sofas and chairs for the cottage were supposed to have been on the ferry, but in all the confusion of Mershan's arrival she'd forgotten to find out if they'd come.

It was time to check on him. Past time.

Stretched out beside the sleeping man, The Cat Dudley smiled, his purrs so loud she was surprised he didn't wake Mershan. Setting the tray on the nightstand, she frowned at the moggie. Silly critter watched Desmond with an adoring expression that said, *Can I keep him?*

"Stow it, I'm kissing—hmm—kicking his arse off the island first thing come Thursday," she muttered to the fuzzy pussycat.

B.A.'s fingers touched the beautiful arm. She was spellbound. It'd been a long time since a man had been in her bed. So many things she'd thought dead within her achingly roared to life. Images flooded her mind, dark imaginings of them together. Of him taking her in the deep of night.

Weakened from the lack of sleep, she fought the heady pull. B.A wondered in a whisper, "Where the hell is Angel B.A. when I need her?"

The tableau seemed too real: her climbing up on the bed, sliding over him, kissing him, tasting him. Him awakening and rolling her under that gorgeous, hard body. His weight pressing her into the mattress.

Dizzy, she jerked. Damn, she was falling asleep on her feet. She'd best get this done. Her hand gently shook his shoulder. "Mr. Mershan."

She flinched at how hot he was. His body glistened with a sheen of sweat that alarmed her. It wasn't normal. His pulse pounded, vibrating his whole body. Were his injuries worse than they'd assumed? Scared that might be the case, she shook him again.

Suddenly, he jackknifed upright. "No!"

B.A. saw his look of horror, empathized with the pain on his face. It took a moment before his eyes focused. Despite concern, her heart kicked into overdrive as she stared. There was a timeless feel to those eyes. Ancient eyes. Eyes of an *auld soul,* Scots called them.

"Are you all right, Mr. Mershan?"

"Just a dream." He rubbed his forehead, then petted the cat crawling into his lap. Even Dudley was upset for him. "I never fooled with cats before."

"I'm not entirely sure he's really a cat." She poured out some iced lemonade she'd brought and handed him several aspirin. "These should help."

As he drained the tumbler, his eyes traveled down her body and back to her face. He lifted an eyebrow over her rumpled state. Swallowing her flight instincts, she struggled against losing herself in those pale depths as she checked to see if they appeared normal. No doubt about it, the man unnerved her.

He bent his knee to prop his arm on it, the corner of that

sexy mouth twitching up in amusement. "Looking into my eyes again, Miz Montgomerie?"

B.A. hated her reaction to him. Around men, she remained cool and in control. She was aware the males of her isle lovingly called her Ice Goddess. So why did this one slip past her barriers?

"I am. Your heart rate alarms me."

B.A. reached, putting two fingers to the pulse in his neck. The pounding was strong. With pantherlike reflexes, his hand caught hold of her wrist. Their eyes locked, and in a breathless moment the rhythm of her blood sped up to match the cadence of his heartbeat against her fingers.

His thumb brushed back and forth across her pulse point, the small touch sending a shiver over her skin. An agonizing touch. "Seems *your* heart rate isn't too stable either, BarbaraAnne."

Like an eegit, her mind grasped for a distraction. "You wanted a meal when you arrived. Would you like me to bring you something to eat?"

He kept up the slow, sensual stroking of her wrist. His grip was loose. She could've pulled back, yet she couldn't break the invisible bond.

Those thick lashes flicked as he glanced at her body again. "Eat? Maybe later. I'm not hungry . . . for food."

Scalded, B.A. jerked her arm back. "Then you should rest."

"You'll be around—in case I need something?"

B.A. thought she heard the sound of a trap spring shut. "I need to check your eyes, wake you every couple hours through the night. To be safe."

"Thank you, it's kind of you to care for me." He slid back under the duvet and settled on his side.

Too jittery to move, B.A. watched him for a moment. Finally she turned out the lamp by the bedside and went to the walk-in closet to pull out extra pillows and blankets. Leaving the low-watt light on in the hall so he could find the loo, she halted in the middle of the floor. She longingly eyed the bed—the only one in the house. There wasn't even a damn sofa to curl up on. Strangely, she didn't fear he'd take advantage of his being alone with her. She feared herself.

After one last look at the bed, she went to the corner of the room and dropped the bedding. As she spread the covers on the floor, Dudley tippy-toed over. The kitty often curled up with her when she slept. His gentle presence helped keep the loneliness at bay. Tonight on the chilly floor, she'd welcome that warm body.

A vibrating hot water bottle with fur, she thought. But instead of crawling under the covers with her, Dudley meowed then did an impatient dance on silent feet. "I get the message, kitty. It ain't happening."

Shooting her a disgusted look, the cat scampered back onto the bed. He executed another little boogie and meowed as if saying, *See, there's plenty of room.* When that ploy didn't work, he started flexing his claws into the duvet, taunting her to come make him stop. Damn cat might as well stick his tongue out and go, *nanabooboo!*

"Traitor," B.A. grumbled. Then she tugged the blanket over her head.

B.A. roused, shivering; still mostly asleep, she searched for her duvet. Fifteen togs, top-of-the-line for winter warmth, she should be toasty under its heavy weight. Then she noticed that scratchy warmth at the back of her throat warning she was taking a chill. Great. Rolling over to find the quilt, her back went into a spasm.

"Ooooo . . ." She remained awkwardly on her elbow, aware she needed to shift to relax the muscles, knowing she didn't dare or it'd seize up completely.

Concerned, Dudley padded over and crawled onto her lap to lick her chin. She tried to push him away, but groaned as the slight movement brought pain. Gritting her teeth, she finally pushed to her feet and shuffled down the hall to the bathroom. Shaking out two muscle relaxers, she washed them down with water.

She glanced at the clock. A little after four. She'd checked on Mershan several times during the night. He seemed tired, though he'd assured her it was from needing sleep and not anything to deal with the head injury.

Going over, she stood by the bed watching her patient. Blessed with a hot metabolism, he'd kicked off the heavy duvet and now slept peacefully. Maybe she'd trade a blanket for the duvet since he wasn't freezing like her.

Innocence touched his countenance, making him appear years younger than his age. She smiled at the long sooty eyelashes. Women would kill to have lashes like that. Her hand softly brushed a black curl off his forehead, then she placed her palm against his brow.

"Just checking his temperature," she murmured to the cat and her gremlins.

She hated to wake him, his slumber seemed so restful. Glancing back to the corner, she nearly moaned. She'd be sick if she slept on the floor. She'd end up with a cold, a sore throat and a stiff back. Michael was spot on when he'd called the bed a bloody parade ground. Four people could sleep in comfort. Carefully she pulled the quilt over his legs.

Aside from all the physical response he provoked within her, her mind whispered that this man was unique. Special. She didn't entirely trust his reasons for coming to Falgannon, yet she held no fear of him. Silly, but she knew this man would never harm her. His threat to her world came in a more dangerous fashion—her wanting him.

She sneezed as another chill wracked her body.

"That does it!" Fetching the king-size pillows, she placed them down in the middle of the bed to form a wall between them. This way, she could keep an eye on him, come awake in an instant if needed. She could catch a nap, not a head cold. If he awoke, she'd jump out of bed and pretend she'd just come to check on him.

Dudley walked down the pillows and started flexing his claws. His purr rumbled as he turned a circle and finally settled down. It's a soothing noise, she thought as she closed her eyes. And as the warmth of the duvet seeped through her cold muscles, she imagined purrs came from her.

* * *

The gray light of dawn filtered around the cracks of the draperies, and Desmond woke up for the umpteenth time. His head was still sore.

What a comedy of errors, yet it had worked to his favor. He reflected on his night in B.A.'s pink bower. She'd been so comical when he dropped his slacks. A gentle soul, she'd been kind taking care of him. How she'd materialized with aspirins and icy lemonade. The ice felt soothing, but he'd needed it on a pain much lower. That had been enough to keep him awake half the night. He smiled, recalling B.A.'s comical muttering to herself and the cat.

Yawning, he noticed two long pillows ran the length of the bed, that silly cat propped up on one. Dudley sat, rumbling a small earthquake. Desmond had no idea cats purred so loudly, but then he'd never had room in his life for a pet.

"Are you the gatekeeper?" he asked.

On the other side of the pillows, in the huge bed was a sleeping B.A. Surprise flooded him, then shifted to an odd surge of anger. Did she jump in bed with strangers so easily?

"I could be Jack the Ripper's great-great grandson."

He patted the rumbling kitty and stared at B.A. slumbering on the other side of her feather bastion. Unbound hair spilled about her in a pool of gold, provoking his body to lurch with a jolt of lust—the kind a man can scarcely control.

Desire goaded him to reach over those pillows, yank her under him and take her in a hundred ways, the driving impulse nearly more than he could curb. A roguish smile spread across his mouth as the notion of pushing a few buttons, testing how far she'd let him go, flittered across his brain. He'd liked her reactions to him and was eager to see her blush again.

On the other hand, he fancied being Ms. Montgomerie's guest for the foreseeable future. He figured acting the perfect houseguest would undermine her opposition to his plans. That didn't include sliding over her and using his mouth in delicious ways to wake her up.

He settled for lifting a lock of her dark blond hair and rubbing it against his mouth. There'd be other opportunities.

Chapter 4

One head rose above the wall. Then a second, followed by an, "Ouch! Ouch!"

Michael and Callum glared at Willie.

"As a writer, *Willa* Macgregor," Michael chided, "you ken stealth dunna include someone bleating like a bloody sheep."

Willie's head popped up next to the Mackenzie cousins, peering over the stone fence that encompassed the official residence of the Lady of the Isle. "Tell The Cat Dudley. 'Tis enough the wee monster of Falgannon gives you his opinion when you're wearing breeks, another to get that vampire bite when you're in a kilt."

Michael snorted. " 'Tis daft, a man crawling around with the wind tickling his family jewels whilst spying like James Bond. Ever see Bond in a kilt?"

Robbie joined the group, then scratched his red head in thought. Dudley jumped up on the fence and pussyfooted back and forth, eager to play this new game. Since Dudley's idea of play differed vastly from the men's, they took a moment to assess what the creature was doing.

"In *On Her Majesty's Secret Service*, Bond donned a kilt—," Robbie began.

The others chimed, "Dinna count."

"That's Lazenby," Callum refreshed Robbie's memory. "The official stance of the "Morn, B.A." Club is Big Tam broke the mold."

"Aye, that Irish laddie sucked eggs," Willie commented.

Michael added, "Better than the new Craig chap."

Murmurs of ayes were uttered with the shaking of heads.

"Last good Bond film was *Diamonds Are Forever*, filmed in Las Vegas." Willie informed them, "Vegas would be grand for a honeymoon. I research my books at the same time."

Michael scowled. "Ever occur, *Willa*, to set your books in present day Scotland? Then no pesky anachronisms."

"Anachronisms? Is that something to do with spiders?" Robbie shuddered. "I have a deep revulsion for anything small and with more than four legs."

Callum nudged Michael with his elbow. "What I want to ken is, can they actually do it on a galloping horse—or is that your fertile imagination, *Lady Willa?*"

The cat came purring by, and the men leaned back to let him make another pass.

Robbie queried, "How come they frag people in movies and we cannot frag The Cat."

"B.A. ruled no fragging Kitty after we got our DVDs of *Full Metal Jacket* and the fragging issue arose." Michael reached into the back pocket of his jeans and pulled out a silver packet, rattling it to draw attention. "Hey, demon from hell, want crunchies? See, Dudley, time for us men to stick together. The Viking Prince has black hair and green eyes. Got to be Irish blood in there somewhere; the lilt is in his voice. Dunna think we'll get a better chance to break The Curse. You need to do your part."

Kitty scarfed down the treats, then meowed.

"Quick, give him more"—Willie nudged Michael— "before he starts caterwauling, or worse, bites me again."

"See anything?" Robbie passed the ancient binoculars to Callum.

The cat suddenly dashed along the walk, up the stairs and into the kitchen through the cocked-open door.

B.A. vetted the tray to see if anything was missing. The Panther Desmond had expressed wanting a meal before the chaos erupted last night, but when she'd asked during the night, he hadn't wanted food. His eyes spoke that he hungered for something else.

She put her hands to her cheeks as images of his beautiful body flooded her memory.

Stop acting like a love-struck teenager, BarbaraAnne, Angel B.A. carped from her right shoulder.

Placing silverware by the plate, B.A. addressed the tiny gremlin of her conscience, " 'Tis just breakfast."

Angel B.A. scoffed, *On Belleck china, with Waterford crystal and a mint-green Irish linen napkin?*

Aye, she's lying to herself. Devil B.A. giggled from the perch on her left shoulder.

That gave B.A. pause, not recalling the Angel and Devil B.A.s agreeing on anything before. "Note to self: Whilst you've a guest, refrain from talking to teeny beings on your shoulders."

B.A. grimaced at the track of her mind. As a child, she'd seen an old *Looney Toons* episode where an angel and devil version of the character kept popping in and whispered chidings. Being imaginative, she'd begun talking to her angel and devil selves and never grew out of it.

Rocking to Tone Loc's "Wild Thang," she dismissed that she'd spent thirty-seven minutes fussing over the tray. Her mouth pursed. It looked like something a lover would carry in on a morning-after.

She glanced to the middle of the room, watching Dudley. His nose was high in the air and his metronome tail swished in contentment, a Harley Davidson purr almost matching the beat of the song.

"Yeah, Wild Thang—that's *you*, Dudley."

Nibbling at her lower lip, B.A. debated if she should forget the whole thing lest the warlock infer she was interested in him. Nonsense. She shrugged. She couldn't care less what The Panther Desmond thought. She would take him breakfast.

Impulsively, she scooped up her pruning shears and darted out the back door.

Michael adjusted the field glasses, then checked if he had the right end. "That wall of mirrored tiles she installed on the closet doors is reflecting the sun." As he lowered them, he spotted B.A. come out the back door and scurry up the walkway to Castle Falgannon's garden.

"Dive! Dive! Dive! B.A. alert!" he warned.

All heads vanished behind the rock wall.

Kitty jumped up on the fence and stared over at them as if wondering what new game they'd thought up to entertain him.

"Shoo, Dudley," Michael pleaded. "Go see what B.A. wants."

The glorious morn embraced B.A. with a warm island breeze, a day so perfect, so rare. There'd be few more like it as winter approached. She inhaled the heady mix of sea spray and peaty earth. Something Yanks in L.A. could never understand. It was damn near intoxicating.

She looked across her island at its breathtaking splendor. Though the view from the castle farther up the hill beyond Rose Cottage was better, this vantage still inspired awe. When growing up, she went to school in the States part of each year. Upon her return, the sheer grandeur never failed to give her pause.

The intense colors of Falgannon left her speechless. Never the same two days in a row, she loved how one could be dark, moody and foreboding, the next sunshine-filled and exhilarating. The low horizons afforded a view over miles of vibrant greens of the rolling countryside to the white sand beaches and tropical colored water.

B.A. had left the back door open to enjoy the music. Also, to keep an ear out if her patient called—though he'd need to bellow over the Tone Loc. Dancing along the walkway, B.A. gyrated through the rose garden leading up the knoll toward the castle.

Pondering which blooms to cut, she inhaled their heady perfume. The music moved her, so she indulged.

"If you can swish your tail, Kitty, so can I." No Robert Palmer girl, she put force behind the sensual rocking. Her long hair swirled as she let the music possess her body. "I wish I had some of those stripper tassels, Dudley, so I could make them go in circles in opposite directions . . ."

Gorgeous lavender tea roses drew her. Pulling one to her nose, she inhaled the citrus scent. As she bent to snip it, Dudley gifted her with one of his vampire bites to her ankle.

"Sir Dudley the Terrible, you're not a feline, but a midget alien in a cat suit. Tommy Lee Jones and Will Smith are looking for you," she teased.

The cat's chubby body cantered up the walkway to the plants profuse with red blossoms. He circled the bush of My Lady's Passion and meowed.

"You think? Men are mad for red. Little red wagons, red cars and sexy red dresses. These blooms are a vivid scarlet—no trace of pinks or purples to muddy the color. The black lacings on the edges remind me of sexy underwear. Okay, Dudley knows best."

Cutting three, she wrapped her silk robe about her and danced back to the thatched house, Dudley on her heels. As she started up the steps, she glanced up at the bedroom window. The corner of her mouth tugged into a smile, and she was glad to see The Panther Desmond wasn't awake to witness her bump-and-grind.

"Grand thing about living out here, Dudley. There's none save you to witness my foolishness."

"You see that?" Robbie whistled, fanning himself.

"I've eyeballs in my head." Michael was stunned. "Our B.A. danced about in her bedclothes in the garden."

Callum nodded. "It's been a long time since our lass was so gay."

"Dunna say gay," Robbie grumped. "Makes me think of Oonanne and Morag."

"Happy, then." Callum stared at the house. "Well, I go for it. 'Tis this Desmond bloke for our B.A. Agreed?"

"Aye," the others chorused enthusiastically.

"A bonnie duo they'll make. The sooner the better," Robbie stated.

"Let's hoof it back to The Hanged Man and report. Map out battle plans. Despite B.A. sashaying, she'll not fancy falling in love as fast as we need. She's a Montgomerie, after all."

Dudley hopped back up on the fence, then yowled as if to say, *What did you decide?*

"I still think the cat needs fragging," Robbie grumbled.

Michael followed the others crawling away from B.A.'s garden, frowning again at his bird's-eye view of what a Scotsman wore under his kilt. "Lady Willa, wear breeks next time we go a-spying. Please!"

Chapter 5

Stepping back from the window, Desmond feared B.A. had caught him looking. His body was rock-hard from watching Ms. BarbaraAnne Montgomerie dance her heart out with the raw sexuality of a stripper and the grace of a ballerina. The pagan rhythm of her movements provoked a hungry heat to ravage his body, to twist his guts into knots. Placing a hand on his groin, he tested how aroused he was.

Desmond sought to recall the last time he'd wanted a woman this desperately—the point where civilized man faded and the primitive took control. No memory jumped to mind.

Too much of his life had been spent struggling to survive. While other kids had worried about bikes or what they'd get for birthdays, his sole focus had been putting grinding poverty behind him. In his twenties, he'd worked eighteen hours a day to ensure his younger brothers received the finest education.

Thus, women had never been a high priority. Oh, there were affairs, numerous affairs, but the women knew going in there was no future with him. It had been for sex, nothing else.

He wanted something more from B.A. Montgomerie. What that *something* was, eluded him. Just *more*. To be defined at a date later.

Conflicting emotions warred within him, spelling trouble. He closed his eyes and leaned his head back. Control that was usually second nature wasn't surfacing.

Images of that gorgeous body swaying as she lost herself to the music, the way her hair brushed the bottom of her derriere, flashed through his mind. When was the last time he'd seen hair that long? Hands itching, he yearned to fist them in the heavy mass, to see her bent over him lost in passion, it cascading around them.

"Quick way to rein in, Mershan," he scoffed.

His desire—too pale a word for the demon growling within him—might play havoc with his plans. He attacked goals in life with the single-minded focus of laying siege to a medieval fortress. No surrender, no quarter given. Plans had beauty in their precision, similar to the blueprints he drew for skyscrapers. The prospect B.A. could cause problems irritated him.

Strangely ungrounded, Desmond fought the urge to reach for his cell phone to call his brothers, to check how they were. It grated that he couldn't have the touchstone of instant contact with the twins, not from this backward island. This had been too long in plotting to let small details such as long blond hair interfere.

Hearing her soft burr speak to the cat jerked him back to the present. Desmond barely dove into the bed before the half-opened door pushed wide.

Carrying the tray, B.A. hummed along with Haddaway's "What Is Love," repressing the urge to jerk her head to the side like The Roxbury Boys. Pausing at the door, she sucked in a breath to control the pounding of her heart. *From dancing like a madwoman*, she told herself.

Who are you kidding? The man upsets your magnetic field, Devil B.A. carped.

The tray rattled as she placed it on the nightstand. She set aside the salt and pepper shakers, along with the pitcher of grapefruit juice, giving him room to eat. "Mr. Mershan?"

He pushed up, revealing that to-die-for chest, setting Devil B.A. to chanting *Tongue bath!*

Flashing a sexy grin, he asked, "Rather formal, considering we slept together."

"It's the *only* bed. They left me the cat as chaperone." B.A. assured herself those bedroom eyes and high-wattage smile did nothing to her knees.

Maybe because you're looking at his bare chest, Angel B.A. rebuked.

Man flesh! Devil B.A. rubbed her hands in glee.

"Some chaperone." Mershan's black brow arched, mocking.

"Watch—sic him, Kitty!" The cat twined between her legs, peeking out from underneath the hem of her gown, a halo above his head. "Bugger, works with the males on the isle."

"Dudley has discriminating taste."

Maybe felines stick together, she wanted to retort. Instead, she asked, "How do you feel?"

"Better. Want to look into my eyes?" When he saw she wasn't rising to his bait, he nodded to the tray. "For me?"

"A bit of breakfast." B.A. wanted to kick herself for going to the fuss. She smoothed the duvet across his lap so she could place the tray over it. Or tried. She encountered a definite lump. Blushing, B.A. jumped back as if scalded. Dudley hopped up on the bed, letting her scold him to cover embarrassment. "Shoo, you big mooch."

"Do you always treat your cat so? He's a live teddy bear."

"Grizzly would be more apt. And The Cat Dudley is *not* my cat," she corrected again.

"I forgot. Maybe you need to check my eyes—my condition might be worsening." He assayed the Irish linen, china and the crystal vase holding three bright red roses, so exquisite they seemed artificial. His brow arched a silent comment on the elegant setup as he lifted the vase to his nose. "Beautiful roses. I love red. First time a woman's given me flowers. I'm touched you went to so much trouble. Thank you, B.A."

She glanced at the cat, who looked like, *See told you?* The red roses were out of place in the pale pink room, a vivid and startling contrast as incongruous and sensual as Desmond Mershan, himself.

"Not much for scent, but the clarity of the red sets the bloom apart."

Rubbing the petals against his lips, the warlock's eyes flashed with blatantly sexuality. "They remind me of red satin underwear with black lace. And they smell . . . not perfumy. Earthy. Pagan."

B.A. almost swallowed her tongue. The expression on his beautiful face nearly provoked her to crawl up on that bed, knock the tray aside and have her wicked way with him. She wanted to see his expression as she lowered her mouth to his, felt his hands rough upon her breasts.

Yeah, bloody shame she was in this stupid virginal cotton gown and not a red satin bustier with black lace. Never had she felt such a grinding, elemental need for a man.

Her intense emotions were amplified by the meeting of their minds, both thinking the rose petals reminded them of sexy underwear. What would it be like to make love to such a rakish man so attuned not just to your body, but your mind as well?

Setting the vase on the tray, he lifted the cover over the eggs sunny-side up and then gestured with the knife to the nightstand. "May I have the salt and pepper?"

Before she realized, she'd handed him the salt. Her fingers flexed in a spasm around the shaker as his hand closed over hers. Och, the bloody warlock—he'd tricked her! Now she'd done it! Maeve would come back to haunt her for being so foolish.

His brows lifted. "Some quaint Falgannon custom?"

"Never mind." She released the shaker. "Too late."

"Perhaps I need to look in *your* eyes. You seem . . . distracted." When he saw she wouldn't explain about the salt, he gestured to the edge of the bed for her to sit. Taking a sip of the juice, he nodded to the books on the dresser. "You read a lot?"

She dragged the chair to the bedside, knowing she dared not get on that bed. "Not much to do on the isle in winter. Whole island's movie mad. We play music. Read a lot."

He paused, the piece of toast halfway to his mouth. "Why do you do it?"

"Read?"

"No, bury yourself on this island. A woman like you should be in London . . . Paris . . . Rome."

Umbrage twisted her mouth. "I dunna *bury* myself. London's fine, I enjoy a trip there. Paris is nice a time or two. If I lived in a big city, I'd choose New Orleans."

He nodded. "A town with an attitude. Shame Katrina did a number on it."

"She'll be back. Food's marvelous, the people warm and friendly. But I couldn't live anywhere except Falgannon. When I'm away, I miss the isle."

"But it's so far away from everything, I'd think you'd be dead bored."

She enjoyed watching Desmond eat. Movements of his hands were deft, precise—like magicians make. He had elegant, long, well-manicured fingers. They were hands she once again envisioned upon her body.

Stop drooling over the man like a ninny, Angel B.A. fussed.

"There's something"—B.A. reached for her exact feelings— "magical about Falgannon. It's in my blood, my soul."

He paused from feeding Dudley bacon, those pale eyes incisive, assessing. It was a dose of ice water hitting her, reminded her that Desmond Mershan was an Outlander, a man passing through. He'd be gone in a month if she permitted his work on the isle, back to the bright lights of those cities he admired. She'd be left with her books, Dudley and the screwball islanders.

She'd be safe.

She'd be . . . lonely.

"I don't think anyplace provides those feelings," he said coolly.

She countered, "A Scot's roots run deep. If I left the island, a part of me would be dreaming of soft nights, of listening to rain on the roof or of walking on white sands at gloaming."

Desmond drank the juice and watched her with those guarded predator's eyes, causing B.A. to wonder what he really thought of her.

"Are we all here?"

Most dawns, The Hanged Man was the domain of what was lovingly called the "Morn, B.A." Club—the elders who came to enjoy tea and bannocks while discussing world events or gossip about Davey and his never-ending battle with his washer-machine. The club acquired its name from B.A. stopping off first thing every day to pick up one of Tam the Baker's pastries to take with her to the store. Naturally, the duffers always wished her a "Morn, B.A."

That B.A. hadn't made her usual stop, and the store remained unopened, was on all their minds. Several topics buzzed about the room. Why had the Vikings come to Falgannon? Had the three Yank lasses arrived, and what did they look like? However, the overriding concern was that the Viking prince had spent the night in B.A.'s bed.

Seeing the ancients—Angus and Callum—at their surveillance post by the picture window, in case B.A or the Vikings showed up, Michael the Fiddle called for order. "Attention, please! Time to shut your gubs!"

"I will, if you will," Brian the Horseman called, causing everyone to laugh.

"Seriousness, please. Matters need sorting out, then furniture has to be hauled to Rose Cottage before B.A. boots the Viking out." Michael tapped on the table with the end of a knife.

"Our gubs are shut. On with it," Tam the Baker barked. "Some of us work."

"He's waiting 'til someone gives him a gavel," Alasdair the Barber smirked.

Michael flashed them a prune face. "First thing I'd bang on would be that pointed noggin of yours, Alasdair, but it'd dent the gavel."

"Och, *on* with it," someone fussed from the far side of the room.

"We assessed the situation at Rose Cottage," Michael began.

Phelan the Lobster demanded, "What did you suss, man?"

"Plenty. B.A. was outside in her nightie dancing and singing."

"*Our* B.A.?" Gasps of disbelief rippled through the room.

Michael glanced to Callum on his left and nudged him for verification. Callum snapped awake to comply. "Quite frisky, too, I'd say."

Willie tacked on, "Mershan has black hair and green eyes."

"The Viking has green eyes?" At the bar, Davie the Weaver exclaimed in shock, dropping his scone into his tea.

"Green as a cat's," Robbie confirmed, "and Eire's lilt is in his voice. Not heavy, but it's there."

Michael watched the murmuring grow as the pertinent facts circled the room, reaching everyone—even the ancients. Almost deaf, they generally missed half of what was said since both were too bloody cheap to turn on their hearing aids.

He picked up the thread. "Her Web site shall fetch lasses to the isle. Only, with The Curse wreaking havoc, it's futile unless B.A. marries the proper man. The Viking prince and she gave off enough sparks last night to power Hamish's lighthouse."

Angus confirmed from the window seat, "Aye, the chap's taken with our lass. That kiss he gave her . . . warmed my old heart to see them."

"The Viking prince for our lass then?" Michael raised his hand in a vote, soon followed by every man in the room. "What, Angus? Not going to cast a no vote as you usually do to be contrary?"

"And bollocks up the thing? Bite your tongue, laddie, I'm a-planning to marry, too. Heard that Anna-Nicole Smith is available again. Have two-thousand pounds tucked up in my sock. I'm sure she'll be interested."

Michael joined the whole room in laughter. "Motion carried . . . unanimously. Mark that down in the minutes. Doubt we'll see it again."

Glasses and cups clinked together, sealing the conspiracy.

A revving engine in neutral, Desmond considered what his next move should be. He eased back in the bed as B.A. removed the tray, watched her, unblinking.

He'd miscalculated, underestimating the obstacle of Ms. BarbaraAnne Montgomerie. He disliked flaws popping up in his meticulous plans. B.A. wasn't what he anticipated.

At Sean Montgomerie's funeral in the spring, he'd seen

her from a distance, sitting at the front of the church with her sisters. Desmond gave the old man credit—good genes ran throughout the clan. Never had he seen seven such beautiful women. Only, an indefinable air about BarbaraAnne drew his attention. Her chin tilted against grief, she'd sat in the pew all prim and proper, that mass of long blond hair in a French-braid, secured with a black velvet bow. Though her sisters were equally stunning, he'd been unable to take his eyes from B.A.

Once she'd turned and looked directly at him, making eye contact. The world held its breath as they stared at each other. Quite odd, disturbing—never in his whole life had he felt that connected to anyone. Then she'd turned away, leaving him cold, with nothing but the festering resentment that forever devoured his soul.

It summoned images of another funeral. The pain of a seven-year-old flooded his mind, the flashback so vivid he nearly screamed, *Father!* For an instant, he'd blinked and then glanced at his brothers, sitting on either side, to see if he'd actually done so. His brother's hand had stayed him from jumping up and interrupting the testimonials to the great Sean Montgomerie—how respected, how loved the man had been. No one spoke for three little boys left fatherless because of the Montgomerie's greed.

Later, outside the family cemetery, he'd watched B.A. from his car, the soft knock of the wipers keeping rain off the windscreen. With a trembling hand, she'd touched the plaque placed in memorial of Evian Deshaunt. In that instant he'd almost hated her for wasting that emotion on a dead man. He'd fought the primitive urge to cross the graveyard and yank her into his arms, to kiss her until he melted that ice castle she'd built around herself, kiss her 'til she knew life was for the living.

Desmond lay back in her huge George III bed and considered Ms. B.A. Montgomerie, sizing up his opponent—surrogate for her grandfather. All the time and money gone into bringing Sean Montgomerie's empire down, and the old devil had escaped Desmond's vengeance. He'd wanted to howl at the moon.

Oh, the financial part of his plans still had the green light. The Brothers Mershan were taking down Montgomerie Enterprises, piece-by-piece, starting with Falgannon; Valinor Revisited, the horse farm in Kentucky; and Colford Hall in England. Nothing could stop them. The Montgomeries would have no idea who was the real power behind Trident Ventures until too late.

He forced a smile, but had a feeling it didn't reach his eyes, because a worried look passed over her face.

"Your head pains you?" she queried in concern.

Desmond curled his fists around handfuls of the duvet, holding tight to keep from grabbing her. She was too close. Her female scent brushed against his mind, nearly letting loose the primitive animal lurking just below the surface. She bent over the tray, the edge of her gown revealing the swell of those perfect breasts. B.A. Montgomerie needed reminding she was a woman and he was more than willing to do it—in every way imaginable.

Instead, he gave a brief nod. "A bit."

Rage and raw pain of that forlorn seven-year-old who'd watched his father pull the trigger ending his life, built inside of him to a dangerous, reckless level. Looking for a venue to vent, he focused on her whiskey-colored eyes. He wanted to see them wide, staring into his as he pumped his body into hers. He wanted to hear that husky voice calling his name as she climaxed with a force her dead husband never pushed her to reach. Maybe then the demons would be silent for awhile.

"You should rest." Anxiety flickered in her eyes.

In a clipped tone he replied, "Fine."

B.A. shook out a couple aspirin and handed them to him with a glass of water.

His control rattled her, he knew, that stillness within him that reminded her of a predator. He scared her in ways Ms. BarbaraAnne Montgomerie didn't want to think about. And like all true predators, he fed off that fear, savored it.

She turned to leave but he stopped her with a question, a challenge. "Don't you want to look into my eyes?"

A faint shudder wracked her body. Then he heard what she

was listening to. Downstairs, the radio played "Would I Lie To You" by Simply Red. Mick Huckhall crooned to look into his eyes and tell him if you believed he'd lie. It was one of those spooky moments, B.A.'s amber eyes stared into his, and he knew without a doubt he'd lie to her with out hesitation.

"You'll do." She wanted to break away, but was held in sway. "Try and rest."

Desmond watched her leave—run. Well, he'd permit her the distance. For now.

Feeling the pain in his head rise, fueled by rage, he closed his eyes and willed his mind to still. So many nights he'd lain awake staring at the ceiling, envisioning Montgomerie's face as he was presented with a fait accompli, that the empire he'd spent his life building would be destroyed with a few strokes of Desmond's pen. More than anything, Desmond had wanted Sean to know who was doing it and why. He'd been cheated of that personal triumph.

He rubbed the knuckles of his right hand, recalling how he put it through a wall after returning from Montgomerie's funeral. His brothers and he had been robbed of a father, of a decent childhood, because of that greedy old man. The one thing that would've conjured peace within him—seeing Sean's face as Desmond took everything from him—was no longer an option.

He'd still destroy Montgomerie Enterprises. He'd lay claim to the horse farm in Kentucky, the going concern in England and this stupid rock in the Atlantic. He'd even relish the pleasure of having Montgomerie's oh-so-beautiful granddaughter under him. He'd ride her hard, give no measure, and though she'd come to him willingly, want him as desperately as he'd want her, he'd be using her. Just as he would take and ravage her precious island.

Why did that suddenly make him feel sick?

Chapter 6

B.A. peeked into the bedroom. She needed clothes and a shower, but that required bearding The Panther. A quick sweep of the room revealed he wasn't about, so she hurried to the walk-in closet and opened the mirrored doors. Intent on escape, she didn't stop to ponder where Mershan had vanished.

Reaching for her jeans, she froze when sounds to the right drew her attention. her vision traveled down the dressing room hall to the spacious bathroom.

The mirror covering the wall behind the double-basins reflected Desmond in all his glory. Well, *nearly* all. The only thing covering that gorgeous body was a black towel around his hips. Leaning over the sink, he stuck out his chin and applied a smooth stroke up his sexy throat with a razor.

Hubba-hubba! Devil B.A. broke into wolf whistles.

She mentally kicked herself for ogling The Panther Desmond, but it had been a long time since she'd had a nekkid man—well, mostly nekkid—in her bathroom. She wished she possessed a dram of Janet the Red in her, as there was little doubt how her friend would handle this situation.

Wistfully, she sighed. Too much good girl was ingrained in her, so she remained flatfooted and tongue-tied. But her heart slammed against her rib cage and desire boiled in her, the ache more agonizing for being a sensation she thought long dead.

Devil B.A. screamed, *Maybe good girls don't, but* women *certainly do!*

Desmond leaned forward and washed off the excess shave cream. As he raised back, his hypnotic green eyes locked with hers as he looked at her in the mirror, their power not lessened because they were a reflection. He snagged a towel and dried his face, then turned. Every ges-

ture was unhurried, each movement measured with that
stillness unique to big cats. He *knew* there was no rush; he
had mesmerized his prey. Exuding confidence, he cocked
his hips and put his hands on them, saying: Look your fill.

B.A. wanted to throw something at him. Arrogant bastard! He stood—a slight smirk on that too sensual mouth
and in that itsy-bitsy towel—assured that he sent her blood
spiraling.

Before she could blink, he stirred, stalking to her with an
animalistic, sensual grace. Angel B.A. screamed, *Don't stand
there! Throw something! Run!* as he moved in for the kill.
Her breaths were short, choppy, pushed her breasts up high
in faint jerks; the heat off his very male body, rolled over her
even though inches separated them.

The feral eyes held her in thrall as Desmond leaned close,
as if going to kiss her. At the last second he whispered, "Do I
smell like pink peonies?"

Peonies, what's a peony? echoed Devil and Angel B.A. in
unison.

She swallowed hard, acknowledging she'd made a fool of
herself. He noted the visible signs she anticipated he might
kiss her, yet stood like a virginal teenager. Both of them were
aware if he'd chosen to follow through she wouldn't have
fought, and that secretly she desired him to do so.

Stop being such a ninny, Angel B.A. rebuked from her
right shoulder. Embarrassment propelled her to step back.
On the opposite side, Devil B.A. groaned and hung her head
in shame.

Smug, Mershan permitted the distance. "Hope you don't
mind. I wanted to wash my hair, get rid of the sticky stuff
from yesterday's adventure."

"I'm sure . . . You dunna-care for the fragrance of my
shampoo?" She stammered.

"*Au contraire.*" Once more, he invaded her space to nuz-
zle against her ear. "On you, the scent's quite seductive. It
haunted my dreams."

Angled open, the closet door reflected their images to the
bathroom mirror and back. Feeling trapped in a house of

mirrors, she suddenly wondered what had possessed her to design a bedroom suite with so many panels of reflective glass. All she'd missed was one over the bed.

Don't go there, Angel B.A. chided primly.

Ignoring mutterings of her guiding conscience, a premonition flooded her mind of Desmond's and her bodies intertwined on silk sheets, the erotic tableau reflected in a mirror overhead.

Well, maybe just one more, Devil B.A. mused, pushing a finger into a cheek to create a dimple in an effort to appear innocent.

Desmond's darker body was clad in the small towel about his hips, standing against her pale body in the white gown, her honey-blond hair, his black—this was a portrait of overwhelmingly salacious contrasts. As if she needed to see them reflected! She drowned in his potent warlock pheromones.

It'd be so easy to take one little step and move into his body. For once not think. To give free rein to the wild emotions rising in her, to the madness shrieking to be set free. Downstairs the radio played Cutting Crew's "I Just Died in Your Arms Tonight." A promise, a lure, taunting her to put a sock in Angel B.A.'s nattering platitudes such as *Men don't buy the cow if they get the milk for free,* and to surrender to the bad-girl side long denied.

No man had ever affected her with such a strong physical pull.

She dredged up excuses: I'm thirty-seven, a widow, surely I can gag that good-girl conscience and indulge in hot sex with The Panther. Agreeing, Devil B.A. broke into a Highland Fling. B.A. sucked in a deep breath to take that step, putting her against him.

Ice water doused her in the form of the front door opening and voices shouting her name. Eyes wide, for a frozen instant she stared at Desmond, nearly hating him for reading her every reaction to him. Hated herself even more for being so susceptible to his potent panther magic.

She dragged the jeans off the hanger and clutched them to

her chest. "Coming!" she called, then dashed from the room, not caring Desmond would view it as running from him.

She paused at the top of the stairs, spotting Brian, Callum, Robbie, Willie and Michael carrying in sofas and chairs. Behind them was Wulfgar with luggage.

"Hi ho, lass," Brian called. "A bonnie day, is it not?"

"Why are you addlepates in my house?" She stormed down the staircase, keen to vent frustration on surrogates.

" 'Addlepates,' she says," Michael addressed the other men. "She plays slugabed this morn, while we've sorted out matters."

Callum and Robbie toted in a chair with Angus sitting there holding Dudley in his lap. "You shameless hussy, prancing around in your nightie!" Then he looked down as if the cat had just materialized. "Go, before you get it in your twisted brain to take a chomp out of me. Shoo!"

"I'm *not* prancing, you invaded my privacy—"

" 'Tis privacy she'd be wanting," Angus chortled. "Likely to wallow that poor Viking more. Ashamed you should be."

Wulfgar the Walking Mountain returned, carrying another case and scuba tanks, which he dropped before her. "These are his," he intoned, then lumbered back outside.

"Wait! Dunna leave these here!" She started to chase after him, only Brian and Michael caught her by the waist, lifted and dropped her to sit on a chair they had just brought in.

"Out of the way, lass," Brian ordered.

"You're *not* leaving his stuff. Fetch him back with you. I played nurse last night," she fumed. "He's perfectly all right."

More than all right, he's absolutely perfect, Devil B.A. purred.

Brian shook his head. "Doc says he's to rest for a week and you're to keep an eye on him. A person can develop *seizures* after a bonk to the skull. You looking into his eyes, B.A.?"

"Why me?" She whipped around, eyeing him with suspicion.

Michael shrugged. "Outside of Janet the Red, we're low on members of the female persuasion to care for him. You really want our Janet soothing his furrowed brow?"

B.A. frowned. Janet had demonstrated a strong yen for black-haired men, over time methodically flirting her way through the males of Clan Fraser while Angus the Ferry wasn't looking. B.A. wanted Desmond out, so that he'd stop sucking all the air from the room and leave her in peace—not devoured whole!

"Janet offered." Brian twisted the burr deeper.

Michael teased, "B.A. is thinking, which never bodes well for us males. Stop lolling about in your gown, lass, or Angus will call you a hussy again. Our Yank lasses are resting, the time difference hitting them. They'll be up soon. You need to be there to welcome them."

"You're certain about the kilts, lass?" Brian quirked an eyebrow.

She ceased nibbling her lower lip over Janet tending The Panther Desmond. "Aye, nothing's sexier than a man in a kilt."

They nodded, bowing to her female wisdom. "Kilts it shall be."

"May we cut them roses from the castle garden?" Michael asked.

"Not roses—a single bud, white or lavender, tied with a tartan ribbon," B.A. insisted, knowing less was more.

" 'O, my love is like a red, red rose—' " Willie crinkled his forehead as he quoted Robbie Burns. "Wouldn't red be better?"

"My Lady's Passion are in full glory," Michael chimed, mischief in his gray eyes.

B.A. frowned. "See, Kitty?" she said to Dudley, referring to their earlier discussion. "Told you."

"Since you're conversing with the wee beastie from hell, ask him to get off." Angus whined, watching Dudley in his lap, "He's kneading me with his tiny daggers."

"Jock the Repair got the blower limping along. Ian, my brother"—Brian winked, speaking of his twin—"said e-mail for our project's full. You need to sort that out. We'll settle the Viking prince. See, not only did we bring the furniture from the ferry, but even fetched a second bed—to save your honor and all."

"What about the furniture for Lady Cottage?" she argued. They'd almost finished installing the paneling and flooring so she could move back into the cottage perched atop the castle. "I have to be in residence by *Samhain*."

"Plenty of time. Stop fashing, B.A., you'll get wrinkles between your brows," Brian teased, obviously taking perverse pleasure in her killing glare.

"Morning," a voice rumbled from behind B.A.

Dudley stopped terrorizing Angus and raced up the steps to twine around Desmond's legs. His bare legs. He stood wrapped in her pink robe reaching only to mid-thigh. Slack-jawed, B.A. stared at his sexy male toes, traveled up his faintly bowlegged but still beautiful legs—to her silk wrapper.

Michael leaned near and smugly arranged the lapel of B.A.'s robe to cover her right breast. The thin white gown little shielded her body's reaction to The Panther. B.A. slapped the hand away, glanced at Brian, then back to Mershan. Then, feeling her blush deepen, she bolted up the stairs, nearly toppling Desmond as she shoved past.

Desmond leaned back against the rail, tracking B.A. as she ran down the hall and into a room. She slammed the door so hard the windows rattled. "She always like that?" he inquired of the Scots.

Michael held out his hand. "Michael Mackenzie." He gestured to the other men and introduced them in turn.

A keen observer, Desmond sensed these men were a tad too eager to make his acquaintance, and not adept in hiding Cheshire Cat grins. For now he let it ride since it worked to his advantage.

"Ignore the lass," Brian said. "I imagine a man in her robe flustered her—not used to it and all."

Desmond grinned sheepishly. "I was without clothing. I guess she took mine and popped them into the washer. These my bags?"

"Dunna be exerting yourself." Michael and Brian jumped for the case before Desmond descended the final steps. "Doc said to relax, to let B.A. tend you. She's to fetch you around to the Marys, so he can look you over this evening before the welcome ceremony for our Yank lasses."

"I'm fine—" he started to say.

The old man interrupted. "Young feller, heed Doc. He may not be much—being a critter doctor and all—but he kens these things."

Desmond's eyebrows lifted. "I was checked by a veterinarian?"

Willie the Writer came forward, his turn to shake hands. "Not exactly. He dinna have time before you knocked him out. Of course, it was B.A.'s fault, screaming like the *bansidhe*."

"You don't have a real doctor on the island?" Desmond turned sideways so they could carry his luggage up to the bedroom, smiling as they automatically installed him there. For whatever reason, these kooky islanders were proving to be allies.

Wulfgar returned, carrying the last of Desmond's belongings. His blond brow arched, asking if arrangements met with Desmond's wishes. Desmond gave Wulf a faint nod. His friend and employee smiled, shaking his head.

"We're a healthy lot, rarely sick. To treat the rare cold we have Morag," Brian said, coming down the stairs. He accepted the cases from Wulf.

"She's a nurse?" Desmond inquired.

"Not a'tall. A healer, an herbalist, I believe they're called nowadays."

Desmond pressed, "And if you have an emergency?"

"They'd send a *helio-co-pator* from the Big Isle." An old man shuffled up to shake Desmond's hand. "Angus Mackenzie, kenned as Angus the Ancient. The men of Falgannon bid you *cead mìle fàilte*, Desmond Mershan."

It'd taken nearly twenty-four hours, but finally had someone said Welcome to Falgannon. Desmond glanced down at the cat standing up on its hind legs, soft paws against his thigh. He meowed as if adding voice to the greeting.

Hmm. Maybe he'd been welcomed yesterday—just in Dudley-speak.

* * *

Leaning against the door she'd slammed, B.A. pressed a hand to her burning forehead. The room was devoid of furniture, so her breaths echoed against the walls.

"Och, 'tis not good, Angel and Devil B.A. The Panther has green eyes and black hair," she muttered. "And the voice—the lilt's there. I knew the situation was precarious when I suddenly thought his toes were beautiful. No sane woman considers a man's feet pretty. They're strange long things with weird toes sort of added as an afterthought. Not Desmond's. I didn't realize it earlier, but his toes are beautiful. Finding his legs beautiful was one thing. They're just right, not chicken thin or fat tree stumps, but sculpted rock-hard muscle. True, they're faintly bowed, but that imperfection only makes him more accessible."

In her mind she heard Robert Shaw in *Jaws* intoning, "*Here's to swimmin' with bowlegged women,*" and though it didn't rhyme as well, there were interesting points about swimming with bowlegged men.

"Finding his legs beautiful isn't *too* alarming. But his toes? Truly a bad sign!"

Rushing into the bathroom, she dropped her clothes on the commode lid, tied her long hair into a knot and stepped under the icy water. She flipped the nozzle over to cold. Drawn from a deep well, the water was frigid, stinging.

She stayed under the spray and let it rinse away the heat from her body.

Desmond locked the door on the pink bedroom. Crossing to the leather attaché sitting on the chair, he ran the zipper around it. First he checked his cell phone to see what he already knew: it wouldn't work. Locating a jury-rigged outlet, he switched the plug to his computer. He groaned at the dial-up speed. After a wait, his e-mail account came up: hundreds of messages—typical—but two with red flags. He opened one, his eyes scanning the message from Jago.

"Des, I arrived in Kentucky and got a room at the Windmill Motel. Talk about stepping into the *Twilight Zone*. This place is in a time warp, stuck in the 1960s. Will let you know when I contact Asha Montgomerie. Called you last night, but was told the phone service to the island was down. A common occurrence, I gather. When I reported it, a sour-sounding Scot said not to bother, they already knew. *Slàinte*."

The second message was so like his brother Trevelyn: short, to the point and a tad cryptic. Jago and Trev were twins, but dead opposite in personalities. "Moving in for the kill tonight. Crashing a gala where she shall be. Sing a requiem for a Raven."

Desmond hit compose and entered two addresses at Mershan International for his brothers, his fingers nimbly typing his message: *I have arrived, much to the imminent distress of Ms. B.A. Montgomerie. The whole bloody isle is some absurd hybrid between* Braveheart *and* Monty Python.

He paused, thinking back on B.A.'s physical reaction to him. Never had he seen a woman so unprotected in her responses. It made him itch to have her in his bed. His body bucked at the notion of her being that open when she made love.

He snorted a harsh, angry laugh. He wasn't going to make love to BarbaraAnne Montgomerie. He was going to screw her—just as he planned to screw the whole bloody isle.

After two breaths to regain control over his body, his fingers tapped out, *She's different than I expected, but foresee no problems.* He hit SEND and watched the messages fly to his brothers' e-mail accounts, wondering if their own plans included bedding the Montgomerie sisters, too.

His lips curved into a hard smile lacking mirth. Touching two fingers to his forehead, he saluted the laptop. "*Slàinte*."

Chapter 7

To be packed into The Hanged Man with over two hundred men and the only one wearing pants was oddly disquieting. Well, pants—breeks, trousers, slacks, any term Scots used for male lower attire.

As Desmond sat at the bar watching the goings-on, he

noted there wasn't one male in the entire pub whose knees weren't flashing. It sort of gave him the willies. While he might lack the same curiosity as a woman, the thought flittered across his mind, what *did* they wear under their kilts? The day had been gloriously warm, but as the sun dropped out of sight—before 4:00 P.M. mind you—autumn's chill made itself felt. The blue flames of the peat in the pub's fireplace were welcome. He couldn't believe they kept warm no matter how thick a wool the kilt was. Backdraft took on a whole new meaning!

Desmond had overheard B.A. tell them to appear in Scots' attire. Since he judged every male on the island would jump through hoops for her, he wasn't surprised to see a few in full Highland regalia. He hadn't anticipated the total male population of the bloody isle to show up as if queuing for *Braveheart 2* auditions, though.

Moreover, he doubted her assertion there's nothing sexier to a woman than a man in a kilt. Hadn't B.A. stammered and blushed when he wore nothing but a towel? On the other hand, observing the Falgannonians give welcome to the three American women, Desmond conceded reassessment of his opinion was in order. Bright eyes and flushed faces attested to the buzzes the ladies got off knobby-kneed islanders.

Sporadically, the islanders came to introduce themselves, flashing smiles, acting a tad too happy. It put Desmond in mind of being at a convention of cannibals and Desmond Delight was the main course. With that parade of white teeth passing before him, it registered the Falgannonians were poster-children for dental health—even Angus the Ancient.

"You don't have a physician on Falgannon, but have a dentist?"

Angus chuckled and then snapped bright teeth at him. "Not a'tall. It's our lass, dragging them Yank obsessions back with her. Don't tell *Herself*, but she might have the right of it this time. When she took over as Lady of the Isle, first thing she did was give us dental floss and fluoride mouthwash. Bossy little thing, even then. We figured it was enough to keep our B.A. happy as she provided for us. Back at the first of the year, we drew the line when she came back with whitening strips. Each time she goes to visit the colonies she returns with some Yank fad to foster upon us."

As B.A. presented each American with a small basket, a tartan ribbon tied on the handle, she drew Desmond's eyes. He inquired, "Who are these women?"

The old man turned his attention to the group on the other side of the room. "The Yanks? 'Tis B.A.'s project. She likely gave them dental floss and whitening strips as part of her welcome basket," he added confidentially.

"Project?" Desmond sipped his iced Pepsi—B.A. refused him alcohol due to "doctor's orders."

"Shoo, Kitty," Angus fussed at the cat when it jumped atop the bar.

The Cat Dudley ignored the old man.

"Is that animal permitted the run of the isle?" Desmond arched a brow, amazed.

"Well, no one tells Kitty anything," Angus barked a laugh. "He dunna listen. Must be a reincarnated Montgomerie."

"So, what's B.A.'s project?"

Angus spotted a man carrying in an ice bucket to refill the bin built into the bar. "Michael the Story, the Viking wants to hear about the project. I dunna ken them computer things. Sort him out."

The handsome Scotsman sat the empty bucket down. Leaning across the oak bar, he flashed another of those dazzling smiles and offered his hand. "Michael Mackenzie . . . and you're Desmond Mershan."

Desmond frowned. "I thought I met—"

"Oh aye, we've a few of them about, six breathing and several dozen in the cemetery. There's Wee Michael, Michael the Greenhouse, Michael the Peat and Michael the Elder. I'm Michael the Story. I teach history to the children here and two other small isles. It was Michael the Fiddle you met this morn."

"The Pete?" queried Desmond.

Michael put a saucer on the bartop and poured out dry

cat food. "Not a'tall—peat as in peat moss. He cuts bricks of the stuff, dries them for heating our homes. Nothing like a peat fire, where whiskey gets its flavor. So, what you want to ken about the project?"

"Our lass thinks it'll work," Angus butted in, "but she's forgetting The Curse."

Desmond smiled into his tumbler, then swallowed the last of his cola. Just what this loony isle needed—a curse! He turned back to Michael the Story expecting to find him laughing, or at least making loony circles in the air beside his ear behind the old man's back. Instead, a worried expression passed over the man's thirty-something face. It spread in ripples to the men standing nearby.

Odd. Desmond possessed the flair for reading people, one of the tools that had seen him rise to the top in the cutthroat world of international business. These men believed in this curse. Not only believed, but *feared* it.

"The Curse?" Desmond prompted on cue, dying to hear this bit of blarney.

Michael drew himself an ale. Stalling? After a swallow, he replied, " 'Tis a legend about Falgannon. We've a shortage, you see, of marriageable-aged females—"

"Shortage!" A male to his right exploded in a snort. "There are *no* marriageable-aged females on the island for the past six years except for Morag the Healer, Oona the Painter and B.A.—and the first two dunna count."

"Not count?" Desmond accepted a refill of his cola.

Michael the Story nodded toward the booth in the far corner where two women—wearing trousers—sat holding hands.

"Since we're in a bind for women wanting to get married, B.A. hit upon the project of importing brides. We have a Web site with a bachelor registry. Ladies read about us—our likes, dislikes—they fill out an application, and if B.A. chooses them, she'll pay their expenses to the isle. They get a two-week vacation, a chance to get to know the island, meet our men." He reached for the silver laptop sitting on the end of the bar and spun it around for Desmond.

The screen filled with the image of a landscape in the

sunset with the Flash header ISLE OF LOVE. Stylish, the layout was by Purple Rain Designs, impressing Desmond enough to note the name for redesign of his Web site for Mershan International. Using the touch pad he quickly shifting through fast-loading pages. There were photos of the island's males with brief bios.

Well, well, BarbaraAnne Montgomerie, owner of Falgannon Isle, was also B.A. Montgomerie, matchmaker. Desmond stared across the pub, covetously tracking B.A., who was setting the nervous Americans at ease. The idea was bloody brilliant and would work better than she imagined. And it was typical of the Montgomeries, who'd poured a fortune into this isle going back to when Old Sean first married Maeve Mackenzie.

Maeve had owned Falgannon, but the old man had had the money. Island-born, at an early age Sean had been sent south to England for an education. In his twenties, he'd amassed a fortune in the stock market, parlayed it into an international conglomerate and returned to claim Maeve. For her dowry, Sean had channeled a chunk of his fortune into dragging the isle into the twentieth century.

Desmond never could fathom this about the old man. A sonofabitch in business, Sean had never done anything without profit margin as his sole motivation. One might argue love had driven him into rebuilding the isle as a small Scottish paradise. Desmond discounted that. Maeve, they said, had lived more for the isle than her marriage. Even in death, they'd returned Maeve's body to Falgannon, while Sean was laid to rest in England.

Evidently, B.A. had inherited the same love of the island from Maeve.

Taking a swig of cola, he used it to wash down the shard of conscience. Yes, B.A. was guiltless, but hers wouldn't be the first life shattered by big business. His mother, twin brothers and he had been innocents; it hadn't stopped Montgomerie from destroying their world. Likewise, Desmond wouldn't let it prevent him from extracting vengeance.

Every night for decades, Desmond had envisioned handing papers to the old man, seeing Sean's face as he comprehended his whole empire was going down the tubes—that Desmond Mershan had orchestrated it and why. He closed his eyes against the vision of his father pulling the trigger. Against seeing blood spatter everything.

Damn Sean to hell for robbing him of the prize, cheating him of the sole purpose for most of his life. It'd still happen. There was no impeding it; wheels were in motion and too much money was at stake. Despite no gratification coming with the hollow victory, he'd at least achieve a sense of closure. Maybe then the demons would stop rattling their chains. Perhaps never again would he awaken bathed in sweat, calling for his father, feeling helpless, alone. Teeth grinding, he forced the emotions back.

Glancing up, as if she sensed him staring at her, B.A.'s luminous eyes sought his. There it was again—that pull, the same connection between them he'd experienced back in the spring at Sean's funeral. In the tartan skirt and black scoop neck sweater, B.A. now stole his breath. Tightness filled his chest. Rubbing the dent in his breastbone, Desmond chalked the sensation up to the gassy Pepsi.

Pushing her buttons this morning had convinced him Ms. B.A. Montgomerie hadn't been with a man for a long time, likely not since the death of her husband. She flustered too easily. Had she been working her way through her own private bachelor preserve, she wouldn't stammer and blush as an untried teen. A woman that sexy used her beauty as a tool, had men ready to kill for her. Whereas he judged every man in the room ready to fight for her, they wouldn't fight *over* her. The whole situation was a paradox.

"I gather why Oona and Morag don't count." Desmond smiled as B.A. blushed and turned away. "But you're telling me none of you are courting B.A.?"

"None of us are daft, are we?" Michael muttered into his glass, then exchanged understanding glances with other long-suffering males.

Desmond conceded it was futile at this juncture, to continue questioning these mad islanders, since they obviously reveled in their insanity. Only, this was digging at him. There wasn't a male in this room—on earth—who wouldn't find

B.A. Montgomerie desirable. One dead husband, or a live one for that matter, was no stumbling block when a man wanted a woman. Desmond had risen to where he was in life by being a keen observer of human nature, of what made men and women tick, of sensing strengths and weaknesses and how to exploit them. That a group of men would place B.A. on a pedestal and worship her as some vestal virgin was contrary to logic and biology. No, it was plain nuts!

" 'Tis The Curse, you see," Angus stated again, as if that explained everything.

Desmond opened his mouth to say, *No, he didn't see*, when Brian the Horseman came to the bar and thumped his hand on it.

"You're up, lad. Break a leg—as the Yanks say in showbiz." He winked. "Do it bang-on and you might win the heart of a fair lass."

Michael skirted the crowd to stand before the fireplace. A hush fell over the pub as the sandy-haired man drew all eyes. "Ages past, the Isles of Britain were joined and located far to our south. The clime was warm, the land a paradise. A race of giants lived upon the shores, and in a time of war they battled each other and shattered the land into many wee isles. That's how the Hebrides came to be. We've heard tales of Sgathach, Warrior Queen of Skye, how she and her sisters taught the Warriors of the Red Branch. Fables retold many times over. However, the Legend of Falgannon is rarely heard outside our shores—a story of love, of jealousy and a curse that never ends . . ."

Desmond's gaze circled the room, marking enrapt expressions. Taking a swallow of his icy soda, wishing it was something a lot stronger, he thought, *Oh great, time for* Romper Room *story hour*. He tried to disguise his sour countenance, but evidently failed because Angus used a cane to nudge his thigh.

"Pay attention, Viking. Now you'll hear."

"The Curse of Falgannon Isle dates back to the time of Sgathach Buanand, Warrior Queen of the Shadow Isle—the Isle of Women. Following in the ancient Pictish belief only women could train men for war, she ran a school and taught the best men from many kingdoms. One day a warrior came, Friseal, sent to Sgathach by the fierce Viking warlord Rolv. Friseal was the son of Rolv, though his mother was an Irish slave. He was beautiful, strong of body and resembled his *mathair* with her black, wavy hair and green eyes. Had Friseal been born of one of Rolv's wives, he'd have been a Viking prince. Even so, Rolv loved Friseal, was proud of his son. As a result, he sent the young man to Skye for training. Friseal proved a mighty warrior, fleet of foot and adept at all weaponry. It wasn't long before the beautiful Friseal attracted the eye of the Queen of Skye, or for her to decide she coveted him for a lover.

"Friseal's older half-brother Olav grew jealous of their father's love for his half-Irish son, saw it as a threat to his birthright, so Olav attacked Skye in the dead of night. Sgathach's female warriors repulsed the assault, but not before Olav stabbed Friseal in the back and left him to die. Fever wasted his body—it seemed nothing could save Friseal. Sgathach sent to fetch Maeve of Falgannon. A great healer, Maeve was one of the Daughters of Anne. Her healing powers came from her being a *cait sidhe*, a feared witchwoman, royalty from the Picts of Cait and Druimalban. Maeve saved Friseal's life; only, whilst tending him, they fell in love. When Sgathach learned of their bond she was furious. In order to escape her wrath, Friseal and Maeve stole away from Sgathach's castle and into the night. Enraged, Sgathach ordered her warrior-women to hunt them down, kill Maeve and bring Friseal back.

"Before setting sail, Friseal put the rest of the boats to flame. Sgathach and her warriors arrived at the shore too late. Maeve's magick was strong. Sgathach could only watch as the Sacred Mists enfolded Friseal and Maeve into its protection. No one landed on Falgannon Isle unless the Lady of the Isle willed it; the mists enshrouded the island, shielding, protecting. Sgathach knew the lovers were forever out of her reach.

"However, a powerful witch in her own right, Sgathach screamed a curse upon the departing lovers—the women of

Maeve's line would forevermore be doomed, their love would see them destroyed. Falgannon's women would birth only male babes, slowly dooming the tiny island.

"Sgathach wanted it far-reaching. The Curse would be stayed for a period of three generations if the woman of Maeve's blood married an Outlander—a man with black hair, green eyes and the blood of the Irish in him. If he took her in any fashion other than love the isle was condemned once more to be an island of men looking across the waters at an isle of women.

"Scoff you may, but to this day, unless our lady marries an Outlander with black hair and green eyes and marries for love, there are no girl babes born to the women of the isle. You three lovely ladies might not believe either. Look around. Count the women amongst us. Visit the ancient churchyard. You might come away thinking a wee bit different."

Desmond felt something queer itching his back—Dudley standing on his hind legs and draping paws over his shoulder. Distracted by the cat, he dismissed the duckbumps snaking up his spine as he watched the guests applaud the oral lore.

Well, women might buy into that romantic garbage, but not a man. Desmond began to laugh until his eyes assessed the males present. A strange mix of emotions was written upon their faces. Acceptance, resolve, and even a touch of desperation. Surely, they couldn't believe this island was cursed? What a bunch of idiots! He knew why there weren't available women on the isle—they were smart enough to hop on the ferryboat and leave this insanity behind!

Wulfgar strolled through the door and slowly made his way to Desmond's side. "How do you feel, other than having a strange fuzzy growth on your shoulder?"

Desmond looked sideways at Dudley. "Where have you been?"

The door opened again and the sexy redhead from earlier poked her head inside. Deciding attention wasn't on her, she surreptitiously claimed a seat at a table near the door. Wulfgar never turned in her direction, but Desmond noted a smug twitch at the corner of his friend's mouth.

"Never mind," he muttered. "You missed story hour."

Wulf chuckled. "Pity that. You make it sound like kiddy time."

"No kid would swallow this hogwash. Is insanity communicable?" Desmond queried.

Wulf shrugged. "Mass hysteria—"

"Not strong enough for this tommyrot."

B.A. rose from the table and crossed the room, pausing several times to exchange snippets of conversation with various men. Her hip-length, gold hair rippled with her movements, her laughter. She stood out in the crowd, shimmered as if anointed with faery dust, drawing Desmond's eyes.

"Old Sean sure bred some sexy granddaughters. Not a dog in the whole pack. Women with the power to make men get down on their bellies and crawl, beg to touch them," Wulfgar complimented.

Desmond ignored the cat flexing its claws a little too spiritedly. He didn't take his eyes off B.A., and gave no visible reaction to Wulf's words. Nevertheless, his stomach muscles tightened; the tenseness radiated up his body to his jaw, becoming a mild pain.

He warned in a silky, ominous tone, "Let the redhead blow you all you want. But when you lean your head back and close your eyes in ecstasy, make sure B.A. Montgomerie's face doesn't come to mind."

Wulf swung around, assessing his long-time friend and boss. Had the man been born with gray eyes, Wulf might liken Desmond to a shark that had taken on human form. Desmond was single-minded in getting what he wanted. He was cold, calculating; he was ruthless—traits of nature's finest killing machine. As a teen in Norway, Wulf had visited Kristiansand Dyrepark Zoo and watched the big cats. They fascinated him: feral, motionless, with intense eyes so absolutely focused. Then the cats moved in a blink, almost faster than vision could follow. Desmond's eyes reminded Wulf of a panther he'd seen. That same control, that preternatural stillness. A predator, a meat eater. To Desmond, women were just another form of meat. They came, they went, none lasting long.

Wulf would bet Desmond couldn't recall their faces within a few months of their passing out of his life. But after two decades of watching him, he'd never seen Desmond look at any woman in this manner.

Deciding to tweak Desmond, he asked with a devilish grin, "Issuing a dare?"

It wouldn't be the first time they'd vied for a woman. Ordinarily, a killer competitor's streak saw Desmond relish the challenge. Winning was all the sweeter for it. Despite that, Wulf had a feeling BarbaraAnne Montgomerie was the exception.

"Hell, she's too big for you, Des—more to my liking. Bet there's Viking blood in that gal. You like those half-starved actresses that grace Cannes Film Festivals."

Desmond's ferine eyes rolled, targeting him, the level stare enough to send lesser mortals to quivering. But not a real Viking.

"*Dra til helvete*, Des."

"I've been to hell, Wulf; I prefer it to Norway—it's warm."

Desmond's body tightened as B.A. stopped before him, her golden-brown eyes searching his nervously. "Sorry that took so long. Are you tired? Head hurting?" she asked.

"My head doesn't ache," he answered. "Want to look into my eyes?"

Ignoring his challenge, she reached out and scratched the kitty still propped on his shoulder. "I thought we'd eat supper here on the porch."

"Good, I'm *famished.*" His response was easy, but she was too close for him to miss the dilation of her eyes as she caught that he meant for more than food.

Blushing, she looked away, noticing Wulf standing there. "Have you eaten?"

Desmond pushed the cat off his shoulder and stepped closer to B.A., placing a proprietary hand on her waist. "Wulf's already eaten. We shan't trouble him."

Wulf's booming laugh sounded, as he thought about what he'd been doing with Janet. "He's right, I shared a good meal not long ago, but thank you for the invitation."

They started to step away when Desmond turned back. "That previous matter—it wasn't a caution. I *meant* it."

Wulfgar saluted him. "You're the boss."

Desmond smiled, but it was hard edged. "Yes, I am."

Chapter 8

B.A. wasn't sure who was the bigger puzzle—Desmond Mershan or the pod-cat the aliens left when they beamed up The Cat Dudley and replaced him with this angelic version. That riddle played through her mind as she toyed with the scallops on her plate, occasionally putting one in the saucer on the chair where the cat had joined them.

She glanced over at the arrangements of white roses accenting the candlelit décor, striking against the deep blue of the Montgomerie tartan tablecloths. In honor of the first three prospective brides to the isle, she'd supervised preparations, her eye to setting the mood for romance. B.A. hadn't intended to be a part of the scenario. The plan had been to sit back and smile while she brought life to her island, content with the role she'd carved out for herself. Who knew, maybe it'd inspire her to pen a romance novel like Willie.

Each woman dined with three bachelors she'd selected from the Web site. Tomorrow she'd breakfast with one, picnic and tour the island with the second, and the third would escort her to supper. Hopefully, by the end of two weeks she'd discover there was a man she saw a future with and stay.

Yet, the bloody Panther upset those peaceful preparations. For all the attention B.A. paid the Yanks and her lads at the other tables, they may as well not be there. Mesmerized, she kept her focus solely on Desmond Mershan.

He carried the conversation through the meal, even touched on the proposed resort. A waste of breath. Unable to concentrate, she little retained specifics. The man was a force, overpowering everything around him. And she couldn't take her eyes off him.

He fascinated her, those beautiful hands. The long, strong fingers moved in elegant magician-like passes, no wasted gestures or nervous ticks. Not soft, they conveyed power. She envisioned them wrapped around a hilt of a claymore, the hands of a warrior . . . the hands of a lover. Amplifying the lack of focus, she battled an odd sense of time slippage, as images of Desmond in chain mail, storming the steps of Castle Falgannon, wove through her mind.

Desmond eyed her as she fed the kitty another scallop. "Your cat's fat."

"He's not mine."

He sat his cup down. "You say that, but he's at your home, you feed him, he's sitting at this table and—once again, you're feeding him. Ownership seems debatable."

She smiled, vanquishing the warrior vision. "The Cat Dudley owns the whole isle, I fear."

"There are other cats on the island?"

"Indoor cats. No one dares let one around him. Kitty's a tad rough on other felines. Rough on dogs, horses"—she laughed—"people."

Dudley blinked at Desmond, halo firmly in place.

"He needs to be on a diet," he insisted.

The cat's ears turned backward as he glared at Desmond. B.A. laughed softly at the kitty's telepathic. *Mind your own beeswax.*

"May I have the salt?" he requested.

B.A. used her knife to scoot the shaker to him.

Desmond studied B.A. This was the second time he'd requested salt and she'd behaved oddly. His curiosity was burning. "You going to tell me what it is with salt and you?"

"A woman must retain some mysteries," she evaded.

Deciding Kitty was already a small bear, Desmond figured another scallop wouldn't matter, so he placed one on the saucer. As a glass-covered cart was wheeled in, Dudley lost interest in the seafood, bouncing on his paws as if to pounce on the tray of desserts.

"Dudley's passing fond of cheesecake?" he guessed.

"Passing fond?" B.A. chuckled. "Oh, aye."

"What would you like for *afters*?" a young man in his late teens asked Desmond, automatically setting a slice topped with strawberries before B.A. "We've fudge-marble cheesecake, Bailey's Irish Cream cheesecake, blueberry cheesecake, 7-Up cheesecake with strawberries and Key Lime cheesecake with raspberries."

"Dudley isn't the only one fond of cheesecake." Desmond arched his brow. Being perverse, he asked, "Anything else?"

Fergus nodded. "A baked apple."

"Cheesecake is a bit of an island obsession," B.A. added unnecessarily. "I collect recipes from around the world. 7-Up cheesecake is nigh on sinful."

Desmond smiled. "I'm game. Sin is my middle name, after all."

B.A.'s wide-eyed expression was priceless. How could a woman live to be thirty-seven and yet remain so untouched? Her long black lashes batted as a blush tinged her cheeks. B.A. Montgomerie was a babe in the woods. That old Sam the Sham song 'Lil' Red Riding Hood' sprang to mind: *You're everything a big bad wolf could want.* She cut off the tip of her dessert, leaned to place it on the saucer for Dudley who was in a tizzy. The deep scoop neck of her black sweater displayed her generous cleavage, enough to make Desmond almost break out in old Sam's lyrics.

After she took a bite of dessert, a crumb clung to the corner of her mouth. Desmond's body clenched, and he craved to lean over and lick it off. Her tongue swiped her lips clean, twisting his gut. *It's going to be a long night*, he thought.

He coughed to clear the dryness in his throat. "Literally, Sinclair is my middle name. My brothers called me Sin for short in their teens."

She choked. "Sinclair?"

"You have some long-standing feud with Clan Sinclair?"

"Not precisely." She reached for her water glass, the sweater slipping off her right shoulder. Clearly turning the topic, she inquired, "You have brothers?"

Desmond forced his mind off the image of him putting a

passion mark on that lovely skin. "Hmm, ah . . . twins, younger by six years, Trevelyn and Jago."

She smiled. "I have twin sisters—Raven and Asha—younger, too. I'm a twin also."

Desmond stared at her over his coffee cup, silently wondering which of his brothers had one of her sisters in bed at this moment. Likely, Trevelyn. He'd move in for the kill with lightning speed. Jago would sit back and size up the situation—a cat giving a mouse the illusion of choice. He glanced at his watch. Trevelyn planned on meeting Raven at some gala. By midnight, he'd bet Trevelyn would have her under him, over him, and in about every position imaginable.

Bedding the Montgomerie sisters hadn't been a part of their plans, but he knew his brothers—they wouldn't resist the fillip. Some elemental quality about these Montgomerie women, a challenge in their eyes, provoked a man to want to dominate them. Possess them. Own them.

"Small world," he replied.

Sipping his coffee, he observed the men and women at the other tables. "You expect your scheme to work?"

"Lonely women will jump at a chance to find love. I have dozens of lonesome bachelors on Falgannon. Bringing the two together seems like common sense."

"Sounds romantic." He couldn't help a faint note of disdain that colored his comment.

B.A.'s amber cat-eyes studied him. "The island, the people mean a lot to me. I do everything I can to see they're happy."

"Even finding them brides? Most men would resent that."

Finished with the meal, she leaned back in her chair. Dudley hopped up onto her lap and she absently scratched his ear. "Scotland fascinates Americans. It's a highly romantic brew: Scotland, men in kilts and a woman having the pick of hundreds of bachelors."

"All because of some ancient curse?" He scoffed. "You really believe it?"

She shifted, visibly uncomfortable. "I'm a logical person, but I'm also of this land. To an Outlander our ways and beliefs might seem—"

"Odd . . . far-fetched . . . bizarre?" he taunted.

"No female children born on the island *is* odd."

He arched his brow. "None?"

A trace of defensiveness twisted her mouth. "Oona and Morag, but—"

"They don't count," he finished. "I've heard. Weren't you born here?"

"I was born at Colford Hall, my grandfather's home in—"

"England. Yes, I've seen it. Impressive," he informed her in a clipped tone. "So, no females that count—for how long?"

"The Marys were the last ones—sixty-seven years ago. None since Maeve married."

"Your men didn't hatch. There had to be women at one time."

"Some marry outside the isle. Women died . . . childbirth, accidents, cancer. Most grow to hate the island and leave. Divorce rate is high on Falgannon."

Desmond pressed. "Your grandfather wasn't—what did the storyteller call it . . . ?"

"An Outlander. Sean was island born and had red hair."

"He didn't believe in The Curse?"

She shrugged. "Sean Montgomerie thought he could re-make the world according to his wishes."

"So I heard."

At the terse note in his voice, B.A. paused, her eyes searching his face. His self-containment clearly unnerved her. On the surface, she'd see a man who was educated, well-mannered—one might even label him charming. He noted the slight breathlessness to her speech, as though it was hard for her to breathe around him. He did nothing to put her at ease, liking how off-kilter she was around him.

"*You* married," he pushed.

"Maybe I ease my guilt with the Web site and sponsoring prospective brides. What better way to fight ancient magic with modern magic—the Internet. As to my husband . . . he was black-haired and part Irish, but had verra blue eyes. I guess Sgathach won't accept two out of three." As if sensing he was going to question her further about Evian Deshaunt, she said, "If you've finished, I need to return to the house. I've e-mails to wade through."

"Fine." He rose and pulled out her chair.

They paused by the tables to wish the American women good night before bidding everyone in the pub the same. Leaving the cozy building behind, they walked into the darkness, Dudley trailing behind them.

As they started across the road, the kid on the scooter came zooming out of nowhere, veering toward them as if to run them down. B.A. calmly put a hand against Desmond's stomach to halt him until the motorbike spluttered around the curve.

"He was trying to run us over!" Desmond gasped, astonished.

"Oh aye—means he likes you. Wee Dougie only pretends to run down people he likes. He calls it virtual bowling. He and his scooter are the bowling ball and we're the pins."

Desmond shook his head and muttered under his breath, "Whole bloody island's crazy."

Pausing by the car, he fished his keys from his pocket. Glancing up at the signpost in Gaelic, he read CEÀRN GNOTHACHAS A' FALGANNON. Another was tacked up to the back, so he leaned to see what it said, only to discover the same sign opposite. He quirked a brow at B.A.

"A joke." She laughed, then translated, " 'Falgannon Business District.' If you blinked, you missed it."

In the moonlight, the madness of this tiny isle seemed infectious. He should be eager to reach the house, check for updates from his brothers. Likely, other business matters needed his attention. Yet he felt no rush—an experience to which he was unaccustomed. His whole life had been so focused on his goals, there had been little time to enjoy the rareness of a moment.

"You know insanity runs on Falgannon?" Desmond expected her to turn defensive.

"Actually, it gallops." Her musical laughter echoed in the still night.

Her smile was mysterious, feline, almost the same expression that silly cat wore, prancing on the hood of the Rover. Moonlight adored her, caressed her. He envisioned Falgannon's Lady dancing on the moor under its pale rays, a pagan goddess calling down mystical powers and using them to ensorcel him, for he could no more resist her than the tides did the moon.

Putting his hand on her waist, he urged her closer. The scent of pink peonies and BarbaraAnne Montgomerie flooded his mind.

Her glittering eyes roved over his face. The corner of her small, full mouth tugged up as she melted against him. His lips closed over hers, brushing softly, then coming to rest. She tasted of cheesecake and strawberries and was more intoxicating than Highland whisky.

Sensing hesitation, he didn't allow her to pull back, but molded her lips to his, gently coercing her to follow his lead. Nibbling, tasting, savoring her. His right hand snaked into that mass of heavy hair, luxuriating in the silken feel, fighting the primitive urge to close his fists in it and drag her to the ground.

She placed a hand on his chest. Whether to push him away or from a desire to feel his heart beating under her palm, he couldn't judge. Trapping it under his, he kept her hand there, letting the pounding of his heart thud out his need for her.

B.A. stepped back, confusion flooding her eyes. Her lower lip trembled faintly.

Desmond's thumb stroked the pulse point on her graceful throat, felt the hammering of her desire. Reaching past her, he opened the Rover's passenger door. She got in without a word. The silly cat hopped in, too.

B.A. glanced up at him, her face an open book. The expression knocked the breath from his lungs, was a fist to his heart.

He closed the door and walked around to the driver side to find Dudley in the seat. "Hop in the back, cat. You don't have your driver's license." Like a steeple chaser, Kitty jumped from the front seat to the back bench, which faced the rear window.

Putting his key in the ignition, Desmond caught sight of the luminous numbers on his watch: 10:43 P.M. He couldn't help wondering if he'd beat his brother, Trevelyn, to being the first Mershan to bed a Montgomerie.

B.A. welcomed the darkness of the car, as it shrouded her emotions. She sat stiffly, shocked to her toes, barely able to buckle the seat belt. This was bad. It had been a tentative kiss. Exploring . . . questioning. A kiss of such sweetness, she fought tears welling in her eyes. He hadn't used his teeth or tongue, only gentle lips. That boiled her blood. Left her hungry for more.

It provoked her to realize this man's touch rocked her the way no man had. Guiltily, she swallowed that fact.

She had loved Evian Deshaunt. Their love had been warm and comfortable until the end. Making love with Desmond Mershan would be anything but comfortable. It'd be as wild and uncontrolled as the winds that swept across Falgannon.

She wasn't sure she was prepared to face that intensity.

It had been seven years since she'd made love with a man, that long since one saw her naked. While she exercised and stayed fit, she wasn't the firm nubile bride Evian wed fourteen years ago. No woman would be at ease with the prospect.

Still, qualms mattered little. When Desmond kissed her it was moonbeams and pixie dust, a magic so rare that a woman would be an idiot not to follow what her body told her. She wasn't asking for tomorrows. Just tonight.

Her stomach tightened in crippling desire, in nagging self-doubt. She didn't take a drink of whiskey often, but craved a dram now to steady her nerves. And och, were her nerves jangling! B.A. spied the cottage coming into view—the drive was too damn short. She was unprepared for this step, but was one ever ready to face a force of nature?

The car coasted to a halt in the driveway and Desmond shut off the engine. In the big hush, B.A. heard the leather seat creaking under his weight. His slow controlled breathing. The jingle of keys as he removed them from the steering wheel. Finally, the release of the handle as he opened the door. Each noise was magnified, yet she couldn't understand how she heard any of it over her heart thundering in her ears.

She watched him through the windscreen, coming around to open the door for her. A momentary reprieve, the cat jumped in her lap and scampered out. Without slowing, he bounded away, up the steps and into the house through his kitty entrance.

"Not your cat?" Desmond mocked.

B.A. smiled, nervous. She explained the cat door: "He stoods in the window and yowled till you let him in."

At the front door he held out his hand for her key, but she'd already turned the knob. The cat reappeared, weaving around her legs. Desmond paused and shook his head.

"You don't lock your doors?"

"We dunna have crime on the isle. There's no need."

"You *do* have a lock on the door?"

"Aye, though I'm not sure where the key is. If you stole anything, what would you do with it? That way of life never touches our shores. When I'm in England or Kentucky I use locks. On Falgannon, doors are for keeping out the weather, not people."

Desmond removed his jacket and draped it across the back of the new sofa the Scots had brought in that morning. B.A. touched a long match to the peat bricks in the fireplace. She was skittish, searching for excuses to avoid him; when the cat meowed from the kitchen doorway, she rushed to feed him.

Slowly stalking her, Desmond finally stopped, coming to lean against the door frame. Sticking his hands in his pockets to still the restless urge to reach for her, his eyes followed as B.A. doled out food to the fat cat.

"Small wonder Dudley's a tiny Goodyear Blimp, he hasn't stopped eating all evening."

She laughed. "When he's eating he's well behaved. Call it bribing him. We see it as keeping him occupied."

"I'd say—looking at this football with legs—he's *occupied* frequently." Desmond chuckled when the cat displayed an uncanny human expression. Kitty clearly said, *Sod off.*

"Can I fix you tea or coffee?" B.A. rubbed her hands together nervously.

"Thanks, no. I'd enjoy a whisky if you have some."

"A Scot not having whisky? Unpatriotic. Only, Doc said no alcohol."

He leaned forward at the waist. "Want to look into my eyes?"

B.A. wasn't fooled by Desmond having his hands in his pockets. She sensed if she got near, he'd kiss her again. Worse, she knew she'd let him. And if he kissed her, there'd be no turning back.

Accustomed to the buffer between the world and her, it was hard to drop the shield. Easier to stand on the sidelines than risk pain that could come from loving. B.A. comprehended if she took this step her emotions would be engaged. There'd be no retreat. She wasn't the sort to indulge in a casual affair simply for physical attraction.

"What's wrong, B.A.? Afraid I might bite?"

A nervous giggle popped out. "I'm sure you bite—all predators do."

"Is that how you view me?" His pale eyes flashed.

"I'd be a fool to see you any other way."

"And that scares you?"

"Not precisely . . ." It *terrified* her. B.A. tossed up her hands, at a loss for words. "Look, I don't fall into bed with every man who comes along."

He nodded.

"It's . . . I don't . . ."

"B.A., shut up and come here," he rumbled.

The moment had come. She could play safe, stay secure in the cocoon she'd created on this isle, or take a gamble. Throwing caution to the wind, she stepped toward him.

Welcome to the real world, Devil B.A. whispered from her shoulder perch, a hand firmly over Angel B.A.'s mouth.

Keeping his hands in his pockets, Desmond wasn't going to make things easy for her. B.A. Montgomerie had too many things in life come easy. Born with a silver spoon in her mouth, precious granddaughter of the great Sean Montgomerie, she'd gone to the best schools, worn designer clothes. Over the years he'd built up a mountain of resentment for B.A. and her beautiful siblings. They'd often made the celebrity section of the newspapers, and he'd kept up with their privileged lives.

He thought of the faded magazine clipping with her picture announcing her engagement, hidden at the back of his wallet. He'd never understood why he cut it out. Why he'd carried it for almost fifteen years—a bizarre touchstone in some sick, sad way.

Not once in her life had she lain in bed at night, trying to ignore hunger pains grinding her stomach against her backbone. She'd never heard her siblings cry for the lack of food. For once in her perfect, protected life, she should want something so much it ate at her insides.

The primitive side of him nearly punched past the civilized uncle, the angry man, reached out and dragged B.A. to the kitchen floor to claim her with all the finesse of an animal. But no, there were demons stronger than mating instincts driving him. He craved B.A. with a grinding need, but he'd do this right. Oh, he'd take her—upstairs in that room of mirrors, on that big George III platform bed in a tussle of sweat and mindless desire. He'd savor her screaming for him, pleading with him to touch her in a way no man had before.

Instead of kissing him, B.A. slid her arms around his waist and laid her head against his shoulder. Disarming him. Though the sexual response was there, and so strong in some ways it was frightening, this was an embrace of solace. As if she sensed the scarred-over pain inside him and offered succor.

For an instant he resented her fae ways, took umbrage as she reached inside of him and cradled his heart. A violent urge swelled in him to shove her against the wall and let loose the primeval male. To stun her with his raw desires.

But then there was an odd ripping inside his chest, and he fisted his hands in his pockets. *He dared not touch her.* But the profound need grew. Desmond closed his eyes, leaned his head against hers and simply soaked up her gentle, over-whelming comfort as the desert would lap up rain. He was coming into the sun after years of darkness.

Finally trusting himself to unclench his fists, he slid his hands around to rub her back. Nothing had ever felt this good, just holding her. Desmond would've stood there until hell froze over, but the phone rang and shattered the magic spell.

His lids lifted; he blinked. Down low, pressed against the bottom pane of the door was a disembodied face. Tail twitching, Dudley was nose-to-nose with the Peeping Tom. Desmond's head snapped back in shock. B.A. jerked as well, due to the shrill intrusion of the phone. She likely presumed he'd done the same.

The face vanished. Desmond stood, trying to decide if he'd imagined it, while B.A. took the call. "Maybe, whatever's in the water of the isle that causes lunacy is starting to affect me," he muttered under his breath.

With a tentative smile, she passed him the phone. "For you." Then, giving him privacy, B.A. moved to the alcove off the kitchen where her laptop was set up.

As he heard his brother's voice in the receiver, Desmond watched her boot the computer. "They *do* have phone ser-vice in that bloody rock. Feared it was a rumor." The voice added unnecessarily, "It's Jago, by the way."

Desmond snapped, "Have I ever confused Trevelyn with you, even on the phone?"

Jago laughed. "You ruined the fun of being a twin for Trev. He couldn't blame me for the rotten things he did, because he never fooled you. Anyway, I'm stretched out on a lumpy bed, staring at cracked ceiling tiles. How go matters on your end? Anything more thrilling than cracked ceiling tiles?"

Desmond strolled to the back door and peered into the night, attempting to spot any movement. He wondered if the Falgannon lads spied on B.A. regularly or if they had adopted nightly strolls due to her having a male under her roof. "Whole isle's friggin' nuts," he said.

"Island inbreeding," Jago joked.

"In this case, the island's under a curse and doesn't have females because of it."

"There you go. No women would work a . . . hardship on the male . . . um, er . . . brain."

Desmond's eyes caught a flicker in the moonlight. Three or more males skulked along the rock wall bordering the rose garden. Kitty stood up on his hind legs and scratched at the door to get out. Desmond cracked it open.

"Sic 'em, Dudley," he whispered to the cat, who bounded down the steps after the lurkers.

Jago queried, "Who's Dudley? Is he nuts, too?"

"Dudley's a cat—of sorts. How's it there?" He didn't say Kentucky. If B.A. picked up that bit of conversation, she'd be suspicious his brother happened to be in the Bluegrass State, the same as her sister, Asha.

"Not a rock in the Atlantic, but strange, too. There are guys called Joe-Bob and Bubba. Versailles is pronounced *VUR-sales*. Rather pretty country. I could learn to like it here."

"I see you one Bubba and raise you a Michael the Story, Michael the Fiddle and several other Michaels."

"Accounts for the strange names here then—Scots settled heavily in this area. Has Trevelyn checked in?"

"You expect him to?"

Jago's laughter came through the line. "How does big brother fare on his end? Is B.A. as gorgeous up close as she was from a distance?"

"Yes," Desmond replied tersely, not wishing to discuss B.A. in the manner of locker room talk.

Missing the clipped tone, Jago plowed on. "Considering bedding her before the big revelation?"

Desmond growled, "Good night, Jago."

"Uh-oh! Wait a sec, Des. I detect something in your voice—sounds suspiciously like solicitousness."

"Good night," he repeated, then he hung up the receiver. Shoving his hands in his pants pockets, he stared out into the night.

It floored B.A. There were so many e-mails from women wanting to be brides! She'd never expected this response.

She nearly danced with excitement. The Web site's design was wonderful, eye-catching, and she had an island full of bonnie males. The site had only been up a month, but it had over five thousand hits today.

"Modern day magic," she said and smiled.

She'd welcomed the interruption of the phone call. The intensity of holding Desmond Mershan shook her to the core. He'd felt so right, his strong muscles under her hands. The radiant heat. The pure male scent headier than any cologne ever distilled. Agonizing sensations flooded through her, warming her after seven years of being alone, cold.

Distanced from him and his panther magic, Angel B.A. blethered in her ear about how things were moving too fast. And she had to agree—such physical desire was scary. Never had she needed a man so strongly, never ached with this soul-deep hunger. But it was more.

So much more. Too easily, she could fall in love with Desmond Mershan.

She could also crash and burn when he walked away.

Desmond strolled into the alcove, pondering the goings-on outside. It was incongruous her islanders would foster him off on their lady if they feared for her safety. Then, why snoop?

As he entered the alcove, he caught sight of his reflection in the far windowpane, the light hitting so it became a mirror. He paused, his vivid green eyes staring back at him. Unsettling, after hearing Michael the Story's spiel about The Curse.

"Your brother's all right?" B.A. queried, glancing up.

He nodded absently, distracted by his reflection. "Just checking in." Shaking a peculiar feeling, he glanced at the computer, seeing she sorted through a flood of e-mails.

She smiled. "Ah, the big brother syndrome. I always want to know where my siblings are, if everything's okay."

Desmond took her wrist, kissed the inside where her pulse jumped, then pulled her to stand. She wanted to protest; he saw her mind grasping for excuses and coming up with none. Instead, she permitted him to tug her into his arms and kiss her. A gentle kiss, a questing kiss, one meant to let her learn the taste of him. To make her relax to the inevitable. Oh, did she relax, molding against him, fitting so well, as if they were two pieces of a whole.

His gut contorted in desire, and Desmond became a ravening beast. He kissed B.A. as he had never kissed any woman: no teeth, no tongue, no wild passion, just true sensual enjoyment of simply kissing. He could kiss her this way for hours. She put her arms around his neck, pressing her body against his.

The sound of a clay flowerpot crashing outside the window made her jump in his arms.

"The cat . . . I let him out," Desmond murmured into her hair, figuring it wouldn't go well for her lads if he ratted on their spying.

"Desmond!" she gasped.

"Hmm?"

There was a second crash and an odd choked off noise, similar to someone crying out only to have it smothered. Desmond saw Callum's face pop up. He swung B.A. around so she couldn't spot the Mackenzie from the corner of her eye, only to discover Willie on the other side of the bay window—likely why she'd gasped. He spun her again so she faced the kitchen. Over B.A.'s shoulder, he bared his teeth at the two men. Their heads vanished from view. Thankfully.

Well, that explains why without hesitation they'd dropped him down in the middle of B.A.'s bed. They were likely camped outside the windows all night.

The phone rang, causing both B.A. and Desmond to laugh. B.A. stepped out of his embrace to answer the call. "Could you hold?" Putting her hand over the receiver she whispered, "It's my brother. This'll take a bit, if you want to go up . . ."

He preferred to remain and eavesdrop, but if he went upstairs, maybe B.A.'s lurking lads would decamp. Come morn, he'd pick a bone with these clowns.

Nearly dashing up the stairs, he grabbed his travel kit and hit the bathroom for a quick shave, not wanting B.A. to get razor burns—anywhere. Finished, he hurried into the bed-

room. Turning out the lights, he opened the shades so
moonlight flooded the room. He wanted to make love to
B.A. bathed in that pale ghostly glow. Stripping off his
clothes, he climbed under the cool silk-covered duvet and
waited.

And waited.

The lights were still on below. He glanced at his Rolex—
three minutes until midnight. The witching hour, when all
things seemed possible, even magic.

Worry crept into Desmond's suspicious mind as minutes
crawled past. Cian Montgomerie, B.A.'s brother, carried a
reputation of being one of the best in corporate law. He was
the head lawyer for Montgomerie Enterprises since B.A.'s father had retired. Still, the solicitor could find out little. Even
if he did, by the time he did it would be too late.

Still, unease bubbled in Desmond.

Lights winked out downstairs, then he heard B.A.'s soft
footfalls climb the stairs and travel down the hall, followed
by noises from the room where the Scots had placed the
other bed this morning. Edginess bit at his patience,
spurring him to stomp down there, scoop her up and carry
her back to this bed. Ignoring surging cavemanitis, he gave
her space. She'd come. She wanted him as much as he
wanted her.

The square of illumination on the opposite wall flicked
out. Seconds later, B.A.'s muffled steps sounded outside the
door. Desmond's heart raced and he held his breath.

She entered the room wearing a prim nightgown and
wrapper, her hair plaited and over her shoulder. She was so
beautiful, the golden girl, the pampered granddaughter of
his enemy. And he wanted her more than life itself.

"Desmond . . . I'd like you and your men to leave come
morn. I'll ring Lewis and make special arrangements."

The world fell out from under him.

"That's it?" He didn't move—*didn't dare*—or he'd spring at
her like a big cat bent on bringing down prey.

"I . . . reached a decision. A resort isn't right for Falgannon. I dunna wish to take the island in that direction."

"Pity that." He breathed deeply to stem his spiraling fury. "Well, I'm afraid you don't have that option, Ms. B.A. Montgomerie."

"I'm owner of the isle. I decide what's needed."

Despite her words, she stood trembling, fragile. She feared him. It was clear she'd jumped at her brother's call as an excuse to distance herself from him. Strangely, he felt a compulsion to go to her, to comfort her, but he suppressed the ridiculous impulse.

"Read the fine print of the papers I gave you. I've put in a lot of time and money on this project. If you cancel, you'll pay the default fee in the contract or I'll sue you."

"Default fee?" she squeaked.

"One-million pounds sterling." Without mercy, he played his trump card. "There's also another paper I hold. Over thirty years ago, Sean borrowed a small fortune, putting up the north tip of the isle as collateral. The loan was never repaid. Through default on repayment I now own a chunk of your island—a shade over one-third to be precise. So Lady of the Isle, it seems there's a new Lord of the Isle, eh?"

B.A. swayed, appearing pale, as if the blood had left her brain. "We . . . shall see." She shakily turned on her heels and fled.

Desmond smiled in the darkness. "Yes, we shall."

Chapter 9

"Och, here she comes. And oh, does she have a mad on!" Willie alerted the "Morn, B.A." Club. Adam's apple bobbing in guilt, he peeked through the blinds of the picture window of The Hanged Man. "I'm sure B.A. spotted me last night. Watch—she'll lash a pound of flesh off my hide. I've been trying to come up with a good excuse for our spying ever since."

"You being a writer and all, ashamed you should be, *Willa*

Macgregor. You seem inventive enough in them ruddy books of yours. Or is it only with people having sex on a horse are you"—Angus the Ancient clucked his tongue, while he stole a glance at the ink marks on his hand—"de-miur-gic?"

Ian Fraser, watching the two over the newspaper, choked on his tea. "Demi-*what*? Looking up big words again, Angus, trying to tweak our Willie's nose?"

The doorknob rattled, sending everyone scurrying. With tea and sticky buns, they took up their normal positions, feigning nonchalance.

Ian arched his brow as the door flung open and B.A. stormed in, her eyes executing a quick sweep of the room. Oh aye, she had a mad on.

She barked, "Where's the bloody eegit?"

"Morn, B.A.," everyone chimed in toneless, everyday fashion, though Ian noticed several struggled to keep their faces straight.

B.A. looked ready to spit nails. "Don't morn me, you gormless pelicans. Where *is* he? I want his head on a platter."

A laugh nearly escaped Ian when Willie snatched the newspaper from his hands and ducked behind it, hoping to escape her notice. He didn't blame Willie. Their lass was a force when her dander was up. Stronger men ran when B.A. had steam rolling out her ears.

She swung around, glaring at all the men, but they bent over their hot buns with singular concentration, projecting halos over their heads. Her frown deepened, as though something had just occurred to her. "Where's Dudley?"

"Being a Montgomerie, she rarely asks," Angus grumbled. "Just demands in her Pictish princess tone. Sean should've beaten her regularly, no doubt," he said once more.

B.A. rolled her eyes. "Oh, put a sock in it, Angus. No one believes you told Sean that."

"You want to ken where Dudley is?" asked Callum, rising to snag another roll as Tam carried them in fresh from the oven.

"A lot of bother over a kitty," Innis sniffed.

B.A. huffed. "Kitty mooches off the Club every morn. Where is he?"

"Could be with the Viking prince," Michael the Fiddle suggested. "He favors him."

"He's no prince," she snapped.

Angus tapped his cane. "Why aren't you taking care of your patient, you scatty harridan? Doc said to watch him closely. You looking in his eyes every few hours?"

"I'm not his bloody nurse."

"Ashamed you should be," Angus badgered in his patriarchal tone. "Not seeing to his care, instead you're here blethering about the cat!"

B.A. nearly growled, "I'm not searching for the cat."

"Then stop fashing and tell us who you *are* looking for, lass." Ian, stirring his tea, eyed Willie again, hiding behind the *London Times*. He leaned over and turned the newspaper right side up, thinking it'd be more convincing.

"I'm hunting Jock the Repair. Bloody phone is out again," she complained. "I've got to call Cian the Brother."

"Jock's working on Davey the Weaver's washer-machine. They thought he'd sorted it out, but Davey's screaming it's creating mounds of suds."

"Want a sticky bun, B.A.?" Michael the Fiddle inquired, waving one under her nose.

"No, I dunna want a sticky bun." But the smell of cinnamon rose from the hot roll. She snatched it away and took a bite, ignoring his smirk. "Tell the MacGyver of Falgannon, he better get it working by noon or I shall . . . ban him from the isle!"

"Dunna think our lass ever banned any of us before," Hamish the Lighthouse said.

Innis huffed, "Got your knickers in a twist, B.A.? Not good for your health at your age."

"My *age*?" She choked on the roll, so Michael slapped her on the back. Enjoying the show, Ian caught Innis winking at Tam the Baker, who picked up the banter.

"Aye, B.A., you're not getting any younger. Willie was reading to us how a woman over forty stands a better chance of being run over by a lorry from Fortnum and Mason than getting married. Edging perilously close to that big four-zero, you are, lass. Since lorries from Fortnum and Mason dunna deliver up here, 'tis a grave concern to us."

" 'Tis true," Callum seconded. "At your advanced years, B.A., dunna let a golden opportunity pass you."

"Aye, we hate to see you years from now, like the Marys, sitting up on the knoll pining over Dudley Campbell. You'll be up in the cottage on the castle and calling your kitty The Cat Desmond. It'd be sad, indeed," intoned Angus.

Clearly exasperated, B.A. stomped to the door. She paused to give them a parting shot. "I'll be at Lady Cottage if anyone needs me. Tell Jock, the *real* MacGyver would make it work with a roll of duct tape!"

"Och, a low blow." Ian lifted his teacup, saluting the closing door. "Guess it's safe to assume our Viking prince dinna carry our lass up the stairs last night like Rhett did Scarlett."

The club all chorused a discouraged agreement.

His cheek being licked woke Desmond from an erotic dream. Seconds passed before it registered that the tongue, akin to sandpaper, wasn't connected to B.A. More's the pity. Seeing the amber-eyed kitty nose-to-nose, he moaned and dragged the duvet over his head. No sooner was he hid from the cat's view, he felt something pounce on his toes and attack.

"Bloody puss needs to go on a diet," he grumbled. "I guess this is Falgannon's version of an alarm clock?"

Rolling onto his back, he allowed the last of the sexy dream about B.A. tied to the posts of this bed to drift through his mind. He'd never been one for bedroom games, thus the dream astonished him. Every detail seemed so real—the sensations, the scents, heat from her body—that it'd nearly been a wet dream. He didn't think forty-four-year-old men still had wet dreams. Peculiarly, it didn't feel like a quirky fantasy but rather a vibrant memory.

He dismissed the unease and lazed as Dudley gnawed on his toes. Half drifting and enjoying the sensual movie playing in his mind, his body responded, bucking against the silk-covered comforter.

Unfortunately, the cat lost interest in chasing mouse-toes and pounced with his tubby tabby weight on the new source of movement under the comforter. Desmond screamed, jackknifing up to remove the playful cat.

"Dudley," he squeaked in soprano, holding up the pudgy pussy, face-to-face. "This isn't how I planned on waking up this morning. Come on, Fuzzball, let's see if B.A. is ready for Round Two."

Hopping out of bed, he grabbed a pair of sweatpants from his suitcase and yanked them on. Then he padded barefoot downstairs in search of Ms. BarbaraAnne Montgomerie.

From the stillness in the house, he sensed her absence. It felt empty, cold. He shrugged, chalking the chill up to the peat fire having burned out. The feline tagged along, dashing ahead to his bowl in the kitchen, hinting he could stand a feeding. Ignoring the pussycat, Desmond glanced around, expecting a note from B.A. with orders to get off her island.

"Hmm . . . no note." Picking up the phone, he discovered no dial tone. He smiled. "Fate loves me, Dudley. Come on, I'll stand you to pub grub as soon as I'm dressed. I've questions for a few of your lads, then we'll run B.A. to ground."

A half hour later, Desmond and Dudley pulled up in the Range Rover and parked in front of The Hanged Man. Looking down the street, he considered going to the store, seeing if B.A. were there. His stomach grumbled, reminding him there had been no breakfast in bed this morning. "Besides," he said to the feline, "I want a tête-à-tête with her lads about their lurking."

Pocketing the keys, he opened the car door. Dudley scampered out and up the pub steps with the accuracy of a heat-seeking missile—only, this fur-covered missile was food-seeking. He noticed as Kitty shot into the inn without slowing; the critter had his own entrance to the pub, too. They'd even painted THE CAT DUDLEY'S DOOR over it in gold letters. Chuckling, he shook his head and used the people door.

"There's Kitty!" Angus declared. "Right peaceful without the wee beastie tormenting us this morn. He's fetched the Viking prince. Come have a scone and jelly, young feller."

Desmond found a chair for himself and one for Dudley. "Thanks. Must be the island air, I'm famished."

"Famished, he is," Innis echoed." 'Tis B.A.'s fault. The hussy. Ashamed she should be, leaving him to fend for himself."

"Aye, the lass needs a walloping with this." Angus raised his cane. "I told Sean, time and again, she needed beating. Did he listen?"

"What did you expect? He was a Montgomerie." Innis shook his head in mock disgust. "You ken Montgomeries never listen."

Desmond frowned as Ian Fraser set a plate of scones and a rasher of bacon before him.

"Och, pay no mind, no one believes he said that." Ian laughed. "That's Angus flapping his gub. No one believe's he'd dare touch a hair on the sweet lass's head."

" 'Sweet lass,' " Angus scoffed. "Dinna she just threaten to boot Jock off the isle 'cause he's no good with duct tape?"

Desmond finished a melt-in-your-mouth-biscuit, then smeared raspberry jam on another. "B.A. was here?"

"Aye, dashed in wanting to ken where Dudley was," Innis answered between sips of tea.

"Wasn't the cat," Callum corrected, "but Jock the Repair and his duct tape she was trying to run to ground."

Desmond fixed Callum with a stare. "Seeing as you're good at keeping tabs on B.A., you wouldn't happen to know where she is?"

The man had the grace to look sheepish. "Oh aye, she's at the cottage on the castle."

That wasn't the first time he'd heard them say it precisely that way. "*On* the castle?"

"Aye," several muttered.

"How do I find this cottage *on* the castle?" Desmond asked.

" 'Tis on the north side of the isle. Take any road—all roads lead to the castle," Ian said.

Desmond cleared his throat. "North side?"

"Tread careful around the lass," Ian cautioned. "She wasn't in a cheery mood when she stormed out of here."

Before polishing off his scone, Desmond broke off a bite of bacon for Dudley. "Now, perhaps someone would explain why you lads were poking noses in B.A.'s windows last night?".

B.A. stood high atop Castle Falgannon, the wind playing in her hair. Placing her hands on the crenellation, she leaned into the breeze and let the warm autumn day caress her face. This isle was so much a part of her heart, her soul.

Passed from female to female of her line since the dawn of time, she was smart enough to know she wasn't an owner but a caretaker, recognized the island owned *her*. She enjoyed visiting her family in England or Kentucky, but the whole time a restlessness niggled in her to return to Falgannon.

B.A. perceived why her ancestors had built the castle on this point. From the vantage atop the hill, she surveyed nearly the entire island. No Viking invaders could approach without being seen—even modern-day Vikings. Why, she was even aware an angry Desmond stomped up the hill heading in her direction.

" 'By the pricking of my thumbs, something wicked this way comes,' " she quoted the Scottish play—only she figured her definition of wicked and Will's varied slightly.

Ignoring the man—or trying to—she stared out across the northern tip of the isle at the white sand beaches, then up the hill to the ancient ring of stones that dated back over five millennia.

"Over any dead body will some Viking raider steal what belongs to my ancestors—even if he does have green eyes. I might be a woman, but I'm also a warrior, as all the females of my bloodline were. No one is taking this castle," she vowed.

The fact he still made her heart go pitter-patter wouldn't deter her one bit.

Desmond paused at the bottom of the stone staircase, which wound up one side of the ancient fortress. He *had* to stop. The view was imposing, breathtaking. He'd been aware there were ruins of a castle on Falgannon, but the lack of information on record frustrated him.

He'd hired aerial surveys done, even attempted three himself with Julian Starkadder, his right-hand man, as pilot. But a dozen endeavors to fly over the isle each met with the same results. As the helicopter sighted Falgannon in the distance, mists suddenly enshrouded it, preventing them from getting closer. When he had complained of the problem, one old seaman called him daft, said the Hebrides didn't have the same trouble with fog as the mainland. Now Michael the Story's telling of the sacred mists enfolding Friseal and Maeve came to mind.

Hence, the majesty of Castle Falgannon now caught him unawares. At first glance he noted the stone stairs as a recent addition, estimating their crafting to have been sometime in the past two centuries. The architect in him admired the castle's brilliance of design, the eight hundred-year-old stone and mortar rivaling anything done today. The foundation showed signs of being constructed atop the ruins of *another* fortress—dating back how long? In this day and age when they imploded half of Las Vegas because the buildings were deemed too costly to repair, that this fortress had endured, weathered, was proud of its heritage, was amazing.

Touching a family-held structure so ancient humbled him. The overwhelming need to own this castle seized him, and it had nothing to do with his plans for developing Falgannon, but for himself. Desmond suddenly coveted this stronghold.

Glancing up, he spotted B.A. framed by the merlons, her gold hair flying in the wind like a warrior's banner. The Lady of the Isle.

Abruptly time shifted, and the weight of chain mail and armor were upon his body, his hand wrapped around the pommel of a broadsword. He stood on another set of stairs, ones much older, the objective burning in him to storm this bastion, to claim Castle Falgannon and its lady. About him he heard the clash of swords, the din of battle. Words echoed inside his brain—this fortress was his and so would she be.

The Cat Dudley brushed against his legs, snapping the

spell, leaving Desmond woozy and shaken. As his eyes followed the cat up the staircase, strangely curving around the outside of the castle and straight to the top, he noticed there was, indeed, a cottage on the roof!

Well, why not? Desmond shrugged. A house atop a castle went well with this dotty island.

As he ascended, he fought that pull, that slippage of time. Reaching the top he paused, agog at the full-size house on the far side of the flat roof. While his architectural curiosity wanted to examine this further, the woman with her back to him, staring out to the sea, drew his eyes.

He'd come to force B.A. to see he'd backed her into a corner. The will to conquer pulsed in his blood, fueled by the need to possess this castle and its lady.

She knew he was there. He saw the awareness in her posture. Ignoring him, she remained looking out at the misty horizon, compelling him to come to her.

Despite the day being unseasonably warm, the skies quickened to gray as though she had summoned a storm to match her mood. He'd never believed in ghosts, déjà vu or witches casting spells, but standing atop Castle Falgannon he found all now in the realm of the possible. His breath held as she turned and fixed him with glowing amber eyes.

He said the first thing that popped into his mind. "What? No kitty door?"

Her eyes followed Dudley across the roof. He leapt up to a cottage window frame and pushed through a pane that had been turned into a cat entrance, barely squeezing his fat body through.

"But he's not your cat," Desmond mocked.

"Dudley's no one's cat," B.A. replied, projecting a sense of serenity, as though she drew power from being on top of this castle. "Some things in life can't be owned."

He rotated to survey the lay of the land, admiring the clever positioning of the castle. Had he been an ancient warrior and planning a fortress, this spot is where he'd have placed it. Desmond stepped closer to where B.A. was using a crenellation to observe the churning sea.

"Some view. Why the house on top of the castle?"

"The Charter says the Lady of the Isle must be in residence of Castle Falgannon from the first of November until May Day of each year."

"And why is that?"

"When Malcolm Canmore re-granted the charter, he added the stipulation the Lady of the Isle must live in residence for that period each year or the island reverts to the Scottish crown. Eventually, the castle needed work—no modern conveniences, floors rotting away and not enough money for repairs. In order to meet the requirement, Lady Cottage was built upon the roof."

"I take it the castle itself is sound?"

"You couldn't blow the bloody thing up. Scots build to last."

He stepped to her other side, eyeing the ring of stones in the distance. "Falgannon has a stone circle."

"Thirteen gneiss stones, standing a millennium before the first Sarsen was raised at Stonehenge."

"May we go see them?"

She shook her head. "Another day. A storm's coming."

Desmond leaned close, invading her space, catching scent of her light perfume and the woman underneath. "So, you aren't having your lads toss me off the isle?"

B.A. wasn't certain how to answer. Too many factors were in the mix, and she hadn't begun to sort them out. Preferring to work with facts, she needed to get a hold of Cian or her father about Desmond's claim of owning part of the island. With the phone out a trunk call was impossible, which left her playing a waiting game.

In some ways she liked that the choice was beyond her control. He scared her. His presence caused her to feel so many things. Even so, she wanted him to stay. Silly, to want to trust a man with your body when signs pointed he wasn't worthy of that faith. Desmond Mershan was one of those bad boys Anne Stuart wrote about, mamas rail against and daughters can little resist. Her whole life she'd been good. A good daughter, a good granddaughter and a good wife. At thirty-seven, a widow, the temptation of this wicked lad was too much to resist.

"Not today," she replied. "The ferry doesn't run until Thursday, and it's too far for you to swim."

His green eyes met hers. "I won't be leaving Thursday either."

She suppressed her smile. "You know, on my word the ferry stops. Should I want to stop you leaving, there's no way off the isle."

He looked amused. "Considering keeping me as a sex slave, BarbaraAnne?"

She shrugged. "That's one possibility. My sister, Paganne, led an archeological team on Falgannon three years ago. They dug up seven corpses in our bog, ages ranging from eight hundred to one thousand years old. My ancestors sacrificed them to the auld gods come harvest. Theory is, they were mates to different Ladies of the Isle and for some reason were ritualistically put to death."

"Not the green-eyed ones!" He laughed, shaking his head. "Lady, I'd love to have you backing me in the boardroom."

"I'm not boardroom material. My life's here, it's where I belong," she stated simply.

Desmond was rattled by her conviction. He considered the scope of his plans, the predicted impact on this island, and he was coming to see how it would affect this woman. Desmond had never known any sense of belonging. After his father's suicide they had moved from place to place, never in one spot long enough to set roots. As he aged, he'd gone where jobs took him. Until he'd put his hand on the rail of this castle, no place before spoke to his mind, telling him this is where he wanted to be.

Wind kicked up, ruffling his hair as he surveyed the breathtaking, almost too perfect to be real vista. The need to possess this castle burned in his gut. A spanner in the works.

"Can we go inside the castle?" he requested, ignoring complications arising from his deep yearning.

"Let me fetch a torch. I'll give you a tour of the areas we can go into." B.A. entered into the cottage's kitchen, pausing to give Kitty some crunchies.

Desmond followed, fascinated with the craft and beauty that comprised the cottage. And while the dwelling intrigued him, and he wished to examine it closely, he was more impatient to see the inside of the fortress.

She led him to the far end of the roof, to the entrance. "Careful, the steps are damp. We plan a roofed entrance over it to keep rain from doing more damage. Stay on the stairs. The flooring is mostly wood and unsound, but we can reach the ground floor and see the Great Hall. The stairs were designed so warriors descending could use their right hand—their sword hand—giving them the advantage whilst hampering invaders. Upper levels were living quarters, bedrooms, the solar—the family room by today's standards."

She rattled off details familiar to Desmond through his schooling on design. Of course, it was one matter to read facts on a page, another to walk through them and touch them. She was right. The castle was sound. Mortar needed repair and all wood would have to be replaced. It'd cost a king's ransom, but to an architect it was just another challenge.

One that ignited his imagination, spellbound his soul.

"The Great Hall was the heart of the castle. The lord's table would've been here." Face alight, B.A. told of life in the huge hall. "Other trestle tables below the salt were taken down each night. They'd have sat around the fireplace, listening to the *seannachie* weave tales."

Desmond couldn't resist. "Tales of Maeve and Friseal?"

Warily, she nodded. "I'm sure that was recounted."

He moved close and she veered away, staying out of reach. He liked stalking her. "Tell me, how many of these ladies found their green-eyed man?"

"Enough. On average one every hundred years."

Every inch the predator, he enjoyed tracking her. "Why didn't you marry a green-eyed man, BarbaraAnne?"

She remained frozen for several breaths, her eyes wide. Again, that strange pressure built within his chest, only this time he wasn't drinking a soda.

Breaking the spell, she shined her electric torch into the fireplace. "The back slides to the side, opening to a tunnel. Logs were tossed onto the fire so no one would ever think to check there."

Leaning over, he checked the hearth. "Does it still work?"

"Aye, the tunnel leads to a sea cave." She watched as The Architect Desmond assessed the hall. "It dunna take a clairvoyant to see what's running through your mind."

He turned, locking stares with her. "You'd be surprised what runs through my mind."

"Part of me is thrilled you view the castle as something other than a pile of rocks. Part fears you consider turning it into a high-priced resort." She awaited his confirmation. When none came, she went on. "Sean left a trust for the island, enough money so I never worry. Along with Evian's insurance, I seldom look at the bottom line in managing Falgannon."

He saw hunger in her eyes. She wanted this castle brought back to life, the same passion that had flared in him the instant he put his hand on the railing.

She tugged her shawl tighter about her shoulders. "I approached Sean with plans to refurbish the castle as a family seat. I learned he held a deep resentment against the castle—maybe it represented a part of his wife he could never touch. Some inner demon drove him to claim Maeve and Falgannon, to show the world the poor islander made good. But in claiming her, he ran into The Curse. Maeve required a fortune to drag Falgannon into the twentieth century. She traded her chance at true love for the wealth Sean offered. He married the Lady of the Isle; she received the funds she needed to save the island. And in the end, neither was happy."

Desmond had been enjoying a companionship with B.A., and he resented the intrusion of Montgomerie's name. It soured his mood.

"You're calculating the cost to restore the castle," she stated.

Challenge was in his words. "If I am?"

"Examine your so-called deed—not I'm admitting it's legit, mind. No matter what part of Falgannon Sean used for collateral, it dinna include the castle or the ring of stones."

"The northern third—which also includes Rose Cottage, does it not?"

"The cottage's on the north third, aye. But no matter, the charter says the castle and stone circle goes with the Lady— a non-breakable trust reaffirmed by Malcolm I in A.D. 945. There's a provision for the tenants to claim their hereditary lands, if they choose, thus, a portion of the island is set aside in trust. The Lady of Falgannon retains ownership of the castle and the stone ring. As far as the area surrounding . . . try changing the land and watch me tie you up with Scottish Historical Trust for decades."

Then she flashed him a sexy smile that spelled checkmate. Damnable woman!

So, why did excitement pump through his veins instead of anger?

Chapter 10

"You dunna understand." Tending bar at The Green Man, B.A. filled orders for Gillis the Younger to bus to the tables. "Mershan claims Sean put the northern tip of the isle up for collateral, then defaulted on the loan."

While The Hanged Man was a traditional pub where everyone gathered to talk, relax or have a good meal, three years ago she'd put in a second tavern: The Green Man. Designed for the younger set, the ambiance reflected that restless energy. "When I'm Gone" by 3 Doors Down blared from the speakers. In another room, two pool tables had games in progress, clacking balls audible as the song switched to Wolfstone's "Ballavanich." A third room was a dance floor, currently used only by B.A. to exercise in off-times when the pub was closed.

Michael the Fiddle paid little mind to her fussing about the invader trying to rob her of part of the isle. He was keeping an eye on Mandy Taggart, who shared after-dinner drinks with Brian the Horseman. The sexy American brunette had given no hints toward which, if any, of her three bachelors she might favor. Since Michael was one of the three she'd selected from the registry, he was antsy, distracted.

At the end of the bar, Willie clicked SEND on an e-mail to a Cassie Gates, who had contacted him through the Web site. Since Jock the Repair had got the telephone working, Willie was taking advantage of being online while it lasted. He also pretended to ignore B.A.

Ian drained his ale and scooted the glass toward her to refill. "I'm not driving, so hit me again, lass."

"You're driving your bicycle," Michael the Fiddle reminded. "You pedaled that into the loch Friday two weeks ago due to too many *Wee Heavys*."

"Eejits, stop with the bicycles and Web site." B.A. passed Ian his ale and held up three fingers, harking that this was his third. "I couldn't contact Cian the Brother about this supposed loan. Any of you ken about it?"

Michael shrugged. "You might try the duffers over at The Hanged Man, but when they have a captive audience, they milk it for its worth."

"Kitty likes him, B.A.," Ian pointed out, rotating on the stool to watch Desmond across the room at the table with the other Vikings.

B.A. raised up from putting ice in a glass for herself, studying Desmond feeding cheese chunks to the golden Dudley. The cat sat in a chair next to Mershan, eyes adoring as if the Lord of Catdom had descended to Earth. B.A.'s heart squeezed at the sight.

"Vote's out on the worth of Kitty's endorsement. He's never liked anyone, so we've no basis for comparison," she pointed out.

"'Tis true," Michael murmured, watching Janet buzzing about the Vikings' table. "Guess Janet's opinion wouldn't matter either, since she has a penchant for men with wavy black hair?"

B.A. knew damn well Michael gigged her with a gaff. The effect wasn't lessened. "Janet can play with blond Vikings, but she'd better leave The Man Desmond alone," she muttered so no one could hear. "Or I'll sic the cat on her."

"What's that, B.A?" Ian leaned on the oak bar. "Speak up, lass."

"Oh, put a sock in it." She tossed a bar towel into his face.

Michael the Story lowered his voice so his comments didn't carry to B.A. "The Viking prince's eyes rarely lose sight of our lass."

Willie nodded and glanced at B.A. "So far she hasn't said a word about me spying last night. I've been keeping a low profile, only . . . I'm not about to let this wait any longer. Wish me luck, gents." Turning the laptop around so she could see the pictures of a pretty girl with freckles, he said, "Could you be adding her to the list? An avid romance reader, she runs a secondhand bookstore in Richmond, Virginia—wherever that is—and is working on her first novel. Her dream is to live in Scotland. She picked me, B.A.—only me."

"Smart lass, I'd say." B.A. patted his arm. "I'll move her to the top of the list and set up arrangements in the morn—provided MacGyver of the East's patch holds."

Michael the Story queried the other males, "We inviting the Viking horde to Thursday night poker?"

"Hey!" B.A. slammed her empty tray onto a stack. "You never let me play."

"Nobody in their right mind plays poker with a Montgomerie." Ian started to push his empty glass to B.A. for a refill, but she held up three fingers and waved them at him. He made a face, grumpy. "You're a cruel woman, putting me on a limit for a month due to me driving me bicycle into the loch. I explained—a kelpie tried to steal me from the mortal world, B.A."

"The waterwitch jumped up and wanted her wicked way with you? Sorry. A five for originality, a two for believability." She set a lemon squash before him on a coaster. "How come the Vikings can come to poker night, but I'm barred."

Phelan the Lobster reminded her unnecessarily, "They're male. You aren't. You ken Thursday night poker is males-only. Besides, no one with all his marbles plays poker with a Montgomerie—they bloody cheat."

B.A. brightened, wearing a suddenly crafty expression. "You're going to leave the yank lasses alone all evening?"

"Och, she has us by the short and curlies," Michael the Story groaned, and the men at the bar crossed their legs. "The occasion not having arisen in the last six years, we hadn't considered what to do with them on Thursday night."

"Never mind. We lasses shall institute a ladies' night. Maybe go for a swim at the springs under the moonlight." She waggled her eyebrows in Groucho fashion. "Nekkid even."

The men on the stools choked on their drinks.

"You're funning, B.A.?" Ian managed to say.

She smirked and moved off to polish the bar.

Willie leaned to Michael the Fiddle. "You're fidgety 'cause Mandy Taggart, the pretty brunette from Oregon, is having drinks with Brian the Horseman. Ian and Brian . . . well-propertied, they are. Their stud breeds hunters that Englanders and Irelanders both fight over. With coal black hair and ice blue eyes, they're handsome devils. A lot to offer a lass. Feeling the pinch of competition, are you?"

Michael shrugged. "A wee bit, perhaps."

Willie sighed. "My fae side says Miz Cassie Gates is the lass for me. So it's more important than ever that B.A. falls for the Viking prince and lives happily ever after—so the rest of the bloody isle can do likewise."

"Oh aye. But being contrary, she's hiding behind the bar, pretending she has to work—an excuse to avoid Mershan. And he's stubbornly sitting with his men, tracking her like a hawk."

"Being a best-selling writer, I'm able to plot." Willie nudged Michael with his elbow. "Get B.A. to dance with you. If the Viking prince sees our B.A. dancing with another man, it might provoke him to do something besides stare. At the same time, it'd showcase you in Mandy's eyes. Women like men who can dance."

Michael seemed skeptical. "You think?"

Willie nodded and took a swallow of ale. "Oh aye, remember in *Strictly Ballroom* when Paul Mercurio danced the rumba with Tara Morice behind the curtains? Even Morag and Oona declared it romantic. Strut your stuff—get back at those eejits for all the teasing you took for taking dance lessons with our B.A."

"We've not danced together for years."

"Like riding bikes. Round up our lass, I'll dig out tunes."

Cornering the bar, Willie pushed by B.A., Michael dogging his steps. When Michael untied the apron about her hips, B.A. looked startled.

"What are you doing, eejit?"

"Not me—*we*. Cannot recall what it's called, *paso doble*, *rumba* . . ."

"You want to dance?" she gasped. "Och, I dunna think so—" The rest was cut off as he dragged her forward.

For some bloody reason, Michael had grabbed her hand and dragged her through the pub, along the aisle through the tables and down five steps to the dance floor. The far wall of the dining area was open so people at the tables could watch. B.A. felt on display.

With a wink, the Story hauled her into his arms. "Those lessons I took because you needed to learn and I put up with teasing from the lads? I'm calling in my marker."

B.A. loved to dance, but she felt she had two left feet until they made their second pass of the floor. Then, each settling into their partner's rhythm, they waltzed to Bryan Adams's "Have You Ever Really Loved a Woman." As they relaxed, their steps grew more playful.

"What caused the urge to play Ginger and Fred? Anything to do with Amanda Taggart?"

Michael shrugged. "Willie suggested lasses favor dancing."

"Willie's a right smart one." She inclined her head in Mandy's direction.

"Seems we have her attention." He beamed.

"You should ask her to dance next."

The arrogant grin fell off his face. "What if she dunna ken how?"

"Teach her," B.A. said with a laugh.

She tripped over her foot as her eyes collided with Desmond's. Even from across the room, his penetrating stare made it hard to remember *one-two-three, side-back-front*. Luckily, Michael was a familiar partner. She finished the dance without turning into a total klutz.

"B.A.," Michael pointed out, "you never blushed for Evian. You do it a lot around the Viking. Whether he owns a chunk of the isle—or *thinks* he does—'tis another reason to keep him about, eh?"

B.A. glanced at Desmond. "If I keep him around, I'm likely to get hurt."

Michael paused at the steps to the dining area. "You might. You could also get lucky. Who kens? Maybe my gran and mum might return to the isle if you married a black-haired, green-eyed man. Now excuse me, I'm about to ask a pretty Yank to dance."

She smiled, watching Michael ask and Amanda eagerly accept. Then Callum and Ian the Radio led Beth and Katie—the other two Americans—onto the floor as well. It was heartwarming to see her plan working.

Sucking up courage, she turned to face Desmond. Butterflies filled her stomach as he rose from his chair and offered it to her.

"Come to look in my eyes?" he asked. He picked up Dudley, then resettled with the cat on his lap. His beautiful hand stroked the cat's back, sending shivers up B.A.'s spine. Enchanted how the man and cat had bonded, she worked to ignore the fire he conjured in her with that simple gesture. How she envied that cat.

"They need checking?"

"Most definitely." Their pale green depths flickered with banked fire. "Fancy footwork out there," he added.

"Thanks, it's been a while since I danced with Michael."

The two blond Vikings rose, pushing their chairs to the table. Wulf gave Desmond a two finger salute. "See you in the morning, boss."

"Please, dunna leave on my account. I stopped by to—," B.A. started to say.

"Look into Desmond's eyes?" the second blond laughed, finishing her sentence. "We're diving in the morning, so we require our beauty sleep. Good night, lovely lady."

With a frown, she watched them go. Recalling Desmond had brought scuba gear, she asked, "You aren't diving? It's too soon after the cosh to your head. The water surrounding Falgannon is warm because of the Gulf Stream, but currents are swift, with strong riptides. It's tricky."

"I'm not diving. Wulf and Dennis are professionals, though, and they'll enjoy the challenge," Desmond said.

Nervous, she used conversation to cover. "So . . . you're getting an invite to Thursday poker night. My lads hope to fleece you and your men—delayed payback for Viking raids on our isle."

"I take it this is a regular thing?"

"Males only, every Thursday—except the last one of the month."

"The last Thursday?" he queried.

"That's the lads' long weekend in Ullapool." She laughed. "As the Marys say—they go tomcatting from Thursday until Monday evening."

Desmond chuckled. "Tomcatting? Quaint way of putting it. Curiosity, since your lads go *tomcatting,* can't they find their own brides instead of you importing them?"

"They tried. For years. Most of them went to university on the mainland. I sent them to Colford Hall to stay. My father gave them jobs at Montgomerie Enterprises local offices so they'd have time and money. Some stayed as long as two years." At a loss to explain, since he had already sneered at The Curse, B.A. equivocated: "They're island-born. Maybe 'tis hard for you to understand, but something about Falgannon roots deep into one's soul. We're never happy for long elsewhere. Most came back brokenhearted. A few did marry. They ended in divorce. As I said, we've a high divorce rate." She fell silent.

They stayed a bit longer to watch the dancing, but then B.A. had to call it an evening. She needed to complete an order for supplies and cut checks since Angus the Ferry left at first light. Also, a new flood of e-mails awaited her.

As they strode from the pub, Wee Dougie's scooter came roaring around the corner. This time Desmond pulled up without her warning. He looked down at the Cat Dudley, who stood waiting, indicating that this bizarre behavior was the norm even to him. "Doesn't that delinquent have anything better to do than try and run people down?"

"He only tries to run down—"

"People he likes. I'm *not* flattered, B.A. Does he go to school?"

"The Marys instruct him, along with the few other children on the isle. Michael the Story teaches them history and lore."

Desmond opened the car door for her, and again the cat jumped inside, hopping over the second bench to sit facing the back window. Desmond lifted a brow. "I see Kitty who's not your kitty is ready to go home."

"He's following you, not me," B.A. replied.

Desmond walked around and got into the driver's seat. As he put his key into the Rover's ignition, he paused. "Would you?"

The question flustered her. Being in the car with him had put her back into that breathless mode. There wasn't enough air. Her heart hammered against her ribs. "Would I what?"

"Follow me?"

She thought of various quips, the old Rowan and Martin's Laugh In, "Blow in my ear and I'll follow you anywhere," or in her thickest burr, "Lay on, Mac Duff." The answer rising from her deepest need was, "To hell and back." Her tongue remained glued to the roof of her mouth.

So much for being witty, BarbaraAnne, Devil B.A. muttered in disgust.

She stared, trying to read Desmond's countenance in the shadows. Her fae voice said for once his guard was down, and she'd miss an opportunity if she didn't reply honestly.

Desmond started the engine. "Cat's got her tongue, eh, Dudley? Pity that. I can think of a few things for which it might come in handy."

Devil B.A. sighed in dejection. So could she.

* * *

As Desmond pushed open the front door, the phone's shrill ringing greeted them.

The first call was the Marys, asking permission to add five rooms to their house. Obviously hard of hearing, the sisters talked so loudly that B.A. had to hold the phone away from her ear, and he caught most of the conversation. With more prospective brides coming, they had decided to turn their home into a bed-and-breakfast, hinting they could be Falgannon's unofficial chaperones to see the "proprieties" observed.

B.A. burst out laughing when Mary Annis yelled from the background, "Sister, you scatty eegit, tell our B.A. we see nothing wrong a'tall with her shacking up with the Viking prince. But we think these Yank lasses need to know they can't have their wicked way with our lads."

That provoked a case of the giggles in B.A., which quickly turned to hiccups. When Angus the Ferry called, reminding her to have the orders and checks ready for him in the morning, she could barely answer.

Shaking his head, Desmond took the phone from her. "Angus, B.A. is having an apoplexy, but she heard."

"Slap her on the back." Angus added, "Our B.A. is the delicate type, so 'tis likely nerves. These high-strung types, like my Janet, need special handling."

"Thank you, Angus, I'll be sure to slap her on the back."

No sooner than Desmond disconnected, Willie rang begging him to remind B.A. to e-mail Cassie Gates. As B.A. got her hiccups under control, her twin sister, Britt, called with news she had a role in a movie.

B.A.'s somber end of the conversation led him to gather the opportunity excited Britt, yet some aspect upset her. From extensive profiles Julian Starkadder had worked up on the sisters, Desmond knew Britt hadn't acted in years, had stopped after the breakup of her affair with some director.

To avoid snooping, he strode into the kitchen, intent on rooting out a whisky. He found several brands of Highland single-malt in a rack on the counter, and Waterford crystal glasses—only the best for Ms. B.A. Montgomerie—in the cupboard.

The cat twined around his feet going *murrrr*, which Desmond interpreted as Dudley-speak for, *Feed me before I pass out from hunger.* He paused, trying to recall where B.A. kept food for the-cat-that-wasn't-her-cat. Dudley, the highly intelligent puss, scratched on a cabinet door. Sure enough, it was stocked with high-priced canned food, a half-open bag of Hill's Science Diet and packets of Armitage Good Girl Catnip Drops.

"Not her cat, huh?" Selecting the dry, Desmond poured din-din into the bowl bearing the name THE CAT DUDLEY. "You need to go on a diet," he said for the fiftieth time.

The cat blinked innocently, then yawned. Desmond assumed he was asking for more, not yawning in agreement.

Watching B.A. talk to her twin, he recalled seeing Britt at Sean's funeral. One wouldn't instantly assume them twins. In the face they were mirror images, but there the likeness ended. Britt's long hair was a dark brown with a heavy mahogany cast, the solemn eyes a hazel gray. Not as tall as B.A., Britt had a more delicate air.

Taking a second tumbler from the shelf, Desmond added ice and Edradour whisky. He paused, watching B.A. She appeared tired. He suspected she hadn't slept well the past two nights. Constantly on the go, everyone wanted this or that from her. She was surrounded by an island full of dotty Scots, was lady of some medieval feudal trust . . . and yet, no one was really there for her.

Going to her, Desmond took her hand, kissed her palm, then curled her fingers around the glass. For an instant, puzzlement lit her expression. Then the corner of her mouth twitched with a brief thank-you smile.

B.A. allowed the Edradour to glide down her throat, spreading warmth through her body. As if she needed to feel hotter being so close to The Panther Desmond! The man was a blast furnace. His tantalizing heat invaded her space, that irresistible male scent brushing against her mind, exorcizing any hope of hanging on to reason.

Pressing the chilled glass to her cheek, she closed her eyes. From behind, Desmond put his hands on her shoulders and began kneading her tight muscles. Singed by his touch, she stiffened, but it didn't take long for those magic fingers to have her head lolling in ecstasy.

Oh, pretty please—does he do a full-body version? Devil B.A. panted from her shoulder.

B.A. loved her twin, who was still talking on the phone, only she had a hard time tracking Britt's words as waves of pleasure washed through her. She wanted to say she'd ring her back later, but understood this was important. Her sister's suicide attempt seven years ago had seen her siblings now take any call seriously. Britt refused to discuss that period in her past, though B.A. always believed Lucien Delacroix, the brilliant movie director, had been behind Britt's self-destructive turn.

"I'd think Hammer doing a remake of *Curse of Glen Gables* would draw good press. The script's good, Lee is big box office after *Lord of the Rings,* and you're more beautiful than ever. What's the prob?"

Britt sighed. "I was high about it, until I went in for pre-pub photos today . . ."

"And?"

"Lucien Delacroix is directing. Talk about being poleaxed." Britt laughed, but B.A. heard tears in her voice.

"Ah, bugger." B.A. groaned.

"I'd never have signed had I known. There's no backing out." Britt sighed. "It's late. You sound tired. I'll ring you later, after I face the devil incarnate. I need to go arm myself with holy water and wooden stakes."

Desmond's eyes traced the lines of B.A.'s face, concern flickering in them. "Trouble?"

Hanging up, she nodded sadly. "My twin—who's nothing like me. She took it into her head she wanted to act in horror films. She did. With her gorgeous body splashed across the screen, and two spreads in *Playboy,* she rose to the top. Britt loved acting in horror flicks. Only thing she loved more—Lucien Delacroix. He directed two of her biggest films. Everyone warned her about him—a maniac genius, he made love to his leading ladies, then cast them aside like trash. She dinna listen. When he dumped her, it destroyed Britt. Hammer Films is staging a comeback. They've set

Chris Lee to star in a sequel to her biggest film, *Curse of Glen Gables*. Britt as the female lead—the same character she played years ago. Same actors—"

"Same director." Desmond ventured a guess.

She nodded. "I'm not sure Britt has the strength to face Lucien again."

Desmond lightly raked his hands up her arms. "From a big brother to a big sister—sometimes we can't stop our siblings from making mistakes."

"Lesson learned long ago. Still, it isn't easy when my sisters keep sticking their fingers in the fan."

Desmond urged, "You're exhausted. Call it a night."

"I have several hours of work to do yet—"

The phone rang and B.A. reached for it, only his long arm beat her to the receiver. "Ms. Montgomerie's butler speaking. She's retired for the evening. Try again in the morning."

"Butler?" The voice laughed. "What's a lady's butler paid these days? Any *side* benefits?"

Desmond's humor sobered. "Trevelyn. Time you checked in."

Kissing him on his cheek, B.A. whispered, "For the drink and the shoulder rub." Then she went into the alcove to handle paperwork, affording him privacy.

"I've been busy, Des."

Desmond's eyes followed B.A. as she booted her laptop, wishing she'd go on to bed instead. "To any purpose?"

"You might say. I'm sitting on the bed of Raven Montgomerie, while she prepares us a late supper." His voice held a note of triumph.

Desmond snorted. "Figures."

"What's with the butler rubbish?"

Desmond evaded. "I'd rather hear details from your end."

Trevelyn laughed. "Not now, Sin. Besides, I'm intrigued by your new profession."

"Trev . . . ," he growled.

"I'd rather not go into details, but the situation's on target." Trevelyn hesitated, then inquired, "You're on track as well?"

Desmond thought back on his life before coming to the island and his purpose for being here. The Cat Dudley twined around his legs, vibrating with a diesel purr.

Was everything on track?

His reply was evasive. "Why shouldn't it be?"

Trevelyn sensed something was off. "You sound . . . different."

Not wishing for more of his brother's incisive probing, he offered an excuse. "I took a tap on the head."

"Hokey smoke, Bullwinkle! Bad?"

"You know me. I've a hard head." He cut Trevelyn off before he could ask more questions: "Check in more—I like progress reports. 'Night, Trev."

" 'Night, Des."

Desmond hung up the receiver, pausing, lost in thought. He stared at the beautiful woman whose lovely face was marred by a scowl as she looked at her computer screen, squinting. He had an idea she needed her eyes checked, was likely waiting until she visited England again. She'd skipped supper telling him she'd catch a sandwich later. She hadn't. He wondered how many times she'd put off eating and then gone to bed with no food, simply because she was too exhausted.

Getting cheese and sliced beef from the refrigerator, he fixed himself a sandwich, sharing a bite of the meat with Dudley. Slicing the bread diagonally, he paused mid-action. He had a strange, sinking feeling that nothing was on track. Least of all, him.

Chapter 11

He stood at the cliff's edge before Castle Falgannon, the wind ruffling his hair. Desmond stared out to sea at storm clouds looming on the horizon. Heavy mist swirled in the air, enshrouding the isle. So much for the Hebrides rarely having fog.

He'd come here, drawn by the ancient fortress and its panoramic vantage. His intent had been to go for a walk, to distance himself from B.A. and refocus on the plans he'd set in motion.

He'd have a hard time achieving those aims after holding her in his arms all night.

The morning had been spent delivering checks to shops on the main circle in the village, their cut of the online catalog sales for *Falgannon.co.uk*. At B.A.'s invitation he'd gone along. After breakfast at The Hanged Man, the first stops had been the pottery store, the bicycle shop, Davie the Weaver's and the art gallery run by Oonanne the Painter. Next came Patrick the Jeweler, who created dazzling gold and silver pieces with Pictish designs. Then the Shoe & Saddle Shop, where to his surprise, he found that outside of Reeboks all leather goods were handmade on the isle. Impressed with the quality, he ended up purchasing the pair of riding boots he now wore. They fit like a glove. The first pair of knee-boots he owned, and yet they felt a part of him, as if he'd lived in them his whole life.

He also wore a fisherman's knit sweater, though it was from Dunmohr, a nearby isle. Not only did B.A. see there was work for all on Falgannon, she organized two neighboring isles. Thus far, the online sales showed a steady clientele.

B.A. also ran greenhouses where they bred and exported hardy tea roses and peonies. Not allowing anything to go to waste, they used the petals to create sachets, soaps and perfumes for popular lines named Mists of the Isle and My Lady's Passion. After the first of the year, she'd launch another for men called Warrior Prince.

For such a small isle, they were quite industrious. The whole island was busy as bees and so bloody happy it nearly made him puke. Desmond couldn't put a finger on why their contentment with their island life irritated him. They weren't living in poverty. Their homes were postcard picturesque. B.A. supplied them with "toys"—DVD and CD players and the latest movies and music. Willie ran a combination book, DVD and CD shop, taking used ones in trade.

The clothing store was stocked with anything the islanders could want, but practical wear, no designer labels—

they were more interested in how long it'd last or how warm it was. The only time they showed interest in who made it was if it came from one of the neighboring isles. When he inquired if they stocked Louis Vuitton jeans and sweaters, the storeowner, Marjorie Mackenzie, informed him she didn't know the man and asked if he was new to the area.

"He'd best contact B.A. She'll add him to the catalogue." After he explained, she fixed him with a pinched look. " 'Tis daft, young feller. A shirt is a shirt, and no putting a name on it will make it any better."

He'd felt like a pretentious jerk.

The island affected him. Desmond hated that it did, but he wouldn't hide from the fact. How could a few days make such a difference? Small wonder the whole community was nuts; he was beginning to think he no longer knew himself. He found it harder to concentrate on why he'd come to Falgannon, more difficult to stay in tune with that predatory instinct of going for the throat.

He'd come out here to center himself, to sharpen his mind-set. Instead, he found he had no anchor. Never had he felt so out of control—and he didn't like it one bit.

He turned, staring at the castle's gray stone walls, trying to see it with architect's eyes, a developer's bottom line. Contrarily, he speculated about the people who had lived there—all the daughters of the original Maeve's line and their search for happiness with their green-eyed men. Had any found bliss? Had the castle walls echoed with laughter?

It surprised him to discover after all these years he still possessed a bit of a conscience. The islanders were so accepting of him. Especially B.A. After he'd claimed ownership of the northern tip of the isle, she hadn't pressed for proof. He knew she'd called her brother this morning. But catching the tail end of her conversation, he heard the tone of her voice was curiosity not urgency. These kooky Scots were too open—*too genuine*. It chafed that he wasn't handling them in the same fashion.

Quashing pointless emotion, Desmond stalked back to the greenhouse to round up B.A. and the cat. After all, it was about time for the ferry to return, then supper and Thursday night poker.

He chuckled derisively. A hot time on the old isle tonight. So, why was he looking forward to it?

The Cyrkle's golden oldie, "Turn Down Day," played over the speakers, the song matching B.A.'s pensive mood as she pruned roses in the greenhouse, the chore a favorite on rainy days. She enjoyed the quiet of the indoor gardens, with Dudley dancing around on the benches. Kitty loved music and often kept her company, but today he surprised B.A. by staying rather than trailing after The Panther Desmond.

Maybe Dudley sensed, as had she, that the man needed space. After the tour of the shops, Desmond had grown silent, brooding. It was troubling.

She'd gotten a trunk call through to her brother concerning Desmond's claim. Cian asked if she'd seen Desmond's paperwork. He'd edged toward livid over her not cornering Desmond for facts. Somehow, that hadn't been foremost on her mind.

The truth?—At this point she didn't care. She was falling hard for Desmond Mershan. It little mattered what had brought him to Falgannon. As she'd told Michael the Fiddle, she might get hurt, but the time for hiding from the world in the safe cocoon of the island was past.

Pulling a perfect white rose to her nose, she closed her eyes and inhaled the citrus scent. Rocking to the music, her mind reflected on last night. He'd been so caring, bringing her the whisky and later a sandwich. It had been a long time since someone did things for her. Years since she'd let them.

When she'd dropped to the computer in exhaustion, he carried her into the living room, laying her on the couch. He'd lit the peat in the fireplace and sat, putting her feet into his lap. There were no words to describe the ecstasy as he put those magic fingers to work on her feet. All tension, knots of seven years, released under his tender ministrations.

Never had anyone treated her with such gentle care, made her feel so precious, cherished. It was silly, but tears came to her eyes. Closing her lids, trying to hold them back, she hoped Desmond hadn't seen. He leaned over and scooted behind her, pulling her back to his chest. He fitted his body protectively to hers. Those strong arms enfolded her, his radiant heat scorching her flesh, seeping bone deep. She'd felt secure, safe.

At dawn, she'd woke to Angus the Ferry tapping on the door. She was tucked up with blankets over her—very alone. The peat fire was barely more than ash.

As she inhaled the flower's perfume, she sighed. Desmond Mershan was a perplexing man, likely perplexing even to himself, though he'd be loath to admit that. And he was oh so hard on a tender heart.

"What to do, Kitty, what to do?" Dudley bumped his head against her arm, assuring her he liked Desmond. "I'm to trust *your* opinion, you arrogant beastie?"

"Talking to a pussycat might lead some to think the kitty's yours." Desmond stood, leaning against the doorway. His midnight hair was windblown, droplets of rain clinging to the curls. Wearing black pants tucked into his knee boots and a fisherman's knit sweater, he appeared island-born instead of the polished businessman who'd arrived four days ago.

Her fae voice whispered: *He belongs here.* Oh, she was in trouble.

Flustered, she waved her hand. "Everyone natters to Kitty. It's when he talks back we show concern." She deadheaded the spent bloom and dumped it into the dustbin on wheels in the middle of the aisle.

Chill, BarbaraAnne, Angel B.A. counseled. *Drooling puddles on the floor is unacceptable behavior.*

Desmond studied B.A., who was pretending his presence didn't affect her. She appeared less tired today, her hips swaying to K. D. Lang's "Constant Craving." The silly cat was doing the same.

"Dudley, my man, they'd have burnt you as a familiar in the Middle Ages." He laughed as Kitty ignored him and continued a *Meow-Mix* chow-chow-chow dance.

Evidently, she'd rested peacefully in his arms last night. Rather surprisingly, so had he. He'd put up with lying next to her, aching with every fiber of his being, wanting her so badly he thought he'd go mad. He'd gritted his teeth and cradled her, so beautiful in peaceful slumber that he couldn't bear to disturb her. Just watching B.A. was reward enough.

At least, it had been last night. Today was another matter.

The queer mood polluting his disposition, he stalked B.A., invading her space, stepping close enough that she'd feel the heat off his body. He breathed the words close against her ear, "Aren't you going to look in my eyes?"

Half closing her own, B.A. shivered. The small gesture empowered him. Lust hit him like a bolt of lightning.

Desmond glanced about the glasshouse. It was shrouded in the thick fog, which coated the glass panels overhead and rolled down the sides. Inside, earthy scents of the plants and a perfume of roses mixed with the more potent aroma that was BarbaraAnne Montgomerie—a lethal aphrodisiac to a man already in hormonal overdrive.

Even snoopy Scotsmen wouldn't be spying in the rain, which meant The Cat Dudley was the only audience—and Dudley was bribable. Besides, Kitty seemed already preoccupied, his nose stuck up in the air as he danced to the music.

"Keep that up, Dudley, and I'll buy you a copy of "Sweating to the Oldies" with Richard Simmons. You can dance away that flubber." He took hold of a surprised B.A.'s hand, twirled her into his arms and started dancing. Phil Collins's "Easy Lover" was playing. "What? Think I couldn't dance?" he asked.

She chuckled. "I think you could do anything you set your mind to, Desmond Mershan."

Rocking to the rhythm, they moved together, each anticipating the other's steps. Desmond sighed, thinking how well they'd complement each other when they made love. The music switched to the slower "He's So Shy" by the Pointer Sisters. He pressed her close, enjoying the sensual sway of their bodies, inhaling the intoxicating fragrance that was pure B.A.

Halfway through the song, he stopped. Brushing the side of his thumb against the faint cleft in her chin, he drowned in those amber eyes. She watched him with a doe-in-the-headlights expression. So luminous. Every emotion exposed for him to read.

Desmond lifted her chin and slowly brushed his lips across hers. Drank in her gasp. Her lips were soft and yielding, tasted of lemon drops. They melted against each other, fitting perfectly, and the world about them spun like leaves in the autumn wind.

He pulled back slightly, unnerved by the power rising between them. No woman before had sent his heart racing with such frantic need. None ever invoked this necessity to possess, to protect. To cherish. A grinding surge of lust pushed him to reach out and take her in the rawest, most elemental way. Yet, as demanding as the urge, his consciousness whispered how special this woman was—maybe too special for his peace of mind.

Controlling his every thought, his every emotion, had been how Desmond survived. This spiraling magic between them was beyond his experience. Outside of control. He was used to taking what he wanted from a relationship, then walking away without a second thought. Terms B.A. would never accept, he suspected.

A lesser man would run, unable to face the gravity of involvement. If a man couldn't accept all the strings that came with her, they'd better back off before she was hurt . . . bad.

He swallowed, bitterness rising in him. B.A. would be hurt no matter what. When the trap sprang shut on Falgannon Isle it'd close around her heart, piercing it as well. For he was a bastard who long ago had sold his soul to the devil in a pact for vengeance. He wouldn't leave her in peace. He'd take her, soak up these moments of sunshine that warmed his cold heart, then use her until that second when those amber eyes stared at him with daggers of hatred.

He shrugged to dismiss a pesky bit of conscience, that bit of Jacob Marley undigested cabbage that rose to nag him, saying if he followed through on destroying her island he'd be no better than Sean Montgomerie. Desmond hated to think he had anything in common with the old man. One viewpoint: He might be worse. He'd be looking into her eyes when she learned of his betrayal. Then who would be the bigger bastard—Sean or him?

Yes, Sean had destroyed his world, but it had been done from a distance. Montgomerie had never seen the pain up close, the hurt, the deprivation. Desmond knew what was coming, what he'd put into action. Since he was no coward, he'd be here to face the fallout when it came down around their heads.

He stared into those glistening eyes, and all other thoughts vanished. The passion smoldering between them was overpowering, humbling, drove all shards of the civilized man from his consciousness. Letting lose the primordial animal. He sensed his mate. Never had anything seared his mind, his soul, with such intensity. He couldn't think. He wasn't sure he breathed.

One last splinter of control kept him from reaching out and taking her with a fierceness that would terrify her. There was a chasm in his psyche, a fathomless darkness, and within that black void lurked a hunger that bordered on insanity. He tried to work the constricted muscles in his throat, to swallow back the crying need before he lost hold on the leash of the ravenous demon.

"I'm not a gentle man. You'd be smart to grab that stupid cat and run as fast as you can." The warning came from a part of him he no longer understood. This suddenly having scruples was a bloody nuisance!

Kitty sniffed, telling Desmond what he thought of the suggestion. Desmond figured Kitty tallied slights against an offender's name and settled up in some manner at a later date. Maybe that was why the cat and he bonded. They were a lot alike in that.

B.A.'s amber eyes traced his countenance with a look that caused Desmond to feel exposed. A Mona Lisa smile curved the corner of that kissable mouth.

"Trying to scare me away, Des? Afraid I might get hurt? Or fear I'll want more than you're prepared to give? I think *you're* the one scared. You've taken women on your terms, but you find I'm different. That rattles you."

B.A. recognized Desmond was a dangerous man. She'd be a fool not to see it. She knew he played some high-stakes game in ever coming to Falgannon. Only, she fathomed something else. Hidden deep under that hard veneer were fleeting glimpses of a little-boy-lost. Those moments moved her, made her want to cradle him. Silly, but her inner voice whispered Desmond was terrified of her. She was outside of his experience. It might be arrogance, but she felt he desperately needed her healing, her love.

"Don't think. Just kiss me, Des."

She leaned into him, letting her body press against him, feeling his intense heat. She brushed her lips against his. The pounding of his heart thundered against her, through her. She paused, enjoying recognition of her power to affect this man. Exhilarated, she slowly slid the tip of her tongue along the fullness of his lower lip.

Clearly afraid of giving over control, he held back. Then, with pantherlike reflexes he moved, seizing her mouth with his. He wasn't gentle. The quickening had hit Desmond— that point in a male when blood leaves his head and travels southward, taking any hope of reason. After the first breathless shock, B.A. decided she didn't want gentle. She yearned to shatter his iron will, to let loose the surging power he fought to deny.

Still having presence of mind to pinpoint her apron was in the way, she reached around to untie it. Before the knot gave, Desmond dragged the strap over her head, growling in monosyllabic grunts that men revert to when their brains are deprived of oxygen-carrying blood. He rained kisses over her neck, stinging kisses that'd likely mark her. Frissons of arousal snaked over her skin, upward to lodge in her brain, then down, tightening her womb into a hard fist.

Pausing, he muttered to the cat, "Scram, beast," for Dudley determinedly butted his head against Desmond's hand on her hip.

Desmond pressed her back against the potting bench, his hands gliding over her shoulders, too fleetingly over her breasts, then her ribs and waist. Rounding over her hips, he lifted her high against him. B.A. gasped. The wooden structure rattled, warning that it wasn't constructed for hot passionate sex, but she didn't think Desmond heard as he wedged his thigh between hers, making her ride it.

B.A. stifled a laugh as visions of them crashing into the rose plants and squashing Dudley to a pancake danced through her brain. "Um . . . Desmond . . . maybe, you should put me down. I'm not a small lass."

Nuzzling her hair, he asked, "Afraid I might drop you?" He let her slip a little, teasing, but his eyes dilated as their bodies rubbed together in tormenting friction. Hefting her back up, he commanded in a rugged breath, "Wrap your legs around my hips."

As she did, he cried out.

"Are you hurt? I told you I wasn't small. Put me down."

"Put you down? Not in this lifetime. Your bloody cat bit me!"

"He's not my—"

"Cat. So you say. I need lessons from Günter Gable Williams." In moving out of Dudley's reach, they teetered.

"Desmond! We're going to crash!"

"Trust me, B.A." In a deft move, he swung her to the long benches on the other side of the aisle and away from the bothersome cat. "Ha! Foiled the cat. No more interruptions. Kiss me woman, I earned it."

His expression was open, not calculating. And it took her breath away. Desmond stared at her in utter awe, as if she were some sort of pastry that he wanted to gobble up in three bites. Expressions such as that did things to a gal's heart.

The man had no idea what he did to her. No, that's wrong. He knew precisely how he set her trembling inside. How she could think of nothing but him.

She kissed him. Oh, how she kissed him! Gone were the gentle kisses shared these past two days, a mere prelude to the pagan fire rising to consume them. He devoured her mouth.

Hot damn, teeth and tongues, Devil B.A. chanted. Angel B.A. fumed about the lack of common sense, how wild passionate sex in the greenhouse was downright dangerous— thorns could get in the trickiest places.

Nothing mattered. Not too many clothes, rickety bench or

garden shears gouging into her hip. Only tasting Desmond. Reveling in his male heat, feeling the sculpted muscles.

Desmond tugged her sweater from her jeans. He broke the kiss, gasping for air. With those clever fingers, he stroked her satin-clad breast. Wickedly, the man watched her eyes dilate in pleasure, brushed his thumb back and forth over her pronounced nipple; she arched into his hand. His touch stilled the dueling voices of Angel and Devil B.A. Skimming the bra cup down, he exposed her soft breast to his skilled assault.

Hunger howled and she complied. Rubbing her hips against his, the apex of her female body fit perfectly over the ridge of his erection. Her head lolled to the side as his sharp teeth nipped the skin of her neck. Sensations and desires spiraled higher as she luxuriated in the bliss of him pleasuring her breast. Aware of her faintest gasp, Desmond instinctively knew what she craved, when to trace circles around her areola, when to add a slight pinch to the jutting nipple, setting desire to electrifying her whole body.

Saturated with ecstasy, it took her several seconds to focus beyond Desmond's shoulder. She needed glasses—more apparently every day. Thinking she'd lost her marbles, she blinked.

"Ahhhhh!" Her scream nearly flexed her body off the potting bench.

The cry was against his left ear, and Desmond flinched. Poor man, he had little time for bereavement over loss of hearing, because when she jerked she knocked the shears off the table and they hit his foot. Dudley, twining around Desmond's legs begging for attention, took umbrage at her scream and the flying metal projectile. He scaled Desmond's leg in protest.

"What?" Desmond moaned. "Dealing with you, B.A. is hazardous to my health."

At B.A.'s shriek, Callum nudged Michael the Fiddle. "Why did B.A. scream? I can't see a bloody thing between the rain outside and them fogging up the glass on the inside."

"You're nearsighted," Michael pointed out.

Willie's nose pressed against one of the large panes, while

the other men rubbed circles for their eyes on the glass. "Not sure . . . is she looking into his eyes?"

Michael waved at the pair as Desmond turned around and spotted them. "More likely, she's checking his tonsils. Think he likes it, too."

Callum, Willie, Robbie, Brian and Ian all waved.

Desmond and B.A. limply lifted their hands in reply.

"Thought the tap on the noggin' was what she was concerned about? Why inspect his throat?" Willie pondered.

Callum made a prune face, frowning at the shorter man. "*Willa*—for a writer, you show a remarkable lack of imagination sometimes."

Willie's chest puffed up. "My imagination lacks nothing. I'm remarkably literal."

Brian sniggered, shoving them toward the doors. " 'Tis remarkable you literally lack an imagination."

Dudley detached himself from Desmond and landed on the bench, then sneezed in utter disdain.

"Someday I might look back on this and laugh," Desmond said. He leaned his head against B.A. to still his rapid breathing. "Right now, I'm considering taking up ritual sacrifice and stuffing their bodies into your peat bog. It'd be that many less brides you'd have to import."

Chapter 12

"Sorry about . . . uh . . . the greenhouse," Michael the Fiddle apologized, holding up two fingers, signaling for two cards. "With the Web site crashing, B.A.'s sister calling and all—"

"Sorry?" Desmond hid his cards, hiding glee over his hand. "Not yet you aren't."

"Thinking of punishing us poor eejits by cleaning out our pockets, Viking?" Brian the Horseman peeked at the single card he'd asked for and then made a sour face.

Not fooled, Desmond shrugged. "I'm considering."

"Consider away, Viking." Michael howled. "See, we're a poor lot, not a fine propertied gent such as yourself. You'd win romance books from Willie, a swayback horse from Brian and Ian or my fiddle. On the other hand, I'd look right dapper in that leather bomber jacket of yours, or that Rolex would make The Cat Dudley a suitable collar."

Desmond eyed the hand of cards facedown before the cat who sat in his own chair. "Who plays Dudley's hand?"

"He plays his own. Kitty, how many cards do you want?" Ian asked the moggie. He got two meows back. "See?"

"I bite. He knew he needs two cards—how?"

"He's psychic," Ian answered, deadpan.

Desmond chuckled. "Fine, how do you know which cards to discard?"

Ian pointed to each card in turn and the cat meowed when he touched the ones to discard. "Kitty's a cardsharp."

"Why didn't I know?" On this dotty island, even a poker-playing cat was believable. Desmond decided to test the waters. "B.A. mention I own the northern tip of the isle?"

Everyone's eyes fell on him, assessing, though not as he anticipated.

Brian nodded. "Herself blethered on about you *thinking* you own the tip. So far, I haven't seen anything says you do."

"You're not adverse to us being neighbors?" Desmond sidestepped the challenge.

Ian grinned. "More time for us lads to whittle down your bank account."

"Not much on the north end of the isle. Just the castle and the stone circle," Michael the Story commented, folding his hand in disgust.

"I want the castle." The words popped out of his mouth before they'd even formed in Desmond's mind.

"Do you?" Brian's mouth quirked upward, his pale blue eyes dancing. "There's only one way to get the castle."

Desmond didn't comment. Neither did they. All knew what was said between the lines.

Desmond won the first hand, deliberately lost the next two, giving himself an opportunity to observe these men, pinpoint their ticks that reveal so much in poker. The fourth he won, lost the three following, keeping up that pattern, winning only enough so they didn't catch on that he forfeited on purpose. Desmond was after something worth more than money—information.

"So, tell me about Evian Deshaunt." He popped the burning question. It had the resounding thud of a brick dropping to the wooden floor. Michael the Story's eyes narrowed in appraisal, recognizing Desmond had fed them a line and now reeled them in.

"What do you want to ken other than he dinna have green eyes?"

The men playing at his table avoided his stare, pretending absorption in the cards. Callum excused himself to get some crisps and drinks. "Want a sandwich, Viking?"

"Later." Not derailed, he focused on Michael the Fiddle—the weakest link. "Come, come, he was married to B.A. for years, and all you can say is he didn't have green eyes? Surely the man left more of an impression?"

Angus the Ancient dragged his chair discordantly screeching over to their table, sat, then nudged Desmond with his cane. "If one cannot speak well of the dead, 'tis best to keep one's gub shut, eh, Viking?"

Interesting. B.A.'s lads held no love lost for her half-Irish husband. "Face it—despite the interruption at the greenhouse and the peeking in B.A.'s windows—I get the impression you lads want me and my green eyes to court B.A. That being the case, I'm owed a few facts to know where I stand."

"We'll not blacken a man's character—may he rest in peace. That leaves little to natter about." Michael the Fiddle leaned his chair back on two legs, rocking. "Will say the cat dinna like him. Only a kitten he was, but Kitty dinna fancy Deshaunt a'tall. Used to piss on his fine Italian loafers every chance he got."

This drew snickers. Desmond didn't blame them; he had a hard time suppressing one himself.

"That's not saying much," Ian qualified. "He hates Callum, too. In fact, outside of the Marys and B.A., you're the first person he likes."

Dudley proudly pushed his chest out, the white patch of

his fur looking like a bib. Desmond rewarded him with some chin scratches and a Cheese Doodle.

After a long silence Ian added, "He hated living in that wee humble cottage atop the castle. Thought it a pile of rocks that should be torn down. Then B.A. could build a fancy mansion on the site."

Willie coughed. "Deshaunt's Plan B. Plan A was to live at Colford Hall, to winter in Italy."

Innis tottered over, carrying a tray with several bottles of whisky and glasses. "From our own distillery. We produce ten casks a month. Thrice distilled, fifty-two-year-old whisky. It'll curl your toes. Good for cutting paint if you run short of turpentine."

The Scot joked. Everyone in the room including Desmond knew Highland whisky of that age fetched several thousand dollars per bottle on any market. Three times that in Japan.

" 'Tis called *Beatha-Stad*—Stop-Breath. Mind now, our lass warned us to keep you from imbibing due to your cosh to the noggin. But a dram is good for the heart. Besides, 'tis time for the men of Falgannon to bid you a true welcome."

Strangely touched, Desmond accepted the glass, holding up the dark amber liquid and studying the color. The hue reminded him of B.A.'s eyes. Something told him Evian Deshaunt hadn't received fifty-two-year-old paint thinner or the welcome from the men of Falgannon.

As he looked around the tables and saw them raising glasses in salute, a pressure swelled in his chest. He lifted his glass in return, then swallowed the heather-and-peat flavored alcohol. It burned its way to his stomach for more reasons than one.

B.A. jerked upright, blinking sleep-crusted eyes, uncertain what had awakened her.

Noting the first shafts of dawnlight filtering through the windows, she glanced down and switched off the computer. Poor laptop, she'd used it as a pillow again.

The house was abnormally vacant without The Man Desmond and The Cat Dudley. So strange, Desmond had only been in her home for a few days, yet his absence already created such an acute emptiness. How bad would it be if he stayed a month?

Ever so faintly, singing drifted in from outside the cottage. Yawning, she shuffled to the front door to locate the ruckus. Peeking through the panes up the side, she saw Ian, Michael and Callum crawling out of the Rover. They were helping Desmond, though mostly succeeded in falling over each other's feet. Behind the wheel—and sober—Dennis sat laughing. He shook his head, got out and came around to aid his boss to his feet. Desmond fell forward, but Ian and Michael caught him and wrapped his arms around their necks. They staggered down the walkway.

B.A. opened the door, and Dudley dashed in wearing a paper party hat left over from Hogmanay. He headed for his food bowl in the kitchen. Hands on her hips, she eyed the singing men, who sobered into sniggers at her dour expression. Desmond stopped before her, flashed a sleepy smile and continued singing in Gaelic. She leaned back from him, fanning the air, the fumes robbing her breath.

Ian winked. "He's murdering the Gaelic, lass, but he's a damn fine baritone."

B.A. heard the unspoken words: *He's trying, which is more than Evian had.* "Mist Covered Mountains" was a favorite of hers. Her heart squeezed at Desmond's attempt to learn.

"You're drunk," she snapped, hiding her smile.

Desmond chuckled. "Me too."

With a sweep of her arm, she stood aside and permitted them to haul him upstairs. She grumped to their backs, following them up the steps: "You gormless pelicans, you fed him. Stop-Breath. Doc said no alcohol. Ashamed you should be."

They dumped him on the George III bed, Michael nearly tumbling onto it as well. "If you're going to lash a pound of flesh from someone, blame Innis. He had to welcome the Viking prince properly."

She leaned her head against the bedpost, smiling at the whole scene, which filled her heart. Never had Evian been drunk with her lads, not once gone to Thursday Night poker.

He hadn't bonded with these men so dear to her, closer to her than even her brothers.

Evian and the men hadn't disliked each other; just as time passed, she grew aware they didn't *respect* each other, though none ever spoke the words. That hurt. Privately, she'd feared Evian had fancied himself the Lord of Falgannon and her islanders his serfs. He often voiced resentment over money she spent to make lives here easier. She recognized when Evian died they shared her pain because she grieved, not due to loss of one of their own.

And Evian had never looked at the castle and seen more than a pile of rocks.

Ian patted her arm. "Get him settled, lass. We'll see ourselves out."

Michael kissed her cheek. "He's a fine braw lad, this one. Damn fine poker player."

"Got green eyes, too." Callum grinned. " 'Night, lass."

" 'Night, pelicans." Tears filled her eyes as she watched them file out of the room. B.A. put the back of her hand to her mouth to muffle the sob. Sucking in emotions on a deep breath, she turned to Des. "Time to roll the drunk Viking-who-isn't-a-Viking off his stomach. Des, help me get your pants off."

"Lass, I've waited to hear you say those words to me since I looked into those gold eyes."

With a panther's grace and strength, he suddenly sprang at her, taking hold of her shoulders. So solid of muscle, he nearly pulled her off her feet. They rocked for a moment, him breathing fumes strong enough to knock her out.

"Whew, secondhand drunk!" B.A. leaned back gasping for air, but he tumbled her to the bed and under him in a deft move for a man totally foxed. She reveled in the weight of his body pressing hers into the mattress.

Dudley hopped up on the bed and poked his nose against her cheek. "Silly, beastie. Here, let's get your party hat off. Des, why is he wearing your Rolex?"

Desmond glanced sleepily at Dudley. "He won it. A mean poker-player Kitty is."

Her emotion burst out in laughter, the kind that tends to

sweep away the cobwebbed corners of the heart and soul.
Desmond traced her lower lip with his index finger.

"You've a nice laugh, BarbaraAnne Montgomerie. You
should use it more."

Dudley insinuated himself between them, licking her
forehead, which set Desmond to sharing her chuckles. She
realized she hadn't heard his laughter either. "You have a
nice laugh, Desmond Mershan. Use it more."

"Feed me fifty-two-year-old paint thinner regularly, I
might." He rolled onto his back beside her. "Whoa, there are
two Dudleys."

"That's the Stop-Breath. Only one Kitty, thankfully. The island couldn't handle two." Seeing his lids drift lower, B.A.
got up on her knees to undress him. "Let's get you tucked
up, then you can kip. Idiot cat, come here so I can take off
the watch." She made a grab at Dudley intending to remove it.

Desmond yawned. "Let him wear it. He won it fair and
square—didn't you, Dudley, my man? The lock's unsnapped
so it's loose enough on his neck."

"He might break it."

"I'll sue Rolex if he does. Guaranteed to take a licking and
keep on ticking." He pushed up on his elbow, his expression
intent, probing. "Do you?"

"Do I what?" she asked breathlessly.

"Take a licking"—he levered higher to brush a soft kiss
against her lips—"and keep on ticking."

Her heart rolled over with a thud. "Um . . . I wasn't aware I
ticked. Besides, I think that campaign belongs to Timex—
maybe's a David Ogilvy slogan."

"Want to find out if you tick?" He breathed against her
neck, setting legions of goosebumps scurrying across her
oversensitive skin.

Oh, boy, does she, Devil B.A. screamed, frustrated only
B.A. heard.

"The Stop-Breath will kick in. You'll pass out any moment." She tried to ignore her body's raging four-alarm fire.
"Let's get you undressed and in bed before you fall on your
face. Then we'll discuss my *ticking*."

"Sounds fair. Eh, Dudley?" He looked about. "Where did my poker pal go?"

"To feed his cat face—with your watch I might add."

Tugging the sweater over his head, she unbuttoned his shirt. Pushing it off those wonderful square shoulders, she fought the urge to do a little licking of her own to discover if Desmond ticked. She frowned at his new boots. "You can't sleep in these. Des?"

"Still here . . . I think."

"I'll straddle the boot. When I do, push with your free foot." Rolling his legs to the edge of the bed, she pulled one between hers, gripping the heel. Glancing over her shoulder, she feared he'd passed out. She didn't want him to sleep with the boots on, concerned his ankles would swell in them. "Earth to Desmond . . . push."

"I love it when you talk dirty." He swung his leg up, nearly knocking her over. After several tries, he managed to find her rump and give a good shove.

She and the boot crashed to the soft carpet. Getting up, she straddled the left boot. Desmond found better control; instead of a nudge, his socked foot gently rubbed across her rear.

B.A. gasped in a trill, "Desmond! Push!"

"Talking dirty again?" He gave her a gentle bump before breaking into song in Gaelic. Dropping the boot, she unbuckled his belt, fighting playful octopus hands. "The woman pitched a tizzy the other night when I removed my pants, now she's yanking them off!"

"Socks, too."

He kept wiggling his feet, but she finally wrested them off. With a shove, she had him on his back and the duvet pulled over him. As she turned to go, he caught her arm.

"Don't leave me." The little-boy-lost stared at her, and it about broke her heart. "Stay. Please."

She nodded. "Let me turn out the lights."

Going downstairs, she pulled the drapes and flipped out the lights. As she turned to go back up, she heard a pecking at the back door. A figure in a gray hooded *ruanna* waited on the other side. Dudley stood against the glass, waving a paw at the newcomer.

B.A. opened the door and offered Morag a smile. "Morn, lass."

"Nice collar, Dudley." Morag held up a jar of her green slime. "Figured your Viking prince will need this. Heard Innis got out the Stop-Breath to welcome him proper-like. I'm making deliveries to the eejits so the rest of us won't have to put up with their moaning."

Accepting the brew, B.A. kissed Morag's pale cheek. "You're an angel."

"I'd let them come begging before doling it out, since they make fun of my goop, only tonight is the *cèilidh*. Whilst having eighty percent of the isle hungover gives Oona, you and me giggles, with the Yank lasses here it wouldn't be a good first impression, eh?" Morag patted Dudley, then looked up. Those pale eyes, the shade of her cape, had always seen beyond the moment. "Sometimes we have to fight for what we want, lass. Remember that."

And with that warning, she vanished into the falling rain.

B.A. took a tumbler from the cabinet. Pouring the thick green gel into the glass, she cut it with ice water from the refrigerator.

Upstairs, she nudged Desmond's shoulder. "Drink this."

"A love potion? Trying to turn me into your sex slave?" He yawned, then seriousness flooded his eyes. "I thought you weren't coming back."

"Morag fetched you some of her goop. Drink it down and you won't have a hangover. I'll go undress."

She paused to draw the curtains on the bedroom window. Rain, heavier now, hit the panes in a steady, soothing noise. Hoping it'd continue so they could get some rest, she went to the walk-in closet and changed into a nightgown—a flannel one.

Chicken, Devil B.A. taunted.

"Hush!" she snapped aloud before she caught herself.

Desmond called, "You telling me or Dudley to hush?"

She flipped out the light. "Um . . . neither." B.A. figured he already thought the islanders were nuts. If she told him about Angel B.A. and Devil B.A., he'd believe her around the bend, too.

Desmond lifted the duvet for her to slide in next to him and immediately pulled her close. Within minutes the tension left his body, his head lolling against hers. The rise and fall of his chest said he slept. Shifting, she leaned her head to his, rubbing her nose in the thick waves of his black hair. Devil B.A. might be pitching a fit about lickings and tickings, but something was so special about cuddling with him, as they'd done on the couch the night before.

Cuddling? When do we get hot and heavy sex? Devil B.A. blared in her left ear with her teeny megaphone. Starting to drift, B.A. smiled. "Put a sock in it."

Desmond roused, murmuring over a yawn. "Talking to yourself again?"

"Um . . . no. . . . ah . . . Dudley."

As if called, Kitty popped up on the bed, walking on top of them. The luminous numbers of Desmond's watch were clear in the darkened bedroom. The cat kneaded the comforter, his ragged purr loud as he settled down to go to sleep, half on Desmond, half on B.A.

Desmond let out with a soft snore. Dudley breathed out a rumbling sigh of contentment. B.A. smiled, her sigh echoing the kitty's.

Sometimes things are just right with the world, she mused.

Chapter 13

A whimper broke B.A.'s slumber. Hardly asleep an hour, she yawned. Warm and comfortable, she resisted waking, gradually becoming aware of what disturbed her.

Desmond.

His heart raced, thudding so hard it vibrated his whole body. His high metabolism was something to which she was growing accustomed, but he was on fire. Sweat drenched his skin. Concern propelled her from her cozy rest, dislodging Kitty. The cat stretched, yawned and then tried to settle down again, only Desmond jerked upright. Rolling the flopping Dudley off her lap, B.A. sat up and put her hand on Desmond's shoulder.

His eyes were open, but he stared straight ahead, lacking real focus. Doll eyes. The eyes of a sleepwalker. Her sister, Raven, had gone through a period of sleepwalking after a rough divorce and miscarriage, so B.A. knew not to awaken Desmond.

Slipping from the bed, she crossed to the closet and dragged out the fan. The lulling white-noise helped her sleep when she was restless; maybe it'd relax Desmond as well. Pointing it toward him, she flipped it to high, then getting into bed again, she closed the canopy's curtains on one side and along the foot so it'd be darkened.

Kissing his cheek, she whispered, "Des, lie down." Surprisingly, he obeyed.

Putting a hand over his heart, she felt the beat, strong and steady. Certainty moved through her: She'd fallen hard for this man, and there was little she could do to protect herself. Refusing to give in to tears, she sighed, combating the panic threatening to swamp her.

The human body replaced every cell over a period of seven years. She'd grieved that long. Perhaps she hadn't been mourning Evian as much as using her grief as a shield, giving herself space to heal, to be strong enough to face loving and the specter of losing again. It had taken this man with his panther grace, one smart enough to take pleasure in a friendship with a fat cat, one with eyes to see worth in a medieval ruin, to make progress past that shield.

"Des, roll onto your stomach," she coaxed. When he didn't react, she repeated the suggestion. Just as she assumed he wasn't going to respond, he rotated.

She'd planned to give him a gentle back rub, to relax him, but Devil B.A. was wide-awake and had her pompoms out. Still, she told herself Desmond had been kind giving her the massage and just holding her the other night; surely she could return the favor.

She stroked her hand along his strong spine. Oh, the man had such a beautiful back. She wanted to bite him! Not a big bite. Just a nip . . . or two . . . or three. To rake her nails across him as he made love to her with that wild, unchecked passion she sensed in him. Lust rolled through her with a power she'd never fathomed.

She'd loved Evian, enjoyed their sex life, treasured their moments of closeness, of really bonding with a man. Still, not once had need eaten at her with such grinding, animalistic force. Swallowing dryness in her mouth, she ran her hand over Desmond's gorgeous back. Each stroke lessened the tension in his body, though increased hers. His heart rate gradually slowed.

Aching until she thought she'd go mad, she slid down next to him and closed her eyes. Thunder rolled in the distance.

Everyone had nightmares, those Freudian dreams of being on the edge of a cliff, fearing stepping off, falling into endless nothingness. It was a metaphor for a fear of failure, the dread of the unknown. It troubled her that a man so powerful, so controlled as Desmond had bad fantasies, and wondered what personal demons tormented him.

How sad: His sleep was haunted when she'd never felt safer than when resting in his arms.

Late afternoon shadows touched the room as B.A. opened one eye, sort of an "up periscope," her brain coming online. Desmond lay on his stomach, awake and staring at her. A sexy feline smile curved those sensual lips. She wanted to kiss him, but she swallowed and knew instantly it was a bad idea.

His left hand reached over and grabbed her waist, edging her close. As he moved to kiss her, B.A. saved his life by putting her hand before her mouth.

"B.A., I want to kiss you." His black brow crooked in puzzlement.

"No you don't. Dragon-breath alert."

He howled. "That bad, eh?"

She nodded. "Aye, something crawled in there and committed suicide."

"I'm probably worse. Let's swap nasties."

"You sterilized everything in there last night with Stop-Breath."

Desmond shifted to murmur into her hair, "Mmmm, we're going to have to stop this."

"What?"

"Sleeping together and not having sex. It's hard on a man's sanity." He leaned over and nuzzled her ear, nipping his way down the curve of her shoulder. It sent a shudder up her spine, straight to the top of her head.

It was tempting to stay, dragon breath and all, especially when he tormented her with little nibbles on the flesh exposed by her gown. Selflessly, she pulled away. No man deserved the kiss of death. She might weaken and overlook the sour-green-nasties in her mouth, but she needed a shower, too. Romance might withstand one or the other, but both meant a rocky start to any courtship.

Desmond grabbed at the edge of her nightgown as she scooted away. Dodging, she dashed for the bathroom. Kitty scampered after her, enjoying the new game.

Brushing her teeth and jumping into the shower, B.A.tilted her head back, the cool water stinging as the spray hit her neck and breasts. As she picked up the soap and washcloth, the shower door opened. A sexy, sleepy expression in his bedroom eyes, Desmond stood in all his male splendor—without even a towel.

B.A.'s eyes flitted to the washcloth in her hand, knowing it was too small to cover her. Taken by that wonderful expanse of male flesh and his rock-hard erection, high and hard against Desmond's taut stomach, her gaze slid up his beautiful chest to those sensual lips.

"It's too small," he said.

B.A. choked. There were many adjectives that rose to mind, but small was not on her list. Her response burst out on a laugh. "You're joking!"

He joined her chuckle. "No. The cloth—the thought crossed your mind to hide behind it."

If he read her that clearly, he surely knew what ran through her head now. "Um, I did."

"I fed Dudley half a bag of dry food. The phone in the bedroom is unplugged. Of course, it might not be working anyway. I put a chair under the door handle. No cat, no ringing, no nutty islanders to interrupt us." Closing the shower door behind him, he wrapped an arm around her waist and pulled her against him. "We both have clean teeth. I'd like that kiss now."

Her breasts pushed up against his chest in the unyielding embrace, leaving it hard to breathe, but then she always had trouble getting air when near him. In his arms, there was no escaping what he compelled her to feel. No hiding from her cowardly self.

She let him take her mouth, the kiss slow and gentle as he savored her. It made her dizzy. The man was hard on her knees.

Harder on her heart.

He backed her under the shower, the slow water pressure raining down on them, nearly turning to steam from their rising body temperatures. Kissing her as she'd never been kissed, he seared all memories from her mind. There was only Desmond. She snaked her arms up his, over the muscular shoulders to weave her fingers in his thick black hair, Arching her body against his, the fit was perfect. A deep inner sense said this was where she belonged.

Her body throbbed as desire pounded through her, rippled within her. Painful. A raw aching, the pulse of her heart, the need to feel him deep inside her, to share that primitive, pagan bond. The physical part of their attraction was mind-blowing.

But the emotional side crashed down on her.

For too long she'd kept everything contained. Getting through each day, contentment was all she permitted herself. It was a good day when she achieved that. Now the walls were down, crumbling under the gentle siege Desmond waged. He'd breached the inner keep where her heart was held in protection. The passion, the need, the love—he pushed her toward all, allowing no retreat. It was agonizing. It was too much. It was not enough.

She was shaking, hadn't realized it until she sensed Desmond reining back. He cradled her in his embrace and kissed her eyelids. "Shhhh . . . easy. Tell me what's wrong."

"It's been—"

"A long time since you've been with a man? I know." He kissed her nose and then smiled. "They say it's like riding a bicycle."

The gentle jest summoned a tight laugh as she fought to keep from crying. B.A. wanted to kick herself, but emotions held under protective glass for years were already loose.

"It's . . . I . . . was . . ." She squeezed her eyes shut, fighting for words that explained her pain, her fear.

"I'm going to kiss you, B.A., and I want you to relax."

There was such tenderness in his eyes that her shaking lessened. He did as promised—kissed her as he had that night by the car, warming every cell in her body, taking hold of her heart, surrounding it, cosseting it. Pulling back, he sighed.

"What set this off? It's not inflating to a man's ego that the woman he wants to make love with is ready to burst into tears."

His erection nudged against her, setting off a short laugh. "Your ego dunna need any more inflating."

She leaned back, sliding her hand down his taut stomach. It wasn't six-pack defined, not even washboard, but trim, hard and sculpted in a way that set her womb to pulsing, tightening with hunger to where it was excruciating. Starting at the base of his erection, she curled her fingers around that magic heat, measured his silken length, then brushed her thumb over the soft tip.

"Mercy . . ." She wasn't sure if the word came from her or him.

Desmond's eyes shut, and he reveled in delicious torment as his body bucked against her hand. When she slid her fingers down, he grabbed her wrist and yanked it away. "Another time I'd be thrilled for you to test my *ticking*, but keep that up and things will come to an abrupt conclusion. And stop distracting me, B.A. What had you ready to cry?"

"Too many things. I've fought to keep my emotions under control for so long. It's distressful when they run amok."

He backed her into the corner of the tiled wall, leaning her against it. He brushed his lips over the faint cleft in her chin. "And?" he prompted.

The truth came out. "I'm thirty-seven, things are starting to . . . sag."

The chuckle rumbled in his chest. "I'm forty-four. Frankly, I don't see a problem."

She grinned, brushing her hips against his groin. "You look ten years younger. I don't see you sagging. No love-handles either."

"I hadn't noticed *you* toting baggage. You've a damn fine arse, woman." He nuzzled her jaw and then chained kisses along the column of her neck. "But maybe my eyesight's failing after that tap on the head. Want to check my eyes?"

She met his probing stare and sighed. "Your eyes are beautiful."

"My *green* eyes?" He challenged. "They look normal?"

Drowning in their jade depths, she was unable to look away.

"Let's see if I can locate this sagging." His hands clutched her hips, his thumbs brushing over the slight swell of her belly to the indentation of her navel. "No sagging here."

The long fingers followed the contours of her rib cage, causing B.A. to suck in her breath. He cupped her sensitive breasts, weighed their heaviness. Her raspy sigh of hunger pushed them against his palms, wanting more. Aching for more. A burning in her womb radiated with a vibrating, pounding plaint. It blotted out the fears clamoring in her head, morphing her trembling into one of need. She nearly melted from the fire he conjured in her.

"Hmm, no sagging there." He nuzzled her neck. "Maybe I need a closer inspection."

Desmond palmed her waist, raising a ripple of goose-bumps, then the arch of her hip. Hooking the back of her knee, he brought it about his waist so B.A. arched upward, open against him. Leaning down, he swiped his tongue across her sensitive nipple. Her gasp caused the corner of his mouth to tug upward. She empowered him.

Enthralled, Desmond tilted back enough to watch the desire play across B.A.'s beautiful face. Then he moved in to tongue her nipple again. Once more he slanted back, studying the response reflected in her dark whisky eyes. If a picture was worth a thousand words, the portrait of B.A. in the grip of passion was more beautiful than all the sonnets ever penned.

Returning his attention to her soft breast, he licked a circle around the ruched flesh. As she assumed he would continue the playful torment, he took it into his mouth, quick, sucking hard, to shock her. She shattered, and an incandescent climax burned through her. Before she came down from its pain-pleasure edge, he thrust his hips and was inside her slick, welcoming warmth, catching her last internal ripples against his flesh.

Her body protested, eyes flying wide, internal muscles that had been dormant for years slow to adjust. Her nails dug into his shoulders. Then her body relaxed to accept his intrusion. Snaking his left arm under hers, Desmond braced them against the wall and waited, giving her a few breaths.

His own gasps were choppy, labored and fighting for a thread of control he leaned his forehead against hers. It took the last ounce of civilized man in him to hold at bay the selfish, primeval beast pounding through his veins. Lust gripped him, possessed him with a force he'd never known. It cost to hold back. But he did it—for B.A.

He took her mouth, kissed her with a hunger that was violent. He'd been with dozens of women. Yet all memories paled, faded to mist as everything felt new, special . . . *connected.*

Unable to stop himself, he flexed his hips, thrusting deeper into her. Then harder. Faster. B.A.'s body tightened around him, ripples of her internal contractions triggering tactile sensations that skittered across his skin and exploded white-hot in his mind. It was nearly enough to drive him over the edge. He wanted to close his eyes, to drown in the sea of emotions raging in him, to surrender to the overwhelming dark grandeur. More important, he wanted to look into her eyes as she came apart around him, to know she saw him and his green eyes and not the memory of any blue ones.

Gritting his teeth, he raised back to draw her attention. Her eyes opened, all emotions there to read. Her pleasure. Her greed for more. Finally, threads of confusion shifted to doubt. She was afraid she didn't please him in some manner. If only she knew.

He kissed her lightly to alleviate her fears. "Look into my eyes, B.A.," he commanded, the words difficult to form through the corded muscles of his neck.

His hands palmed her wet hips, then in a quick jerk, he lifted her high, bracing her against the wall. B.A.'s lips made a sweet O as he planted himself to the hilt. *Deep enough to touch her heart.* He blinked, unsure if he'd spoken the words aloud or not.

"Not too small?" he teased, flexing his hips to move within her.

"Arrogant man."

"Damn right," he replied, the smile predatory.

Hips hammering against hers, she scorched him with her silken heat. He lost all semblance of sanity, driving them to a height neither knew was possible. B.A.'s fierce climax rippled along his flesh, pulling him into that swirling vortex with her.

It was a little death that shook him to his soul.

Chapter 14

Desmond absentmindedly blow-dried his hair, watching B.A. in the mirror's reflection as she shimmied into her long skirt. He sighed. B.A. shimmied well.

"This isn't going to be one of those affairs where the whole island—except Oonanne and Morag—run around showing their knees, is it?"

B.A. zipped her plaid skirt and pulled the leather belt through the loops. "I could ask one of the lads for a loaner . . ."

Dudley jumped up on the counter, walked over and

butted Desmond's arm for attention. He ruffled the cat's thick fur. "What do you think, pal? Me in a skirt? Think I'll pass."

B.A.'s eyes danced. Putting her hand on his stomach, she watched as the muscles contracted from a jolt of lust. She snaked her fingers up his chest. "You'd wear one for me. Wouldn't you, Des?"

I'd jump through hoops for you, woman. Desmond fought the pounding in his body—a losing effort. She set his blood to boiling and there was little he could do but stand like a fool and enjoy it. He grabbed her hips and yanked her against him.

"We can discuss me wearing one for you—in private— another time. Keep rubbing my chest and we won't make it to the party."

She rocked her hips with his and whispered against his mouth, "*Cèilidh.*"

He grinned. Strange, he knew he'd smiled many times in his life, but this grin seemed to reach every pore. "*Kay-lie* be damned, I've a better idea how we can spend this evening."

He opened his mouth to kiss her with every ounce of the rapacious hunger she provoked in him. Only, she put her index finger to his lips. Undeterred, his tongue darted out and swirled around the digit. He sucked it into his mouth, drawing on it rhythmically to convey what possessed his mind.

She croaked, "Hold . . . those thoughts . . . for later. You'll not talk me out of the *cèilidh.* I want to waltz with you, Desmond Mershan."

With a groan of regret rumbling in his chest—and a *pop* as she pulled her finger from his mouth—she spun out of his arms and vanished into the bedroom.

Drinking in the image of her walking away, Desmond leaned back against the counter edge, afraid his legs might not hold him. Dudley head-butted him. "She wants to waltz with me, Dudmeister. Think we'll make a striking pair?"

Kitty meowed an emphatic yes, nodding his head.

Desmond chuckled. "Well, who am I to doubt a poker-playing cat?"

* * *

It was nearly dark as Desmond pulled up with B.A. and Dudley before the town hall. He glanced at his watch and sighed, unused to night falling in the afternoon. A crowd filled the hall, and on the small stage two men played accordions, harmonizing with one of the Marys on piano. Two younger lads with flutes and Michael the Fiddle backed them.

Not one for accordion music, Desmond was surprised by the sound they created, which was more like muted bagpipes. The music was haunting, sending prickles dancing across his scalp.

B.A. led him through the gathering, causing Desmond to wonder if he'd ever held hands with a woman before. No instance came to mind. He glanced at their interlaced fingers, feeling that urgent need just to touch her, even in a small gesture. An addiction now.

He tugged her hand to slow her. "No real bagpipes?"

She laughed over her shoulder. "Och, pipes are for outdoors, instruments of war. Our ears wouldn't stand them inside."

Tables were arranged on either side of the door leading to the kitchen. Covered dishes were lined up on one, while the second to the right had bottles of Pepsi, 7-Up, Wee Heavy—Scottish ale—and several brands of scotch. On the opposite end was a large crystal bowl where Innis mixed punch.

"Evening, Desmond. B.A and Kitty fetched you to our monthly get together, eh?" Innis grinned as his eyes fixed on the loose grip Desmond kept on B.A's hand. " 'Tis a grand night."

"She wants to waltz with me." Desmond checked over the selection of drinks.

"A bonnie duo you'll make on the dance floor." Innis lifted a cup in salute. "Fix you anything to drink—the hair of the dog? Though you dunna look the worse for wear."

"Fifty-two-year-old paint thinner agrees with me—though it might also be that green junk Morag brought."

Innis shuddered. "I have to hold my nose, but it'll fetch you 'round with nary a hangover."

"She'd be a millionaire many times over if she bottled the stuff and sold it." Desmond suggested. "She should consider it."

Innis shook his head. "Nah, wouldn't interest her a'tall. Says she has to put something special in each batch for that person. Not sure I want to ken what *special* is. She's happy with her herbals and creating perfumes for B.A.'s commercial lines. So, what will you be having?"

"How about a dram of Stop-Breath?"

Innis looked briefly regretful. "Not with the philistines over from the other isles. We lock the private stock away." He winked. "After you waltz with the lass, come back and I'll sneak you some fine Edradour or Highland Park. Get you learning a proper palate for fine malt whisky."

Desmond noticed the pile of sleeping bags in one corner. "Why the camping gear?"

"B.A. holds the *cèilidh* once a month and people from Dunbeag and Dunmohr come over. Our lass won't let them drive their boats back in the dark. They have a fine time, then kip in their sleep-sacks here and breakfast in the morn. After, she holds the Counting, giving them their share of the online business."

A tall, handsome man sauntered in, giving Desmond pause. "That's—"

"Jock the Repair, MacGyver of the East. There's naught he cannot repair, though B.A. insists he's not good with duct tape."

Desmond knew the old theory that there's a double for every person somewhere, but this was amazing. "He's a dead ringer for—"

Michael the Story reached in front of Desmond to snag a paper cup. "Oh aye, bloody git. There's a long list of ladies hoping to come to the isle, waiting to meet the eejit. But after falling down in the duct tape department, our lass will put him at the end of the queue."

B.A. tugged on his hand. "Come on, Des, time to waltz."

Desmond followed B.A. through the crowd ringing the dance floor. Dudley trailed after them. An odd excitement hummed in his blood as people stopped him, shook his hand and introduced themselves. He'd thought he'd feel an interloper tonight; that feeling of never belonging was something he'd carried his whole life. Contrary to expectations, he was warmly welcomed.

Desmond had been many places in the world, worked, lived and socialized, yet he always remained apart, the lone wolf. In his world, people judged by how you dressed, what car you drove or where you lived. These kooky islanders cared nothing about his apparel, didn't demand to know his heritage or bank balance. They just accepted him.

Once again, the back of his mind insisted he was still that lone wolf among sheep. They wouldn't welcome him if they knew why he'd come to their isle.

As the band played "Mist Covered Mountains," B.A. stepped into his arms. "I warn you, Mershan, I love to dance."

Instead of sweeping around the dance floor movie-style, this waltz was slower, a focused partnering that kept them at the middle. As in the greenhouse, their movements were in tune with one another. As if they'd danced a hundred times before.

Desmond grew aware all eyes watched, smiles and nods of approval on everyone's faces. Even so, a slight dizziness spiraled in him. This was a simple waltz, a man and a woman—and a cat—out on a dance floor. Yet somehow it was so much *more*.

He stared into B.A.'s eyes, images assaulting his mind. The world spun, tilting on its axis. Out of the blue, B.A. wore a white gown and a chaplet of white roses in her hair, a vision of a bride that rocked him to the core. Shocked, he blinked his eyes.

Then another scene crowded his brain. He stood in the Great Hall of the castle. It wasn't the ruins, but furnished and aglow from flames of the fireplace. Peculiarly, he saw himself as a spectator, yet in the same breath was a part of the man in the vision, witnessing a tableau so detailed it blotted out his surroundings.

This other him stood staring into the fire's bluish flames, lost to contemplations. He wore chain mail, a red surcoat, and a red and black plaid across his chest diagonally, fastened by a large Pictish brooch. His head snapped up as B.A.—at least, she looked like B.A.—entered the room wearing a white gown in a medieval style. It fitted her body, flaring at the hips. A gold chain girdle circled her waist, nearly reaching the floor. The low-cut square bodice hugged her full breasts. Her long blond hair was unbound, a simple gold circlet adorning her forehead.

She was so beautiful he forgot to breathe.

"Des, are you all right?"

For a second, the medieval version of BarbaraAnne shimmered before him. The vision faded, revealing B.A. in her navy sweater and tartan skirt. He almost blurted out that he wanted her wedding gown designed in that medieval style, so strong were the images still haunting him.

He blinked, striving to dismiss it. Likely, it was that fifty-two-year-old paint thinner's lingering effects, or that green goop from Morag. "I'm fine. Want to look in my eyes to be sure?"

"Actually, I do. You're glassy-eyed. I feared you might pass out."

The music ended. They stood staring at each other for a long minute. Desmond leaned forward and brushed his lips against hers, not caring they were the center of attention. When every male in the place burst into applause, Desmond stepped back and shook his head.

"Only on this dotty island!" he joked. "Do we take a bow?"

She linked her fingers with his and led him toward the tables. "You need feeding."

At the F-word, Dudley's ears perked up and he pranced like a trick pony ahead of them.

"Now you mention it, last thing I ate was Cheese Doodles just before Innis brought out the Stop-Breath." Desmond took the plate she handed him, seizing on hunger as an explanation for the bizarre images that assailed him on the dance floor. Stepping so his thigh brushed the side of hers, he nuzzled her hair against her ear. "Some daft lassie dinna feed me all day."

"Och, B.A., 'tis ashamed you should be," Cedric the Doc

chimed behind Desmond. "Lass, dinna you ken the way to a man's heart is through his tum?"

"She knows, Cedric." Desmond stared at the mountain of food B.A. heaped on his plate—enough for a small army of Dudleys. Glancing down at the cat, who was doing a rumba on his hind legs, he added, "Come on, Dudley, we have our work cut out."

The evening passed in a blur of delicious food, dancing, great music, whisky and fun company. Desmond couldn't recall ever having a better time. B.A. was asked to dance often. It surprised Desmond, each time she checked with him before accepting, her eyes lingering on him as if she hated to leave his side even for a few minutes.

Doing his stint as a proper gentleman, he asked one of the Marys to dance. She blushed as she put her hand in his.

On the dance floor, he passed B.A. dancing with a pimply faced teenager. He winked at her. Wearing a witchy smile, she winked back. Dudley had a hard time dividing his time between his two people.

Mary-Annis exclaimed, "There's Kitty! Haven't seen him all week."

"Sorry, he's taken to following me around," Desmond admitted.

"Och, no worries. We dunna see him that often. He generally trails after B.A., only coming to mooch at lunchtime," she answered.

"I thought the cat was yours."

"That's B.A.'s gub. She got him when he was a wee thing, but ended up asking us to take him. Dudley didn't get on with B.A.'s husband. I always said, if a man dinna get along with a kitty, get rid of the man. Moggies are good judges of character. After Deshaunt's death she dinna feel right asking for him back. Think also, B.A. couldn't stand having something to love at that point. A miserable lass she was, especially after Roarke Deshaunt pulled that stunt at the memorial service."

"Stunt?"

"Ashamed he should be. He was grieving, but that dinna

give him leave to attack our B.A., blaming her for Evian's death. Right there at the memorial services, mind you."

"He did that?" Desmond's hackles went up, imagining B.A. distraught, barely holding herself together, and having some selfish bastard heap guilt upon her.

"He blamed her, said if she hadn't insisted on living on Falgannon, his brother would be alive. The "Morn, B.A." Club couldn't boot him off the isle fast enough. Lucky for him, because the Fraser twins and the Michaels were ready to learn him some manners, Highland style. Our lass has seen too much sorrow. She needs someone to love her, to cherish her, to ease the load off her shoulders. This island's a big responsibility and she carries it alone."

Desmond heard the warning.

He used the times B.A. danced with others to learn about Falgannon. Over drams of Highland Park, Desmond discovered B.A.'s online catalogue; selling their quilts, sweaters, kilts, leather goods, jewelry and the two perfume lines saw steady employment for all three isles. The seasonal harvesting and shipping of roses provided extra income for dozens of islanders.

Guilt ate at Desmond's insides. He'd like to chalk it up as too much whisky, maybe even the start of an ulcer, but it was his conscience that plagued him. These people were so happy with their quiet lives, content in this pocket of the world that was near paradise. And his plans would destroy that. He'd bring in outsiders and they'd lose their sense of security. Their children rode scooters after dark, never fearing someone would hurt them. Likely, none of the residents of the three isles—same as B.A.—bothered to lock their doors. His development would see strangers coming, a type of people they didn't know, shouldn't trust.

Downing a dram of Highland Park, he savored its unusual taste, not of peat fires but something wilder, untamed, a balefire for pagan invocation. Alarmingly, another bizarre vision exploded into his mind. This time, it was of the snake in the Garden of Eden. Only it twined around the Falgannon business district sign, and the blasted serpent had his face!

The room spun as he heard B.A. calling from a great distance.

"Des, you're sick?" She leaned toward him, putting a hand on his thigh.

He swallowed the emotions lodged in his throat. "Maybe you need to look into my eyes."

"I am! That's why I'm concerned." Pulling him to stand, she suggested, "Let's walk out and sit on the swings. The fresh air might do you good. If not, we're calling it an evening."

After they donned their jackets, B.A. led him out to a lawn glider at the side of the town hall. It had two benches facing each other, but he settled into the corner on the same side with B.A. and pulled her into his arms. The night was cool, but they generated enough heat to keep cozy.

Setting the swing to rocking, he nuzzled her hair. The faint scent of her peony perfume saturated his senses. Closing his eyes, he floated on the peace she brought him, yet in the same breath exhilaration fluttered in his chest.

Opening his eyes, he caught sight of the sky. It glowed, shimmered, danced with all the colors of the rainbows. "Does Falgannon have night rainbows?"

B.A. leaned back, her head cradled in the curve of his shoulder and neck. "The Aurora Borealis. Haven't you seen it before?"

"Nope. I've never sat and stared at the stars before."

The corner of her mouth lifted. "Maybe those bright city lights have blinded you to magic. Lore says it's the reflection of the Valkyries' armor as they ride the night sky."

The puttering whine of the kid on that blasted scooter shattered the tranquility of the moment. They heard Wee Dougie coming halfway around the island, slowly heading in their direction. He finally drove up and pulled to the other side of the yew bushes.

"I suppose he's waiting for me to step out so he can show how he likes me?" Desmond guessed.

B.A.'s soft laughter rumbled in her chest, moving through him. "He waits for the *cèilidh* to break up every Friday to have a go at the old duffers. He read a quote—Cagliastro, I think—saying man sleepwalks through life and isn't truly alive unless he's under deep stress."

"Took that to heart, Wee Dougie did?"

"I bought him a helmet and insisted he wear it. It has a futuristic design, so he got it into his noggin it's a virtual helmet. He'd just watched *Lawnmower Man,* mind. That's why he calls it virtual bowling. And yes, he tries to run down the people he likes to make them feel alive."

Desmond chuckled. Inhaling the pure island air, he flexed his arms around her, pulling her close. "Know what makes me feel alive?"

"What?" She turned.

"This." He lowered his head and brushed his lips against hers.

As he softly kissed B.A., he felt her heart race under his hand. It'd be so easy to cup her breast, to feel the soft weight. If he did, he'd ignite a fire in them and he'd end up taking her here on the swingset. Sex on a lawn swing definitely had merits—but for a different occasion, a safer locale.

He ran his tongue along the seam of her full lips, tasting her, savoring her as he might a fine wine. She made a kittenish noise in the back of her throat and opened for him. His gut clenched as her tongue followed his, setting up a duel that nearly made him forget where they were.

The sound of running feet broke the magic. Someone took hold of the swing, stopping its rocking. "Da! The Viking is pillaging again!" Wee Gordie's voice.

"Gor, she's wallowing our poor Viking prince again." Angus the Ancient tottered over, his cane clacking on the stone drive.

As Angus made it halfway between the town hall and the swings, Wee Dougie went barreling at the old man, the high *rat-tat-tat* of his two-cycle engine full throttle. At the last second, his scooter swerved and Dougie reached out and tagged the old man on the hip, counting coup. Then he drove off.

Angus shook his cane at the vanishing bike. "That's it, B.A., I want that delinquent tossed in the jug."

"Angus, we dunna *have* a jail," she pointed out playfully.

"Then put him in the stocks. Surely we still have those."

Desmond leaned his head back, closing his eyes. *Only on*

Falgannon. Laughter vibrated in his chest. The more he suppressed it, the more his body jerked.

"Och, B.A., dinna realize you were giving our Viking that PVC again. Hey, Doc, he's having seizures!" Angus shouted.

Cedric came running outside, and in his wake was Innis, carrying a bottle of fifty-two-year-old scotch. "This will fetch the lad around."

Behind them trailed the population of three islands. Wee Dougie made his return and chased people left and right. The Escape Artists dashed up, barking and nipping at the wheels of the scooter.

The only character not outside was The Cat Dudley.

"Someone come fetch Kitty," Angus the Ferry called from the doorway. "He's on the table scarfing down ham."

Innis shoved the Stop-Breath into Desmond's hand. Then Cedric stepped up to the swing to look into his eyes, only one of The Escape Artists latched on to the hem of his kilt and hauled him backward. Desmond could no longer contain his laughter. It roared from him so hard that his ribs hurt. Tears came to his eyes. Never in his whole life had he laughed like this.

Looking at B.A., a sobering thought raced through his mind. He downed the whisky in one gulp, not realizing until done that the tumbler had been full. Fire spread through him.

Even so, the kick of the alcohol couldn't combat the sobering question that had risen to his lips as he stared at B.A. The words, burning inside him hotter than the scotch, were: *Will you marry me, B.A.?*

Chapter 15

Whomp, whomp, whomp.

The sound rattled the windows of Rose Cottage, the pummeling noise felt not just heard as it drew closer. Outside, readying for a dive with Dennis and Wulf, Desmond paused from checking his scuba equipment. Shielding his eyes with his hand, he attempted to examine the source, but the helicopter headed at them with the sun behind it.

B.A. came out the back door, then hesitated upon seeing Desmond prepping the diving gear. She frowned, her large eyes haunted. Turning away, she waved to the Fraser twins, who had cantered up on horses—one pure black and one snow white. The animals were nervous and sweating. Even Dudley twined around her legs, wanting soothing because of the whirly monster.

Ian patted the side of his white mare to ease the horse's fear. "The berks are circling the isle?"

"Third pass," Desmond confirmed.

Muttering "Where's the bloody fog?" under his breath, he recalled the times he'd tried to fly over Falgannon with Julian Starkadder, but had been prevented. "Company's coming," he teased drolly.

Ian joked, "Not sure Falgannon can stand three invasions in one month, especially if these are more males. B.A., can we institute some sort of immigration policy limiting invasions to females only?"

"Aye, B.A." Brian winked at her. "What's the use of importing lasses if we end up sharing them with Outlanders? We only let our Viking prince stay 'cause he has green eyes."

Glancing at B.A., Desmond asked, "Expecting anyone?" Prickles of panic crawled up his spine as possibilities rose to mind. None good. The biggest fear—the helicopter carried B.A.'s brother Cian, riding in like the cavalry to save the day.

The helicopter buzzed low, further scaring the animals. B.A. picked up Dudley to cuddle him, while the Frasers used their skills to restrain their mounts. The black reared, nearly unseating Brian. Slowing, the machine spiraled a descent, aiming for the castle.

"They're starkers! They can't land there!" B.A. vaulted off the porch, determination filling her face.

Desmond tracked their path. "That's what they're doing."

She shoved Kitty against his chest, then rushed to the Frasers. "Give me a horse."

"It's that Pict princess coming out in our lass again," Ian

told Desmond, swinging his leg over the horse's neck to dismount, still holding the reins. "Maeve dinna ken the word *please* either."

B.A. snatched the reins and stepped barefoot into the stirrup, her skirt billowing in the breeze as she mounted. "Stupid gits! They want to land on the cairn?" she raged, kicking the horse's ribs.

"B.A., damn it. Stop," Desmond shouted. "Idiots, stop her! She'll get herself killed!"

"Och, she's a Montgomerie. She never listens to anyone," Ian warned.

Desmond shoved the cat at Ian and demanded of Brian, "Let me have *your* horse."

The twins exchanged questioning looks. Then Brian hopped off and tossed the black's reins to him. "Any chance he knew Maeve, Ian?"

" 'Tis our B.A.'s ugly Yank manners rubbing off," his brother replied.

The mare reared as Desmond set his heels to its ribs. "I'm going to thrash her!"

"Angus would approve!" Brian called out dryly, sporting a quirky grin as he and his twin watched Desmond gallop after B.A. "I like our Viking more all the time."

"Oh aye." Crossing his arms over his chest, Ian nodded. "A sight to see—our Desmond trying to paddle our lass. Ten pounds say our lass flays the bloody hell out of him."

Brian spit in his hand and held it out to seal the wager. "Done."

They slapped palms and shook on it.

It had been a while since Desmond had ridden a horse. He leaned forward in the saddle, pushing to overtake B.A. Blasted woman rode like the wind, blond hair flying behind her, a Valkyrie headed for battle. He'd been around Wulf long enough to know the Norse translation of *Valkyrie* meant "Chooser of the Slain." He judged B.A. not only wanted to do a little choosing, but planned to slay as well!

B.A. cantered her horse up the oddly ramp-shaped plateau, then stopped in the middle of the artificially flat-

tened land. Fighting to keep the horse there, she blocked
the helicopter from landing. The animal bounced on its
hind hooves, but determinedly she chanted words in Gaelic
to soothe and control it. Though terrified, the horse obeyed.

The rotors whipped the beast's mane and B.A.'s hair, an
image of terrifying beauty that burned into Desmond's
mind: a Pict warrior-goddess ready for battle.

The pilot got that she wasn't backing down. He waved
and headed toward the next knoll. Flush with success, B.A.
nudged the horse into action, barreling down the inclined
path.

As she flew down the hill and straight at him, Desmond
reached out and caught a rein. She jerked it away.

"B.A., damn it, stop!"

"Let go!" she screeched. "I'm going to kill them!"

Using her reins as a lash, she slapped the neck of
Desmond's mount. It shied. Not the rider B.A. was, it took
him all his skill to hold his seat, allowing her to get away.
Recklessly she galloped toward the helicopter, not pausing
to see how dangerous the situation was. A scared horse
could panic, rear and toss her into the rotors.

Desmond urged his mount to a faster pace. B.A. was
halfway up the knoll before he overtook her. Drawing
abreast, he leaned over, wrapped his arm about her and
dragged her from the saddle. Off-balance, the horse
dumped them both.

Struggling to protect her, he softened her fall with his
body. Air slammed out of his lungs, still he refused to release
his grip. Faring better, she scrambled to her knees. He
grabbed her wrists and dragged her to the ground again.

The witch tried to kick him, but with one angry push he
had her on her back. She was strong, furious and a handful
to restrain without hurting her. Pinning her arms over her
head, he struggled to draw breath, to allow the hammering
in his heart to subside.

He snarled, "Damn it, B.A, stop! Want to get yourself killed?"

His heart pounded from the exertion, but more in fear at
how her anger had blinded her to peril. Once she stopped

struggling he eased his grip, only to have her try to knee him in the groin. He dodged, absorbing the blow to his thigh.

"You really want to cripple me there, luv?" He used his hard male muscles on her frailer female body, pressing until she found it difficult to draw air. "Dealing with you is going to put me in the hospital one of these days."

She barked, "*Leig dhomb!*"

"Which means? One of us doesn't speak Gaelic."

B.A. huffed, blowing stray hairs from across her mouth. "It means, let me alone."

"So you can play Russian Roulette?" His eyes searched her beautiful face, light-headed over how carelessly she'd acted. "Damn it, woman, rearing horses and helicopter blades don't mix!"

The emotion in his words finally reached her, causing her to search his face. It registered how upset he was. She closed her eyes, and he saw her mentally kick herself.

"Sorry," she offered. "I have the devil's own temper."

He nodded, combating the Neanderthal within him. B.A. had released a massive dose of testosterone in his blood, an adrenaline cocktail that left him with a major buzz. And it was sexual. He wanted nothing more than to extract payment for his fright in the most primitive way possible. On the other hand, if he gave in to the retro-caveman act and shagged B.A. here, no doubt a bloody horse would decide to sit on him, Wee Dougie would putter up to ride circles around them, and The Escape Artists would be chasing his wheels.

Judging it best, he let her up. He glanced at his hands, which were trembling uncontrollably. Not since he was a small child and he'd witnessed his father take his life had anything terrified him so. Now he understood B.A.'s panic over his diving with Wulf and Dennis.

"I lost ten years of my life," he muttered.

B.A. accepted Desmond's proffered hand. Noticing how he shook, in a gesture of reassurance she reached up and caressed his cheek as he helped her rise.

Clearly tongue tied, he grabbed her upper arms, his mouth covering hers in a bruising kiss that stole her breath. She tasted cinnamon from the gum he'd likely swallowed chasing after her. She tasted anger, fear.

She tasted love.

B.A. smiled against his lips, wondering how long before Desmond recognized it himself.

He released her and warned, "Do something that dangerous again and I'll turn you over my knee. And don't think your lads will intervene. They'd cheer. Angus would pat me on the back and say it was about time someone took you in hand and beat you regularly."

Poking a finger into his chest, B.A. accused playfully, "You drank too much Stop-Breath last night."

"At this moment, I haven't drunk enough."

She grabbed his neck, yanking him down for a kiss to knock his socks off. Not holding back, Desmond's mouth worked hers until her knees were weak. Her hand clung to his waist, loving the feel of him. The man sure was a kisser!

Releasing him, B.A. stepped back. She tried to calm down, seeing the helicopter had landed. Its blades slowed and then came to a stop.

As she took a step, Desmond gave her a swat on the rump. She jumped in surprise and turned. Laughing, she winked at him, but kept on toward her target—the people in the helicopter.

"B.A., you lack your face painted blue and a claymore slung over your back—like Mel Gibson," Desmond called after her.

Two men climbed out of the helicopter, followed by three women. One was male, straight from the cover of *GQ*, flashing a fake, magazine smile. He held out his hand. "Hallo! Gareth Davies, BBC. I'm looking for B.A. Montgomerie. We want to do a special for the *Tales of Ancient Britain* series, about The Curse and the fact that there are so few women on Falgann—"

Hands on her hips, B.A. growled. "Who gave you leave to be landing here?"

Desmond came to stand beside her. "Yeah, Falgannon is a private isle. No one lands here without written permission."

"I tried to ring—" Davies's eyes shifted from B.A. to Desmond.

"W-R-I-T-T-E-N—it means you write me and I write back. *Maybe.*" B.A. pointed at the offending machine. "So hop in that bloody whirlybird and get the hell off my island—"

"*Our* island," Desmond corrected, then gave her a crooked smile.

B.A. glanced at him with a mix of perplexity and pleasure. "—before I arrest you for trying to destroy historical ruins. You nearly landed on an ancient cairn." And with that, she turned to go back down the hill.

She heard Desmond say, "I'd guess *welcome* wasn't a word Maeve used often either."

"Wait! This is a great opportunity—," Davies yelled to B.A.

She turned, saw Desmond put his hands on his hips. Mimicking the island brogue, he said, "Och, dunna waste your breath. She's a Montgomerie. Montgomeries never listen to anyone."

B.A. coasted her bike to a stop behind the Rover. Setting the kickstand, she helped Dudley out of the handlebar basket. He often rode with her, provided she kept a sedate speed. Today she could've entered the Tour de France and Kitty would've hung on for his fat life.

"You're not letting that picnic basket out of your sight, eh?"

Undoing the bungee cord, B.A. packed it together with the blankets. She descended the cliff path, careful with her footing. Dudley dashed ahead.

This morn had not been smooth sailing on the romance front. After the *cèilidh,* she'd noticed Desmond mentally retreat, distancing himself from her. He'd done the same on Thursday after they'd delivered checks to the shops on the village circle.

"Silly man is feeling too much and dunna leen how to cope. TM—Typically Male. The power of his emotions scares him witless, so he back's off. Circles his wagons, as

Willie would say in one of his Westerns," she told the prancing cat.

She'd permitted Desmond space. A moody person, she granted others the same right to retreat into themselves. His drawing back bothered her, but males never adjusted quickly to these overpowering forces.

Ignoring his mood, she'd busied herself this morning passing out monies to the Dunmohr and Dunbeag people, seeing that they ate breakfast and then sending them on their way back to their isles. Returning to Rose Cottage, she'd discovered Desmond doing a check of his scuba gear, prepping to dive with Wulf and Dennis.

Perhaps the dread churning in her was irrational. It brought back the too terrifying reminder that in loving a man you opened yourself to the possibility of losing him. That tightness around her heart increased with every breath.

"Kitty, his tanks could run out of air, he might experience a cramp, or Cecile the Seasick Serpent—Nessie's cousin—could want a Desmond appetizer for his elevenses. All valid concerns!" she assured Dudley. "I offered sound logic why he might forego diving today, such as a kelpie might come to spirit him away from the mortal world. Being an Outlander, Des wasn't impressed with that possibility. You ken what he told me? Not to worry, he wasn't driving a bicycle."

She spread her blanket on the pure white sand. Pulling the basket to the plaid's edge, she took out peat bricks and unwrapped the plastic. As she scoop out sand for a fire pit, she talked.

"I have six brothers, mind, so I've had time to study men, warts and all. No matter their age, start telling them things—for their benefit—and suddenly they get this kindergarten stubbornness to their chin and a mommy-can't-make-me look in their eyes. From that point on, reasoning with them is useless. They'll do as they damn well please to spite you!"

The pit dug, she placed the earthy rectangles in the center and lit them. The soft breeze caught the smoke, spiraling it into the air. "I should've kept him in bed all day. But no,

Des went diving despite my protests. Tears clogging my throat, I had to watch him drive away, Kitty. Well, the day's not over."

She smiled as Dudley scampered off to play tag with the surf. So comical: The tide would roll out, he'd chase it. Then it'd return and he'd dance beyond the high water line. The silly cat so enjoyed life.

Growing restless, B.A. kicked off her shoes and strolled along the water's edge, watching the tide ebb. The white sand was damp under her bare feet, and the beach appeared as if the *Sidhe* had stole in and swept it clean. Quite rare, at gloaming on hot summer evenings, the sandbars almost sang. The crystal and shell grains soaked up so much heat, they sounded similar to distant wind chimes when you walked upon them. It was magic found only on Falgannon.

Gathering her skirt to her hips, she sat and wrapped her arms around her knees. She propped her chin on them, listening to the soothing sounds of the water against the shore.

"Oh, Dudley, I never intended to love again. There—I said the L-word! I'm falling for Des. Having lost Evian, I never wanted to set myself up for that pain again. This time it's more dangerous. I loved Evian. Those emotions pale beside what Des makes me feel."

A tear rolled down her cheek as she stood. Then another. She watched them hitting the sand. The tide lapped at them, stealing them away from the mortal world, absorbing them into the endless sea; it receded as five more plunged to the crystalline sand.

"Seven tears to summon a Selkie." She sighed to the turquoise water that had claimed his life. "Oh, Evian, I'm sorry. Only, Des touches me in a way you never did. He sees the castle with ancient eyes. As it was, as it could be again. My lads like him. They get drunk together, play poker. Even Kitty loves him. Already Des belongs to this isle in ways you never did. I'm powerless against that."

She exhaled, not sure what she expected. Some sign from Evian that his spirit had moved on, didn't begrudge her a new love? The only answer was the lulling wash of the surf pulling away her tears.

Blinking against the glare, B.A. thought she spied a seal. Often they came up to the shoreline, so cute, so unafraid.

Seven tears to summon a Selkie, her mind echoed.

The seal morphed—the head and shoulders of a man rising from the surf, like the fabled creature of Hebridian Lore. It took seconds to realize it was a non-Selkie Desmond. The breath she'd held all afternoon released; her heart started a steady thudding. She watched him pause, waist deep, and bend to remove foot fins.

Two more heads reared up behind him, Viking sea gods from the deep. They overtook Des when he lagged. Laughing, Dennis hooked his arm and hauled him toward the shore. They rushed up on the beach, dropping their flippers and removing their hoods and tanks.

Desmond's eyes found her as he rolled the neoprene cap off his head and then shrugged out of the harness of the double tanks. Dennis caught them as if they were too heavy for Desmond.

Des nodded. "Thanks, Dalen."

"Welcome, boss." Dennis grinned. "If we'd have let you drown, we'd have a hell of a problem collecting our paychecks."

B.A. inhaled sharply at the full impact of the words.

Drown?

Desmond flinched, his eyes locking with B.A.'s amber ones. Trouble on the horizon. The last thing he'd said to her was that nothing bad would happen to him. Next time he went diving, she'd be even more worried.

His thigh had suffered a spasm due to the fall off the horse and the bruise where B.A. kneed him. Without Dennis and Wulf's help he would've had trouble making it back against the strong riptide. After her tizzy this morning, he didn't want her to know what caused it, fearing she'd blame herself.

He took in the romantic setting. Nevertheless, he feared

YES! ☐

Sign me up for the **Historical Romance Book Club** and send my TWO FREE BOOKS! If I choose to stay in the club, I will pay only $8.50* each month, a savings of $5.48!

YES! ☐

Sign me up for the **Love Spell Book Club** and send my TWO FREE BOOKS! If I choose to stay in the club, I will pay only $8.50* each month, a savings of $5.48!

NAME: _____

ADDRESS: _____

_____

TELEPHONE: _____

E-MAIL: _____

☐ **I WANT TO PAY BY CREDIT CARD.**

☐ VISA   ☐ MasterCard   ☐ DISCOVER

ACCOUNT #: _____

EXPIRATION DATE: _____

SIGNATURE: _____

Send this card along with $2.00 shipping & handling for each club you wish to join, to:

**Romance Book Clubs
20 Academy Street
Norwalk, CT 06850-4032**

Or fax (must include credit card information!) to: 610.995.9274. You can also sign up online at www.dorchesterpub.com.

*Plus $2.00 for shipping. Offer open to residents of the U.S. and Canada only. Canadian residents please call 1.800.481.9191 for pricing information.
If under 18, a parent or guardian must sign. Terms, prices and conditions subject to change. Subscription subject to acceptance. Dorchester Publishing reserves the right to reject any order or cancel any subscription.

JOIN NOW!

GET UP TO
4 FREE BOOKS

You can have the best romance delivered to your door for less than what you'd pay in a bookstore or online. Sign up for one of our book clubs today, and we'll send you **FREE* BOOKS** just for trying it out...**with no obligation to buy, ever!**

HISTORICAL ROMANCE BOOK CLUB

Travel from the Scottish Highlands to the American West, the decadent ballrooms of Regency England to Viking ships. Your shipments will include authors such as CONNIE MASON, SANDRA HILL, CASSIE EDWARDS, JENNIFER ASHLEY, LEIGH GREENWOOD, and many, many more.

LOVE SPELL BOOK CLUB

Bring a little magic into your life with the romances of Love Spell—fun contemporaries, paranormals, time-travels, futuristics, and more. Your shipments will include authors such as LYNSAY SANDS, CJ BARRY, COLLEEN THOMPSON, NINA BANGS, MARJORIE LIU and more.

As a book club member you also receive the following special benefits:

- **30% OFF** all orders through our website & telecenter!
- **Exclusive access** to special discounts!
- **Convenient** home delivery and 10 day examination period to return any books you don't want to keep.

There is no minimum number of books to buy, and you may cancel membership at any time. See back to sign up!

*Please include $2.00 for shipping and handling.

there would be a helping of crow to eat before the evening was over.

B.A. walked toward him, concern etched on her face. The anguish he saw in those golden-brown eyes twisted his gut. He'd tasted that fear earlier when she rode that horse into danger. He regretted his actions caused her pain.

Knowing she was upset, he'd considered postponing the dive, but in the end he'd chosen to work off some of the residual adrenaline. Being honest: He'd escaped, trying to distance himself from what she provoked him to feel. But the effort had proved futile. The insular feel underwater only permitted his mind to reflect on everything that had happened since coming to the isle.

B.A.'s eyes traced his face as an artist might, learning every shadow, each curve. Her hand reached out and brushed a curl off his forehead. He nearly hated her ability to see past his guard, leaving him exposed. He grabbed her by the shoulders and kissed her hard, stopping the witch from stripping his mind of every secret. Once he had her breathless, he stepped back.

"I take it The Cat Dudley, you and I are dining alfresco?"

A smile formed on her lips. "Thought you might enjoy watching night rainbows."

He brushed his mouth against hers. "Let me get my clothes and give Wulf some last-minute instructions on a report I want him to write."

Dennis offered, "I'll take the tanks up, boss."

"Thanks." Desmond rushed up the trail with Dudley bounding after him.

Dennis hoisted the scuba gear by the straps, then scooped up both pairs of fins.

"Mr. Dalen?" B.A. called, causing him to turn back.

"Yes, my lady?" His blue eyes flashed with a devilish twinkle.

His bright smile was infectious. This was a man B.A. would enjoy having as a friend. She adored males. Surrounded by them her whole life, she loved their moods, their reversion to childishness at odd times, often their inability to verbalize emotions and their time-honored chivalric code toward women. They provoked, fascinated and flabbergasted her. Her fae sense said Dennis could easily fit in here with her lads. His endless amusement at every situation went well with the quirkiness of Falgannon.

"I feel too formal addressing you as Ms. Montgomerie, too forward as BarbaraAnne. 'My lady' fits," he said.

"How about calling me B.A. then?"

He nodded. "I'd be happy to, if you call me Dennis."

She held out her hand to shake. "Done. Dennis, might I ask a favor?"

"Funny, I've been waiting to approach you as well with a request." Dennis held her hand for a moment, then released it. "You first."

"Could you please tell my lads if I see the first face peeking about the cliffs or hear Willie going 'ouch, ouch,' I'll truss them up with Jock the Repair's duct tape and yank it off."

Dennis laughted. "A pleasure. Want me to take the cat with us?"

It was her turn to laugh. "Brave soul. Kitty dunna like being 'taken.' So, what's your request?"

"I'd like to live here . . . permanently."

Her eyes widened. Yes, men did the most astounding things! "Make a home on Falgannon?"

He nodded. "I've plenty of money. Desmond pays well. I've saved nearly everything. I've been around the world with him seven times over, but I'm tired. I want roots. I know you don't want another man on an island of males, but I'd love to retire here. There are things I want to do so I'll retire come spring. With your permission, I'll buy a plot, build a home and settle here. This place is paradise."

She digested the information. The island had plenty of land not being used. "It's doable. You've spoken to Des about this?"

"Not yet. He knows I'm tired of travel. "I've known my dreams for a long time, just not where to find them. I want to write. Viking tales. I talked with Willie. He's excited to have another writer on the island. Also, I spoke with Hamish the Lighthouse. Said he'd enjoy splitting chores with me. My grandfather ran a lighthouse and I've fond memories of that place. Hamish said I could bunk there this winter. Come spring we can take turns helping build real homes." He laughed. "Sorry, I guess you'll need to add me to your Bachelor Registry—end of the line, naturally. I want to get my first book done and my home started before considering marriage."

"You *have* thought this out." She'd have no trouble finding eager ladies when he was ready. She held out her hand to shake. "I'm sure Innis will toast you officially with paint thinner, but welcome, Falgannon's newest resident."

His smile turned to a grimace. Looking down, he saw Dudley had returned. "Your cat nipped my ankle."

"Kitty's sealing the bargain."

Desmond grabbed the jogging pants and jacket from the back of the Rover, then went to the passenger side to unlock the glove compartment. B.A. might not lock her doors, but habits died hard with him. He inserted the key, paused, realizing he *had* forgotten to lock it. Strange, he always locked the glove box. Guess he'd been too upset about B.A. Dismissing it, he pulled out his wallet and turned to Wulf.

"Shame about the location. It's ideal for a deep water harbor." Wulf pushed his bright blond hair from his face.

Desmond dismissed the problem with a shrug. He should be ticked. Wulf was right—it was perfect. His original plans had called for the deep harbor to be built at this point.

"B.A. would keep us tied up in courts for decades—and win. Since the beach was directly under the castle, she's not passing an idle warning about the checkmate with Scottish National Heritage. I'm not going to cry over spilt milk. Once we locate another spot, I'll press B.A. to trade my parcel of land for another chunk of the island." He held out several large bills.

Wulf's left brow arched. "Bribing me?"

"You have plans for the evening with a certain redhead, if I know you. Get Dennis to stand B.A.'s lads to drinks. I don't want to see the first Michael or Ian."

"A challenge, since there's a surplus of both." Wulf slid behind the wheel. He looked as if he were contemplating whether to say what was on his mind. "Des, there are alternatives. There are, what—hundreds of isles with no people on them out here?"

Muscles in Desmond's jaw twitched. "Plans are set. You know the costs involved."

"There'd be a price for pushing it back as we hunt for another site. But with the takeover bid for Montgomerie Enterprises coming, you'll be able to take the hit and move on."

Desmond closed the door, his stare impassive. "This is about more than money."

Wulf nodded. "Revenge? My friend, there are many ways to achieve that, some sweeter than others. You're fighting a ghost—fighting yourself. If I were you, I'd marry that lass, change her name to Mershan, then keep her pregnant with Mershan babies. All hail, Clan Mershan. That'd set old Montgomerie rolling in his grave."

With a wave and a laugh, Dennis appeared and climbed into the passenger side, slamming the door. Wulf started the engine. Desmond stood watching as the car drove off and vanished over the knoll, trying not to let his friend's advice take root.

Why did B.A. Mershan have to sound so perfect?

He watched B.A. poking the peat bricks with a long stick, absently stirring flames. His mouth quirked. She stared, a dreamy look in those whiskey-colored eyes, while he unzipped his wetsuit. Wind stirring his hair, he rolled one side off his shoulder, then the next.

"What's the going price tag on thoughts these days?" he asked. "I'm curious about that Mona Lisa smile." Sitting on the blanket, he rolled the blue-striped, black neoprene down his legs, then yanked the jogging pants on before B.A. could see the massive bruise on his thigh. Unzipping the jacket, he shoved his arms into the sleeves.

B.A. looked as if she wasn't going to tell, then he saw her change her mind. "The way you rolled off that wetsuit reminds me of how a *Selkie* sheds his skin, so I was pondering if you're part *Selkie*. You're beautiful enough to be one."

"You hear that, Fuzzball? She thinks I'm beautiful," Desmond chuckled to the cat.

"My grandfather, many generations back, was said to be a *Selkie.*"

Though still in a black mood, Desmond couldn't help but smile. "Did he have green eyes?"

"Of course."

"Is green eyes a Scottish passion?" Desmond dodged Dudley, who'd crawled into his lap and was trying to lick his chin.

"No—a passion for Mackenzie women." She brushed her mouth lightly against his. "And only ones with black hair. Lucky you."

"Very lucky me." He inclined toward her, intent on taking her mouth in a bruising kiss. Only, Dudley meowed and bumped noses with him.

"He missed you."

"No, he *hit* me." He laughed, rubbing his nose. "Did you?"

She opened her picnic basket and took out plates and glasses. "Miss you, you arrogant man?"

"Hm. I recollect the last time you called me arrogant."

"After you rest and eat, I'll let you remind me."

Pushing Kitty down, he scooted so his chest molded against B.A.'s back, nuzzled her hair. "And he asks, why not now? He's more than up for the task." Dudley jostled back into Desmond's lap, causing him to wince as the fat pussycat stomped on his bruised thigh.

"Because, Mr. Arrogant, your leg cramped. Dennis and Wulf hauled your arse back." Her voice cracked.

"B.A." He took her hand. "That's why you dive with partners."

"And that is why you're going to rest, eat something and enjoy the show nature will soon put on for us."

Desmond was unaccustomed to relaxing. He had a feeling it might be a lot of work. Lying back on the soft plaid, he was willing to give it a go. Besides, he hungered to learn about B.A. "So tell me: What's a *Selkie*?"

"A seaside fae, native to the Hebrides. Legend says they

can shed their sealskin and appear with perfect male or female form, their features alluring and beautiful." B.A. talked as she prepared their food. "Often, they came ashore and took mates."

"So great-umpteen great-granddaddy came ashore and took a lover?" he said.

"Annie Mackenzie was to marry Sean Ogilvie, but he died. Disconsolate, she walked into the sea, intending to end her life. Near death, something saved her, pushed her to the shore. When she reached the beach, she saw a seal. Mad that the meddling beastie interfered, she grabbed a piece of driftwood to throw at it. A hand closed over hers, preventing her. Annie's eyes lifted to behold the most beautiful man she'd ever seen. His name was Cian. He told her life was precious, to value it, then he disappeared into the sea."

"But he returned?"

"For weeks, Annie went back to the shore, hoping to see this mysterious man again. As she lost hope, seven of her tears hit the sand and the tide carried them out. Lore says seven tears shed into the endless sea summons a *Selkie*. Cian answered her call. They became lovers. Annie bore him a son, though she soon learnt the legends were true. Cian could not linger on shore with her for more than a year and a day. He didn't want to leave, but had no choice. He gave her a strange orange-brown candle, telling her to burn it in the window at midnight when she could stand the pain of separation no longer. Eventually, the candle was replaced with another and another. Annie and Cian had thirteen children. When she died, the candle was in the window. That candle has been preserved for over three centuries in my family."

Desmond sat up as she handed him a plate. "May I see the candle?"

B.A. poured him a glass of wine. "Sometime. It's in a vault at Colford for safekeeping."

Desmond's jaw flexed at the mention of Colford Hall. "The candle belongs to Falgannon?"

"It does."

"Why is it at Colford?"

"Sean deemed it safer there."

"Even England returned the Stone of Destiny." A spark flared to life in his soul. "Perhaps it's time for Annie's candle to return to Falgannon."

B.A. stared at him sharing his dinner with the golden cat. "Yes, maybe it is time for Annie's candle to come home."

Chapter 16

Members of the "Morn, B.A." Club raised their heads as Dudley flew through the kitty door of the Hanged Man, stopped and shook his fur dripping with rain. Seconds later, the people door opened and B.A. danced in followed by Desmond. They were both laughing, sharing an umbrella and holding hands.

B.A. started toward the kitchen, only Desmond pulled her back to him. They stared at each other for a long moment, lost in the wonder of their emotions. Then B.A. gave a witchy smile, her eyes bright with joy.

Leaning forward, Desmond brushed his lips over hers, tasting sea spray and rain. It was clear he would've deepened the kiss, unabashed by the audience, had Kitty not delivered one of his vampire bites to his ankle.

"Ouch! Your cat bit me again." He playfully swung at Dudley, who pogo-ed out of reach.

B.A. repeated as expected, "He's not my cat."

Desmond raised his eyebrows. "Come out with that one more time, I'm going to think you're a habitual liar."

"Kitty's telling you he's hungry."

"That's not news. Kitty being finicky—CNN would post that as a news bulletin." He trailed after B.A. toward the pub's long bar. "Since food's mentioned, I'm famished, too. Feed me woman, before I go into a Dudley faint."

"You and the cat go sit. I'll be out with food for you both."

Michael the Story grumbled over his cup of tea, "No idea

why they're smiling so. Never got around to shagging last night. Ashamed they should be!"

"Aye." Robbie mimicked Callum's pruned face, and informed those who didn't already know: "They picnicked on the beach, curled up like spoons and watched the northern lights. He got frisky several times, but our lass smacked his hand. At high tide, they awoke and went to Lady Cottage to inspect the work and watch the sunrise. After, they walked for hours in the rain. 'Tis enough to give a man the blues."

Ian sighed. "Still, there's an invisible, elastic bond between a man and woman in love. It's damn fine to see that electricity between our lass and the Outlander. Bodes well for Falgannon's future. To my way of thinking, so what if the Viking prince owns the tip of the isle? The castle belongs to Herself. Ain't much the man can do without her finger being in the middle of it. And if Mershan owns part of the isle—or *thinks* he owns it—he'll be staying."

"Gor, it *has* to be love." Phelan the Lobster sighed. "Wish they'd get on with it. We ain't getting a better chance to beat the Curse."

Willie suggested, "We need to natter with Morag, get her to brew a love potion. I received an e-mail from Cassie Yates this morn. She's coming next week. I'd like to see B.A. and the Viking sorted out so I can concentrate on my own romance. In my fifth book—*Love's Dark Savage Fury*—The hero and heroine had a shotgun wedding. Maybe we need to slap iron, saddle up and wrangle B.A. so our Desmond can brand that heifer."

"Gor," Brian shook his head as if dizzy. "Willie's gone cowboy again."

Angus waved a finger. "B.A. catches you comparing her to a cow, she'll make you a tunic."

"That's eunuch, Angus." Ian sniggered.

Willie flinched. "Wouldn't want to imagine what our B.A. would do if she ever caught wind I used poetic metaphor for her being a cow."

Robbie nodded, and went back to the problem at hand. "You ken B.A. is a Montgomerie. It's hard to get them set on anything—stubborn being their middle name."

"Them bloody Vikings figured they'd get us shite-faced so we couldn't go spying last night." Michael the Story chuckled. "They dinna ken you cannot get drunk for two days after taking Morag's goop."

Willie grinned and buttered a scone. "We had a fine time watching *them*, though. Vikings are funny when they get foxed."

Sniggers rippled through the group.

"Think we should show mercy on them, fetch Morag to mix up a batch of the goop for them?" Hamish inquired.

Everyone paused, thought for a second, then shook their heads no.

Desmond came over and pulled out a chair. "Morning. You lads look pretty chipper."

Ian folded his newspaper and fixed the man with a stare. "Considering your two Vikings poured half the pub down us?"

Desmond sipped some tea innocently. "Where *are* the children of Loki?"

"In the backroom, on cots, sleeping." Michael the Story pulled pictures off the bulletin board. He flashed the pictures of the two tall, bare-chested Norsemen, faces painted blue and wearing kilts, sprawled on narrow folding beds. "That green stuff Morag gave you after Thursday night poker? It fetches you around, all right. Only it does something strange to a man's innards."

"Only men?" Desmond questioned.

Brian shrugged. "Not sure—lacking a supply of females to experiment upon. Fixes you so you can't get drunk for forty-eight hours. The alcohol they kept pouring might as well have been water. They're the only two that got drunk."

B.A. sashayed in and set a plate stacked with buttermilk scones and another with eggs sunny-side up and rashers before Desmond. "No bacon for Kitty," she warned.

Dudley flashed her a glare before butting his head against Desmond's elbow, taking his appeal to a higher court.

"B.A., them BBC people are pains in the bum. They blethered 'til I feared my ears might bleed listening to that Davies git," Willie complained, then added, "Get along lil' doggie," under his breath.

"B.A., your lads picked on my Vikings," Desmond teased, holding up the photos.

Laughter bubbled forth from her. "I told you, they're working off residual IOUs for all those Viking raids."

Desmond chomped some bacon, then asked, "So what did you do with the latest set of invaders?"

"The Marys tucked up the women. The pilot took a sleep sack to the town hall and kipped there. Mr. Big Teeth paid a hundred pounds to sleep in my bed." Willie beamed.

"B.A., you've gotta sort out them Beebs." Jock stacked his cup on his plate. "One of the females accosted me. Thought I was Richard Dean Anderson. When I explained I was younger and better looking, she said, *fine*. Never saw a woman so intent on grabbing my *fearchas*."

Desmond eyed B.A. "Is that what I think it is in Gaelic?"

She snatched away the bacon he'd slipped to the cat. "Hope she dinna leave fingerprints, Jock."

"B.A., the Beebs are talking nonsense, wanting to take blood samples of everyone." Robbie shuddered, showing his aversion for needles.

B.A. blinked. "Whatever for?"

"Since hemochromatosis is getting press, they wonder if a quirk in our chemistry is behind Falgannonian women having only male bairns," Willie grumbled.

" 'Tis not right, them disrespecting our curse." Angus muttered. "Bloody English, always wantin' to perpetrate atrocities on us poor Scots."

Desmond slipped Dudley more bacon when B.A. wasn't looking. "What's hemochroma . . . whatsis?"

Ian leaned back his chair, rocking it. "Hemochromatosis—a condition where the body stores too much iron in deep muscle tissue and organs. People of Scot-Irish ancestry stand a one in four chance of carrying the gene. The Beebs think if the Picts-Celts-Gaels have one, maybe they have another."

Angus bellyached, "B.A., I dunna fancy some *Sasunnach* bugger prodding me like a pincushion. Boot them off the isle. We dunna need a chromomosomeme adjustment. Falgannon will be fine as soon as a certain lass marries a green-eyed man."

Everyone's eyes fell on Desmond, causing him to choke on his scone.

The phone rang and Brian answered it. "B.A., some rock group called Five O'clock Shadow has written a song about The Curse and Falgannon. They want to come to the isle to film a rock video."

B.A. rolled her eyes and picked up Desmond's plate to get more scones, slapping him on the back with her free hand. "Tell them, wrong number. As for the Beebs, you lads have fun ejecting them from the isle after breakfast. Jock, watch your *precious*."

Desmond poured more tea to wash down the lodged biscuit. "I was up at the castle checking the cottage. Will the work be finished by Halloween?"

"Enough so B.A. can move in," Brian replied.

"Could you use another hand?"

Ian folded his arms over his chest. "Might muss up those manicured nails of yours. I ken you're an architect 'n all, but this is hammering, sanding and such. Any experience?"

"I've hammered a few nails in my day," Desmond answered, then sipped his tea.

B.A. placed more hot biscuits on the plate, pausing to give Tam the Baker a buss on the cheek. "No one in the whole world makes scones as good as yours."

"Our Viking prince sure scarfs them down, lass. Has a fine Dudley-style appetite." He beamed at the praise.

The door swung open and Wulfgar stumbled in, looking like a little boy who'd just awoken from a nap. Well, as much as someone nearly seven-foot tall, with his face painted blue and wearing a red kilt could, B.A. thought. Befuddled, the poor man blinked as if seeing two of everything.

She took his arm and led him to a stool, pushing him to sit, wondering how he'd react when he noticed he was in a kilt and had received a Pictish facial.

"I'll fetch Morag—"

The back door opened and Morag breezed through. "Speaking of the devil, were you?" Shaking the rain off her *ruanna*, she hung it on a peg. "Heard our lads drank the Vikings under the table, knowing my antidote kept them from getting polluted." She stopped when she saw Wulf, snorted, then steepled her hands over her mouth to prevent further laughter.

Wulf's head jerked up, absorbing her words. Morag set about mixing a glass of the green gelatin. Wulf eyed her suspiciously as she set it before him, then gave a monosyllabic grunt.

"Watch him, Morag," Tam teased, pushing rolls into the oven. "Animalistic noises are first signs them Vikings are going berserker. Ain't you seen *The 13th Warrior*?"

Wulf grumbled, "What's this junk?"

"Morag's magic." B.A. patted him on the head. "It'll fetch you around."

Dennis stumbled in and over to where Wulf sat. "B.A., not complaining, that stuff they poured down us last night—it truly was paint thinner."

B.A and Morag started chuckling again.

Dennis croaked, "What's funny?"

When B.A. didn't reply, the men looked at each other. Both sets of blue eyes set in blue-black faces went wide. Knowing they were in Morag's gentle care, B.A. picked up the plate and was almost through the door, when she halted abruptly.

"They gave you Stop-Breath?"

"Yeah, I told them about my plans to move here. Then Wulf asked if he could stay, too."

Tam grinned. "Our Wulf has sisters, so the lads voted to adopt him, too."

"Sisters?" B.A. perked up.

Wulf nodded, then grimaced. "Three. Triplets, twenty-one-year-olds. The men at home run from them. You're welcome to them, B.A. I'd put them up for sale on eBay, but think there's a rule against it."

Tam shook a finger. "Had he told us that first, we might've skipped painting him blue."

"Hmm, methinks you both best break the news to Desmond about your defection ASAP. Gossip has wings on Falgannon." B.A. backed against the swinging door, watching Wulf and Dennis both groan and hang their heads—their *blue* heads.

"Come on, my braw Vikings. Down the hatch. Then we'll set about turning you a nice healthy pink again." Morag set goop before Dennis, then winked at B.A. "I do love this part."

Rain poured down as Desmond pulled into the drive of Rose Cottage and shut off the engine. He reached into the backseat for the umbrella, but paused. Leaning brought him close to B.A. He felt the heat from her body, the scent of the rain on her skin. Almost more than he could stand, he fought the primitive urge to drag her under him and take her right there on the bucket seats.

"Don't bother with the brolly," B.A. whispered breathlessly, "it's just a dash."

"You're sure?" He brushed his lips across hers. "Ummm, you might melt."

"We're already steaming up the windows." She stroked his chin with her thumb. "I stand a stronger chance of melting here with you."

As Desmond opened the driver door, Dudley dashed between his legs and up onto the deck. Not slowing, he barreled in through the kitty door.

Chuckling, they both rushed up the steps and onto the wooden porch themselves. Desmond wasn't sure why he was laughing so hard. Being out in the rain and getting soaked was not a cause for such happiness. He held out his hand for B.A.'s keys, then recalled.

"Silly woman, never locking doors."

B.A. looked up at him with those whiskey-colored eyes, robbing him of breath. His heart did a slow roll as he reached past her to grasp the doorknob. Initially, he meant to turn it. Instead, he maintained his grip and backed her against the doorframe. He leaned into her, rubbing his cheek against her soft hair, and the rain releasing her peony scent kicked him into hormonal overdrive. Closing his eyelids in ecstasy, in agony, he savored the sense of being against her.

What was he going to do with this woman?

His mind had no answers. At least, none he was ready to face. In less than a week, she'd turned his world upside down. Likely, he could reason out what would happen between them, but he knew he wouldn't appreciate the answers. Wouldn't like the loss of control. For the first time in his life he could only breathe for the pleasure of the moment. And right this moment, he was going to kiss B.A. until her toes curled.

He opened his mouth over hers, relishing the taste of scones and jam. At first he kept the pressure light, again amazed how much he enjoyed just kissing B.A.

Kissing, stroking and cuddling were important to females. At an early age, men gleaned that these were tools used to lure ladies down the primrose path. Males were sprinters, he knew, *ready-set-go* where sex was concerned, but since the days of cavemen they'd comprehended a woman would have none of the stallion-covering-a-mare routine.

Hmm, Desmond made a mental note on his list of *101 Things to Do with B.A.* Playing horsey with his Scots lass held a definite lure!

Though men acquired the necessary skills to woo a lady into bed, they often didn't linger on what his mother had daintily called "the preliminaries," when she'd embarrassedly told him of the birds and the bees at age thirteen. So, why did he feel he could stand here kissing B.A. forever?

"Ouch!" Desmond growled, "Guess who."

B.A. looked down to see an annoyed Dudley snapping his tail. "He's impatient," she remarked.

"Kill Kitty." Desmond made a swipe to grab him, but the cat crammed his pudgy body back through the cat door.

B.A. spun and ducked under Des's arm, pushing the door open. "We need a fire, to get out of these wet clothes and into a hot shower."

"Mmm, good clean fun. I'm game."

"You light the fire, I'll feed the bottomless pit." B.A. saun-tered into the kitchen.

Desmond dropped to the arm of the sofa, watching her walk away, barely remembering to breathe. B.A. looked damn fine in those clothes plastered to her by the rain. She switched on the radio, Cutting Crew filling the air, and her hips swung to the music as she opened a can for Dudley.

Desmond was content to sit there like a sap and soak up the images and essences that were B.A., only when the singer hit the lyrics of how it "Must have been some kind of a kiss" and he "should've walked away," the blood left his brain. It was that damn specter of conscience rising again.

Yeah, he should've walked away from B.A. It would've been best. She was a warm, loving, honest woman. Not once had she spoken to him about Evian. There was no need. He'd seen her at the Colford graveyard as she touched the bronze plaque in memory of Deshaunt. He'd witnessed the pain, the agony, the guilt as sobs wracked her whole body, her soul.

And he was a bastard for planning to take so much from her. Soon would put her world at risk. She didn't deserve what he was going to do to her, to her island.

The song changed to the dreamy "I Want to Know What Love Is" by Foreigner. The words flooded through him, hit-ting him with a power as no song had ever done, the lyrics speaking to every need within him, possessing him. Like a sleepwalker, his steps carried him to the kitchen. The few feet seemed miles down a darkened tunnel. The light at the end was B.A. Walking away from her was *never* an op-tion.

She raised up, surprise spreading over her face as she as-sessed the dark mood etched upon his countenance. She opened her mouth to speak, but he took hold of her wrist and pulled her to him. He kissed her. Searing heat re-placed the cool of their rain-soaked clothes. He kissed her hard, not playfully. His kisses spoke of the emptiness inside him, of the soul-deep hunger and how only she could van-quish it.

The ravenous beast had slipped its leash. No pulling back. There was no tenderness in him, no gentleman to apologize as he captured her other wrist and backed her to the refrigerator, pinning her against it. Holding her hands at the side of her head, he ground his pelvis against hers, feeling her arch like a cat, seeking even more.

Flashing a feral smile, he released her wrists. Hands sliding down her body to her firm rear, he jerked her up and against him. Taking a step, he balanced her on the counter, leaving her legs dangling over. Her arms encircled his neck and held on.

He fisted his hand in her damp hair and forced her head back, their eyes locking, as if the final shard of civilized man sought to glean if this dark side of his nature terrified her. Sensing he needed reassurance, she locked her legs about his hips and dragged him to her, rocking against his groin, clearly relishing the delicious friction. Her hands fumbled with the zipper of his jacket and pushed it off his shoulders.

He kissed the strong column of her neck, fed on the radiance that was her, absorbed her fae essence that branded his soul. His left hand palmed her breast, squeezing, feeling the pebbled nipple. He struggled to undo the buttons on her sweater, but heard them popping and ricochetting against the opposite wall as he shoved open the front, baring her breasts to the coolness of the house.

Pausing a moment, he drank in the beauty of her body, her ruched areolas. Her chest rose and fell in short breaths, telling him her arousal matched his. She was with him all the way. So in tune, whether in gentleness or raw animalistic passion, they fed off the mood of each other.

Soul mates.

Crashing overhead thunder rattled the whole house. In the same instant, the lightbulbs in the kitchen and living room exploded. B.A. jumped. Her hand accidentally caught the cord of the radio draped down the side of the refrigerator and yanked it from the wall. Left in the dimness, in the heavy silence, their labored breaths were clear.

Sliding her long skirt up her damp legs, his thumbs drew slow circles on the soft skin of her inner thighs, rising close to where she most wanted his touch. He felt her shudder. Her hips flexed, inching nearer to his thumbs. Lightly, he dragged the back of his knuckle over that sensitized pearl at the apex of her female core. B.A. nearly bucked off the counter.

When his other hand stroked her firm derriere and felt she wore a thong, he nearly came undone. He should've slid it down, taking time to draw out the anticipation, pushing her to the point she'd beg for him to take her, but the beast wanted no part of prolonged foreplay. He ripped it, making a vague mental note to order her a dozen—two dozen—from Victoria's Secret when they came up for air.

Leaning into her, he took the tip of her tight breast into his mouth, sucking hard. He'd mark her, likely mark her many more times before this madness spent itself. The civilized side of him might flinch at the animalistic treatment of a woman who deserved moonlight and roses, merited reverence. But the beast took and took.

Her head lolled back as his teeth raked her sensitive nipple. He watched her ride the hard crest of the pain-pleasure threshold, her lids half lowered. Yanking her to the counter edge, he spread her thighs wide.

Fumbling with the drawstring of his sweatpants, he drew in the scent of her arousal, the female fragrance clouding his brain to the point of insanity. He jerked her forward, impaling her on his hard length of flesh. For a brief moment, shaking, he held still, savoring the sweet sensation of being inside B.A.'s hot slick body.

Of coming home.

Then the beast howled. He withdrew and then slammed into her again and again. Still, it wasn't enough. Wrapping his arms around her hips, he lifted and swung her up against the blank wall on the other side of the refrigerator, pinned her there. His hips flexed over and over, riding her hard, pushing her higher.

"Show me," he half growled, half begged as he pounded into her.

Desmond wanted this agony, this ecstasy, this dark glory to last forever, but her body tightened in a hard spasm as she climaxed with a near crushing force. Her internal muscles clenched around him, dragging him with her into the swirling maelstrom. He could no more hold back than not draw his next breath. His body exploded, pounding in his blood to where he nearly lost consciousness.

Holding on to B.A. like a lifeline.

Drowsing, B.A. rested on her side on the sofa, staring into the peat fire. His radiant warmth surrounding her, Desmond spooned against her back, his beautiful arm draped over her waist as his hand palmed the curve of her stomach. He was so quiet. So peaceful.

She ran her fingers over the back of his hand, contemplating how violently he'd made love to her. Being TM—typically male—*he'd* likely refer to it as having sex. Or something even a bit more graphic. Men! She smiled. Desmond would shy away from saying "made love," the L-word a bête noire.

Only, the two words he'd uttered during the throes of passion spoke volumes. *Show me.* The part demand, part plea stemmed from the song that had been playing just before the light bulbs exploded. He wanted to know what love was, and he wanted her to show him.

Show me. Those two words told her everything she needed about Desmond Mershan.

Chapter 17

Parking her bicycle at the path leading to the castle, B.A. glanced up at the gray stone fortress. Hearing the hammers and saws, she smiled. With All Hallows' Eve nearing, it wouldn't be long until she was officially in residence at Lady Cottage. Anticipation hummed in the nippy autumn air. The future was a vague, scary mix of dreams, hopes and a touch of fear, for she couldn't imagine living there alone now that Desmond had come into her life. Instead of existing day-by-day, for the first time in years she looked forward to Halloween and beyond to Christmas and New Year's.

The past few weeks had settled into a comfortable pattern as autumn's colors kissed the landscape. Desmond took to working on Lady Cottage with her lads. Passion lit his eyes when he worked with wood, his hands almost making love to the grain, sculpting elaborate designs in the molding with the router. B.A. noted admiration in her lads' eyes as they watched him, knew it forged another link in their friendship. Before lunch he'd carry his sketchpad outside to draw the castle's exterior.

At first he sketched the fortress as it looked now. However, his series of intricate drawings had evolved into how it would've appeared in its prime. The details were beyond talent and imagination, yet she held back asking Desmond where he got his inspiration.

Wulf and Dennis broke the news they were becoming residents of Falgannon. Desmond's reaction was hard to read. He seemed surprised, but she couldn't judge if he was against the idea or not. After they'd informed him of their intentions, they moved their belongings into the lighthouse, the first step to planting roots.

Wulf called his sisters to inform them they were moving to the island come spring after graduating university. He reported they weren't happy about moving to "the ends of the earth," until he mentioned there were over two-hundred single males to torment. Ingrid, Astrid and Raghild would visit over Christmas holidays, so in five weeks Falgannon would experience its second Viking invasion. At dawn Wulf went out with Phelan the Lobster to check the lobster traps. Afternoons were spent working on the old bulldozer, figuring with Falgannon's imminent housing boom it'd come in handy.

Willie was delighted to have another writer on the isle. They'd taken the ferry to shop for beds suitable for tall men and picked up a wonderful desk and tables at a small antique shop on Lewis. Willie offered to help Dennis critique his novels, but B.A. feared Willie might have Dennis penning lusty Viking tales under the name of Denise Dalen before he was done.

In her quieter moments, niggling doubts about what had really brought Desmond and his men to the isle rose in her mind. She figured it little mattered. They didn't stand a chance against her nutty islanders, The Cat Dudley and her. The three Outlanders fit so perfectly into the rhythm of Falgannon. They belonged. Oona had even screened Dennis and Wulf navy sweatshirts with *BORN AGAIN FALGANNONIANS* in red plaid across the chest.

If only Desmond would make the same commitment to the isle.

She sneaked up behind him, trying to be quiet so she could watch him sketch. He was an amazing artist. There was little doubt he was a brilliant architect, but she thought his true talent lay in his art. The man was an undiscovered genius with a number-two pencil and art-gum eraser.

Secretly, she'd showed Oona his sketches. Her friend agreed the drawings were incredible, suggesting they could be produced in lithographs and sold—for a hefty price. B.A. debated how to approach Desmond about selling his works through Oona's gallery. Woman's intuition told her Desmond likely discounted his talent and wouldn't take her seriously.

Covering his eyes with her hands, she whispered against his ear, "Guess who."

He paused from sketching, wiggling the pencil back and forth rapidly between his fingers. "What do I get if I'm right?"

"A hot date with the lass of your dreams?"

"What if I'm wrong?"

"Hmm . . . you have to wear a kilt on All Hallows' Eve," she teased.

His chest rumbled with laughter. "No choice, Ms. Montgomerie."

She kissed him on the neck. "Not going to discuss the kilt?"

He set the sketchpad on edge against the chair and pulled her onto his lap. Rickety, the folding chair protested the extra weight. "You could ply me with feminine wiles. I love to be plied."

"I think you love Tam the Baker's scones more," she pouted.

He rolled his eyes as if considering. "Um . . . a toss-up. Maybe to score points with me, you could learn to make them."

"Dream on, Mershan. Why bother when Tam is a genius with the shortening? Of course, there's an alternative."

"Something wicked, I hope." He nuzzled her neck. "Do tell, I am all ears."

She wiggled her bottom against his lap. "Not quite *all* ears."

"B.A.!" Willie called as Cassie Yates and he pedaled down the hill on bikes.

"Company." Desmond groaned, dropping his head against the soft curve of her shoulder.

"Hush, Cassie's going to be my first success story," B.A. proudly pronounced.

"A bit premature isn't it? She only came on Monday."

"A TM response," she sniffed.

"TM? I could be wrong, but figure that isn't praise."

She nodded. "TM—typically male. Men are quick to doubt love at first sight. I've a feeling Willie and Cassie will be the first of my matchmaking efforts to tie the knot."

Desmond scowled. "Ever wonder where the expression 'tie the knot' comes from?"

"Pre-Christian marriages, part of the pagan ceremony. The bride gave a piece of her clothing and the man added his. They tied them into a knot, meaning the two were bound together as long as the knot remained. Part of handfasting rites. On a year and a day, if there wasn't a child and either party decided to end the marriage they untied the knot, releasing them from their bond."

Desmond started to joke, saying she tied him in knots, but then he stopped, got a far-off look, like he was having a vision.

"Des, are you all right?" B.A. called.

He came back to himself, blinking, then smiled. "Just famished. I need food, woman."

B.A. was disturbed by Desmond's odd behavior but distracted by Willie and Cassie running toward them, holding hands, their faces were happy and shining with love. It warmed her heart, gave her hope. She'd set up the Bachelor Registry and Web site out of guilt, feeling she'd let her lads down. To see it working made her want to cry.

"TF," Desmond breathed against her cheek. "Women get teary when romance blooms."

B.A. elbowed him. "Hallo, you two. Enjoy the tour of the isle, Cassie?"

"She loves the isle, B.A.," Willie exclaimed with a breathlessness that had nothing to do with pedaling about the island.

Cassie spun in a circle. "My fondest wish has been granted. The island's picture perfect. It must've cost your grandfather a fortune to modernize it."

B.A. noticed Desmond turn his head away, his expression hardening as if he tried to hide his reaction from her. It gave B.A. pause, but once again Cassie reclaimed her attention.

"Willie showed me the wind machines on the drop-off of the mountain—so clever. You get power from them, yet they don't intrude on the isle's beauty hidden there. And the lighthouse is an artist's dream. I wish I were a painter. But the castle . . . *it* takes my breath away. Shame it hasn't been restored."

"It's my fondest hope, but beyond my means."

Cassie continued, "It's a shame. You and your husband would be the perfect lord and lady for the castle."

"Oh, I'm not her husband," Desmond corrected, a wicked dimple appearing at the corner of his mouth. "I'm her green-eyed man. The Lady of Falgannon always—well, occasionally—has a green-eyed man. Sort of her own personal sex slave."

"Sex slave! That's it!" B.A. elbowed him, setting the chair to wobbling. "I'm tossing Tam's scones into the *cuan*."

"A *cuan* is a bay," Willie explained.

Cassie hugged his arm. "Willie can teach me Gaelic. I've always wanted to learn."

"I can sing in Gaelic." Desmond rubbed his hand up and down B.A.'s spine, making her shiver.

"B.A., may I take Cassie into the castle?" Willie requested.

"Careful going down the steps, and stay in the areas that have stone flooring."

"This'll help me with my book. It's set on an island off the coast of Scotland. Fate, don't you think? If you don't mind, I want to use you and your husband as models for my heroine and hero. You're so beautiful, so perfect for the medieval period. Maybe I can get Oona could do a bookcover with you as models." A shadow crossed her face. "That's okay, isn't it? I'm sorry. This is so exciting!"

Desmond fought a queer feeling creeping up his spine when Cassie brought up the medieval period. To cover, he resorted to teasing, "I'm not sure I'd make a fit medieval hero. I'm much too modern. I like modern conveniences, like electricity and toilet paper."

Cassie giggled. "Writers skip over the toilet paper problem. But you'd be a dashing hero. In mail and a surcoat, with a plaid across your chest—a red tartan, I think. It'd go so well with your black hair. I see it in my mind. The cover would be super!"

Desmond flinched at her mention of the tartan, thinking of the visions he'd been having of himself and B.A. in medieval times. Three-fourths of the plaids in Scotland were red and black.

"Do you know the history of the castle?" Cassie asked, then rolled her eyes. "Silly me, of course you do. Could you tell me if there were any great battles fought here? Maybe some warrior came to claim an earlier Lady of Falgannon?"

The perplexing sensation spread in Desmond, provoking him to run his mouth. "Nah, only Vikings invaded this isle."

B.A. eyed him. "Ignore, Des, he's light-headed from the lack of food."

Desmond attempted to turn the topic, panicked to hear B.A. speak. Somehow, he knew what she would say. "I'm in a Dudley faint. Speaking of which, where is Kitty? You starving him, too?"

"Thursday is lunch with the Marys. They make hash." B.A. tilted her head, clearly puzzled at his clownish behavior.

"We're going to have lunch, would you two like to join us?"

Willie shook his head. "We picnicked outside the cave. I'll take Cassie on a tour of the castle while you feed our Desmond. You can tell her about The Sinclair coming to claim our Deporadh later."

Desmond stiffened. It burned to breathe. Something snapped. Desmond feared it was his sanity, until the chair gave way under B.A.'s and his weight, tumbling them onto the ground. He lay there, a slat of the chair jabbing him in the hip, barely able to draw air. Yep, someday soon, loving B.A. would see him in the hospital.

Loving B.A. The words echoed in his mind, their enormity more than he could accept.

Ian and Brian cantered up on their horses, The Escape Artists yapping around the mares' hooves. One hound ran to Desmond and licked his face.

"Uck! Dog PVC, as Angus would say." Desmond groaned as B.A. rolled off him.

"Och, she's wallowing that poor man around again." Ian spotted Willie practically dragging the Yates girl to the castle. "B.A., I'll have you know, I bathed this morn."

"Your hygiene isn't the concern. He's fearful you might turn Cassie's eye," B.A. pointed out. "He's not risking pro-longed exposure to the Fraser twins' virile beauty."

Brian laughed, jumped down and offered Desmond a hand. "B.A., you ought to take better care of your man."

Desmond pulled a face. "She won't feed me either."

"I'll feed you—a knuckle sandwich." She began running her hands over his body to see if he broke anything. When she made a swipe along his zipper, he jumped.

"Damn, woman, show a little modesty!"

"I just making sure nothing vital was bent or broken." She batted her eyes innocently. "Des is making noise because he dinna want to hear about Deporadh Mackenzie and Iain Sinclair."

Ian carried the basket and blanket from the bike. "Willie should write *that* as one of his romance tales. Better than them yippee kiye, lust-in-the-dust Westerns. I'd read that one."

"Why does our Desmond not wish to hear about Deporadh and her green-eyed man?" Brian helped his twin spread the blanket.

"A Sinclair man coming to claim a Mackenzie woman rattles him a bit, does it not, *Sin?*" B.A. replied.

Desmond ignored her, picking up his sketchbook to close it. His eyes lingered on the image of the man and woman half-drawn on the stairs of the castle. He flipped the cover down, hiding the drawing.

B.A. opened her hamper and took out four glasses—lucky she'd brought extra, as the twins weren't showing any signs of leaving. "Falgannon's own," she announced, pouring the wine.

"B.A., you're the only one who likes that dark purple grapeade."

"So, why does the story of Iain Sinclair and Deporadh Mackenzie alarm our Desmond?" Brian prodded.

"Desmond's middle name"—B.A. lifted her glass in salute—"is Sinclair."

Chapter 18

B.A. wiped down the oak bar in The Green Man while observing Morag push a glass in front of Wulf. The woman ordered, "Drink this one."

"No!" Wulf snarled, then turned back to B.A. and asked for the eleventh time, "You didn't answer me. Are any of your sisters available?"

B.A. took a sip of Pepsi, pretending to ponder his question. "Available for what?"

"To marry."

"Outside of my twin Britt, none of the sisters seems to fall for blonds. And after meeting Lucien Delacroix, the director who drove a stake through my sister's heart, I suppose there might be a good reason for that aversion."

"You said your sister is acting again?" Wulf grinned, held up his hands before his chest and bounced imaginary boobs. "Great actress. I want a big, buxom wife. You'd suit me fine, but Desmond wouldn't like me to court you. He goes jungle cat on me whenever I mention your name. Growwwl."

He burped and then giggled. A seven-foot giggling Viking was a sight, B.A. thought.

"If you call one of my sisters buxom, they'll deck you," B.A. warned. "Come to think of it, *I* might deck you. Males and females have a different connotation of that word."

"Gor, this batch of the goop dinna work either, Morag." Michael the Fiddle sniggered.

In fact, all the men along the bar—except Dennis and Wulf—were having a fine time. They'd gotten the Vikings foxed again at Thursday night poker, and twenty-four hours later the two were still drunk. It stymied Morag. Her magical antidote no longer worked on the Norsemen, and actually seemed to keep them inebriated despite adjustments in her formula.

"How many does that make?" Ian the Radio queried, looking squeamish. "Don't blaw in here, Wulf. It'll resemble Steve McQueen's *The Blob*."

Shoving his glass to B.A. for a refill, Jock the Repair mused, "That film's black-and-white. I was never certain what color the blob was. Could've been green."

Morag put glass number seven before Wulf, determination clear in the set of her jaw. Her goop had never failed before. The Norwegian rolled his eyes as she edged the glass closer.

Sipping some cola, B.A. wondered how long it'd be before her lads were taking bets on whether Morag or Wulf won this Battle of the Goop.

"B.A., you have plenty of sisters. Surely, you can spare one," Wulf said, continuing on his bride quest.

"I have six." She ticked them off. "Catlyn is getting married in a week. Britt is dealing with the big love of her life again, so dunna need any complications. LynneAnne lives in New York in a tiny apartment—which rules out keeping a pet Viking. Asha dislikes big men *and* blonds—and if you call *her* buxom, you're dead meat. Raven would only like you if you posed nude for her paintings. You might interest Paganne, but you'd have to dress up in the horned Viking hat, chain mail and spend four hours discussing the merits and flaws of *The 13th Warrior*."

Janet the Red pinched B.A. and muttered lowly "No sisters for Wulf."

"Oh?" B.A. turned and lifted her brows.

"Angus wants to quit Falgannon, divorce me and to go back to that woman he still visits in Ullapool. We talked last night and decided it's time to stop pretending. I thank him for getting me out of that nowhere village in Ireland, but he's too nice a man to not be happy. He thinks if you break The Curse maybe he and his lady love can be happy on the mainland. His cousin Jamie wants to take over Ferry. So— no sisters for *my* Viking."

B.A.'s eyes flicked to the door, watching for it to open. Desmond had gone off on a *males-only* errand with Callum, Brian, Ian, Willie and Michael the Story. Her female curiosity itched to know why.

"B.A., how come you chucked those three parachutists off the isle yesterday?" Tam the Baker pointed at the WEE HEAVY sign, signaling he wanted an ale. "They were female and had already imported themselves. Less work for you, I'm thinking."

"She dinna like that one smooching our Desmond," Phelan goaded.

B.A. rolled her eyes. "Those parachuting ladies are the latest trouble from the Web site. I hadn't counted on a down side of this project. Those women had more money than sense. They hired a small plane to fly over Falgannon to get a jump—no pun intended—on the competition."

"Och, admit it. You're ticked that one ran up to our Desmond and kissed him on the mouth, leaving smears of her dark red lipstick, and claimed him as hers."

"I dinna like that they cheated and ignored my rules. Besides, they weren't interested in living on the isle, they only wanted boy toys."

"Maybe you should've asked us if we wanted to be toys," Innis huffed. "How did you get rid of them?"

"Told them we dinna have indoor loos. They ran screaming to the ferry."

Dennis lifted his head from the bar as Morag pushed a glass of green slime nearer him. He turned a similar shade, then groaned, *"Jeg tror jeg må spy."*

Jock leaned forward, observing Dennis's face. His eyes shifted to B.A. "Is that Viking for, he's going to blaw?"

Wulf grumped. "No, it only means he *thinks* he's going to throw up."

Dennis made a mad dash to the bathroom.

"Guess he decided." Jock eyed Wulf. "Five-to-two says our Wulf lasts an hour."

"Done!" Innis slapped the counter.

Setting down a tray of dirty glasses, Janet chimed in with a saucy come-hither challenge, "Three-to-one our Wulf dunna blaw a'tall."

"You can't bet, Janet the Red. Males only."

"Thursday night poker is your male bastion, not betting. Stop putting *male only* on everything or B.A. and I are going to organize Women's Lib and protest. Aren't we, B.A.?"

"They only have males-only rules everywhere because it's been six years since they've had other females to deal with," B.A. pointed out.

"Dunna remind us, lass," Innis and Robbie groaned, the last two to receive divorce papers served through the mail.

Phelan waggled his eyebrows at Janet. "B.A.'s always corrupting us with items of Yank pop culture. Maybe it's finally time for the Women's Movement to hit the isle."

At the end of the bar, Davey the Weaver stood up on the rungs of his bar stool. "Now hear this! Now hear this! Women's Lib has arrived on Falgannon."

"Going to burn your brassieres, Janet?" another man called from one of the tables.

"I'm betting Wulf has a strong Viking tum. Any of you brave lads putting your pounds where your mouth is?" Her impudent smile had them all lining up.

B.A. shook her head, then glanced toward the door. She missed Desmond. Her lads had borrowed him an hour ago, with promises to return him unharmed. Curiosity was killing her. If they brought him back painted blue, she was going to be brassed off. Worse, she hoped they hadn't taken it into their pea-brains to have a brotherly what-are-your-intentions-toward-our-B.A. natter.

Looking at the clock, she muttered, "I'll wrap them up with Jock's duct tape and pull it off slowly if that's the case."

Desmond crossed his arms and leaned back against the counter in the tailor's shop, glaring at Callum, the two Frasers, Willie, Michael the Story and Cam the Tailor. Bolts of rich tartans filled the store, along with other materials and items falling under the label of "notions." Cam custom-made clothing, specializing in kilts. The work was exquisite and B.A. said he commanded a hefty price in the Falgannon on-line catalog.

Crossing his legs at the ankles, Desmond replied, "Does 'No way; José,' ring a bell?"

Cam looked perplexed. "Who's José? Have the Spaniards invaded?"

They started in again with arguments, but Desmond just lifted his brows. Dudley jumped up on the counter and draped himself over Des's right shoulder for support.

"Takes a real man to wear a kilt. B.A. would think you braw in one," Cam assured.

"Braw? Thought that meant puke," Desmond pretended.

"*Blaw* is puke. Braw means muckle fine. 'Tis a compliment," Ian translated.

Desmond leaned near Dudley and muttered, "Even when they translate they wander off into Scots lingo."

"Our B.A. thinks a man in a kilt is verra sexy," Willie pressed.

Desmond yawned. "B.A. thinks I'm dead sexy in pants."

"We install B.A. in the cottage on the castle next week," Michael informed him—as if that made a difference.

"I see no connection between her moving into Lady Cottage and me wearing a skirt."

"It's a big ceremony. Starts out at noon. B.A. and her guard ride around the isle on horseback, visiting the crofts and marking her boundaries," Michael explained.

"What boundaries? She owns the whole bloody isle." His smile turned feline. "Minus my third, of course."

Ian eyed him. "Jury's still out on that."

"Possession is nine-tenths of the law. Besides, Dudley votes with me."

"Stop changing the subject." Michael shook a finger at Desmond, but Dudley leaned forward as if to bite it so he backed up. "Bloody attack cat. At dusk B.A. and her van approach the castle—"

"Van?" Desmond yawned again, having stayed up late last night playing poker. He smiled at the memory. This time he'd mercilessly cleaned the pockets of B.A.'s lads. "I thought she was on horseback."

"Aye, she is. Van—medieval term for vanguard, her personal escort."

Desmond tugged on Dudley's paw. "They've gone medieval on me, Dudmeister."

Michael ignored Desmond trying to derail the conversation. "Her captain helps her off the horse, then the Ancients present her with the pennant for the Lady of the Isle. The captain follows behind, carrying the Falgannon Sword. They're piped up the long steps to the roof. B.A. attaches the flag to the pole, signifying the Lady is officially in residence. Then she goes inside Lady Cottage, where the captain gives her the sword and she places it in the holder over the fireplace."

Desmond tilted his head in ennui. "Sounds interesting, but I've heard no reason for me to shiver-me-timbers in a skirt."

"*Kilt,* laddie! We figured you'd be B.A.'s captain this year," Brian stated.

"Not if it entails me—"

"Wearing a skirt." They tossed up their hands in frustration.

"Especially if you expect me to ride a bloody horse!"

Ian winked at his twin. "Fair enough. Desmond passes on the honor. We can get someone else to heft B.A. up and down on the horse. Maybe since the Vikings are now Falgannonians, one of them would do the honors."

Desmond arched a brow at Ian, who signaled his brother with a thumbs-up.

Brian continued the attack. "I'm sure our Wulf will be happy to do it. When I left The Green Man, he was badgering B.A. if any of her sisters a available."

"A braw lad such as him won't have trouble turning a lady's head," Michael concurred with a smile.

"Any of you ever stick your hand in a beehive?" Desmond knew they were prodding him, but it was working. "I'll play B.A.'s captain, but *no* kilt."

"It's tradition," Cam insisted.

Desmond shrugged. "Start a new one. *No kilt.* I'm not riding a horse in a skirt. I'm not bloody Mel Gibson."

Willie, staring at Desmond's boots, tilted his head. "Maybe . . . I have a solution. Remember my cover for *Flame's Burning Dark Passion*? They had my hero in leather pants."

Desmond warned, "As long as it doesn't involve me wearing a skirt—"

"You'd be in pants," Willie said. "To quote B.A. when she goes Yank on us: 'Chill.'" He gathered three bolts—a tartan, one of black leather and one of white linen, then placed them all on the counter next to Desmond. "See, gents, a superior mind always prevails."

Desmond frowned at the red-and-black tartan, knowing without asking it was Sinclair plaid, the same pattern as he'd seen in his . . . whatever they were. He *hated* using the word "vision." He didn't have visions. But damn if he knew what else to call them. Maybe he'd done more damage than he thought when he'd cracked his skull. If they kept haunting him, he'd zip over to the mainland and have his head x-rayed.

"Careful patting yourself on the back, Willie, lest you get a cramp," Tam advised. "Impress us with your bloody brilliance, Writerman."

"B.A. shall adore this and Desmond, and his no-kilt rule, will be satisfied. Let me unfurl this against his legs. See? Leather pants, poet's shirt and a plaid across his chest. We need a big fancy brooch to hold the tartan."

"Patrick the Jeweler finished some new Penannular brooches." Tam caught the concept and unrolled the tartan. He draped it across Desmond's chest and shoulder, displacing Dudley. "Sort of neo-Scot pirate. Damn fine idea—one of your bookcovers come to life."

"Leather pants?" Desmond queried, feeling as if everything had spun out of his control. Though it was an improvement over a kilt.

"Think of B.A.'s expression when she sees you."

"Oh, aye." Cam pulled out his tape measure and ran it along Desmond's inseam.

Desmond eyed him, trying not to be goosey. "Watch it there, how do I know you haven't been hanging around Oona and Morag?"

"Hold still, lad, and we'll sort you out." Cam continued measuring.

Ian beamed. "Desmond will start a new fashion trend on the isle."

"Damn sight warmer than having your arse flapping in the wind." Desmond patted Kitty. "What's your opinion, bud? Will B.A. think I'm dead sexy in leather pants?"

"Meow!"

"My thought, too." Desmond winked at the beast.

He opened his mouth to say, "What a man wouldn't do for a woman he lo—" but caught himself before the dreaded L-word popped out. He'd almost admitted he was in love with B.A., but feared the power it placed in her hands.

Yet no matter how he might avoid the word, he suspected he already knew there was no evading the fact. He was in love with BarbaraAnne Montgomerie.

Watching the group surrounding Wulf, B.A. dried the tray and placed it back in the stack. Only five minutes to go before Jock's hour bet was up, and her lads were keeping a close eye on him.

Jock slid the newest glass of Morag's goop closer to Wulfgar. "Come on, try Morag's latest batch."

Wulf turned a shade of gray-green.

"You dirty cheat!" Janet tossed a bar towel in Jock's face.

All at once, Desmond and her lads filed back into The Green Man, wearing smug expressions. B.A. therefore ruled out the Intentions Speech, and Desmond was still the same shade as when he'd left, so she was curious what they'd been doing. But she wasn't going to give them the satisfaction of asking. Ignoring them, she pushed through the swinging door into the kitchen, intent on fetching ice to refill the bin. She opened the machine and used the scoop to shovel the crushed ice into the bucket, muttering under her breath in Gaelic.

"*Bheir aon fhear each gu uisge, ach cha toir a dhà-dheug air òl*," she muttered, reaching for the pail's handle.

A hand closed over hers, lifting. Desmond's eyes were so close she could see the small black etching within his iris. She nearly melted, lost in their vivid hue. Oh, how the man had the power to rock her.

"Which means, lass? Dudley might understand Gaelic, but I'm not so learned."

"A Scots proverb says, One man can lead a horse to water, but twelve cannot force it to drink."

He arched his brow. "I'm the horse? And there were five, not twelve. I take it you missed me?"

"Arrogant man."

He carried the bucket back out to the bar and poured the ice into the bin, leaning close so his voice didn't carry. "I can remind you of three occasions when you called me arrogant."

"I suffer memory lapses." B.A. leaned close enough to nip the corner of his sexy chin.

"I'll remind you later." His thumb rubbed the inside of her wrist as he flashed a killer smile. "Maybe while we play horsey."

Callum saw the electricity in the air between Desmond and B.A. Passing a Wee Heavy to both Michaels, he smiled smugly before taking a swallow from his own.

Michael the Story studied him for a moment, then glanced to his left at Michael the Fiddle. "Usually when one of you knows something, so does the other. It's like you share one brain. But I see your better half dunna ken. So, why are canary feathers hanging from your mouth there, Callum?"

"If you must ken, I fitted our Desmond's Rover with a bicycle rack today."

"Bloody hell. That ranks up there with Sean Connery coming to vacation on Falgannon." Michael the Story grinned and clanked his bottle against Callum's.

"Aye." Callum beamed. "He figured he's always running B.A. to ground on her bike, so it'd come in handy. While B.A. was at the store, he had me install the rack on the Rover."

The men swiveled on their barstools, their eyes following as Desmond led B.A. to the dance floor and started dancing to Bob Seger's "Come to Papa."

"They sure move well together," Michael the Story sighed.

"A bonnie pair," Callum concurred.

"See how they anticipate each other—as if they've danced together for years. Hits a man *here*." Michael the Fiddle thumped his fist to his heart.

Picking up his bottle of ale, he ambled to a table where he could watch the couple dancing. Soon, the others followed.

"I've partnered B.A. for years, so I recognized something rare and special exists between those two people." He was pleased, but the words were tinged with sadness. "B.A. has always been ours. Even when she married that arrogant bugger, Deshaunt, she still belonged to us. I think someone has finally touched our lass's heart the way no one has before."

"Oh, aye." They all nodded.

"Och, stop with the long faces! Time to celebrate. Our lady has her green-eyed man." Phelan the Lobster nudged Ian the Radio. "Go put on some sexy tunes, get a little dirty dancing going here. Speed things up."

B.A. noticed her lads sat watching, wearing sappy grins. "We've an audience," she said.

"Why not? I'm an excellent dancer." Desmond said with a wry grin. "And I have green eyes."

"Where did you learn to dance?" There were a thousand questions she still wanted to ask; she was eager to know everything about him. Des had been slow to give up answers, like most men.

He shrugged. "I paid a woman to teach me, figuring I needed to blend in at social settings. It came in handy, as I've lived around the world and was expected to dance with clients' wives."

"You lived in the States?"

"We moved there when I turned nine. I was born in London. My mother was Irish, my father was half-English, half-French. After his death we moved to Ireland for two years."

Desmond kept the smile plastered on his face, though the muscles felt taut. After his father's suicide, they'd returned to his mother's people in Ireland. They'd lived in a thatched cottage on family land. His grandfather, a bitter, hard man and an alcoholic, hadn't welcomed them. He viewed Katlyn and her three sons as millstones around his neck. He forced his daughter to scrub floors on her hands and knees, treated her like a servant. In one of his drunken tirades, he'd died of a heart attack.

His mother wasn't well educated. Marrying at an early age, like many women of her generation, she'd expected her husband to care for her. Desmond's father had loved and pampered her with a grand lifestyle. Being part French, he'd encouraged a clinging dependency. A delicate woman, she'd died inside when he killed himself. Afterward, she was only a shell, keeping herself together enough to care for her three sons.

Their situation had been harsh, so remote from everything, they hardly seemed to exist in the twentieth century. A lady from the United States was vacationing nearby, a writer researching her next book. Fortunately, she'd taken an interest in the lad who did her yardwork and felt for the plight of his family. She'd hired his mother as housekeeper while she summered there. When she left come autumn, she'd paid his mother the bonus of tickets to the United States, saying Katlyn stood a better chance there of breaking away from the grinding poverty of the small Irish farm.

Pushing himself to ignore the demons rattling their

chains, he said, "I've lived in every large city in the United States, London, Paris, Rome, Hong Kong—even in Norway and a dozen of places in between."

B.A. tried to make her next question sound casual. "Ever considered settling down in one place? Wulf and Dennis are tired of the globe-trotting."

He started to reply, but the image of him standing at the bottom of the castle steps with his hand on the stone railing rose in his mind. Maybe such dreams were futile, especially knowing what was coming down the road.

He answered, "No, never," though he wanted to say *never before*.

He saw the light in her amber eyes dim. B.A. was so open, so trusting, he almost wanted to kick her. She needed someone to protect her and this Pollyanna island from their faith in the goodness of people. A worldlier woman would take pleasure in this relationship yet shield herself against men generally being bastards.

"Until I put my hand on the railing of the castle." The words were almost torn from him; he'd been unable to keep them from her. And Desmond again had the strange, sinking sensation his life was out of control.

Chapter 19

Peeking out the window panes of the front door, Oona called, "What ho, the lads from *Riverdance* are here."

Confused, B.A. and Janet rushed to the door. Desmond and four other men jauntily strode down the walk, the heels of their boots sounding on the stones.

"A year for breaking traditions, eh? You've a new gown for the first time, B.A., and our Viking prince is striking a blow for male fashion," Oona said in her dry tone. "Do love the leather breeks. Think I'll have Cam knock me off a pair."

None of the lads wore in kilts. Each wore black breeches,

knee boots and poet's shirts. Tartan sashes swept diagonally across their chests. Arranged in a phalanx behind Desmond, their tartans proclaiming their heritage: the Fraser twins represented Clan Fraser, Michael the Story stood for Clan Mackenzie and Jock for Clan Grant.

Her lads were handsome, but Desmond drew B.A.'s eyes like no other. In the month he'd been on Falgannon his hair had grown longer on his neck, the waves stronger. His hair was done with plaits, small braids starting over the ear and going back in chief's braids. He wore his blousy shirt with a pirate's élan, the sleeves soft and billowing. The tartan crossing his chest proclaimed Clan Sinclair. A gold cathead brooch held it in place at his shoulder.

B.A.'s eyes traveled down his long, muscular legs clad in leather, and she nearly swallowed her tongue.

B.A. fanned herself. "Those breeks should be outlawed." Summoning composure, she uttered the formal welcome: "*Ceud mìle fàilte* to the men of Sinclair, Grant, Mackenzie and Fraser."

Ascending the steps, Desmond held out a white rose. He took a deep breath and, in a burr so thick it made her smile, said, "Tha men aye Falgannon hae come fer tha Quine aye tha Isle." *The men of Falgannon have come for the Lady of the Isle.*

Oona's head snapped back. "Gor—they fed him Stop-Breath again!"

Desmond took the cape Oona held out. Sliding it about B.A.'s shoulders, he fastened the catch at her neck. B.A. noticed how his hands trembled, his thumbs gently brushing her skin just above her breasts. Desmond stepped back, but raised his hand to cup the side of her face.

Looking into his eyes, emotion slammed into B.A., almost driving her to her knees. What Desmond forced her to feel was devastating. Fighting tears, B.A. leaned her head against his palm, basking in the power of her love for this man.

Dropping his hand, Desmond turned on his heel and offered his arm. They descended, though B.A. wasn't sure her feet touched the ground.

Desmond asked, "Where's the wee beastie?"

"Helping the Marys cook. Dunna worry. Kitty'll show up when food's served."

"We planned to stuff him in leather pants, but he ran off. I'm afraid he's angry at me."

"There's not much you can do wrong in Kitty's eyes."

B.A. shared Dudley's sentiment.

Desmond lifted B.A. up on the horse, settling her in the sidesaddle. He paused, staring at his hands upon her waist.

Flummoxed best described the emotion that hit him upon seeing B.A. in the medieval gown. The black garment was a stunning complement to her long blond hair. She shimmered as if blessed by pixie dust. Still, he was relieved the dress was black and not white, for otherwise it was identical to the gown she wore in his visions. He wasn't sure he could've handled her in white. Her long hair had a hint of a ripple, and the image of the medieval maiden kept crowding his mind.

He could only stand and stare at her. B.A. was heart-breakingly beautiful.

Desmond knew when his brain worked again he'd face weighty questions. He floundered in emotional quicksand and feared only one answer existed to the dilemma.

"Damn it, B.A.!" Oona dashed inside and back with two gold slippers. "Eegit, you're wearing tennies."

Oona passed Desmond the gold slippers while she unlaced the sneakers, since B.A had already arranged her legs on the sidesaddle. He slipped the dainty gold shoes on her, feeling much like Prince Charming and Cinderella.

His gut twisted, knowing he was no prince. Time was running out. Soon B.A. would know that as well.

"Bloody hell." No words came to Desmond's mind. The few half-formed floated away, far short of conveying his thunderstruck emotions while standing at the pinnacle of Falgannon.

In a leisurely pace they'd ridden up the hill, past the castle, then to the high plateau where the stone ring sat. Desmond sensed tangible power radiating from those pagan stones. A magnetic disturbance in the air. Whispers of ancient voices. The thirteen stones, nearly fifteen feet tall, were some of the oldest in Britain. Sunlight reflected off alternating streaks of crystals imbedded in the gray stone. Magic.

Several times B.A. had put off his request to visit them. After going there, Desmond understood her reticence. A Doubting Thomas, the experience unnerved him, the silvery stones almost mocking him: they'd been here thousands of years and would be thousands more, long after he was dead and forgotten. Standing before them was humbling. And as he'd woven between the slabs of gneiss, he savored their eternal riddle, easily envisioning pagan celebrants dancing ancient rites under the pale moon.

The stones emitted an aura, a cross between a hum from a tuning fork and static electricity. They taunted him to touch them. He had. His mind flooded with so many images it'd been painful. He'd jerked back, dumbfounded. Visions of a past life, for lack of a better term, had increased since touching them, even invading his dreams at night.

Though the stones' pull was strong, their command dwarfed when compared to the panoramic vista now claiming his attention. He glanced over his shoulder to the perfect village far in the distance. The rolling lands of Falgannon were arrayed at his feet, so green, yet gilded with the painter's brush of autumnal colors. On the horizon, other islands were thin ribbons of majestic purple scattered on the turquoise water. Dunbeag and Dunmohr were closest, only a few miles to the west. Falgannon's rear dropped off, fingers of rocks jutting from the sea in a connect-the-dots from the isle to the two others and showing that they had once been joined.

Desmond swung from his saddle, glancing between the two faces of Falgannon. Showcased before him were thirteen square miles of manicured, perfectly maintained farms and homes, reflecting B.A.'s love. In contrast, raw, untamed sea was at the isle's back, high waves crashing against the ancient rocks.

Tearing himself from his dumbfounded awe, he lifted B.A. from her horse. So high up, the winds were buffeting. Bespelled by the landscape, he didn't notice she took his hand until B.A. tugged, leading him to a single stone.

Not as tall as the ones in the ring, it was hardly more than five feet high. The odd form resembled a woman in a hooded cape, with her hands before her as in prayer.

B.A. said, "The Lady Stone. Legend holds she was the first Lady of the Isle, one of the Daughters of Anne. I presume Anne to be the Pict-Celt water goddess Annis. The lady angered Annis somehow. For punishment, Annis turned the lady to stone. Here she remains, watching over the isle."

A brown twig was stuck in the soil before the stone. Ian yanked it from the ground and tossed it away. Untying a small pack from his saddle, he took out a bottle of water and a trowel and passed them to Desmond.

B.A. and he knelt before the stone. From the lads' instructions, he knew to dig a hole a foot deep. B.A. plucked the leaves from the lower stem of the rose he'd given her, exposing two buds. She held it at the center of the pit he dug, while he raked and tamped the peaty soil back. B.A. took the bottle and carefully emptied the water on the dark earth.

A small act, but Desmond sensed deep significance attached to the ritual.

"Every Samhaine we come to Lady Rock and plant a white rose," Ian explained. "If the Lady of the Isle has found her green-eyed man, and he has black hair and Ireland in his soul—and if he takes her in love—the rose will root and grow strong. If not, it withers and dies."

A question flickered in Ian's ice blue eyes: Would this rose flourish or be a twig a year from now? Desmond met Ian's challenge with a poker-face.

His heart burned. A callow knave, he'd come to Falgannon under false pretences. That was bad enough, but to permit this relationship with B.A. without being honest with her was beyond the pale. And as Ian studied him, Desmond feared this man he'd come to view as a friend could read his guilt.

Worse, he craved to be B.A.'s man. Her green-eyed man. The one to summon the magic that would see Falgannon thrive. He wanted to make this same trek next fall and see white roses blooming.

Pragmatic, Desmond realized he could no longer hide from the questions arisen this past month on Falgannon.

Desmond offered B.A. his hand. She smiled, those amber-brown eyes so open, full of trust. He felt a blow to the center of his chest, as if all the air had been knocked from his lungs.

Desmond stared flabbergasted out at the sweeping horizon in both directions. This island was pristine. Such beauty, such perfection was to be protected with the heart of a warrior. Falgannon was well-served by its lady. Only, the lady deserved a protector.

He stood buffeted by the breeze. The opposing forces of Falgannon's winds were an invisible undertow, holding him, trying to drive him right into the soil. Telling Desmond he belonged here.

B.A. pushed through the wind to reach him. Desmond grabbed her, drawing her against his chest, wrapping his arms around her to absorb the heat from her body. Glancing over her shoulder, she watched his face.

He stared down on the undulating farmlands and the cobbled road leading to the neat horseshoe-shaped village, struggled to find words to describe the impact of being up here, of sharing this with her.

Her smile was witchy. "It affects me that way. The power never lessens."

He leaned his head against hers. "My God, B.A., you can see forever from here."

And he meant that literally—*forever*.

Nearly midnight, after all the ceremony, Desmond stood in Lady Cottage, his hand caressing the pommel of the sword, a soul-deep ache in him. The broadsword called to him as the castle did—as B.A. did. This island was changing him. He'd be a fool to deny it. At this late date in his life he'd discovered there were things money couldn't buy. Items beyond price tags. Biting the bullet would cost him big time, but the bottom line was that only an idiot ignored what stared him in the face.

I'm in love with B.A.

He'd never believed love existed until now—still hated using the word. But what else could he call this consuming emotion? Before, women had intrigued him, but after having sex with them several times, his interest waned. Being male, he'd found pleasure in the emotionless couplings. But never had he caught himself thinking of a woman, aching to be with her every minute.

He'd spent four weeks with B.A., almost continuously in her company. It should've stifled him. When she was out of sight, images of their time together inundated his mind. He hungered for her, and not just for their lovemaking. Meaningless flashes: her licking the mayonnaise off the spoon after she'd made sandwiches, her falling asleep on her laptop, or when he'd caught her dancing with Dudley to the Moody Blues's "The Story in Your Eyes."

He was a Doubting Thomas brought to his knees by a Scottish witch.

Accepting the certainty, he had to act fast to set their relationship right. Work he'd already scheduled on Falgannon would start after the first of the year. Before then he needed to confront B.A. with the truth. She'd likely take this sword to him when he revealed his plans.

Yet he knew one thing—he'd got to B.A., too, dug under her skin as badly as she affected him. The power between them was rare, special. He felt confident they'd weather the coming storm.

He tried to pinpoint the moment he'd taken the tumble, that second he'd fallen headlong in love with B.A. Montgomerie. He'd been fighting it for a long time. Maybe it it had even been that breathless instant he looked into those amber eyes when he first arrived on Falgannon. Or was it that first night he'd awoken to see the cat propped up on the pillows between them, B.A. slumbering, trusting, as if they belonged together? Had that fae blood of hers sensed this destiny from the start?

Possibly it was before, at Sean's funeral—that pause in

time when she'd turned, locked eyes with him and the world shifted on its axis.

He removed the sword from its rack. Holding it out, he relished its weight, its balance.

Ridiculous! But perhaps when he clipped B.A.'s engagement picture from that magazine, he'd started down this inevitable path to her. He should've gone after her years ago. They'd be happy on this tiny island, likely have half-grown children by now. How had he been so blind?

Well, he wasn't dimwitted enough to make the same mistake twice. He wanted B.A. in his life. No matter the cost, he'd move heaven and earth to have her.

"That sword belongs in your hands." B.A. strolled in, carrying two glasses of whisky.

Reverently, he settled the sword back on the wall rack. "I hope I wasn't breaking some Lady of the Isle rule by handling it."

"Not a'tall. In that snazzy outfit you look the Highland warrior. The sword's natural in your hands. You're a warrior, Des. You don't use a sword, but you wage war, don't you?" Her cat-eyes stripped his soul bare.

He'd formulated his intent to claim B.A., but not *how* he'd broach the subject. He wanted this magical night, to use their passion to bind her to him before facing the cold facts of tomorrow. Thus, it seemed prudent to divert the topic. "How old is the sword?"

"Two centuries, cast from the original sword of The Sinclair—Iain Sinclair. He came to claim Deporadh Mackenzie, Lady of the Isle in 1457."

"Sinclair . . ." He steeled himself. "Tell me of Deporadh and this green-eyed man."

She gave him an amused look. "How did you ken Iain had green eyes?"

He shrugged, not ready to discuss his visions. "I'm wrong?"

"Nay, he had green eyes."

"And they lived happily ever after?"

"After a rough wooing." Her laugh was musical.

Accepting a glass, he swallowed some peaty Scotch. "Tell me about this rough wooing."

"Deporadh borrowed money from Iain, Laird of Dunstrathraven, offering a piece of Falgannon as collateral. She failed to repay The Sinclair. He came to claim his chunk of the isle. When she blocked him from landing, he stormed the castle and took her prisoner."

Prickles crawled over Desmond's scalp, seeing the story in his mind as a memory, and recognizing the striking parallel to their lives now. Pulled back to the sword, he ran his index finger along the cross-guard. "Kept her prisoner?"

"Locked away for months. Deporadh refused to deed the land to him. It became a battle of wills. You might say he won, claiming her and the castle. But I'm convinced Deporadh saw he had green eyes and not repaying the loan was the quickest way to get him to come after her."

"What about the Irish blood?"

"His mother was Irish, a Fitzgerald."

Desmond choked on the whisky.

B.A. patted him on the back. "Des, are you all right?"

He nodded, observing her reaction. "My mother's a Fitzgerald."

"And Sinclair blood is in you." B.A. cocked her head.

"Yes. Paternal grandmother."

"Interesting, how you have both Fitzgerald and Sinclair blood—and green eyes."

He focused on the sword. "Where's the original?"

"In the safe—"

"At Colford," he guessed. "Damn it, B.A! First Annie's candle, then The Sinclair's sword. What else does Colford have that belongs to u—?"

She licked her lips, eyes dancing. "*Us,* Des?"

He didn't know why he was so irked, but: "Falgannon's history belongs here."

She put her hand on his arm. "*Us?*"

"Well, I own part of Falgannon."

"So you claim." Flashing him a look that said coward, she sat on the arm of the sofa.

Too restless to sit, he raised his glass. "Here's to pixie dust, ancient curses"—Dudley hopped up on the couch's back, coming to pester B.A.—"and kitties that play poker. But most of all, to BarbaraAnne Montgomerie. She takes my breath away."

A tear glimmered in B.A.'s eye. Removing the glass from her hand, Desmond set it and his own on the coffee table. His lips found hers, brushed them, the tenderness causing a small gasp to escape her. Taking advantage, he deepened the kiss.

A racket broke out from below the castle, causing them both to jump.

"Bar bar bar bar Barbara Ann
Bar bar bar bar Barbara Ann . . ."

B.A. groaned. "I'll kill them. Will save finding them brides."

"This isn't part of the official Lady of the Isle ceremony, I take it?" Curious, he followed her onto the roof.

Going to the east wall, they looked down through the crenellations to see the Michaels, the Fraser Twins, Jock and Callum singing an off-key rendition of the old Beach Boys' tune. At the rear of the group were two tall blond men. Wulf had his arm draped around Janet.

Wrapping B.A. in his embrace, Des asked, "Might the castle still have vats of boiling oil?"

"A chamber pot would come in handy." She stuck her tongue out at the men below. "When I was growing up, anytime they wanted to get on my nerves, they'd break out in that song. They haven't tormented me this way since . . ."

When she hesitated, Desmond finished, "Evian's death?"

She nodded, smiling sadly.

Desmond noticed Dudley chasing his shadow across the roof, more active than he'd ever seen him. A power, an energy radiated atop this castle. Kitty sensed it. The first day he'd come here to confront her, he'd recognized how it affected B.A., witnessed her drawing strength from it.

That force now charged him. For the first time in years, he felt so . . . light. As though the troubles, pain and driving need for vengeance within him had been grounded and neutralized. He wanted to chase shadows across the castle roof with Dudley.

Tightening his arms about B.A., he asked, "Will that caterwauling go on long?"

She rubbed her shoulders against him. "You have plans?"

"How about having our own 'installing the Lady' ceremony?"

"Could you be more specific?"

His body jerked. "My mind wonders about those winter months when Iain kept Deporadh prisoner. I'm curious about this rough wooing."

"I dinna say it was wintertime."

"I've a good imagination," he evasively replied.

He took her mouth, basking in the pounding she set loose in his blood. Scooping her up in his arms, he swept her inside Lady Cottage and up the stairs to the loft bedroom. He wondered if Iain Sinclair had felt that same drive to claim Deporadh Mackenzie.

Desmond lowered her to her feet, kissing her like he was a drowning man and only she could save him. He smiled in the kiss, feeling her knees go wobbly. Her fingers bit into the muscles of his arms, hanging on—just the reaction he wanted to draw from her. In the morning he'd face telling her about his plans, of the North Atlantic oil rigs. Tonight he'd make love to her, bind her to him so she'd know they belonged together no matter what. Brand her so she'd never let another man touch her.

Breaking the kiss, Desmond turned her and lifted her long hair over her left shoulder. Slowly, he drew the gold cord through the laces on the back of her gown, exposing her lustrous skin. He chained kisses down her spine, smiled when she shivered, the shudder crawling over her skin. He savored it, felt it under his mouth.

He wanted to draw this out, to delight in every magical second, only the need to mate thundered through his body. He pushed the gown off her hips, revealing a red thong.

"Do you buy them by the gross?" He whistled, turning her. "Mercy, you're not wearing a bra, just that scrap. It's hard on my system, lass."

Placing his hands on her hips, he slid down against her until his knees were on either side of her feet. Her breath inhaled on a sharp intake as he glided his hands up, cupping the weight of her breasts. His thumbs brushed circles around her sandy-colored areolas, then across the stiff peaks of her nipples, jutting more with each stroke. She was so responsive. He took one breast into his mouth, not suckling like a babe, but as a man, drawing hard, laving his tongue against the tiny bud. As she swayed, he wrapped his arms around her derriere, lifted and tossed her diagonally onto the bed.

B.A. gasped, "Desmond!" then laughed.

He grabbed his poet's shirt and yanked it over his head, tossing it into the shadows. B.A. watched as if he were her personal Chippendale heading for the Full Monty. By her flashing eyes he saw she was turned-on by the leather pants. He owed Willie for that.

He climbed on the high bed and then straddled her. Keeping his weight on his knees, he asked, "Ever wonder how Iain handled his Lady of the Isle? Would Deporadh have cowed in the corner and quivered in fear, or would she have fought him?"

"Mackenzie women have always been warriors," she replied cautiously.

Rays from the full moon beamed through the skylight, partially banishing the darkness of the loft. The silvery glow caressed them, rendering them enchanted beings. She was pinned beneath him. But then, trying to escape appeared to be the last thought on B.A.'s mind.

"Buckle up, baby, it's going to be a rough ride." He flashed his teeth in a predator's smile.

"I do like these breeks." Sitting up, she put her hands on his leather-encased thighs. She snaked them up his body, tracing his contours. His stomach muscles contracted as her thumbs stroked his erection defined against the leather. "I wonder if Ian took her prisoner, or if he fell into *her* trap. I think she lured him here and—"

"Made him her sex slave? A longstanding tradition with you Mackenzie wenches." He pulled her hands from his groin. "Ah, no touchy-touchy the sword of The Sinclair, wench. You'll prick your thumbs on the sharp blade."

"Prick my finger on a prick!" B.A. fell back, howling with laughter.

Often men thought of laughter in the bedroom as out of place. From B.A. it was perfection, like healing sunlight pouring into his dark soul. He leaned forward to caress her breast, which was damp from his mouth.

"Responsive wench." He kept circling it with his thumb, watching the areola ruche tighter, relished her raspy sigh of delight. As she closed her eyes, he stopped toying, took the nub between his finger and thumb and gave it a light pinch, then rolled it. Her hips bucked, but not in pain. Too lost to the sensual buzz vibrating in her blood, the razor-edged desire rose another notch.

He pushed her arms over her head. Before she fathomed his intentions, he caught her wrists and wrapped the gold cord from her dress around them. "I think The Sinclair would've been cautious dealing with a Mackenzie lady."

"Desmond?" She yelped as he hooked the cord around the post of the headboard.

His eyes roved over her body—arched so beautifully, a pagan offering. He smoothed his hand over one breast and down her stomach, which quivered under his palm.

"Going to leave the boots on, Des?" Her body quaked with suppressed laughter.

Desmond had always had a strong sexual appetite, but even baser, animalistic needs drove him. Play and laughter never had a place in the bedroom before. With B.A. everything seemed new. This capricious banter only sharpened his need to be close to her, sharing—and not just physically. Closer to her mind, heart and soul. He'd use their bodies to create a white-hot blaze, fuse them together so tightly she wouldn't know where she ended and he began.

Once more, images besieged his mind, flashing to the morning after B.A. first ordered him off her island. He'd awoken to an erotic dream of her tied to the bedposts. He'd assumed it was the bed in Rose Cottage. Only now, reality slammed into him. It was *this* bed, the oak wood he'd seen in his vision, not the antique white frame, this same gold cord binding B.A.'s wrists.

"Desmond, you pass out with me trussed up like a Christmas goose and I'll bite you," B.A. teased, but he saw quizzical flickers in her eyes.

Pushing the images away, he brought his mouth down to

hers, nibbling along her lower lip. "Silence, wench, you're about to be ravished."

She bumped her hips against his, provocative. "What's the hold-up, Des? Ravish away!"

"I'm considering if I need a pair of golden spurs. Knights of Auld wore spurs, didn't they?" he teased to cover his confusion.

"Spurs aren't required accoutrements for ravishment."

"Willie might have a different opinion on that."

B.A. drew a ragged breath as Desmond slid down over her body, his mouth catching the sensitive peak of her breast. His tongue swirled around the crest, teasing, tormenting, while those magician's fingers tended the other one. Her body bowed against him, her desire an ache that twisted inside her, her need for this man devastating. The longing went deeper than the flesh; it reached to the timeless soul, touching her in a way no man before had. The way no man ever would. Only Desmond.

She wanted his hard body pressing her into the mattress, wanted to be over him controlling the pace. Wanted him inside her. The thud of his heart slammed against her thigh as he continued the downward slide. Frustration rising, she wanted to howl as the golden cord kept her stretched, open to his pleasure. She wanted to feel her hands on those wonderfully sculpted muscles, to clutch the arch of his spine as he entered her.

Then his mouth moved on her, on her hot core of need. Incapable of thought, she drowned in the blinding pleasure, the rough lap of his wicked tongue. She splintered into a thousand pieces, coming against his mouth. She feared there'd be no putting Humpty Dumpy back together again.

Desmond reared back and yanked the slipknot on the gold cord. Releasing her, he unlaced the front of his leather pants . . . and cursed.

B.A.'s eyelids batted. "What's wrong, Des?"

"Hang on, love, you're getting ravished by a man in leather pants. The bloody things are glued to me. My skin's too hot and sweaty to get them off."

"Ravished by a man in leather pants!" B.A. grinned. "Am I lucky or what?"

Desmond laughed and finally slid into her slick, welcoming heat.

And ravish her he did! Thoroughly, blissfully, through the night. Once fast, rough and furious, like a summer storm breaking over Falgannon. Next, so slow and tender it brought tears to her eyes. When he set her atop him, she seized the chance to turn the tables. Undaunted, he'd pushed her from one shattering climax to another. Each time she thought she had nothing left to give, he bucked his body into her, harder, deeper, more frantic, until she did his bidding.

She surrendered every response he commanded, leaving her wrung out, shaky.

Nearing dawn, B.A. rested half on her stomach. Desmond kissed the small of her back and spooned his body against hers. Flexing his muscles, he pressed her into the feather mattress. She sensed by his breathing he half-drifted, yet he couldn't stop touching her, kissing her. He stilled, his body relaxing, heavy upon her. It was a weight she relished.

She thought him asleep until he whispered, "B.A.?"

"Mmm?" She stroked her hand over his, resting against her stomach. He lifted it slightly, lacing fingers with hers.

"Don't tell your lads, but I don't have a drop of Viking blood in me."

"They'd forgive you. You've something better, remember. You've Sinclair and Fitzgerald blood."

"Yeah, I do, don't I?" He sighed. "Will you forgive me?"

"Des, I'd forgive you anything," she murmured, her eyelids too heavy to keep open. She savored Desmond's body around hers. Felt safe, protected. Loved.

He squeezed her hand, then noticed the thin gold band with the oval peridot she always wore on her ring finger. She never removed it, not even when she showered. He slid it off and transferred it to his left pinkie finger as if sealing a pact. "Remember that promise, lass. I'm going to hold you to it."

Chapter 20

Sliding across the huge bed, B.A. discovered Des was gone. The feather mattress was cold under her hand. Though the plaint for sleep was strong, she needed to see him. To reassure herself? Of what? Their lovemaking had been beautiful, exciting, consuming—a fantasy brought to life. Yet, underneath, prickles in her blood warned some dark urgency had driven Des, as if he needed to imprint his very essence upon her soul.

An ostrich burying her head in the sand, she hadn't pressed Desmond about anything, not wanting such details to intrude upon their relationship. Why he'd come didn't matter. Still convinced she didn't want Falgannon changed by the flocks of tourists he'd prefer, she'd avoided bringing up the subject. The longer he stayed, the more he became a part of the island. The harder it'd be for him to leave or change it.

Yawning, she ambled down the staircase from the loft. After a quick inspection she established neither Desmond nor Dudley were on the castle—something she instinctively knew. Her cozy little home felt empty, cold without their bright sparks. The bottomless pit and Desmond were probably off in search of Tam's scones.

Hearing a car door slam, she rushed out to meet the pair. Smiling, she watched her men trod up the steps. Desmond carried a warmer tray from The Hanged Man. Dudley hopped in an uneven gait, never taking an eye off it.

No hello, not even a good morning kiss, Desmond launched into a question: "Where's the original flag of Castle Falgannon?"

"There are several older flags put away to preserve them. The winds are harsh here." She slid under his free arm and kissed him a proper good morning. "After last night, the first thing the man asks about is a pennant? Ashamed you should be."

"Where are they?" He wasn't derailed.

"In the vault—"

"At Colford," he growled.

"Don't grit your teeth, Des, you'll get a headache," she teased. "Yes, they're at Colford."

"Falgannon's history belongs on Falgannon, B.A."

"Rather possessive—and suspiciously like a threat." She chuckled, taking some pleasure in that Desmond was so concerned about what belonged to the island. Whether he recognized it or not, he was setting down roots. "What set you off about the pennant?"

"This flag's wrong."

She glanced at the pennant flapping in the breeze, studying it. It was a navy field with a gold cat rampant—inside the gold lozenge, denoting it was a lady's flag. "What's not right about it?"

"The cat's missing faery wings." He blinked, noticing she was dressed. "I was going to feed you breakfast in bed."

"That can be arranged." She took his hand and pulled him inside Lady Cottage. Dudley scampered after them.

A rainbow arched over the island as B.A. spotted Desmond at the castle's crenellations, staring out at the white beach below. Though they'd whiled away the better part of the day laughing and making love, Des seemed haunted. Whatever was biting at him was coming to a head. It tore at B.A., made her wonder again what demons drove him. Panic fluttered in her chest.

She went to him, troubled by the shadows in his eyes after seeing his current series of sketches. They centered on the castle, but these were of people. The woman looked like she herself had in the medieval gown she'd worn yesterday. At first she assumed he'd gotten up during the night and drawn it while she slept. Then she saw the date. Desmond had sketched it a week ago. The other sketch was of a man with long wavy black hair and wearing chain mail and a surcoat.

He stood atop the castle and in the background was a flag—
the cat rampant with wings. A nontraditional heraldic sym-
bol, denoting the *cait sidhe,* faery cats.

Desmond was drawing images from the past. To a man
rooted in logic, that would be hard for him to accept. Did he
even understand why he had got these flashes from the
past? Her eyes studied the solitary figure, debating whether
to broach the subject with him or wait until he came to her.

Desmond sensed B.A. as she approached. "You mentioned
turning Rose Cottage into a honeymoon lodge." Leaning
into a crenellation, he stared down the hill to the cottage.

"I thought it'd be a lovely spot for newlyweds."

"Don't."

Possessiveness boiling in his gut, Desmond didn't want
someone else in that house where he'd first made love to
B.A. He knew she had to be in residence in Lady Cottage
from November until the end of April, but he saw them living part-time there. "Is there a problem with that?"

She kissed his cheek. "No . . . I'll make other plans."

"I'm toying with the idea of adding on some rooms, so I
could have an office."

B.A.'s heart leapt; he could see the erratic pulse in her
neck. "That's . . . doable."

They stood in silence, enjoying the shimmering rainbow.
He finally worked up enough nerve to say what was eating
at him. "Ever wish you could wipe clean the slate, start
over?"

"Des, you're troubled. I'd be a fool not to see it. You awake
bathed in sweat. Memories that deep hurt because you've
buried them. Talking might help."

"Talking *can't* help. This month here with you . . . I don't
know myself anymore. I have no control."

She stroked his arm. "No one could ever take control from
you. You're seeing life away from the glare of bright city
lights. Things have different values for you than a month ago.
We can't erase the past—good or bad, it defines us, molds
us. But we can change the future if we're brave enough."

"Yes, the past made me as I am." He stroked the back of his hand against her cheek. "I'm unsure how to say what I want."

Desmond lightly bit the inside of his cheek to stop the words ready to pop out. He fought himself, the selfish part of him that desperately needed B.A.'s light in his life. It pushed him to come out and ask her to marry him, to bind her to him in every way possible, and damn whatever lay down the road. Maybe a gentleman would lay out the plans for Trident Ventures' leases on the North Atlantic oil wells, plans that had been in motion for so long. How after the first of the year, he would be the new CEO of Trident. Admit he'd planned to use Falgannon as a base for housing, supplies and storage for the wells, changes that would destroy the perfection of this tiny island.

Perhaps he was arrogant enough to believe what was between them could see them through the worst of times. Maybe it was desperation. He knew with B.A. at his side he'd battle wizards and slay dragons. For her he could face anything, even the demons within himself.

Conceit, selfishness, fear—whatever drove him, he couldn't pull back. He needed B.A. in his life, to know he'd be able to hold her in his arms at night come what may.

"The most direct route is the simplest. B.A., will you ma—"

A helicopter rose from behind the north side of the isle. It loomed over the hill and then swooped around the castle like some prehistoric warbird. Desmond's stomach dropped as he saw the big M on the side. The white Sikorsky S-76C was designed for offshore oil rigs, and as the manufacturer said, *It flies like it means business.* It traveled at speeds of 175 m.p.h., could hover even in heavy crosswinds. Seating was for twelve passengers in deluxe comfort, and at its nine-million-dollar price tag, it damn well better, Desmond thought. He knew who piloted it—Julian Starkadder. Julian handled that baby as if it were an extension of himself.

Curving in a circle, Julian pointed the nose at them, hovering to make eye contact. He rakishly saluted Desmond before turning the bird toward the flat area near Rose Cottage.

"Smart enough not to chose the cairn, at least," Desmond muttered to himself.

Cold dread filled him. Why had Julian come? A dozen scenarios flooded his mind, and none were good. He'd thought he had a few weeks, at least until New Year's, before everything would come crashing down on his head, but time had just run out.

"M for Mershan?" B.A. said. "I'm impressed. I know the price tag on that cute little bird. Cian checked around for a used one for the island."

The rakish, black-haired man stepped from the helicopter, removing his reflective sunglasses. His small gold hoop earring glinted as he strode up the hill to meet them.

Julian Starkadder was a throwback to a time of buccaneers and pirates. No one knew much about his past, and with black hair and hazel-green eyes, people often assumed he was a Mershan. Besides his brothers, there wasn't a man Desmond trusted more. In some ways his bond with Julian ran deeper, since Julian had been privy to some of Desmond's darker dealings while he'd kept Jago and Trevelyn's hands clean.

Yes, Julian's arrival on Falgannon spelled trouble. Desmond glanced nervously toward B.A. In the past few weeks he'd pushed aside reality. He hadn't expected the world to intrude so soon.

Panic edged up his spine as he watched Julian walk toward them. He wanted to rage at the the possibility his idyllic time with B.A. was at end. He wanted to grab her and scream *Mine*. Instead, he stood frozen with dread.

Julian's eyebrow arched at Desmond's longish hair, fisherman's knit sweater and knee boots. The other brow rose as he saw the fat cat curving around his boss's ankle and hissing. "Des, your expression matches that rottweiler cat's."

Desmond felt like hissing. "Trouble?"

Julian's countenance revealed nothing. B.A.'s lads would be in trouble if he turned Julian loose at Thursday night poker. "Sorry, you have to come back."

B.A. smiled and offered her hand. "Welcome to Falgannon Isle. You must be one of Desmond's brothers. Jago?"

Turning on a high-wattage smile, he oozed charm. "Not Jago or Trevelyn. Julian Starkadder. I'm Desmond's—"

"Personal assistant," Desmond snapped, irritated by Julian's effect on women.

"You favor Des." B.A. glanced between them, trying to tune in to the nuances of their silent communication.

Julian laughed. "I'm prettier. I hate to be a bother, but could you arrange some hot coffee and sandwiches for me? We don't have much time. I've been on the go most of the day. I'm starving and I'd kill for a cup of coffee."

"Certainly." B.A. sensed she was being dismissed. She didn't act as if she minded. Both men's eyes followed her up the staircase and out of sight.

Julian worried the gold hoop in his left earlobe. "Wow. Wonder if the other sisters have that same effect on a man. Standing near her is like taking a blow to the chest."

"Want a comparison to be sure?" Desmond snapped.

Julian joked, "Your expression is as hostile as that mangy cat's. And cats spray things when they want to mark them."

"There are other ways of marking a woman." Desmond eased up now that his territory was staked. "What's the trouble? Problem with the oil rigs?"

Julian's eyes clouded. "Your mother's dying."

Desmond looked around to see if he had everything. He was only taking some clothes, his briefcase and computer. His teeth gnashed as he fought himself from going to B.A. and telling her the real reason he was leaving.

He could hardly breathe. If he spoke the words, he'd shatter to a thousand pieces. He closed his eyes willing his racing heart to slow. *God, it can't be true.*

Anger and resentment against Sean Montgomerie surged again like a volcano within him. Those emotions had faded this past month. Now they were back, raw, more dangerous. Once out, there'd be no turning back. He wanted to put his fist through a wall.

Julian had apparently reached Trevelyn in London, who'd be waiting in Ireland when they landed. Jago faced the longer flights from Kentucky-to-Atlanta-to-New York, then a transatlantic to Manchester, and finally to Ireland.

Impulse was to tell B.A. the truth. But that was a mistake.

She'd insist on coming with him; she was that giving. If he permitted B.A. to accompany him, he'd be torn by trying to keep things hidden from her. Her presence might cause problems with Jago and Trevelyn, even upset his mother. The mere mention of the name Montgomerie could bring on one of her panic attacks. Also, at the moment he feared the wild emotions careening inside him; the beast was about to break the chains. He didn't want B.A. anywhere near when that happened. It wouldn't be pretty and she didn't deserve what might spill over onto her.

"Sorry, Des." Julian's eyes took in the huge oak bed and its rumpled state. "I judge you've been happy this past month, really happy. You've not had much happiness in life."

Dudley pussyfooted in and curled around Desmond's leg, then hissed at Julian. "Had you said that before I came here, I'd have called you crazy. I didn't know what happy meant." Sadly, he smiled at the fat pussycat, wishing he could stuff him in the suitcase and take him with him. Even Dudley would be a comfort in the coming days. "Yes, I've been happy here."

"You're in love with her," Julian stated simply.

Desmond started to deny it, his typical knee-jerk male reaction. He bit back the words. "Damn me, fool that I am, yes."

"Let nothing stand in your way, Des, especially not the past. It's not worth losing something so rare, so special. I'd give my left arm to have a woman look at me the way she does you."

Desmond studied his friend. "I would've bet you didn't believe in love."

"I didn't—until I saw how B.A. looked at you and you looked at her. That's magic. Don't throw that away because of the past. The past is dead—" Julian flinched.

"Not quite dead." Desmond's resolve hardened.

"Sorry, a lousy choice of words. Revenge will leave you with nothing. *Nothing*, Des."

"Tell that to a dying woman." Desmond closed his eyes, feeling as if his heart was being torn asunder.

B.A. came in carrying a large thermos. "You sure you don't want a hamper of sandwiches? It would be no trouble."

"The one you fixed will tide me over. The coffee's appreciated." Julian took it from her. "It's nice meeting you, B.A.

Next time it won't be such a rush, though you should chain up that cat. He doesn't like strangers."

"He welcomed Des with open arms." She smiled, but Desmond saw her troubled eyes checking the closet to see if he'd left belongings; how she relaxed when she spotted some clothes.

"Well, I'll go get the bird chirping." Julian left, giving them a moment alone.

Desmond started to follow, not trusting himself to be alone in this bedroom with B.A. The scent of their lovemaking still seemed to hang in the air. One breath and he'd drag her back to the bed and bury himself in her heat, the only heat to keep at bay the coldness in his soul. One breath and he'd go down on his knees, wrapping his arms around her.

He dared not touch her or he'd never leave. A tear refracting in her eye nearly undid his resolve.

"I could go with you. I won't take time to pack. I could buy what I need."

He forced a stiff smile. "Who'd feed Dudley?"

"The Marys will." The quaver in her voice was an arrow to his heart.

"I'll call." He kissed her hard on the forehead, then started to push past, only Dudley wrapped his legs around Desmond and scaled his thigh. "Damn it, Dudley, not now!"

B.A. bent down to unstick the cat. Holding the beast tightly, she followed Desmond outside.

A crowd hovered out of range of the helicopter; even Angus was there. It touched Desmond to see the long faces. The Fraser twins came forward to help him with his bags, putting them into the back of the Sikorsky.

Both patted him on the shoulder and shook hands with him. As he climbed into the passenger side, Ian called, "Dunna fash about the lass and the wee beastie. We'll mind them 'til you get back."

Hearing the question. *Are you coming back?*—Desmond nodded, unable to speak. If he spoke, he'd break. He'd need all his strength to face this coming ordeal.

Hand on the door, he caught sight of B.A. standing to the side, alone except for the fuzzy cat in her arms. He met her eyes, knowing this would be hell on her. Not just his leaving and their separation, but he was going away in a helicopter—not much different than a plane.

He stared at B.A. Could only see her. Not thinking, he climbed out of the Sikorsky and stalked to her. He pulled her into his arms and took her mouth with all the passion that burned between them, barely aware he was crushing the squirming kitty. If he could stand here and kiss her forever . . .

Only, there was a fragile woman whose life was slipping away second-by-second. He broke the kiss, leaning his head against the side of hers, inhaling that faint peony scent.

"I love you, lass," he whispered, but was unsure if she heard him or not over the noise of the helicopter. Tears flooding his eyes, he stopped back. He was too damn close to losing it. And Desmond Mershan never afforded himself that luxury. Never in his whole life.

Swallowing, he reached out for the pudgy pussycat. Holding Dudley up in the air, he stared at him nose-to-nose. "Take care of her, Fuzzball." He kissed the silly beast on the head and then shoved him back into B.A.'s arms.

Closing the door on the helicopter, he nodded to Julian. "Get me the hell out of here."

He watched B.A. as the machine rose higher, then Julian kicked the monster into full speed. Her small figure vanished in the gloaming.

Chapter 21

Bing . . . bing . . . bing . . .

That blasted hospital pager caused Desmond to grind his teeth, part of his endless waking nightmare. Desperate for a moment of solitude, he'd come out to sit in the hallway.

The doctors came and went, shaking their heads, resigned to doing little more than making her comfortable. Comfortable? What a joke. They gave her near lethal doses of morphine to ease the pain, and it blocked her consciousness. To Desmond's deep horror, he grew cognizant it didn't block her subconscious from being awake—and in pain. During lucid moments Katlyn succinctly repeated conversations his brothers and he had, yet she'd been knocked out at the time.

By the time Julian had rushed him to his mother's bedside, Desmond had assured himself all his emotions were under control, reined in; questions and worry over B.A. and Falgannon were neatly labeled and compartmentalized. Even so, nothing could've prepared him. Laying eyes upon Katlyn's emaciated body, his mind jumped to the conclusion they'd shown him to the wrong room. This woman was nearly bald. Her thick, wavy black hair, so like his own, was gone; only wispy white strands remained. Her skin was pale, translucent, similar to a woman in her eighties or nineties. Her face was almost blank.

When she'd opened those Irish green eyes, the floor fell out from under him. Reality slammed into him like a brick wall. She'd called him Michael. It broke his heart that she thought he was his father.

Her room was private, so they were able to stay around the clock. In the beginning they wore themselves out keeping a deathwatch. Despite the doctors' assurances she wouldn't last a day or two, she clung to life with a determination that amazed everyone.

They'd taken to staying in shifts. Business needed attention. The world didn't stop because one small woman lay dying. Julian handled problems arising, saw the brothers supplied with clean clothes and dragged them off for decent meals.

Desmond couldn't come to terms with losing her, even though she'd been under nursing care for several years. When he'd visited her in late September, she'd started chemo and responded to the treatment, so he'd hoped—damn, he didn't know what he'd hoped. A good old case of denial. They'd warned him the chemo would likely do little to stem the tide of the cancer.

She'd had a tumor for some time, and had hid the fact until she collapsed a year ago Christmas. When they operated, it busted, sending cancer cells throughout her body. He later learned the cells hit her liver, causing a secondary cancer. When she responded to treatments he'd told himself if they could keep her alive long enough some brilliant researcher would discover that miraculous cure.

The chemo was a Catch-22. While it curbed the cancer, it destroyed her heart and kidneys, forcing the doctors to cease the treatments. Once stopped, she'd slipped into decline within weeks. His fortune could buy her the best medical treatment available, but it couldn't save her.

Bing . . . bing . . . bing. . . .

Desmond leaned his head back and closed his eyes, trying to still the noise inside his head. He was tired. So bloody tired. Sounds about him receded as darkness claimed him.

He stood trembling, cold. He was scared, though unsure why.

Strange men had come to talk with Father. Fraught with emotion, their voices had been raised, angry. He sat on the upstairs landing, his face half stuffed between two stair rails, eavesdropping. The discussion escalated to shouting, then the men stormed out of the house.

Mother went in to soothe Father. She'd always had a magical touch to make him smile, though often no one could do that for her. Father's low mournful words, his mother's voice—edged with hysteria warned one of her moods was upon her. Their murmurs spoke of a desperation that carried to him.

Abruptly, the library door flung back, and Mother—so beautiful in that red velvet gown—dashed down the hall and into the drawing room. Heavy mahogany doors muffled her wracking sobs. Des stood helpless, his heart clenching with each moan torn from his mother.

He glanced toward the library, seeing the door half-open. Maybe he should go tell Father that Mother was so sad, though surely Father heard the crying. Still in Mickey Mouse slippers, his feet carried him into the library.

Father was on the phone, talking to someone, pleading.

He listened to the words, thick with emotions foreign to Desmond's sheltered world. The whispered desperation grew louder.

"Montgomerie, you can't do this!" He held up pieces of paper. "You put up the land on Falgannon, the Kentucky farm and Colford Estate as collateral. Don't tell me you didn't understand the land wasn't yours to promise. You knew, damn you. The only thing that can save me is the lands you promised. You lied! Sean Montgomerie, I hope you rot in hell!"

The receiver dropped from his father's hand. Michael Mershon sat there, a waxen figure like the ones in Madame Tussaud's. He didn't seem to breathe, just sat holding the papers.

Desmond walked toward that big desk with the carved lion heads. "Father?" he queried, uncertain, needing reassurance. Hesitantly he tugged on his father's sleeve, trying to gain his attention.

Michael Mershan turned, seeing his son and yet clearly not comprehending the young boy's panic. His chest rose and fell. Relief flooded through Desmond with that small movement of normality in the man he so loved. Soon, his father would lift him up on his knee, ask Desmond what was wrong and then make everything all right.

Michael Sinclair Mershan did none of those things. Warmth left Desmond as he saw a tear rolling down his father's cheek. His father was crying!

Upstairs, one of the twins wailed. Barely a year old, both babies were cutting teeth and cranky, but no one went to answer the fretting.

"Desmond, you're such a handsome lad. So strong. You must be a big boy now. Go to your mother and help her. Promise you will take care of her and your brothers now."

Desmond nodded, unable to force the words past his tight throat.

His father seemed to shrink within himself. Dismissed, Desmond turned to walk away, hearing a drawer open behind him. He stood trembling, hidden by the tall winged-back chair, his father likely thinking he'd gone. In Desmond's mind, he could see his father open that big deep drawer he kept locked and had forbidden Desmond to open.

Desmond had, once, when both his parents were gone. Putting the key in the brass lock he'd opened the drawer. Inside was a heavy box with a gun with a pearl handle. He'd known better than to touch it.

Apprehension slithering up his spine, he looked around the chair as his father raised his right hand and placed that gun to his temple. Frozen in horror, Desmond heard a sharp report—oddly muffled by the thousands of books covering the library walls—then his father's body jerked.

His mind couldn't absorb the enormity of his father's action. At age seven, he had no way of comprehending how that single moment would so shape his future.

Father's hand fell over the chair arm, twitched, then the gun dropped to the floor. For a shattered instant, the distant eyes struggled to focus and seemed to see his son hiding by the chair. His mouth trembled, trying to form a word. He never spoke it, though Desmond always believed his father had been trying to say, *Sorry*.

Distantly, over the strange buzzing in his head, his mother's scream reverberated through the house . . . through his mind. Beyond a child's awareness, Desmond sensed his world die in the same instant his father drew his last breath.

Bing . . . bing . . . bing.

He jerked awake, blinking against the harsh brightness of the hospital. The damn dream. No, not a dream—nightmare. One that had haunted his whole life. Now, he lived through another. And once again, he was helpless and failing to protect his mother. He'd promised Father he would. He'd promised.

"Mr. Mershan." The nurse materialized before him and said with hushed urgency, "She's asking for you."

Rain fell steadily, though Desmond little noticed. He had no concept of time; he'd walked endlessly. Fleeing his inner demons.

He was tired. So bloody tired.

He found himself standing before a small store—a jewelry store—but he had trouble seeing the items in the window. After minutes, it dawned why he couldn't focus clearly—he was crying. Strange, not to know when one cried.

He blinked away the tears, his eyes fixing on the display of gold Irish wedding bands. One in particular called to him, with the words *Mo Anam Cara*. He sounded out the words. *My soul mate*. The band wasn't expensive. He could afford to give B.A. diamonds that would make Liz Taylor envious. He doubted that would interest her. A second one had a golden topaz, making him think of her whisky-colored eyes.

A plastic sign in the window said, OPEN, so his feet carried him inside. Bells tinkled as he entered, reminding him of Falgannon's store. He missed B.A. Missed that silly cat.

"We're closing," the lady called in a musical lilt, coming from the backroom. Her eyes took in his appearance, softened with concern. "Sir, are you all right?"

He blinked, unsure why he'd come. The ring. "Won't take long. It's a sure sale. The *Mo Anam Cara.*"

" 'Tis a lady's ring you'd be wanting?"

"Oh aye." A faint smile tugged at the corner of his mouth as the island cant slipped naturally into his voice. "The one with the topaz heart."

"Do you know her size?" She pulled out various rings in a velvet tray.

Fool. It had never crossed his mind. Then he glanced down at the thin band of gold with the peridot on his pinkie. He'd taken it from B.A. the last time they'd made love. Reluctantly, he pulled it off. "Match that."

On the third try, she found one. *Third time's the charm*. He needed all the luck he could get. She passed it to him and he slid it on his finger. It went on and then off with the same amount of resistance as B.A.'s ring.

"Will that one do?"

"Perfect." He replaced B.A.'s ring, feeling the comfort of

the warm metal, a tangible piece of her he could hold. Taking out his wallet, he removed his Platinum American Express card. "Do you have engagement rings?" Strange, he glanced over his shoulder expecting the words had come from another.

"I've put them away. If you give me an idea what you're looking for, a price range . . . ?"

"An oval diamond would look lovely on her hand."

She locked the front door. "I have a 4.3 carat that may be what you're looking for. A loose stone. It'd need mounting. I could have it by tomorrow afternoon if you're in a rush."

"I am."

She came back with a velvet box. Opening it, she took out several small pouches. The third and fourth were nearly the same size. Perfect oval diamonds.

"Have the smaller set in a simple platinum band and the larger as a pendant. Can both be ready tomorrow afternoon?"

She pulled out her receipt book and wrote up his order, chuckling again. "Your lady is lucky. Rarely do I get to supply a perfect stone for a perfect lady."

"I don't deserve her."

She handed him the sack with the soul mate ring and the receipt. "Most men aren't worthy of a woman. Ask yourself one question—are you willing to give up *everything* for her? You answer yes, you're worthier than you think."

An hour later, Desmond was still asking that question when a car pulled to the curb. Wipers running, Julian turned on the flashers and waited. Desmond opened the passenger door and slumped into the seat.

"How did you find me?"

"Sherlock Starkadder at your service. I figured you'd head for a jeweler. Second choice was a pub. Lots of pubs in this neighborhood, fewer jewelers."

"I'm tired." Desmond closed his eyes, listening to the rhythmic slap of the wipers.

"You're also twisted with grief and depressed, my friend. So, how much did you spend?"

"I bought a gold Celtic ring and a special stone for a special lady. I hope she won't throw them in my face."

"I doubt it." Julian smiled. "She'll love them. Now ... something to consider when you have to confront what you're going to do about your plans—Jago's in love with Asha, about as bad as you have it. Trevelyn's in over his head and refuses to admit it, but I wouldn't like to come between Raven and him. These Montgomerie sisters really must be something special. I feared the four of us would grow old together, doddering codgers everyone hates. How many are left? Three sisters?"

"Kat recently married. Britt's twin is battling an old flame from the past. But there's always LynneAnne in New York and Paganne, the archaeologist."

"Rule out the archaeologist, she'd bore me to death. And I'm not setting foot in New York again, not even if delicious LynneAnne was waiting naked and wrapped up with a big red bow."

"Wulf and Dennis are retiring, both moving to Falgannon," Desmond said absently.

"Cool, I can come visit for the hols and your kids can call me Uncle Julian."

"Children?" Desmond sat up so fast his head crashed into the top of the car. "Gor, B.A. has the power to cause me peril even at a distance."

"You'll get used to the idea, Daddy Des."

It had never occurred to him to ask B.A. if she used birth control. He doubted it. And his package of condoms sat untouched in his suitcase. Desmond leaned back, calling himself a bloody idiot. He had never let that detail slip before. The image of B.A. pregnant made him feel strange inside. Scared him spitless.

Yet, something stronger rose inside him, as powerful as the demons that haunted his soul. He'd never imagined himself a father. Never wanted to be one. In many ways he'd been both a mother and father to Jago and Trevelyn; raised them, saw they had the best life he could give.

Desmond thought back when he turned fifteen and

landed a job with Bentley Construction by lying to the owner and saying he was seventeen. He'd needed money—not teenager's wages, but a man's pay. The twins had needed glasses and new clothes for school in the fall. He'd wanted to see them with the best, not hand-me-downs as he'd had. He recalled coming in after a long day of hammering, his body aching with every fiber.

Yes, he'd used up all his fatherly urges before his twenty-first birthday. Contrarily, a grinding hunger now awoke within him, one that hoped B.A. was pregnant. It was a tie that might bind them when he destroyed her family's holdings.

Chapter 22

Chilling rain whipped around Desmond, lashing his face. It would be a simple matter to tilt the umbrella for more protection, but that required caring. He was dead inside. In a dark corner of his soul, the beast growled in rage, in frustration . . . in madness. Numb, he just stood, holding a blood-red rose, and stared impassively. Trevelyn and Jago watched him, concern in their green eyes, but it was too much effort to reassure them he was all right.

He *was* all right. Wasn't he?

Jago crossed to him and placed a hand on his arm. "Come on, Des. It's not necessary to stay while they fill in the grave."

Desmond couldn't move. He felt rooted to the spot. Sounds of the shovels tossing the wet dirt into the hole was the only noise the three graveyard workers made. They raked the last clumps on top, then laid the sod rolls and finally the elaborate wreaths. One from each son, one from Julian.

Somehow, Desmond had failed his mother yet again. As a child he hadn't been able to lighten her sorrow when the black moods seized her. A simple country lass, she hadn't been prepared to raise her sons alone. Katlyn Fitzgerald

Mershan had been a beautiful, fragile lady, as delicate as an orchid—and as easily crushed.

He was grown before he understood what afflicted his mother, realized there were treatments for what they now called bipolar disorder. Back then, it was labeled manic-depression. Few spoke of the condition.

Through hard work he'd made something of himself, seen his brothers raised with every advantage. But his money could do nothing to ease her pain and suffering.

"Des, it's over." Jago squeezed his elbow.

Desmond jerked away. "It's *not* over. Not 'til we take down Montgomerie Enterprises."

Uneasy, Jago glanced at Trevelyn. He said, "You wish to go ahead with the plans?"

Rage boiled inside him. "You ask that? She's barely in the ground—a woman whose life was ruined by Sean Montgomerie."

"If Montgomerie was here, I'd strangle him with my bare hands," Jago pressed, "but taking the son-of-bitch's mistakes out on his granddaughters isn't the way, Des. Two wrongs don't make a right."

"I'm not 'taking it out on the granddaughters.'" Desmond swallowed back shards of conscience. "I'm merely claiming what Sean put up as collateral. Move the plans up, I want it done."

Stepping to the grave, Desmond raised the red rose to his nose. Images of B.A. and her white rose shimmered in his mind. B.A.'s rose before Lady Stone was purity, the hope of a future touched by magic. The promise of happiness. In contrast, he stared transfixed at the rose in his hand—a blood-red rose. *Blood vengeance.*

Pain lanced his heart, his soul. Quashing down his questions, his doubts, he kissed the red rose then placed it atop his mother's grave. Not looking back, he stalked off into the rain. Alone.

B.A. dragged the stepladder over to hang the mistletoe at the archway of The Green Man. Her eyes glanced to the calendar on the wall, hardly believing Des had been gone nearly a month. Butterflies of doubt fluttered in her stomach. She muttered under her breath, "He's coming back."

"The Curse is punishing our B.A. for importing females," Callum announced to the pub. "I told you this would happen, B.A."

Ian snagged a Wee Heavy from the cooler and sat on a stool, eyeing Falgannon's voice of doom. "You didn't tell me." He looked to his twin. "He tell you?"

Brian leaned the pool cue against the wall. "Not me."

"Nor me," Jock added. "He tell you, Angus?"

"Ehhh?" Angus squinted, trying to hear.

B.A. laughed when Ian leaned over and said loudly, "Dunna ken why you squint because you can't hear. *Turn on your trannie.*"

Angus rapped his cane on the floor. "B.A., tell this pup there ain't need to scream at a body. Don't need the thing on if everyone would stop whispering."

Tugging on the garland—which had a cat attached to the end of it—she watched the men around the bar drinking pints, their faces a mixture of emotions. They wanted to laugh at Callum's dire pronouncement, yet were fearful in the same breath it had a ring of truth. One didn't trifle with The Curse.

"While we all want to get married, we like our peaceful ways. During the past few weeks our quietude has been put asunder, B.A.," Callum continued. Everyone muttered *aye* and nodded in agreement.

"Boy, had they got that right," B.A. sniggered.

She hadn't foreseen the lunacy the Web site would bring to the isle. The paratrooping incident had just been a beginning. The past two weeks, boatloads of crazed females sporadically patrolled the shores, waving and yelling, trying to discover where to land. Once, three jumped off the boat and swam to the pier. Then there had been the Blond Brigade—five amazons who landed in a hot air balloon. It didn't stop there. Two more used a hang-glider pulled behind a boat, and another Jet-Skied in after being dropped by a cruiser.

B.A. had let the last stay. The woman decorated the Jet-Ski

to look like Splendid Mane, the mythical seahorse of Man-annan MacLir. When the woman landed, she offered a tale of how Splendid Mane had carried her away and brought her to this beautiful isle. Originality and knowledge of Celtic lore earned her enough points to stay.

The phone rang, drawing B.A. Part of her hoped it might be Des, but he generally rang late at night. Seeing as her hands were full, Ian started toward the phone.

She told him, "If that's Katie Couric again, tell her I moved to Poland."

" 'Tis Cian the Brother." Ian held out the receiver.

B.A. groaned, climbing down. She'd dodged her brother's calls for three weeks. "Cian. What a delight. How's Dad? Getting ready for the hols at Colford?"

"Damn it, B.A., I've left dozens of messages. Why haven't you returned my calls?"

"Busy. 'Tis the season. A lot of decorating and shopping to do."

B.A. stuck her tongue out at the phone; her brother expected the world to drop to its collective feet and grovel whenever he snapped his fingers. Holding the phone between her head and shoulder while unwinding the garland proved a struggle, as Dudley was intent on killing the glittery snake monster and wouldn't let go.

"Have you seen Mershan's paperwork yet? Can you fax it?"

She said evasively, "I don't have a fax, Brother mine. We're lucky to get Internet. Never needed to fax anything."

"You have a scanner?"

She could care less what had brought Desmond to the island. If he wanted to claim part of Falgannon . . . well, she intended to be Mrs. Mershan come spring. The question of ownership would be moot then.

"B.A., I need those papers."

She sighed. "Cian, I don't want a hotel. I've been clear on that. Anything else—it dinna matter. I plan on marrying him."

"*Marry?*" Her brother's stunned voice came through the wire. "He's asked you?"

B.A could barely hear Cian for the racket of her lads clinking glasses and laughing over her declaration. "No, but I'm a

Montgomerie. I never listen to anyone. I'm going to marry him. He'll come around to the idea."

"You hardly know him. Damn it, B.A, the man is a shark."

"What shark? He's an architect." She wiggled the garland for Dudley.

"He's also head of Mershan International. He and his brothers buy a lot of businesses on the skids, turn them around and sell them for huge profits."

"Good for them. Think of the jobs saved. You should admire that, since Montgomerie Enterprises the same."

"You're not going to listen, are you?" he accused.

"Och, we Montgomeries never listen. Ask anyone on my whole bloody isle."

"You haven't introduced this man to the family."

"My family *here* adores him. That and how I feel tells me all I need to ken. Anything else dunna matter—only details Des and I can handle together."

"Bring him for the holidays, B.A. Give the family a chance to get to know him."

"Sorry, I want to spend our first Christmas on the isle."

"I still want copies of his paperwork."

"First chance I get." *Maybe after the marriage,* she vowed silently. "Must go, Dudley and I are decorating the pub. Tell everyone there I love them. Ta."

Desmond stared out the car window, watching water stream down the glass. The rain, the swooshing of tires on the wet pavement, was soothing. *The soft,* B.A. called this type of rain. As he rode in the back of the black limo through London, he experienced a strange nothingness in his heart. He welcomed the lack of emotion, but knew there were too many things outside his control waiting to crowd inward, to disturb this mental solitude.

Aware of his brothers' furtive glances, he feigned ignorance. Jago was stoic, maintaining a stiff upper lip. Red-eyed, Trevelyn kept tears at bay, replacing the pain with a desire for vengeance. Like Desmond, he blamed his mother's death squarely on Sean Montgomerie.

Retreating into himself, Desmond sighed. He hadn't

rested much for weeks; even then, the sleep had been haunted. Nightmares and B.A., neither was ever far from his mind. A schism had opened in his psyche, a crack down the middle of him that he didn't know how to stop. He feared what would happen when it reached his care. He ignored his dread by hiding in the vacuum where no emotions existed.

Trevelyn had his briefcase open, was studying blueprints for the triple oil platforms. "I see no earthly reason not to push this through. I say we step up the timetable for the Trident Ventures takeover bid of Montgomerie Enterprises, then we can go public with Mershan International buying out Trident. I'm tired of this hanging fire. I want it done. Finished."

Desmond let the words roll off him. Rain beaded the tinted windows as he watched the passing city streets. Everywhere were signs of Christmas. Store windows glistened with miles of red, green and gold tinsel.

"Trev, there's no sense messing up everyone's holidays. A few weeks won't matter." Jago rubbed the back of his neck, clearly exasperated.

"*Our* holidays were messed up. Years of them. You think Mum looked forward to Christmas knowing there was little she could give us? I recall one Christmas we were damn lucky to have something to eat, because she came down with pneumonia and couldn't work. She needed to be in the bloody hospital, but wouldn't go—"

"What I recall was Desmond getting up sick and doing his paper route before school so we could eat." Jago glanced at Desmond. "I'm so sick of this song and dance that 'we had it hard growing up.' Yes, we did. But we stayed together as a family, thanks to Des. It's past, and has been for a long time."

"The point being how our mother suffered—what it did to her health. It put her in the grave," Trevelyn snarled.

"Maybe we should drop it." Jago gritted his teeth. "We can't live in the past. There are other things to worry about now."

"If we get this business done, we can have closure."

"Sometimes I find it hard to believe you're my twin. You're so thick—"

Traffic stalled, bringing the limo to a halt. Desmond pushed open the door. Leaving it standing wide, he walked down the street.

"Where the bloody hell is *he* going?" Trevelyn said.

Ignoring his brothers, Desmond walked to a pet store, peered inside. A pretty blond clerk opened the door, holding it for him. Desmond walked in and stared at the kittens on display.

"We have some gorgeous Seal Pointe Siamese . . ." the clerk suggested.

"I want a tabby." He studied the cats, fought the urge to take them all, but one dark gray caught his attention. It sat trembling, so scared. "*That* one."

The clerk opened the pen and removed the cat by the scruff of its neck. Desmond frowned and snatched it away, as though he suspected she planned on feeding it to the dogs on the other side of the room. The kitten snuggled down in the curve of his elbow and sighed.

"She's taking to you," the blond commented.

"Cats love me." Desmond glared at Trevelyn, who'd appeared and smothered a laugh. "I'll need a pet carrier, food, bowls . . . toys."

Trevelyn glanced at his watch impatiently, but Desmond just smiled. His brother rolled his eyes as collars, bags of catnip, wind-up mice, climbing perches, cat beds and a clawing post were also purchased.

"Oh, and two cases of the catnip bubbles." Desmond pointed.

Trev closed his eyes and shuddered.

B.A. pushed open the door to Patrick's shop, her eyes dancing over the glass cases of gold and silver jewelry. Breathtaking torques, cuffs, brooches and rings twinkled under the lights.

Boxing an item to ship, Patrick smiled at Kitty, who jumped up on the glass and left paw prints. "Hello to you, wee beastie. Evening, B.A. Let me guess why you've come."

"Evening, Patrick." She chuckled. "I'm that big a pain then? Sorry, I want these gifts to be perfect."

"I have the ring." He leaned back in his chair and yelled into the house, "Skylar, our lass is here."

He opened a velvet case, showing a heavy gold ring. A one-of-a-kind design, it was precisely as she'd envisioned it: a gold winged faery cat over the onyx stone, edged with the Celtic loveknot border.

"Patrick, it's stunning!"

"Wait till you see Skylar's handiwork."

Footsteps sounded on the stairs as Skylar bounced down. He said, "Expect she's here about this." He carried a blanket like it was wrapped about a baby. "I think she'll be satisfied."

Pushing Dudley aside, he placed the plaid on the glass case and unfolded it to reveal a gleaming sword. Skylar was right. B.A. was satisfied and knew her expression reflected it.

The claymore was five-foot tall, and while Patrick's ring was beautiful, the sword was magnificent. In her soul she knew the blade would be treasured by Des, a gift to speak of her love for him. She recalled him reverently holding the Sword of The Sinclair. Soon, he could hold one that was his own. The pommel was engraved with the Faery Cat rampant, matching the ring, while the hilt was wrapped with the same black leather Tam had used for his pants. A fitting touch, she thought, a smile spreading across her face.

It was beautiful. It was exquisite.

"Does it please you?" Skylar asked, knowing full well he'd done magic.

"Oh aye, the Sword of The Mershan pleases me."

Chapter 23

"Harrods is supposed to have *everything*." Desmond's words sounded like a threat.

Strolling up, Julian assessed his boss's mood. Sacks and boxes were piled everywhere. Turning, he arched a brow at the Mershan twins. "He trying to buy out the store?"

"Good you came." Jago stopped trying to sort out all the parcels. "We'll need the Rover to load this stuff. With the cat carrier in the limo—"

Trevelyn chuckled at Julian's scowl. "Don't ask."

Desmond was hounding the poor clerk: "Isn't that what you advertise?"

At a loss for words, she made helpless circles in the air. "Cowboy chaps aren't in high demand in Britain, and I'm not sure what a ten-gallon hat is, sir. We're metric."

"Don't forget the spurs that go jingle-jangle-jingle," Desmond reminded with a glare.

"Of course, sir. How could I forget?"

Julian eyed Desmond, clearly not believing his ears. "He's gone cowboy?"

"Gifts for a Willie the Writer." Jago gestured to the dozens of boxes, some already wrapped with Christmas paper and bows. "He's shopping for the whole bloody island."

Julian took out a stick of gum, and put it in his mouth. He kept his words low so they didn't reach Desmond or Trev. "And he still thinks he's going to destroy Falgannon?"

"He's in denial, not even thinking. Grief will hit him like a sledgehammer. Once he gets past that, he'll have to face the problem of B.A. Montgomerie and her island."

Julian suggested loudly, "Let's pack up the shopaholic and send him back to B.A. She's what he needs."

Trevelyn turned around and gawked. "The Pod People get you?"

Julian met his level stare. "B.A.'s one hell of a woman, and he's in love with her."

"I thought you didn't believe in love," Trevelyn scoffed.

"Desmond didn't. Jago didn't. *You* didn't." Julian shook his head. "Tell me you don't believe in it now."

"Where's the manager?" Desmond glared at the poor clerk, who backed up.

"Des, stop harassing the poor lady." Julian shoved a package into his boss's hands. "You forget the magic of the Internet. Gather the part of the store you now own and we'll head to the hotel. We'll get Google the best set of chaps and boots we can find."

"Please!" Jago gathered several stacks. "I thought he'd never get out of the woman's lingerie department. He bought five of everything."

"Thought *we* wouldn't get out of the lingerie department." Trevelyn shuddered. "The women were circling like we had price tags on us. Shopping is a form of torture!"

Julian laughed. "You didn't enjoy the fellowship?"

"Bah-humbug." Trevelyn threatened, "If I hear another Christmas carol, I'll puke."

Julian lowly began to sing "Christmas, Christmas time is near, time for toys and time for cheer . . ."

Desmond glanced at the kitten chasing its tail on the king-size bed. Watching her brought a peace to him. He tossed her the cap off his pen, and she delighted in pouncing on it. In the chair next to him, Julian surfed the Net, buying lizard-skin cowboy boots, spurs and a felt cowboy hat.

"What's with the 'head 'em up, move 'em out' routine?" Trevelyn shifted dinner plates from a tray to the table.

"The cowboy is done. What's next, Santa?" Julian asked.

Desmond stretched, then yawned. "A motorbike for a kid—something for on-road and off. Have it shipped to Falgannon. Tomorrow order another Rover—dark blue or green—and see it's ready for me to drive as soon as possible."

"Ho ho ho, your wish is my Google." Julian clicked the mouse.

"Who's the bike for?" Jago poured a whiskey-and-water

and sat it before his brother. Desmond tapped his fingers at Jago's mother hen routine, but accepted the drink and took a sip.

"A juvenile delinquent who needs to be locked up."

Jago laughed, shaking his head. "A new bike will punish him."

"Actually, it's to keep my sanity. If I have to listen to Wee Dougie's *putt-putt-putting* much more, I'm apt to toss the lad and that sewing machine engine into the *cuan*."

Jago laughed, "Our brother dear has acquired a bit of a burr."

"Desmond, here's one: 125cc Enduro style motorbike delivered to your door." Julian spun the laptop around to show the picture.

"Perfect. Also, order a helmet—something that doesn't look like a virtual reality helmet."

Julian chuckled. "I'm not asking."

Desmond reached for the bottle of scotch only to have Jago snatch it from him.

"No more until you eat. You look like hell, Des."

"I feel like hell. Will all this stuff fit into a Rover?"

Julian stopped clicking keys. "Two people, a cat and half of Harrods? Sure."

"Two people?"

"Jago goes back to Kentucky, while Trevelyn returns to Colford," Julian said. "He'll be nearby so he can handle things for a few days. So, guess who's elected to see you get to Falgannon in one piece?"

"We might have a problem. Asha's talking about coming to England for Christmas." Jago let that sink in. "Problems will arise if Trevelyn and I both are invited to Colford."

Trevelyn paced to the window, his face drawn. "I've already been."

"Is Asha serious?" Picking up a knife and fork, Desmond started eating.

"Maybe. She's furious at Daddy Dearest for selling the horse farm." Jago looked glum.

"Sweep her away to Hawaii for Christmas," Desmond suggested.

Jago shook his head. "She's not the Hawaii type."

Trevelyn crossed his arms and then raised a hand to run his thumb across his lower lip. "If we put our plan into action, then if Jago and I were in the same room, I wouldn't have to exclaim 'What ho, my long-lost twin the gypsies stole!'"

"Trev, you're daft." Jago slammed his glass down on the tabletop, showing his first display of emotion through the whole ordeal. "You're silly buggers if you think Raven or Asha will ask either of us anywhere after all this comes down."

Desmond lost his appetite. Placing his silverware on the plate, then put his elbows on the table and steepled his fingers. He was bloody tired. "Let's put the timetable to a vote."

Julian poured a glass of ice water, eyeing them. "Vote on *this* issue first—anyone not in love with a Montgomerie sister raise his hand."

Julian sat down and held up his, then looked around the room.

Ringing shattered the night's stillness. Grumbling because Jock hadn't put a phone jack in the bedroom yet, B.A. dislodged Dudley and rushed downstairs.

"Sorry to call so late, B.A."

Not Desmond. "Cian. I was just watching the rain on the skylight. Everyone all right?"

"They're fine. I'm just disconcerted with trends on ME stock."

She laughed. "You picked the wrong shoulder to cry on, wee Cian."

"You call me that because you're at the other end of Britain," he growled, then sighed. "B.A., something's hinky. Sean destroyed boxes of documents, which sets off warning bells to me."

"Doesn't matter." B.A. sat on the leather sofa, Dudley crawling into her lap. "I'm going to marry Desmond."

Her brother cleared his throat nervously. "I also did some digging on Mershan International. They keep a low profile.

Your Desmond designs skyscrapers with big price tags. He was in the running to rebuild the Twin Towers in New York, but abruptly pulled out. Rumors are he's pooled his resources for a big project."

She teased dryly, "Cian, you know Des isn't a conman, so why this late night call?"

"Someone's buying up ME stock left and right. People were approached off market, asking if they'd sell. I'm guessing they have about thirty-four percent of the stock. Someone's positioning for a hostile takeover."

"The family retains fifty-one percent of the stock. So?"

"I learned who's behind the offer on Valinor. Trident Ventures. They deal with petroleum speculation. What would a petroleum firm want with a horse farm in Kentucky?"

"Maybe they want to get into horseracing—a tax write-off."

"The tax laws were tightened. It's why Dad wants out." Cian paused. "I really dislike Mershan showing up. Maybe it's coincidence, but I don't believe in them. If you do, you're apt to get bitten in the arse."

B.A. joked, "Des has permission to bite my arse anytime he takes a mind."

Cian conceded, "You sound happy."

"I love Desmond. Nothing else matters."

"Please, B.A. Change your mind. Bring Desmond for Christmas. Let the family meet him."

"Sorry. Our first Christmas will be on Falgannon."

He sighed. "All right. It's been a long time since you sounded happy. Night, B.A."

"Night, Cian." B.A. hung up the phone and patted Dudley. "Race you back to bed."

Desmond stood in the darkened hotel room, staring at London's stormy skyline, the phone ringing in his ear, and mentally kicking himself for calling B.A. at three in the morning. Knowing how she pushed herself, he hoped she'd eaten. He should hang up and let her rest. But he couldn't. He needed to hear her voice.

"Cian, go to bed," came her sleepy words.

"If I didn't know Cian was your brother, I might be jealous."

"Des?"

"Forgotten me so soon, B.A.?"

She laughed. "I have, but The Cat Dudley hasn't. He wants to ken when you're coming home."

Coming home. Her voice poured through him like liquid heat. He'd been a month without her. What he wouldn't give to hold her now, to smell the haunting fragrance of pink peonies. "Soon."

"Can't be soon enough for Dudley . . . or me." She said, "I miss you. I'd say the whole island misses you, but this is the lads' long weekend in Ullapool."

"I've missed the lads, the silly cat . . . you." Desmond brought his hand up, seeing his reflection in the glass. He touched his fingertips to the mirrored image, feeling like he was touching not the reflection of his hand, but B.A.'s.

He still experienced visions, but no longer doubted they were memories from Iain Sinclair. He'd never believed in curses, kitties that played poker or love, but B.A. had taught him all these things. Regardless how it might go against logic, he felt the hand of destiny upon his life.

All that had come before merely led him to B.A. From the day he locked eyes with her in an ancient Norman kirk, to when compulsion pushed him years ago to clip her photo from that magazine and carry it in his wallet.

To have B.A. in his life required breaking a promise to his mother, one made hundreds of times as a child and repeated in the hospital by her deathbed as her frail hand grasped his, her eyes beseeching. If he lost B.A. over fulfilling that vow, it'd kill something inside him. Forsaking the oath he gave to his mother would see him die, too.

"Des, are you all right?" Perceptive B.A. Even distance didn't lessen her fae quality, the connection between them.

Leaning back, he shut his eyelids. Fought tears. He wasn't all right. And he had no idea how to set things straight. He wanted B.A., needed her with an unfathomable ache. At the same time, he couldn't shut out images of his mother, her pleas to make the Montgomeries pay.

"I'm not sleeping well," he said.

"Come *home,* Des."

Home. Home and B.A. "Soon. I'm going to get a few hours' sleep. Night, B.A."

"Night, Des. I—"

He hung up, cutting her off, fearful she was going to say she loved him. As much as he craved to hear the words, he knew he couldn't accept them without saying them back. Right now, that would be a knife in his heart.

He remained staring out into the rain-soaked landscape for a long time.

Chapter 24

"Eh, B.A., I think you missed putting garland on The Escape Artists," Ian teased as he watched the foxhounds race by the storefront.

Balanced atop a rickety stepladder, B.A. stuck out her tongue. Tacking garland around the door to the back room, she yanked on the strand, but it was snagged. Again. Turning, she frowned.

"Kitty, dunna shred that. You want everything special for Desmond, eh?"

At the name, Dudley dropped the garland and ran to the bay window. Crawling up into the display, he pressed his nose to the glass, peering intently down the hill to the harbor. Poor thing seemed convinced Desmond would show up soon.

B.A. sighed, hoping he was right.

"Tree's up, B.A." Ian held it upright while Brian fixed the base.

"Thanks, I appreciate you sorting it out for me."

Brian grinned. "Hope our Desmond likes decorating trees. Plenty waiting." Both pubs, the store, Rose Cottage, Lady Cottage and the town hall . . .

"Okay, I can take the hint. I plan to enjoy this holiday sea-son, to celebrate every one of the twelve days of Christmas." She glanced about the store, now decked with fancy gar-land. Her lads deemed her tinsel-mad, but she didn't mind.

A blast from the ferry horn announced its arrival. She leaned to see past the rack of Walkers' crisps to the dock. Nearly dark, she observed little more than lights, but the pat-tern was different. The glass was starting to fog up around the edges, so it was hard to tell, but she thought a pair of headlights on high beam shone off the ferry's rear.

A ruckus arose as the door to The Hanged Man flew open and the "Morn, B.A." Club piled out. Within seconds, The Es-cape Artists dashed up, barking and chasing the old men. Naturally, Wee Dougie puttered up on his scooter, hoping to make everyone feel more alive.

B.A. laughed. Looking out the window, Dudley vibrated like a tuning fork. How *dare* the islanders do anything with-out him being smack in the middle!

"Hasn't been such a brouhaha since our Vikings invaded." Ian followed Brian to the door.

Dudley darted out as Wee Gordie flew in, crashing into the counter. "Did you see, B.A.? The isle has another Rover. It's loaded with stuff. Did you order it, B.A.? What are all the boxes for? Did you buy me a present?"

Car lights came up the steep hill and stopped before the store. The islanders crowded around a dark sedan. B.A.'s heart flipped and she nearly fell from the ladder as the crowd parted and she spotted the black-haired man.

With Dudley leading, the man came through the door, The Escape Artists circling his legs. Surprisingly, he didn't trip. He hesitated, shot a fleeting look at the new jars of sweets, then glanced upward to see if any dangerous ob-jects were suspended overhead. His eyes locked with hers and the world shifted on its axis. His virile perfection stirred B.A. as no man had, no man ever would.

She descended the wobbly ladder as he strode to the counter with a panther's grace and bent to set his leather duffle on the floor. Dizziness buzzed in her blood as she girded herself to face him for the first time in over a month. Would he feel the same? Would their passion burn as bright?

Then he raised up, meeting her stare . . . and everything stilled.

His eyes, those pale green warlock eyes, were capable of freezing with the arch of a brow or of burning her with a lover's passion. Lifting her chin, B.A. fought a frisson as their gazes locked. Pestered by the moggie on the countertop, Des ran his hand along Dudley's spine. The gesture triggered vivid memories of that hand upon B.A.'s body, stroking with the same sensual magic. She was right. He was a bloody warlock. *Her* warlock!

The Cat Dudley arched under his hand for maximum contact, turned and head-butted his arm for more pets. Desmond's gaze narrowed on her, shocking B.A. with its heat. They slowly raked over her face, the dark gold hair fanning about her shoulders, down to her breasts and then lower—a path of scorching fire that traveled back up to lock stares with her. His appraisal finished, he watched her, knowing things about her, secrets they'd shared, things he *dared* her to forget. The well-formed lips parted. Arrogant man.

Eyes dancing, he said, "I'm looking for B.A. Montgomerie, Lady of the Isle."

Her traitorous body roared to life. Breasts heavy, tips sensitive, without glancing down she knew the thin silk of her red blouse outlined the crowns of her nipples. The bloody man had that effect upon her! And the external reaction was nothing compared to her rampant emotions.

She lifted her chin. "What might you be wishing with B.A. Montgomerie?"

Gently pushing away the persistent cat, he smiled. "We've business. I presume you're expecting me?"

"You need written permission to land," she challenged.

"I don't need it. Ask Dudley. I own a third of the isle."

"So you say."

"You haven't investigated that?" he asked in surprise.

"I've been . . . busy." She shrugged, then gestured. "Decorating."

His eyes took in the naked tree in the corner, the garland framing the windows, and the strand halfway around the door, half on the floor. "I see. With Dudley helping."

"I'll check . . . one of these days."

"B.A.," he rumbled. "Shut up and come here."

"Gone a month and thinks he can come in here—"

B.A. squealed as he hopped on the counter and swiveled his hips, his feet coming down on the other side. Dudley sprang, joining in the new game. Grabbing her waist, Des spun her into the store office and deftly kicked the door shut, blocking out all the nosy islanders peering through the windows.

Her nagging doubts faded as he pinned her against the door. The distinct scent belonging to Desmond made her light-headed. Closing her eyes, she relished the weight of his lean, hard body—sensory overload after a month without him. He lowered his head to kiss her slowly, gently, thoroughly, her body burning with his fire.

Breaking off, he complained, "Your cat is biting me."

She glanced at Dudley gnawing on his ankle. "The wee beastie missed you."

"I missed you both." Reaching down, he ruffled Dudley's fur. "Did *you* miss me, B.A.?"

"Not a'tall, you arrogant man."

"You know what happens when you call me arrogant." The tip of his index finger traced the line of her jaw, throat and down the red silk blouse to circle the tip of her breast.

Shuddering, B.A. stroked his face. Blind excitement over his coming home ebbed, and she registered how drawn he looked. His face was leaner, harder; shadows under his eyes denoted little sleep for weeks. B.A. blinked at how gaunt he appeared. Her fae voice whispered Desmond had been through emotional hell this past month.

Hiding her concern, she slid her leg along his inner thigh. "Refresh my memory."

Kitty scaled Desmond's leg like a lumberjack. "Ouch, varmint," he gasped. Removing the kitty, he held Dudley up nose-to-nose. "I'm going to lock you—wait a minute, I bought a present for you."

He shoved the cat at B.A. and dashed outside.

B.A. looked Kitty in the face. "We'll take him home, fatten him up with Tam's scones and love those shadows from under his eyes. Now let's see what the Magic Man brought you."

Desmond returned, toting a cat carrier. B.A. chuckled to herself, thinking she'd like to see Des *try* to put Dudley in that. But setting it on the floor, he opened it. Dudley and she drew the same conclusion—the carrier wasn't the gift, but what was inside. B.A. pressed her hands together over her mouth, fearing what would happen.

Dudley arched like a Halloween cat. Of course, since Dudley resembled a fur-covered football with legs, he was very comical striking the pose.

A puff of dark gray fuzz peeked out. Seeing Desmond, the kitten exited.

B.A. gasped. "Oh, she's precious! But Des, watch the cat. Dudley dunna do competition."

Desmond held the kitten before him. Dudley inched forward, acting as though Des held a tiny cobra. "See, Pal? She's a wee lass. We'll have to watch out for her, protect her. Females are delicate and can be hurt easily."

Desmond glanced at B.A., wariness in his eyes. That little-boy-lost look. Was he insecure about her feelings? How silly. She'd been an easy mark for Desmond. Despite all fears and trepidations, she'd fallen into his arms with hardly any effort on his part.

"What's the kitten's name?"

"Annie."

"The Cat Annie?" She squatted down and stroked Desmond's cheek.

So much love was in this man, aching to get out. He was close to his brothers, a brilliant architect, a powerful businessman, only she doubted anyone had been there for him. Whatever troubled Des, her love and Falgannon's magic would soothe him.

His friend Julian came in, immediately faced by Dudley in attack cat mode. "I see the Grendel of Falgannon still hates me. How's he taking the dust bunny?"

"He hasn't attacked, so we're progressing well." B.A. rose, offering a smile. "Are you going to stay awhile?"

Desmond stood, clutching the kitten. "I've invited Julian for the holidays."

B.A. beamed. "Wonderful! What about your brothers? Plenty of room at Rose Cottage. I'd love for them to come."

Desmond placed the kitten in the carrier. "I believe they have plans."

"Maybe next year," B.A. suggested hopefully.

Touched with sadness, Desmond's eyes met hers. "Maybe."

Desmond found it strange being back on the island. His month on Falgannon had sped by too quickly. The month away felt like a lifetime. Pulling into Rose Cottage's driveway knocked him off kilter. Exhaustion pulled at him, though his heart was warmed by the peace of coming home.

As his eyes adjusted, he noticed the cottage's shape was different. "You let the Marys turn the cottage into a hostel for brides?"

"The lads did a little work. Come see."

Julian climbed out the car, lifting his brow when B.A went inside without stopping to unlock the door. Desmond shrugged and followed. He noticed a door in the living room wall; beside the base of the staircase now led into a large room.

B.A. took his hand. "You mentioned wanting an office . . . You now have a wonderful view with a bay window, and a second fireplace to keep you cozy." When he stared, he saw her grow afraid she'd gone too far. "Well, let me get Julian settled—"

"Not in the master bedroom," he growled.

She kissed his chin. "The other bedrooms are furnished now."

Desmond looked about the room, touched by B.A. creating this space for him. The wall where the room joined the house had been turned into bookshelves. He envisioned his desk cattycornered, his drafting board over by the window where he could work yet enjoy the beauty of Falgannon. He envisioned B.A. sitting in the window seat reading while Dudley lazily napped, his tail snapping as The Kitten Annie chased it.

A sinking sensation hit him, feeling as if a part of him was lost. He wasn't sure how to find it . . . but if he didn't, he'd never be whole again.

B.A. lifted her arms about Desmond's neck as he slid his own around her lower back, pulling her against him. Nothing had ever felt so right. Their bodies were perfect together. This was where she belonged.

Skin to skin she pressed against him, reveling in his feel, his scent. She hungrily watched those green eyes. So many things were in there. Lust was foremost, but she also saw surprise, wonder, challenge . . . awe.

The corner of her mouth quirked with womanly knowledge. While she was humbled by the power of what rose between them, she accepted it, surrendered to it. She'd known love before, known the security of belonging with another, to another. B.A. grasped how special this bond was between them.

Love. Pure and bright.

Desmond had no idea what was hitting him. Like most men, they tended to think with something lower than their brain. Love sneaked up on them, surprised them. Not that she was arrogant, she sensed Desmond had never experienced true love before. Males had a propensity to be cautious, to fear the enormity of emotions beyond their control. Men—especially powerful men used to absolute rule—were scared by this. They couldn't face how helpless they felt before the force of such overwhelming, consuming passion. The sexual side they could handle, but the emotional need was beyond their dealings. Some men ran.

Des wasn't a runner. He'd step up to the challenge. That sexy mouth twisted into a crooked grin, so she nibbled on his lower lip, then bit down slightly, feeling his body buck against hers.

Desmond tumbled them into bed and set her atop him. He smiled at the mass of her blond hair cascading around them. With some deft work he was inside her, but remained still, clearly luxuriating in the tight fit.

She leaned forward and ran her tongue along the seam of his lips. Pulling back she asked, "Slow or fast?"

He rolled so their positions reversed. Flexing his hips, he grinned a panther's grin. "Oh, slow, I think." He backed out gradually, agonizingly, excruciatingly. Keeping that nerve-racking pace, he thrust inside her again. "Very, very slow."

B.A. moaned breathlessly. "You . . . arrogant . . . man."

A little while later B.A. rolled onto her side, watching Desmond feign sleep. His breathing betrayed him. He was awake.

One question had been answered: the passion was still there. Blistering, white-hot, burning as brightly as before. But Desmond had suffered deeply this past month. While he'd missed her, The Cat Dudley and the island, and he couldn't escape the bewitchment cast by Falgannon, something was wrong.

"Des?" She leaned against his back, nuzzling his neck. "My great aunt from Kentucky would say you're playing possum. Are you ignoring me?"

"Yes," came his sleepy reply.

"Too bad." She nipped his shoulder playfully, then brushed her fingers through his raven black curls. "We share our bodies. Can we not share each others' problems?"

He sighed, rolled over and resettled with his arm about her. "It was a rough month, B.A."

"Business?" she asked, putting a hand on his heart, startled how it jumped.

He bit out, "Yes. Old business."

"Care to talk about it?"

"I want to *forget* about it." He took her wrist and dragged her across his body. His *green* eyes were lasers, burning into hers. "Make me forget, B.A." His hands grasped the back of her knees and guided her astride him.

"Talking might help."

"*This* will help." His strong back arched up and he pushed his hips back on the bed, moving them both so he was propped against the headboard. Wrapping his powerful arm around her waist, his mouth met hers with unleashed power, and one thumb worried the tip of her breast.

She'd like to push the issue, certain Desmond needed to discuss what bothered him, but the man conjured ecstasy with that beautiful hand. Her body burned, needing him inside her again, to be a part of him. He increased the pressure, giving her nipple a tug to push her desire higher.

"Make me forget, B.A." He shifted to impale her once more on unyielding flesh. In near desperation, he drove into her, shattering her mind in a thousand pieces. Not giving her space to come down, he slammed into her harder. "Again, B.A."

Again wasn't possible. But then he tilted a bit, moving his body with his sure strokes. She couldn't hold back, jerking, climaxing harder, stronger, longer, shocking with its force. The beautiful agony wracked her body and escaped her in a moan.

Instead of following her into that bliss, Desmond increased the energy of his thrusts each a masterful piston of his hips dictating her release. He drove her into an ever-tightening coil, until she lost track of how many times he pushed her to climax—over a dozen. It was hard to count as one often went right into another, each magnifying the waves of pleasure of the one to follow.

"Make me forget, B.A.," he said again. He buried his head against her breasts. He exploded within her, his climax towing her to join him once more. The velvet release went on forever.

Distantly, B.A. grew aware that tears hit her breasts.

"You scare me, Des." B.A. stroked his beautiful back.

He sat on the bed's edge, awoken by another bad dream. Cocking his knee, he faced her. "It's only a nightmare. Sorry I disturbed you."

Putting a hand to his heart, its force alarmed her. "*This* disturbs me. I sense things in you, dark things. It's reflected here." Her index finger traced the lines bracketing his mouth. "You've lived hard, I think."

Stillness in him intensified. Underneath was that panther waiting to slip its leash. "Are you saying because I had a hard life, a life not as privileged as yours, I'm not good enough for Sean Montgomerie's precious granddaughter?"

She drew back. "Where'd that garbage come from?" She would've chuckled, but saw he was serious.

He jumped up and went to the window. "I had it rough, B.A., but nothing compared to what my mother suffered. Hardships have a way of wearing a person down, someone like her. Frail, frequently sick, bronchitis seemed to hit every winter, turning into pneumonia. She missed work because of illness. More times than I care to recall, she was fired for it. I'm sure you noticed I'm faintly bowlegged. I had rickets as a child."

She came to stand behind him, stroking his shoulder.

"Rickets!" He laughed, but it wasn't in humor. "In this day and age *no* kid should have rickets. Not enough milk and Vitamin D in my diet, B.A. Know why?"

Fighting tears, B.A. trembled, fearing she wouldn't like the answer. She was unable to speak as his intense pain washed over her.

"Often we didn't have money for food—simple stuff . . . bread, milk, eggs. When my mother wasn't looking, I divided my milk between Jago and Trev. They were babies, they needed it more. With your privileged life you've no idea what it's like to lie in bed in the middle of the night, hungry. To hear your baby brothers crying for the same reason. I recall one job she had, a waitress in a greasy spoon in some jerk-water town in Alabama. She earned minimum wage—$1.55 an hour at the time. Sixty hours a week earned her ninety bucks, so she took in ironing. She came in after working ten hours and pressed clothes half the night."

"Why didn't she seek public assistance? Programs exist in the United States to help single mothers see their kids never go hungry."

"Pride. Fear. After my father's death we lived with her father on a farm in Ireland. Life was harsh—worse after he died. I was working before I turned nine, got a job weeding flower gardens for a woman, Grace Delacourt. Like your Willie, she was a romance writer, was there for a year while she wrote her next book. She was kind, caring. My mother became her housekeeper and when it was time to return to the United States, she sat Mum down and discussed sponsoring her for permanent residency in the States. Grace took us with her. Life was good for a while: steady pay, food, a roof that didn't leak over our heads. Before my eleventh birthday, Grace was killed in an accident. Life wasn't so good after that. My mum feared they'd deport us to Ireland, so she moved—and moved. Anytime we were in a town long enough for someone to ask questions, we'd move again. She worked menial jobs. She wasn't strong physically. Always sick, she never went to a doctor because it'd take the few dollars she had for food. Worse, she needed treatment. She was manic-depressive. Her moods . . ."

He tilted his head upward, blinking back tears. B.A. stared. Her insides were raw because this pain was his. Her arms encircled his waist. She laid her head against his back, cradling him with her love.

"She lived, one moment bright and gay, telling me the good things that'd happen to us when she got a better job. Next, she'd cry as if she'd never stop." He snorted in disgust, but she felt the quiver of pain lance through him. "You can't imagine how it was. Not enough food to last from one payday to the next. I was old enough to understand. The twins were toddlers. You can't explain to a child who's hungry he has to wait. Luxury was having a mustard sandwich for supper Thursday nights."

Desmond wrenched away from her, but B.A. slid her arms around him. Her tears fell on his back.

"When I was fifteen I worked in a construction crew. I intended to quit school, work full-time. I didn't want my brothers wearing hand-me-downs as I had. When the time came to return to school, I asked to be kept on. The owner, John Bentley, asked why. I explained I had to help my mother raise my brothers. He made a deal—stay in school and I could work five hours every night and a full day on

Saturdays. I forced Mum to get medical treatment, refused to give in to her panic when her black moods hit, when she wanted to pick up and run. Even after John helped me straighten out our legal status, she often slipped into irrational fear we'd be sent back to Ireland or the authorities would take the twins away. When I turned eighteen, John paid my college tuition. I went to the local college so I could live at home, still work . . ." He trailed off, his tale done for the time.

B.A. hugged him tightly. "I'd wish for something better for you. But it's who you are, what made you the man you are." *The man I love.*

And then B.A. cried more, seeing what Desmond was doing in his mind. Her soul twisted with that child's anguish, that pain he'd carried so long. She wished to comfort that frightened, hurt boy. The Child Desmond was still very much in pain. She prayed that time and her love would help heal him.

Chapter 25

Desmond's arm hung loosely around B.A.'s shoulders as they watched the pontoon plane cut its engine and coast toward the harbor mouth. Keen to see B.A.'s sister, the Fraser twins were in a dinghy, already rowing out to fetch LynneAnne.

Desmond was unsettled by the visit. LynneAnne had chosen to come to Falgannon for the holidays instead of Colford, and this was the first time Desmond had faced any of B.A.'s siblings. While thankful it was a sister and not one of her six brothers, he was leery of LynneAnne's reaction to him.

Dismissing his anxiety, Desmond teased, "You have another female for matchmaking."

B.A. slid her arms around his waist. "I thought of Ian and Brian long ago. She adores them, but as brothers. Though both would've been good choices for her."

Desmond laughed. "Both?"

She chuckled, too. "*Either*. Leave it to a man to latch on to that."

"Sorry, men wish for twins, not to be one sharing a woman."

"Don't spin dreams of my twin and me." She dragged her finger down the middle of his chest and lower. He snatched her wrist, preventing the wandering digit from moving past his belt. "When we sisters each turned thirteen, Maeve gifted us with little curved knives."

"Yeah, I noticed yours. It's on a plaque by your desk."

"They're replicas of ones Pictish women carried. After Viking raiders were defeated, the women used the knives to castrate prisoners."

He laughed and kissed her forehead. "Understood. No fantasies about twins."

The dinghy pulled alongside the dock, everyone anxious as LynneAnne climbed up the wharf's ladder. When she popped over the edge, B.A. rushed up to her. Desmond gritted his teeth. Having experienced B.A.'s welcomes, he feared both ladies might end up in the drink.

He watched, curious if the sister shared B.A.'s sex appeal. Likely, Julian knew, having spent several weeks trailing her in New York, reporting on her life. Desmond's glance flickered to his friend. Speculation flashed in Julian's dark eyes, but his expression remained typically aloof.

LynneAnne wasn't as tall as B.A. Her build was similar, with well-rounded breasts and shapely hips. Her dark auburn hair was in a French-braid, reaching past her waist, the style accenting her lovely face. She had the same features—that Montgomerie chin, the model's cheekbones—though the witchy cat look to her eyes was stronger.

Sisters linking arms, they walked forward. Desmond felt the incisive power of LynneAnne's amber eyes, her gaze direct, assessing.

"Ian and Brian blethered on about Vikings invading. Looks more like pirates have overtaken Falgannon." Her shrewd gaze skimmed over Julian, then dismissed him with a flick of her long black lashes. She zeroed in on Desmond, noting Kitty curved around his ankle. Stepping close, she met his stare. "Cats are good judges of character. But then, Dudley isn't a cat."

Desmond couldn't resist. "What about the two-legged kind? Are they a good judge?"

Her eyes shifted to B.A. and back. "Tell me, Desmond Mershan, has my sister told you the legend of the *Cait Sidhe*?"

"I know about the selkie and kelpie—but I don't ride a bicycle so I'm not worried."

Her smile spread. "Women of our line supposedly descend from the *Cait Sidhe*—"

"A race of Pictish witches, I recall."

"It's told how females of Maeve's line came from one woman—"

He cut her off, to irritate her. "I've been to the Lady Stone."

"Have you?" Her dark brow lifted. "And planted a white rose?"

B.A. slid under his arm, hugging him. "We did."

LynneAnne grinned as the Michaels came over to hug her. Then she winked at B.A. "So are the lads taking bets if the rose blooms?"

Michael the Story tugged her braid. " 'Tis not a betting topic, lass."

"He dunna ken about the *Cait Sidhe*, Michael." She shook a finger at him. "You're falling down as *seanchaidh*. Ashamed you should be."

"LynneAnne, say hello to Julian Starkadder." B.A. did the pretty. "Julian, this is my younger sister. She builds—"

"Carousels." He extended his hand. "Someone mentioned it."

LynneAnne's expression turned cool. "What do you do as Mershan's pet pirate? Force his enemies to walk the plank?"

Desmond shook his head, laughing under his breath. "Wrong move, LynneAnne." Julian took her hand. A blush tinged her cheeks as he held it. She blinked, losing the staring contest. Julian smirked. Instead of kissing her hand, he faintly nipped it. "What do I do? I *bite*."

LynneAnne shivered. "Mershan, I hope you see he gets his shots."

* * *

Desmond lifted LynnAnne's suitcases out of the Rover and said to Julian, "B.A. told me about her curved knife. They're based upon ones Pict women carried. After battles, they castrated prisoners with them. I'm thinking of hiding B.A.'s."

"She was telling you this . . . why?" Julian laughed.

"Admonishment to keep my baser male fantasies in check—but also, I surmise, so I'd pass the advice on to you."

"Never fear, after seeing the effect Montgomerie sisters have on you Mershan brothers, I want no part of one." Julian shoved a piece of gum into his mouth. "You got the pick of the litter. Someone who spends days carving wooden horses must be boring as dirt."

Desmond hesitated, seeing LynneAnne come up behind Julian. He waggled his eyebrows at his friend. When Julian looked behind him, she flashed him a look that'd kill.

"Give this boring-as-dirt woman her suitcase."

She reached for it, but Julian took it. "Allow me."

"Let go. My suitcase is probably boring, too," she snapped, trying to wrestle it from him.

Desmond stepped back. This was like standing between two spitting cats ready to tangle.

"I've got it. Stop the hissy fit," Julian ordered.

"Mershan, tell the hired help to keep opinions to themselves. Besides, for a man with an earring in the wrong ear, he shouldn't care if a woman's boring or not."

Julian blinked, puzzled. "It's in my left ear."

"Right is wrong, left is right," LynneAnne quoted in singsong tone.

Julian shrugged. "Right."

"See?" She stuck the tip of her tongue out at him.

"*Right is wrong* means a guy is gay, LynneAnne."

"Precisely, it's in your right ear."

He tugged on it. "*My* left, not yours."

"So you're not gay."

He slowly shook his head. And leaning close he added, "Want to find out what else I do besides bite?"

Yanking her case from his hand, she muttered, "Bloody pirate." Then she headed inside.

Desmond took the last case out and slammed the back door on the car. B.A. came storming out of the house, hands on hips.

"What did he do to my sister?"

Desmond commented to Dudley, "Looks like the hols won't be boring, Fuzzball."

Four nights later, Desmond surveyed The Hanged Man, jam-packed to both welcome LynneAnne and celebrate Yule. To Desmond's relief most of the males, save Cedric, were in pants. And for the first time in six years, new women were scattered among Falgannon's lads.

Desmond lifted B.A.'s hand to his mouth and kissed it, watching her beam with delight.

Cassie had stayed. The "Morn, B.A." Club were running bets when Willie and she would make the announcement. The two were inseparable.

The first three prospective brides had returned home, but Amanda Taggart was coming back to Falgannon after she settled things in the States. Two new candidates were present, as was the daring gal Jeannie Burroughs, who'd Jet-Skied to the island claiming she was carried off by Splendid Mane.

Wulf's sisters—Ingrid, Raghild and Astrid—were white-blond Viking goddesses. They'd led B.A.'s lads on a merry chase since arriving yesterday on the ferry, Falgannon's second Viking invasion for the year. They'd blown Thursday night poker all to Hell.

"Get a mop. Your lads are drooling again," Desmond teased, watching Callum, Hamish and Patrick making cakes of themselves by dancing attendance on Wulf's sisters.

Under the table, B.A. nudged his leg with her foot. "Hush, Michael's starting."

Indeed, the handsome man with long sandy hair and poet's eyes claimed the attention of all as he began his tale of ancient lore. Standing before the fireplace, he hypnotized with his words. "Lore holds that the Daughters of Anne are descended from the *Cait Sidhe*, Faery Cats—Pictish witches with magic in their blood. Each possesses the ability to transform into a catamount nine times. She may change eight times and retain her human form by never taking the shape of a cat again, but if she morphs into a feline the ninth time, she is condemned to remain as such for the rest of her life. Anne, daughter of Anne, married Thane Fhitich. When the Northern invaders came, Anne and Fhitich led their people in a fight for this isle. In the heat of battle, Anne discovered her husband surrounded by the Danes. Fearing his slaughter, she transformed into a catamount and frightened them away, saving Fhitich. Unfortunately, she'd transformed eight times before, and was thus was condemned to remain a cat for the rest of her life. The Auld Ones were touched by her deep love and sacrifice for her husband, so they granted her the power to come to him in human form on the seven nights of the full moon. On Lughnasadh, the first of August, she was permitted to remain in that form for the whole day—the only time she could walk in sunlight as a woman. To this day, the females of the line are reputed to have this ability. Scoff, but look in their eyes, you'll see they are truly cats having assumed human form."

Desmond arched his brow at LynneAnne. "This is what you wanted me to hear? B.A. is half-cat?"

LynneAnne grinned, wiggling in her seat. "What did you think, Mershan?"

Desmond snorted. "A load of cobblers, worse than tales of green-eyed men."

LynneAnne stared at him, then laughed. "Mershan, you're whistling past the graveyard. I bet he's a good poker player—nearly as good as The Cat Dudley, B.A. You should ban these two from playing cards with your lads. Your lambs aren't prepared to handle such cutthroat pirates."

"Pirate? I thought I was a Viking." When Dudley fussed to get in his lap, Desmond gave in and settled the beast on his thighs. "A prince, at that."

"One with Sinclair and Fitzgerald blood," B.A. agreed. She hooked his calf with her stockinged foot and secretly ran it up the inside of his leg.

"Sinclair and Fitzgerald? Impressive. Shame he scoffs at The Curse." LynneAnne's witchy eyes studied him. "Viking Prince? Pirate? What other masks do you wear, Mershan?"

B.A. pushed her foot the rest of the way up his leg and against his groin. Des reached for his drink, but B.A.'s sensual foray and LynneAnne's cat eyes boring into him shattered his composure and he spilled his whisky. It spread across the table and into Julian's lap. Julian jumped back, dabbing at his thighs with his napkin while B.A. rushed to the bar for a towel.

LynneAnne nearly purred, thrilled.

Desmond leaned forward and crooked his finger for LynneAnne to come closer. "You try coming between B.A. and me and I'll tie you up, gag you and toss you into the peat bog," he warned.

She didn't look worried.

Later, B.A. and LynneAnne hung the ornaments everyone brought forward. The tree in The Hanged Man was the "family" tree. Each person had their name and a small image of them hand-painted on the bulb. At Yuletide, these were hung. Oona's grandmother had created the oldest ornaments. Oona kept up the tradition.

B.A. eyed the door, waiting for the men to return. They'd gone to fetch the Yule log. Desmond had made noises the rite was nonsense, but she saw it pleased him to be included.

She asked her sister, "What did Des say to you?"

LynneAnne glanced up from tying a decoration. "The louse threatened to stuff me in the bog if I interfered between you!"

"Good," B.A. chuckled. "He needs a tough skin to deal with us meddling Montgomeries."

LynneAnne stared at her. "I'm glad Desmond broke through that wall you built . . ."

"But?" B.A. prompted.

Her sister shrugged. "He's a lot of man—the kind sane women run from. I worry about you. I don't want you hurt."

"I won't be," B.A. assured. "Only thing Des could do to hurt me is leave. Of course, then I'd stop the ferry from running and keep him as a sex slave. Do you think he'd threaten you if he dinna care deeply?"

LynneAnne shrugged.

B.A. stopped, worried. "Do you *like* Desmond?"

"I don't know him. He gives off pheromones, which make me uncomfortable, itchy. That's why I poke at him. He'd make a ninety-year-old granny itchy. I see that silly cat adores him, the way your lads respect him. That tells me a lot."

The truth hit B.A. "You dinna like Evian. LynneAnne . . ."

"Okay, I kept my mouth shut and always regretted it. He wasn't good enough for you." LynneAnne sighed. "Desmond is always looking at you, touching you. I wish a man would feel that way about me."

The door opened and the men pushed through with the log, Dudley capering at Desmond's feet. The men dusted snow off their hair and shoulders.

LynneAnne snorted. "You call that a Yule log? It's pitiful, like that tree in the old Charlie Brown cartoon!"

"Don't be insulting our log, lass," Ian warned, "or Angus will be saying you should've been beaten regularly."

"Tell Angus to stuff it. No man ever raised a hand to a woman on this isle. Everyone knows that."

B.A. smiled at Des as he snaked his arm around her waist and kissed her. She leaned into him, relishing the taste of man and whisky. All else faded as she clung to him, their kiss so tender, so sweet, tears came to her eyes. Her mind whispered, *I love this man, love him, love him.*

"Da, our Viking's pillaging again," Wee Gordie called at Desmond's elbow.

He glared at the smiling kid. "If I bribe this munchkin, will he go bother someone else?"

B.A. stroked Desmond's cheek, noticing the shadows still haunting his eyes. She dusted the flakes off his hair. "It's snowing?"

He nodded. "Heavy."

"I want to go enjoy it, but first you must put your ornament on the tree."

"You can't see the branches as is," he teased.

But there was sadness in his eyes at not being a part of this Falgannon tradition. After hearing about his childhood, she presumed Christmastime had been hard. Going to the bar, she fetched a box from under the counter. She held it out, fighting a tear as Des hesitated. This little boy lost hungered for that box; Desmond the man wouldn't open himself to it.

Wee Gordie pushed Des forward. With a slight tremble, he finally accepted the white box from B.A. and pulled off the lid. A portrait of him from waist up with Dudley sitting in his lap was on the gleaming silver bulb.

Desmond couldn't move. Never had he received so precious a gift. B.A. lifted the ornament by the hook and together they fastened it on the tree.

"You like?"

He nodded, forcing the words past the lump in his throat. "Very much."

Oona came over, admiring her handiwork. "I did a nice job, if I say so myself."

"It's beautiful," Oddly, he felt like breaking down and crying—maybe crying as he never had his whole life. "Thank you, I'm chuffed."

"Speaking of beautiful, did B.A. talk to you about me representing your castle drawings?"

Desmond blinked, confused. "My drawings?"

"Sorry, Oona, I keep forgetting." B.A. smiled, embarrassed. "Oona wants to turn your drawings into lithographs and sell them through Falgannon Gallery."

He scoffed, "No one would buy those."

"They'd snap them up," Oona assured him. "Come by the gallery when you have time."

Desmond let out a gasp and whipped around, glaring at Oona as she sauntered away. "You're sure she's gay? She goosed me!"

"Take me out into the snow, Des." B.A. dragged him to the door.

The ground was white, with more big flakes falling thickly. Dudley peeked out his cat door, sneezed, then scurried back inside. B.A. danced out into the road, allowing snowflakes to hit her face.

"Isn't this beautiful?" She held her arms out, embracing the weather.

Desmond slowly walked to her. B.A. looked at him with those luminous, all-seeing eyes that bored straight to his soul. Then a sad smile crossed her mouth.

Leaning up, she brushed her lips across his. "Whatever causes the shadows, Des—it little matters. Nothing matters but us."

Pulling her into his arms, Desmond held her tightly, wishing with all his heart he could believe that.

Desmond stretched out on the sofa, then crossed his legs at the ankles. He sipped hot cider while critiquing the tree B.A. and he had finished decorating for Lady Cottage. The crystal bubbling lights were the perfect accent for the French blue frosted bulbs. Elegant. But then, each tree she decked was unique.

B.A. picked up the empty boxes with the kitten under her feet. Dudley lay along the sofa's back, eyeing the other cat with disdain. Like Desmond, he was a little jaded, since this was their fifth tree and another was in the offing. "It's gorgeous. But then, so were the other four."

"Going bah-humbug on me?" She dangled a ribbon for the kitten. "Rose Cottage will be the last. Thought I'd cook supper for LynneAnne, Julian and you. Then we could decorate the final tree and have a quiet Christmas Eve."

Desmond's eyebrows lifted in doubt. "Cooking?"

"You say that as if you think I can't."

"Tam assures me I 'won't starve.' From that I inferred, you've a lacking in the culinary arts."

"You'll see tomorrow."

"You're cooking, not serving up what Tam sends over?" he teased.

"I'll make you eat those words." She tossed a throw pillow at him, missed and hit Dudley, knocking the cat off the sofa. The kitten jumped on Dudley's neck and bulldogged him. The cat stared at Desmond in disgust, clearly saying, *This is all your fault.*

"Words?" He expelled a breath as she sat in his lap. "Not food? Haven't you learned the way to a man's heart? The lads tell you, but being a Montgomerie, do you listen?"

She leaned forward and kissed him until steam poured out his ears. "The *only* way, Des?"

He attempted to roll her under him, then instead tumbled them onto the thick rug before the fireplace. "I've always wanted to make love to a gorgeous blonde on a bearskin."

"It's not real bearskin." She wrapped her arms around his neck as he loomed over her.

"Faux bearskin, but real blonde." Kissing her, he shifted onto his hip so he could unbutton her sweater. Breaking the kiss, he stared at her teal brassiere. He flipped the snap. "Bet the inventor of front-closing bras was a man."

He slid down her body to put his hot mouth to her breast. Not pausing for playfulness, he drew on it hard, causing her hips to arch in instant hunger.

"Maybe it was a woman . . . who couldn't undress fast enough," B.A. gasped. "I wish I could wiggle my nose and my clothes would disappear." She grabbed his belt buckle.

A scream came. "B.A.!"

Desmond dropped his forehead against hers. "B.A., what this isle needs is ritual sacrifice." He struggled to re-snap her bra. "I think a green-eyed man should have that right."

"B.A!" The door flung open.

"You and unlocked doors." Desmond glowered while she hurriedly buttoned her sweater, then offered his hand to help her stand.

Out of breath, Willie asked, "May we use the phone? Where's the phone, B.A.?"

"Willie"—B.A. showed him to the hall table—"is someone hurt?"

"Och, no. Cassie needs to use it."

"Cassie?" B.A. looked to see Willie's girl standing outside the door, obviously cautious about entering uninvited. "Come in."

Desmond muttered behind B.A.'s back, "Yeah, everyone else does."

"Sorry, B.A." She wrung her hands. "But I wanted my mother to be the first to know, and the other phones aren't working—"

Willie grabbed Cassie's arms and danced her in a circle, his face aglow with excitement. "We're getting married, B.A.!"

Cassie laughed. "Okay, mother's third."

"I'm happy for you." B.A. hugged Cassie as Willie shook hands with Desmond.

"B.A., can we wed on New Year's?" Willie inquired as Cassie placed her call.

"Sorry." B.A. stepped into her study and picked up her day-by-day calendar. "I've downloaded Form M10. You both take it to the Registrar's Office in Stornoway. Once the Registrar is satisfied, she'll issue a marriage schedule."

"What happened to saying 'I will' over an anvil?" Willie sulked.

"I'm sure Cassie will want a beautiful wedding," B.A. hinted.

Cassie's mother wanted to talk to Willie, so B.A. went to the bar and took out glasses and poured drams of whisky. Desmond, on the sofa arm, caught B.A by the waist and tugged her back to him. Nuzzling her shoulder, he kept his voice low.

"It's driving me nuts wondering if you have on a teal thong."

"The delay in getting a permit to marry works out fine," Willie said, coming back to the living room. "She wants to fly to Falgannon for the ceremony!"

B.A. passed everyone a drink. "To my first success at matchmaking."

"To a match made in Heaven," Desmond toasted. "And to a lock on that door."

Willie beamed. "A match made on Falgannon—even more special."

Desmond's heart squeezed as B.A. looked at him with love in her eyes. "Much more special."

Desmond walked down a long dark hall. Heart-wrenching sobs tore at his soul. He paused, helpless against the grief gripping his mother. Sometimes he wanted to lie back on his bed, close his eyes and never awaken. But who'd care for her and the twins?

As he moved forward, the darkness seemed to extend forever, the cries always just a little ahead. After his father's death, they'd never lived in anyplace with more than a few rooms, so it seemed odd to walk this endless corridor.

Finally, he pushed open a door. His father sat, staring at a piece of paper, his face waxen. He lifted his head. "You're the man of the family now, Desmond. Your mother needs you. Your brothers need you. Everything's up to you." His father raised the gun to his temple and pulled the trigger.

Behind him, Desmond heard a scream. It reverberated through his head. His mother's hand reached out, grasping his so tightly it was painful. The scream went on and on. Arm throbbing, he struggled to pull away. Still she held on, as if she let go there'd be no way back from the torment.

"Mother, you're hurting." She squeezed harder. He cried, afraid she'd break bones. "Please let go."

Her claw-like grip increased. Growing lightheaded from the pain, he fought the darkness and passing out. The hand was no longer the beautiful hand of his mother. The flesh had wasted away to nothing, tissue thin skin over bone. His head jerked up, the staring face of Katlyn as he'd last seen her: bald, featureless, unrecognizable except for those green eyes dulled by the touch of death.

"You promised, Desmond, you promised."

Soaking with sweat, Desmond jerked awake; his heart hurt. He closed his eyes, grimacing from the pain.

B.A. pushed Dudley and the kitten off her legs where they'd cuddled. Sleepy, they snuggled back down together without the cat noticing he cradled the kitten. She scooted behind Desmond, leaned her head against his shoulders and wrapped her arms around his waist. "It's exciting about Cassie and Willie. Can I talk you into wearing a kilt for the wedding?"

His tension eased as he realized she wasn't going to ask about his dream. "Wanting to put me into a skirt again?"

"I'd think you dead sexy in a kilt."

He glanced over his shoulder. "I thought you loved the leather breeks."

"I do. Only, I think Willie wants you as his best man. I'm sure he'll wear a kilt, so his best man will need one, too."

"I've an ace up my sleeve." He shifted so he could kiss her. A slow tender kiss. When he pulled back, he brushed a strand of hair behind her ear. "Sometimes you amaze me."

"Amaze you good or amaze you bad?" She slid down the bed as he rose over her.

"You don't push. I thought women drove men nuts with questions." His pale eyes searched hers in the dim light of dawn.

"I'm curious, even nosy. But living on an island of men I've learned you can't prod them into things. Try, and they'll get stubborn. I bide my time. 'All good things come to those who wait.' "

Desmond slid over her. "Let's see how good I can be when I make you come."

Chapter 26

"What did he do to my sister?" B.A. stared at Desmond and Julian as LynneAnne sailed by them. When neither man answered, she pecked Des on the cheek and headed down the steps. "Bloody pirate," she tossed over her shoulder at Julian. She paused, tugging on the handle of the car several times before it finally opened. "Des, this damn thing is sticking again."

"Wulf's ordered a replacement."

B.A. glared at Julian again, then climbed into the navy Rover on the way to fetch groceries.

Julian appeared bored. "They're in agreement of their opinion of me, it seems."

With a smile, Desmond watched B.A. reverse the car and slam out of the driveway.

"I'm not sure you should've given B.A. the Rover. She drives like a bat out of hell," Julian commented.

"She makes love the same way . . . lucky me." Desmond turned to him. "So what *did* you do to LynneAnne?"

"Nothing." Julian leaned back against the porch railing.

"She doesn't want to cut out your liver and feed it to The Escape Artists for *nothing*."

"Escape Artists?" Julian queried.

Desmond pointed at the pack of foxhounds.

"Ah, The Escape Artists—long-legged beagles. Are they "The Dog" something or other?"

"Only Dudley gets a personal 'the.' Now stop avoiding my question."

Julian insisted, "*Nothing* happened."

"Ah . . ." Desmond smirked. "The big nothing."

Julian tapped the end of his nose with his index finger.

"Losing your touch? Never knew a woman to turn down a night in your bed."

Julian stared impassively. "Actually . . . I did the turning down. Figured you wouldn't want me playing tag with B.A.'s sister."

"You're adults."

Julian shrugged. "I tried to be honorable, but little Lynne-Anne wanted to play knick-knack on my drum."

"As in knick-knack-paddy-whack, give the dog a bone?" Desmond laughed.

"So now she's back to accusing me of wearing the earring in the wrong ear."

Desmond tapped his friend's upper arm. "Come on, while they raid the store, Patrick's letting us in through the back of his jewelry shop. I want to buy LynneAnne a present."

"A bribe?" Julian accused. "Smart idea. Maybe I'll buy something as well. Might keep her from using a meat fork on me."

Climbing out of the Rover, B.A. eyed her sullen sibling.

Something had occurred between Julian and her sister last night. She liked Starkadder, but wasn't sure he was brother-in-law material. Still, love struck and you either grinned like an idiot or ran like hell.

Which piqued B.A.'s inquisitiveness. LynneAnne was neither grinning nor running.

They ran a gauntlet of silly dogs and pushed into the store. Dudley rushed to the stack of Kookamunga Catnip Treats and meowed as B.A. passed. Shooting her a glare when she ignored him, he knocked over a tub, bit into the plastic lid and ripped it off. B.A. chuckled.

LynneAnne glanced at Dudley. "The hog in fur is eating the inventory," she remarked.

B.A. placed honey in the basket. "Aye. I let him steal them. Makes them taste twice as good."

"I don't think *taste* comes into Dudley's decision-making process."

B.A. cut to the point. "Planning to tell me what Julian did?"

"Nothing." LynneAnne stared at the cans. "Anyone eat this stuff, or do you sell it for doorstops? I mean, *canned* haggis?" She shuddered.

"Kitty loves it."

"B.A., that's not a recommendation."

B.A. fixed LynneAnne with a glare. "What did Julian do?"

"I told you: Nothing!"

"Ah. Nothing." B.A. worked to hide her smile. "Details?"

LynneAnne threw up her hands. "Watching Desmond and you made me . . . *itchy*."

"So you decided to let Julian scratch?"

"You and Mr. Dark-and-Sexy give off enough pheromones to raise the dead. Seeing Starkadder's a bloody pirate with a stupid earring, I figured he'd be up to a little yo-ho-ho." She picked up the haggis, pretending to read the minimum daily requirements.

"And was he up?"

LynneAnne slammed the can down. Dudley jumped. B.A. figured the poor dear probably experienced a flashback to the night of Desmond's arrival.

She loaded everything she wanted to buy into her basket. "So?"

"It's embarrassing." Opening a jar, LynneAnne took out a sucker. "He'd fallen asleep on the sofa. He looked so wicked, yet so innocent. I went over and kissed him. Oh, boy! He kissed me back. Slow, deep and like he wanted to climb into my skin. Tears came to my eyes."

"And?" B.A. hefted her basket, then flipped off the lights.

LynneAnne followed her and climbed into the car. "He said, 'I don't know you and you don't know me, maybe we should leave it at that.' Then he went upstairs to his bedroom and closed the door. Have I acquired leprosy?"

B.A. sighed. "Likely he's keeping his distance because he's Desmond's employee."

"What's working for Desmond have to do with the price of canned haggis?" And LynneAnne fell into a sulky silence.

B.A. knew her sister. This wouldn't be the end of the matter. Of course, if LynneAnne decided to set her cap for Julian, maybe they'd settle on Falgannon. Smiling, she took the curve in the road.

The silver Rover pulled into the drive ahead of them, and the two sexy males got out. "Men hard on a woman's heart," B.A. sighed.

LynneAnne exhaled noisily. "Bloody pirates."

B.A. basted the goose while Dudley and Annie meowed at the tantalizing aroma. Desmond came in, laughing.

"Dinner!" he said.

"Where'd you go earlier?" she asked, pushing the bird partway back into the oven.

He opened the refrigerator to fix a lemon squeezy. "We dashed to The Hanged Man, mooching some real grub from Tam to tide us over until the *cèilidh*."

She waved her baster at him. "You'll have a helping of crow with supper."

"That's crow? I thought it was a goose." He sniffed the bird, then tried to snag a wing, only to have his knuckles slapped.

"You'll get worms." Replacing the foil, she shoved it back into the oven. "I'm doing a Yank Christmas supper—goose, dressing, yams, cranberry sauce, rolls and pumpkin cheese-cake."

"Mustn't forget the cheesecake. Fine Yank tradition." Desmond took her wrists, hauling her against him. "Can I bribe you to wear that apron for me later?"

"If you grovel for insulting my cooking."

He lowered his head to kiss her, only the phone rang. He groaned. "What *is* it, B.A.? Some microchip alarm hidden at the back of your neck goes off every time I touch you?"

B.A. untangled herself to take the call, heard her brother's voice. "Cian, are you calling to wish us a merry ho-ho?"

"Christmas? Oh yes—Merry Christmas, B.A."

"You sound distracted." She accepted the lemonade from Desmond.

Cian sighed. "That's putting it mildly. I'm tracking down siblings."

To her delight, Desmond massaged her shoulders as she talked. "Aren't they at Colford?"

"LynneAnne's with you. Asha and Liam are in Kentucky. I'm sending proxies for LynneAnne and you to sign. Trident Ventures is gearing up for a hostile takeover. They bought up a big block of stock—near forty percent. I'm waiting for the shoe to drop."

"The family holds fifty-one percent—"

"Father owns eleven percent, as do I. The remainder is spread among grandchildren. You have five percent and our brothers and sisters each have two. LynneAnne, Asha, Liam and you own eleven percent of the stock. I *need* those proxies."

"You'll get them."

"Okay. Merry Christmas, little sister. Wish the same to everyone from me."

"*Nollaig chridheil huibh* to all from Falgannon."

Hanging up the phone she paused, lost in thought.

Desmond smoothed the furrow in her brow with his thumb. "Keep frowning like that and Dudley and I will cart you to the mainland for Botox injections. Something wrong?"

B.A. looked at him, unease filling her, yet not certain why. "Do you know anything about Trident Ventures?"

* * *

Desmond stared at the goose on his plate, sick to his stomach. He feared he'd vomit if he took the first bite. He needed a scotch to steady his nerves.

B.A. had nearly taken him out at the knees with her earlier question about Trident. For a breathless instant he'd thought she knew everything. When she said she didn't understand how a takeover bid worked, he drew air again. He'd mumbled an ambiguous reply, which satisfied her, though he couldn't recall what he'd said.

"Des," he finally realized B.A. was saying. "Is something wrong with the food?"

He shook his head. "No, it's great."

"You haven't taken a bite." She kissed him lightly. "Please eat. You worry me when you go spacey."

He took a bite of goose, not tasting it. "Just a slight headache."

Ever solicitous, Julian jumped up and fetched aspirin. Desmond thankfully accepted the pills and whisky, welcoming the alcohol's warmth.

Julian sat and ate. "B.A., this is delicious."

She stuck her tongue out at Desmond.

The front door burst open and a racket ensued. The cats hissed and ran under the table as Ian and Brian came in. Unfortunately, The Escape Artists sandwiched themselves between the twins and nearly bowled Ian over.

B.A. headed them off. "Eegits! Evict the hounds from hell."

"Sorry, lass." Brian laughed as a foxhound knocked him onto the sofa. " 'Tis Ian's fault. He was to lock them in the kennels."

Ian had two hounds by the collars, dragging them out the door. He glared at his brother. "Och, you dirty liar! It's your turn to tuck them up."

Angus came in, holding a large jar above his head. "Out of me way!" He fussed at the dogs, who were jumping to grab his eggnog. "B.A., ashamed you should be. The Escape Artists will give the kitties tiny livestock."

"Tiny livestock?" Julian choked.

"Fleas." Desmond said with a laugh. He welcomed this typical Falgannon chaos, used it to mask his panic.

After much ado, the dogs were ejected and the door shut firmly.

"How did those dogs earn their nickname?" Julian asked.

Ian explained. "They learnt to flip handles with their noses, so they're always out."

Desmond pulled up chairs for the newcomers. "Ever consider a *lock* on the kennels? Locking doors keeps all sorts of things in—and out." His eyes flashed at B.A. in a private joke.

Ian came forward, holding an empty plate. "Endless apologies, B.A. We brought a haggis to contribute, but the pups got it."

Desmond sniggered. "There is a God."

Angus eyed the goose and trimmings, then winked. "Glad to see our B.A. learnt the way to a man's heart. Must be the first time a Montgomerie *ever* listened to anyone."

The Frasers and Angus departed, complaining they'd eaten too much. It had been a lovely family supper. Laughing, teasing—plenty of food and eggnog. Even the kitties had Angus's nog. Passed out, both lay before the fire. At one point the kitten stretched, resettled, cuddled up against Dudley. The cat opened an eye, glared, then went back to sleep.

B.A. was on one sofa, head contentedly in Desmond's lap. LynneAnne curled up with a pillow on the other couch, pretending to drowse. But B.A noticed her sister tracked Julian like a hawk. Julian slouched in a recliner, feigning interest in a DVD. His hooded eyes shifted to LynneAnne when she wasn't looking.

B.A. sensed a torrid romance brewing.

The clock on the mantel chimed midnight. Hooking her arms around Desmond's neck, she moaned, "I'm too cozy to move."

Julian rose and went to the tree, poking around until he found two small gifts. He squatted before B.A. and held out a box wrapped in gold foil. "Merry Christmas, BarbaraAnne."

B.A. undid the bow and paper. Inside the box was a pair of white gold earrings, Pictish in design. She kissed his cheek. "Thank you, Julian, they're lovely."

Covetously observing B.A. and the earrings, LynneAnne didn't notice Julian turn and hold out a box to her. He tapped her arm twice to attract her attention.

"For me?" She looked up at him, surprised.

Julian rolled his eyes. "No, the cat." He rattled the box. "Cripes, it's not ticking."

LynneAnne unknotted the red bow. In the box was a gold cuff bracelet with Pictish drawings. Lovingly, her fingers traced the intricate patterns on the metal.

"Do you like it?" Julian asked.

B.A. grumbled when Des made her move. He got to his feet and patted Julian on the shoulder. "Down boy."

Barely containing her excitement, B.A. had hidden the sword at the back of the tree, so she had to work to get it out. The kitten joined in the fun, dashing in among the presents and then straight up to the treetop, peeking out—a live Christmas angel.

Shaking, she held her box out for Des. She couldn't breathe as Desmond carefully undid the tartan bow, the gold foil paper and finally the lid. He sat frozen, staring at the magic crafted by Skylar's skill. Angel and Devil B.A. both screamed, *Does he like it or not?* B.A. bit back the urge to tell them to put a sock in it. "Des, say something or I'll pass out."

He put his hands around the pommel of the sword and lifted it. "This . . . is . . ."

"Is what, Des?" She stared at the man she so loved, holding in his hands the sword forged for him. He looked perfect gripping the weapon, her modern-day warrior.

He answered, "Words fall short for what I see in this."

You see my love, her mind whispered.

He leaned to kiss her, but she held up the small box to make her gifts to him complete. "*I'm* opening this one." She laughed. Hand shaking, she ripped the beautiful paper. Reaching out, she took his left hand and slid the ring matching the sword onto his index finger. "Merry Christmas, Des."

He put the sword down and brushed a kiss against her lips. "I've never received presents so special."

Needing reassurance, she searched his eyes. She wanted

desperately for this Christmas to make up for all the sad ones he'd ever faced. He pushed her to sit on the footrest.

"Close your eyes."

B.A. vibrated with anticipation as Desmond sat behind her. He lifted her hair over one shoulder. Then he draped a chain around her neck and fastened a catch.

"Can I open my eyes yet?" she asked.

"No, impatient woman." He took her left hand.

Breath lodged in B.A.'s throat. She thought, *Here it comes*. But instead of a ring on her third finger, he placed one on her pinkie. Her eyes opened, staring at the delicate ring. So convinced he would give her an engagement ring, she felt let down. But that faded as she read the Gaelic around the band—*Mo Anam Cara*. My soul mate.

Thrilled, she forgot about the necklace until she put a hand to her throat. Jumping up, she rushed to the mirror by the closet door to see. The delicate choker was two hearts. One platinum encircling a smaller golden heart with a diamond at the center.

Their eyes met in the glass reflection. "It pleases you?" he asked.

B.A. turned to kiss his mouth. He deepened it. Being in his arms felt so right.

My soul mate. The ring said everything.

"Hey, do I get any presents or a lump of coal?" Julian called.

LynneAnne shoved her foot across the sofa and kicked him. "Bloody pirate."

B.A. chuckled. Her hands clung to Des for a second, not keen on losing the closeness. Then returning to the tree, she took two large boxes and set them on Julian's lap. She tapped LynneAnne's auburn head. "Stop kicking Julian when he can't kick back."

Her sister made a face, and as she turned, B.A. spotted LynneAnne kick him again.

Julian shook his head. "She's ticked because I won't let her kiss me," he said.

"You arrogant son of a shoat!" LynneAnne turned bright pink.

"Shoat? I won't ask." He opened his gifts from B.A., a fisherman's knit sweater and knee boots—her hint that he belonged on her isle like Des. "Thank you, B.A."

"She's trying to make you a born-again Falgannonian," Desmond warned, handing Julian two envelopes.

Julian sliced them open with his pocketknife. "I can think of worse fates," he said. His hazel-green eyes skimmed the papers, clearly stunned.

"Planning to tell us what they say, *Jules*?" LynneAnne grumbled.

Julian flashed her a scowl. "Brat."

"Pirate."

"Whatever. The first envelop contains adoption papers." He eyed his boss. "Desmond has . . . gifted me with ten percent of Mershan International."

"He dunna believe in token gifts." LynneAnne waited a minute then kicked his thigh again. "What's the other say?"

B.A. observed the two men staring at each other. Julian looked overcome. "Thank you, Desmond."

"Grrrrrrrr. If you don't spill it, Jules . . ." Again, LynneAnne pushed against his thigh with her socked foot in warning.

"The other is a promissory note." Julian read the words from Desmond: " 'Anything you want, anytime, anywhere—just ask.' Again, thank you."

Desmond nodded. "No—thank you, Julian."

Julian eyed LynneAnne stroking the bracelet. "You intend to put that on?" he asked.

She frowned. "Thank you. It's beautiful, but I can't keep it."

Julian growled, "What? Afraid I'll ask for sexual favors?"

She kicked him again. "Not bloody likely when you run from a kiss. I'm telling you, it's because you wear that bloody earring in the right ear. I've heard about the *brotherhood* of pirates."

"The right ear is left," Julian said through gritted teeth.

"Yeah, you have it in the left," she sneered.

"My left is *right*."

Desmond shoved a package between them, tired of the

silliness. "Believe me, LynneAnne, Julian's not gay. You should see the gorgeous string of blondes he's dated."

"Blondes?" LynneAnne growled.

Julian glanced at her sideways. "Yeah, I don't like redheads."

LynneAnne smiled at Desmond. "Thank you, the earrings are lovely."

"They'll go well with that bracelet Julian gave you," Des replied.

"But I can't keep that." She looked sadly at the cuff in her lap.

"You keep his gift, but mine has to go back? Desmond . . ." Julian appealed.

Desmond turned to B.A. and said in the same tone, "B.A.?"

B.A. laughed and did the same to her sister, "Lynne-Anne . . ."

"I don't have a gift for Julian." LynneAnne pouted. Then her expression brightened and she dashed upstairs.

"Bloody redhead," Julian muttered.

Rushing back, LynneAnne crawled onto the sofa, leaning over Julian. "Hold still, Pirate." Shaking, she removed the hoop earring from his ear. In its place she inserted a small diamond on a gold post. Julian held still while LynneAnne secured it. "There. I like that better. Now you're a high-priced pirate."

"You'll accept the bracelet now?" he asked.

LynneAnne nodded, slipping it on her right wrist.

B.A. looked around to see the kitten chasing Dudley, Des holding his sword, and the squabbling Julian and Lynne-Anne. Her heart was so full of love and happiness, it hurt.

After tidying up the papers and serving mulled cider, B.A. slumped to the sofa, reclining against Desmond. It was a perfect Christmas Eve. Well, almost. If only Desmond had asked her to marry him. She stared at the twinkling amber stone of the soul mate ring, satisfied nonetheless.

Take the silly man prisoner and keep him until he gets down on his knee! Devil B.A. sniffed in disdain at B.A.'s lack of foresight.

She toyed with that option. A vision danced through her head, not of sugarplums, but of Desmond chained to her bed.

Angel B.A. whispered, *Leap year is coming.*

Yeah, that was the ticket. B.A. brightened. In 1288, Scotland passed a law allowing women to propose marriage to the man of her choice on February 29. Desmond had until then or she'd ask the silly man!

Sometimes the world can be a bloody beautiful place, B.A. decided as she closed her eyes and drifted to sleep. Images of Desmond bare-chested, in leather pants and chained to the bed in Lady Cottage, filled her dreams.

Sighing, she thought she heard an angel singing a Christmas carol. She smiled when she realized it was just Devil B.A. singing the B-52's "Love Shack."

Chapter 27

At dawn's first rays, B.A. slipped out to head for the Lady Stone. Today being St. Brid's Day, she turned her mind to what she'd avoided for over three months. Had the rose planted on Halloween survived? She was scared, but this was a bridge she needed to cross alone.

During the holidays and then while planning Willie and Cassie's wedding, she hadn't found time to sneak away. Curiosity had nagged, but she'd focused on preparations for the first wedding stemming from her Web site, and Hogmanay—the Scottish New Year.

The lads voted Desmond to be the *first-footer*. Scots lore said if a black-haired man crossed your threshold after the stroke of midnight on Hogmanay, good luck would be granted for the year. Hedging their bets, Scots always shoved a black-haired man out into the night with a bottle to keep him company, and no one else could come in until he'd put his first foot over the threshold after the stroke of twelve. Desmond protested his selection, pointing out the Frasers had black hair, and with twins they'd double the luck. The lads remained adamant the privilege fall to the Viking prince. When put that way, Desmond couldn't resist. He'd grabbed a second bottle, shoved it at Julian and swore, "You're black-headed. Misery loves company."

Such times were seared into B.A.'s memory, cherished, for she knew how precious they were.

After New Year's, the islanders had thrown themselves the wedding. B.A. had cried, naturally. Willie was in his cowboy hat, chaps and boots. Desmond winked at B.A. saying, "Told you—no kilts!"

But now the time had come to find out if the rose lived. No longer able to find excuses, B.A. escaped to the Frasers' barn at first light. She saddled the white mare and rode toward Falgannon's stone ring. Still a bit of a pagan at heart, the symbolism of this day wasn't lost on her. The world awakened from its long winter slumber. Life began anew.

High upon the hill the breeze was brisk and unseasonably warm. Spring had come early to the island. She dismounted, looking around. Patches of mist stirred, restless ghosts on the dawn horizon. Desmond was right. You *could* see forever from here. Taking the small pack from her shoulder, she removed the bottle of water.

"What do you think, Angel and Devil B.A.? Will it be green?" she whispered in the stillness, her eyes closed. Afraid to see.

Shaking, she lifted her lids.

Strange, she put so much stock into Falgannon's lore. A modern woman, she considered herself a logical person. Yet with The Curse and how she was bound to this isle, she'd found herself accepting it unreservedly.

The clouds broke and a sunbeam shone like a spotlight on Lady Rock. Light-headed, she stared at the small rose bush. Trying to breathe, she feared her mind conjured the island magic. Yes, the weather had been unusually warm for weeks, but this was a miracle. Kneeling before it, her shaking hand caressed the green leaves, and finally the tiny start of a bud. The rose would bloom soon. In her heart she'd prayed to find it alive, but never had she anticipated this beautiful wonder.

"Thank you, Lady Anne," she whispered to the silent rock, the penitent woman forever frozen in time. She wiped away tears of joy with the backs of her hands.

After watering the growing rose, B.A. returned to mount the mare. It was an effort to keep from setting the horse to run back. She wanted to ride to the castle and awaken Desmond with the wonderful news. Only, she knew Brian and Ian would have her hide for not cooling the mare.

As she cantered to the stable, Brian strolled out. "You're up early this fine morn."

She dismounted, rushed to him and bussed his cheek. "You sexy man, cool the horse for me and I'll make it up to you later."

"You rode her, rub her down." But a twinkle in his eye said he'd do it.

"Oh, Brian, the *Samhaine* planting . . . is a bush. There's a bud that could bloom in a couple weeks!"

Brian's smiled widened. "Why dinna you say? Run tell our Desmond the news!"

She did just that—ran the whole way to the castle.

Desmond wiped the shave cream from the mirror and looked into his haunted green eyes. Each day saw the lies between B.A. and him eating away at his soul.

Julian and he had worked these past weeks to find alternatives. He wished he could stop the project, but feared that avenue might not be an option. Whatever choices, he had to tell B.A. The dread that she'd discover his deceit was more than he could handle.

The nightmares were worse. Pains now rippled through his chest after waking, taking an hour for them to ease. It frightened him.

He needed to confer with the Trident transition team, bring them up to speed on alternatives he now considered. When he flew to London next week, he'd check with a doctor, run some tests to be on the safe side . . . maybe even talk to a psychiatrist. The dreams were of the past, but they hurt him physically.

Stepping into the steaming shower, he was resolute. He

had to face B.A. Every time he touched her, he felt guilty for not being honest. He exhaled, girding himself for the coming storm. Tonight he'd do it—enlighten her about his plans, what had brought him to Falgannon. The driving force of his whole life.

Then he'd get down on his knees and beg her not to leave him.

Shrill ringing greeted her upon entering the cottage, and her impulse was to ignore the phone. Only, her inner voice said she didn't want to answer it; she *had* to. " 'Lo?" she panted.

"B.A.? Thank God."

"Catlyn?" She glanced at the clock on the wall, frowning, wondering why her sister would call so early. "Is everyone all right?"

"No . . . yes . . ." Cat paused. "Desmond Mershan has two brothers, I believe?"

"Something's happened to them? What, Cat? Tell me." Panic surged in her.

"Nothing's happened yet. Trevelyn and Jago? Those are their names?"

"Yes, dammit Cat, if you dunna tell me—"

"This isn't easy. Raven's involved with a Trev Sinclair. She's in love with him. Last night they had an argument after she discovered something about Trident Ventures."

"The group threatening the takeover?"

"Trident also bought—"

"Valinor." B.A. recalled how puzzled Cian had been about that.

"Yes. They paid a good price, too."

B.A. was light-headed. Trevelyn was in England, using the name Trevelyn Sinclair? He had connections to Trident and they'd bought the farm in Kentucky—where Asha was. "You asked about Desmond's other brother. Jago."

"We learned from Liam this morning that Asha's fallen for a Jago Fitzgerald."

B.A.'s stomach knotted. "That's their mother's maiden name."

"I thought . . . you might talk with Desmond."

"Desmond?" she echoed. Then reality set in. "Yes, Desmond."

"B.A." Cat's voice broke. "I'm sorry. The Mershans are using Asha, Raven and you. Somehow. It can't be a coincidence—"

Phone slipping from her hand, B.A. felt her knees give way. She didn't faint, instead crumpled like a rag doll. Barely able to breathe, she felt her head fill with a strange buzzing. She needed stand and face the music, but her legs wouldn't obey.

She finally comprehended the shower was running in the upstairs bathroom—why Desmond hadn't heard the phone.

She rose, slowly considering what she needed to do. Why was that so hard? Desmond's attaché wasn't here. He kept it and his computer in his new office. The sound of the shower shutting off propelled her outside and down the castle steps. B.A. didn't stop until she opened the door at Rose Cottage. Ignoring her burning lungs, she headed to the office with quiet steps, hoping not to wake Julian or LynneAnne.

She clicked the banker's lamp on the oak desk and sat down. Lifting the laptop lid, she pushed the power button, then clicked Desmond's avatar—a chess piece.

"How fitting."

Trying to log in, her fingers shakily typed SINCLAIR as a password. Nope. DUDLEY. Nothing. "Well, piss. Same thing for lying, two-faced pirate."

After two dozen tries, she shifted her attention to the briefcase. Silly, it was a three-number combination lock—it only kept honest people out. Her first attempt was 666.

"Guess he dinna want to be obvious," she muttered to herself. "What do you think? 1-2-3? Too simple for a man so complex?"

Her idiot brother Cian kept his set to 000. Desmond would never take that chance. Nor would he use his birth month and day. Out of ideas, she tested one last time. 1-0-1. October 1. The day he'd come to Falgannon. The day they'd met. *Snap.* The catches released.

A tear welled in her eye. "Oh, Des—you shouldn't be so sentimental for a lying Viking pirate."

With a fortifying breath, she opened the attaché. Maps were easily recognizable as Falgannon. She put them aside, along with dozens of complicated blueprints. Unfolding a file labeled Trident, she hit paydirt with a single sheet of paper. *The key.*

On letterhead for Trident Ventures and addressed to Desmond, it confirmed everything would be kept under the table until Trident's takeover of Montgomerie Enterprises. Afterward, announcements would be released that Mershan International was buying out Trident. In essence, Desmond would be CEO of a company, with Trident Ventures and Montgomerie Enterprises as subsidiaries.

"Oh, Des, how could you?" The final nail in his coffin—the envelope she'd thought she mailed to her brother weeks ago with the proxies. Without them, Cian could only vote forty-four percent of M.E. stock. Desmond had offered to take it to the ferry. He'd kept them instead.

"Bugger!" B.A. made a sour face. She wanted to cry. Wanted to scream. She wanted to take her Pictish knife and play tic-tac-toe on all the Mershan brothers. "Bloody friggin' pirates. The whole lot of them."

Needing time to clear her mind, she rammed the papers into the briefcase, little caring they crumpled. She had to get away, to calm down to be able to fight Desmond.

"I don't care what plans for Falgannon the low-down, lily-livered varmint has in mind,"—only Willie's western patter fit—"I'm going to make him sorry he thought to use my beautiful isle for his oily schemes."

Hearing footsteps on the stairs, she rushed to get out of the room.

Julian came through the door. "Desmond, you're . . ." He pulled up short. "B.A."

"No, it's *not* your lying, two-faced boss," she choked out.

Julian's arms caught her, his solid body blocking the door. Deep sorrow filled his eyes. "Why don't you sit, B.A.? Let me fetch Desmond."

"Let go of me," she growled.

"B.A., let Desmond explain—"

"That he's a bloody pirate out to ruin my island? Bad enough he wants to screw my family over, the Mershans sink to screwing my sisters and me—literally. You picked the wrong man to call boss and the wrong woman to placate." She grabbed his nose between two fingers, giving it a twist.

"Damn it, B.A.!" He sounded funny with his nostrils clamped. "That hurts."

Busy trying to pry her hand away from his nose without hurting her, he was easy prey. She slammed her knee into his groin. Turning purple then green in the face, he doubled over, emitting a horrible retching noise. "I like you, Julian, hate being mean to you, but that's what you get for having a pirate for a boss."

As she pushed by him, she heard LynneAnne call out then ask Julian, "What did you do to my sister?"

B.A. didn't slow. She fled Rose Cottage as though the devil was after her. "That's silly. The devil is atop the castle."

She stared at the castle, then turned and ran in the opposite direction.

Wrapping his towel about his waist, Desmond walked from the hot bathroom into the chilly bedroom. The drop in temperature was noticeable. Reaching for his robe, he headed downstairs to build up the fire. Halfway down the steps, he noticed light shining oddly into the living room. Alarm bells sounded as he rounded the banister and saw the open door and the phone off the hook.

Going to the door, he stared across the roof. The only thing stirring in the breeze was her pennant. He yelled, "B.A.!"

Footsteps sounded up the staircase, then Julian's head popped into view. "B.A.'s been in your briefcase," his friend called out.

Desmond's knees nearly buckled. "What did she see? Where is she? What did she say? Damn! The proxies!"

"No idea where she is. Your lass is a dirty fighter. She nearly ripped my nose off, then busted my balls. I'm doing my best not to puke, and LynneAnne gives me this '*What-did-*

you-do-to-my-sister' stuff. I couldn't reply, so the witch kicked me in the arse. I want hazard pay, Des!"

Not listening, Desmond pulled on pants and a sweater. Dudley jumped on the dresser, watching him dress. "She can beat the bloody hell out of me, Fuzzball," Des promised, "as long as she doesn't chuck me into the peat bog. Come on, Dudley, let's run her to ground."

He spent the whole day chasing B.A.

First she'd hidden at Willie's empty house. Willie and Cassie were in Vegas on their honeymoon—Desmond's wedding present to them. She'd gone out the back as he came through the front door. Phelan suggested he try Morag's. She wasn't there, but the third teacup in the kitchen said he'd missed her again.

That was the pattern of the whole day.

Cresting the knoll, Desmond heard music coming from The Green Man, confirming what Ian told him: B.A. had headed this way. Stepping onto the porch, he noted the windows vibrated from the force of the music. Inside must be deafening. He twisted the knob, knowing it would be unlocked.

Turning the corner, he spotted B.A. She danced in beat-up ballet slippers, her long hair swirling around her. Madonna's poignant ballad "You'll See," about a woman wronged, filled the pub. The fine hairs on his neck prickled. She seemed at peace, dancing within the heartrending song. Yet, something was wrong.

B.A. mesmerized him, her movements were sheer poetry torn from her soul. She mourned. And it scared the bloody hell out of him. Blood draining from his face, it was as if he'd taken a blow to the chest. Did she already grieve for something she perceived as dead?

The tune switched to "Don't Speak" by No Doubt. He didn't dare breathe, fearing she'd sense him. B.A. danced to blow off everything, seeking solace in the frantic movement. The tune started slow and soft, then flowed into something harder that carried her away. Her dancing conveyed the edgy pain of fearing to lose someone you love. B.A. was sensual, ethereal—her every step was etched with emotion she both embraced and rejected.

Des dropped his coat on a table, his feet carrying him down the steps and across the wooden floor. Focused on the music, B.A. didn't hear him. As the song hit its crescendo, she crumpled to the floor. Her body jerked in small spasms, and she sobbed.

Compelled to touch her, he reached out. He put his hand on her shoulder; her head whipped up, startled. The eyes of a frightened doe watched him, filled with pain, accusing.

Squatting, Desmond took her into his arms and cradled her, her agony slashing his heart. She shocked him by hugging him tightly, as if she never wanted to let him go, her body quaking with silent sobs. He permitted that for a time, but was alarmed when it went on and on. She needed to break free of this crippling pain and face him like the warrior she was. He rose, pulling her to her feet.

He stared into that beautiful face, tears trickling down her cheeks. Nothing in his life had ever hurt him as deeply. To know he'd caused this made him close his eyes in shame. Opening them, he searched for the right words to ease her torment, to explain his own.

"You lied," came her simple accusation.

Swallowing the knot in his throat, he nodded. "Yes."

"You wanted to *use* me." She choked back a sob.

"Yes," he agreed, offering no defense.

"As Jago is using Asha and Trevelyn is using Raven."

"Yes."

"I'll use Maeve's knife on Trev. Asha and I are strong. We'll survive this. Only, Raven is fragile. If anything happens to her, Trevelyn will wish he'd never been born. I don't know what this is about. And you know what? *I don't bloody care.* Nothing can justify using my sister."

"He's in love with her," he stated softly.

"And Jago's in love with Asha?" she sneered.

"Yes."

"How convenient. I'd looked forward to meeting your brothers. Any men like you had to be wonderful. Oh, now I shall meet them—but it will be to take payment for hurting my sisters."

"I'm sure your sisters will extract their own measures of reprisal."

B.A. shocked him again by stepping close. She nipped at his jaw. Desmond's body roared to life, thrumming like a Ferrari engine in his neverending sexual need for her. That silly male side responded, ready-set-go, pedal to the floor. But a niggling doubt warned this was too damn easy. B.A. Montgomerie was many things. Easy wasn't one of them.

She leaned into him as if she wanted to crawl into his skin. Her mouth brushed his, setting off fireworks in his beleaguered, desperate brain. The kiss spiraled as her hungry hands roamed over his body, seeking, scratching at his cashmere sweater. She rubbed her knee up the inside of his leg, making him widen his stance, then rocked her bent thigh against his throbbing erection. Oh, mercy, the wanting roared through his body to the point of agony.

B.A. shifted again, but his idiotic male brain was stuck in one mode, besotted with his soul-deep ache for this woman. Then she slammed her knee into his groin, and white-hot pain wracked his body and mind. He collapsed to his knees, writhing in torture. Mother Nature's cruel joke on males.

"I should've remembered Julian!" he choked out.

She sat on a small stool and changed into her Wellies. The witch started humming along with Blondie's "One Way Or Another." Boots fastened, she clomped by, leaving him to his blistering misery. Suddenly her steps returned and, before he knew what she was up to, she kicked him in the behind, sending him sprawling to the floor.

"Bloody Viking," she snarled.

He tried to laugh. "I'm arrogant, too."

But the door slammed, and Blondie sang, "*I'm gonna get ya, get ya, get ya . . .* "

"I think she got me all right," he agreed. Dudley hopped onto the middle of his back, purring, and settled down for a nap.

* * *

"What I don't need is the bloody Scottish Mafia." Desmond hesitated when he saw the men gathered at the bottom of the castle. "Great. Round Two, Dudley, and half the silly isle will be in the middle of this. I'm surprised the Michaels aren't selling tickets."

They'd naturally see B.A. as the heroine and him the dastardly villain. He *was* the villain, so they had every right. Only, it hurt that these men he'd come to see as friends would turn from him.

They eyed him. Not in anger, as he'd anticipated, but rather typical Falgannon eccentricity. There was a smirk or two, a male empathetic, *Better thee than me.*

Ian called, "Eh there, Des, you're limping."

His twin's eyes danced. "We should've warned our Desmond that Montgomerie lasses are dirty fighters. The rules: Never let them behind a wheel of a car when they're pissed, keep them away from sharp objects, and foremost . . . protect your *breall.*"

"Now you tell me." Despite everything, the corner of his mouth lifted into a half smile. Something was so soothing about life on Falgannon. Chaotic when it should've been smooth sailing, unruffled and all giggles when times were bad.

Something flew over the edge of the castle roof and floated to the ground. His clothes. Evidently, B.A. was evicting him. More apparel followed.

Brian asked deadpan, "Wash day at the castle?"

"Go ahead, laugh." Desmond quirked a brow. When his cashmere sweaters came next, he growled and started for the steps.

Ian caught his arm, pulling him back. "What's your rush, Des?" He handed over a flask. "A wicked temper our B.A. has, only she can't sustain it. Let the sweet lass toss what she wants over the crenellations. You can afford it, I'm thinking. It'll wear the darling out."

Desmond nodded, seeing the wisdom. "Thanks for the whisky and the advice."

He took a sip, puzzled by their continued friendship. He'd feared their animosity.

Michael and Callum came over. "Instructing him in *B.A. 101*?"

"Aye, can't be having our Desmond face our lass unprepared. Wouldn't be fair." Ian shared the flask. "How's betting?"

Desmond looked aghast. "Bets?"

"Not much won't draw a bet on the isle. You versus our lass." Callum smiled, rubbing his hands together in glee. "There'll be wigs on the counter tonight."

Desmond accepted the flask again, his tension easing now that he saw these men—his friends—wouldn't look at him in loathing. "Wigs on the counter?"

Callum held up a pound note showing a man in a wig, issued by the Royal National Bank of Scotland.

Desmond shrugged. If you couldn't beat them, enjoy the lunacy. "How am I doing?"

"Five-to-three our lass chucks you out with the laundry. We also have bets where you sleep. Here you're a dark horse, Des. Twenty-to-one says you're in Rose Cottage before midnight."

"I figured you lads would form a phalanx for B.A.," Desmond said.

"Och, our lass wouldn't appreciate us butting in. She's handled an island full of males for years. One Viking dunna require our help." Ian watched as pairs of Desmond's shoes whizzed through the air, one just over their heads. "B.A. sure has a mean overhand throw," he added.

"It's them Yank ways," Angus pronounced. "Corrupted her. Probably played that baseball while she was in the States.

Another shoe zoomed perilously close. "Maybe we'd better move out of range," Ian suggested.

Suppressing chuckles, Angus held out a stick to Desmond. "Here. A proper-size stick to beat our lovely lass."

"Proper?" Desmond accepted it.

"No bigger around than a man's thumb." The old man made a thumbs-up sign and winked.

"Look out below!" B.A. called, then hefted his empty scuba tanks over the side, sending them crashing down.

"That's it. If you'll excuse me . . ." Desmond stalked off, slicing the stick through the air. Reaching the stairs, he paused and watched his wetsuit follow the tanks. Taking the stick in both hands he broke it over his knee, flung it away and then took the stairs two at a time.

Just as he neared the top he heard Angus moan, "I told Sean Montgomerie. He dinna listen. Now our Viking ain't listening either. Best up the bets in favor of our lass."

B.A. locked the house against him. She saw him coming across the roof, squeaked and dashed inside, slamming the door.

"*Now* she locks it," Des muttered.

B.A. glared at him through the window. Not sure of the new game, Dudley had used his kitty entrance and now waved a paw at him.

"B.A., open the damn door!" he ordered

She stuck her tongue out at him.

"Don't push me, B.A. Open the bloody door. Now."

"*Pòg mo thòin,*" she snarled.

"Have the decency to at least insult me in a language I understand." He pounded on the oak door, then stalked to the window.

"It means 'kiss my arse.' " She stuck out her tongue.

"Gladly—let me in. You don't lock your doors here, remember?"

"My Yank ways are reasserting."

"Open the door, B.A., so we can talk."

"About what? How you plan to destroy my island with cheap track housing? An oil storage area? A deep-water harbor? You'd bring oil to this isle risking the seals, fishing, our beautiful white shores? You bloody pirate! Hiding behind Trident Ventures. You *are* Trident Ventures!"

"Not yet. I'll acquire Trident after the takeover bid."

"Och, big difference. Well, go ahead and waste your money battling Cian. He's your equal. But you're planning on ruining this island. *My island.* And that I won't let you do." She dropped the blinds, cutting off his reply.

Dudley squalled as the shade hit him. The kitten jumped on and tried to bulldog him. "Yeah, Pal. This isn't a good day for handling females."

Sighing, he headed to the kitchen window where the

pane had been removed to make Dudley's entrance. He pushed his arm through the opening to the shoulder, to reach the lock. "There's more than one way to skin a cat—no offense intended, Dudley."

B.A. dumped his belongings in a bin bag. She glanced at the dresser at Desmond's personal items: cufflinks, watch, billfold. She'd just picked up the wallet when she sensed his presence, was startled, and it flew out of her hand to crash against the wall. Two yellowed newspaper clippings and a sleeve of plastic fell out.

B.A. stared at Desmond. Fixed on the items, he was unable to draw breath. They both lunged. Closest, she snatched them away. His longer arms reached her wrist, manacling her in a grip that was uncomfortable but not painful.

"Playing bully isn't earning points," she warned. He held on for a moment, as if savoring her back against his chest, comprehending that contact would be all that was permitted him. "Des . . . let . . . go."

She felt him shaking. That rattled her. Desmond was so strong in her eyes. Right now, she didn't need to see him vulnerable, didn't need to weaken in her anger.

He nodded and stepped back, then leaned against the dresser, clearly lacking strength to stand. His pallor concerned her.

Strangely, B.A. felt more in control. Turning over the plastic sleeve, she studied her own face from fifteen years ago. The photo portrait had been made when her engagement to Evian was announced. A lifetime ago. Questions rushed at her, only she was in no frame of mind to sort them out. Biting her lower lip, she considered this damning piece of evidence—a photo protected from age by sealed plastic. He'd obviously carried it for years.

The tiny square had the power to overwhelm her heart.

"You knew who B.A. Montgomerie was all along. I sensed you did, but couldn't fathom why you'd lie."

He opened his mouth to speak, but tears gleamed in his eyes and obviously clogged his throat. He tried to speak, then looked at the ceiling and stopped.

"Why the charade?" she begged.

"The truth?"

"Nothing less," she growled.

"I came into the store. You stood, so beautiful, so un-reachable behind a wall of ice. I wanted you more than my next breath. I wanted to provoke you, to rattle those walls you built to keep men at a distance."

B.A. swallowed back tears. She ignored the significance of him carrying her picture all that time, unable to handle it. Neither of them was in the mood for twenty questions. He was hanging on by his fingernails.

"I'm not stupid, really." She attempted to make a joke, but her voice cracked.

Desmond watched her. "I never thought you stupid, B.A. Too trusting, maybe."

The more she talked, the calmer she became. "Let's skip *why* you carried this for now. That loan Sean defaulted on—was that something you made up?"

He shook his head. "Outside of pretending I didn't know who you were, and forging letters between Sean and myself, I haven't lied to you. I just never told you everything."

Fear edged up her spine as she picked up the newspaper clippings. One was her grandfather's obituary. Even older, the second was an obituary as well. She needed to sit, but couldn't move as the headline leapt at her: MICHAEL MERSHAN, FINANCIER COMMITS SUICIDE. She read details of the man's death, but all blood drained from her when she reached . . . *pulled the trigger in front of his seven-year-old son, Desmond.*

Chapter 28

Desmond sat, the scrap of newspaper on the table before him. Emotions swirled in his haunted eyes—determination, anger, pain, sadness. Underneath, B.A. sensed terror. Rocking the chair, he steeled himself to an ugly task.

"Sean used lands he didn't own as collateral to back risky

ventures. Emerald mines in South America, oil in the Middle East. When one venture paid off, the windfall backed another, each bonanza bankrolling the next. An empire built on a house of cards. Everything turned to gold for Midas Montgomerie. They called him that, you know."

"I think I heard it."

"Midas Montgomerie's luck turned. Rebels took over the mines, Arabs seized oil wells, coal mines in Wales were closed due to working conditions. Dozens of investments soured."

Nausea hit her, leaving B.A. certain she didn't want to hear this.

"Know what a pyramid is?"

"I know they're illegal."

"Sean ran a high-stakes pyramid. My father, poor fool, made a lot of money through Sean's early investments. Sean convinced him to lure his friends and associates into the spiraling game. He helped get Sean huge loans using the horse farm, Colford Hall and Falgannon as collateral. Everyone tossed in their life's savings, borrowed to get shares. And when things crumbled, my father believed everyone was protected because of Sean's collateral."

B.A. shivered. "Sean never owned Falgannon. Colford was in trust for my father until he inherited. The farm in Kentucky was purchased by my father for my mother."

"The house of cards collapsed on my father and his bank. That piece of paper deeding one-third of Falgannon was a shill. The bank lost, the investors lost . . . my father lost." He touched the paper, his hand trembling.

Desmond was trying to control the anguish and fury of unhealed wounds, the pain he'd carried his whole life. Despite resentment for him using her, and for his brothers going after her sisters, B.A. loved this man. Love was like that, she knew. You couldn't flip it on and off like a switch. What he felt reached into her, past the hurt, past the sense of betrayal. She ached for him.

"I was seven, no idea what was happening. I knew my father looked pale, drawn. He'd hardly slept or eaten for weeks. Mum's mood swings were more alarming. Then one day I sensed it was worse." His eyes beseeched her. "B.A., I . . . I need you to understand."

Pain lanced through her. "I do. Trevelyn targeted Raven, Jago went after Asha and you came to the island. The Mershans set out to claim the properties Sean put up as collateral."

If she hadn't known it before, in that instant she understood just how much she loved this man. If destroying this beautiful isle would bring Desmond the healing he needed, she'd step back and, hating every second, she'd let him finish what he'd come to do. This isle was part of her soul. Even so, she wouldn't hesitate a breath in choosing between Desmond and Falgannon. Part of her would die, but Desmond was that important. She'd walk through fire for this man.

And yet, she couldn't permit Desmond to destroy this magical rock in the ocean. Bringing his vengeance against Falgannon, against her—surrogates for years of rage against her grandfather—would never bring him peace. He'd destroy the isle and her people, bring noise, pollution, and the special purity would be despoiled to feed his revenge. But then what? Once he discovered his schemes couldn't heal his pain, it would be too late to put Humpty-Dumpy back together again. The isle would be lost for nothing.

He moved to stare out the window, this man who had carried hurt for so long. Given time, her love could heal him. Only, she had to reach him first.

"Desmond, I love you," she said softly.

He whipped around, his ice green eyes lashing her. "And what's the price tag, B.A.? Nothing in life is free. Payment for your love is I stop my plans?"

She shook her head. "No conditions, no price tag. I love you and ask nothing in return. Loving you is part of me. It's who I am."

"You won't beg me to give up these plans? Offer yourself as compensation?" His words were cruel—the panther flexing its claws.

"I *love* you. It's a simple truth. One I'll live with no matter what you do. I won't ask you to stop, but I won't let you rape this island to soothe your wounded psyche. I warn you, Des—"

"Warn me?"

"Take legal action against my family's holdings for what Sean's cheating cost your father, sue for the mental hardship it placed on your family. I'll stand beside you. I'm lousy at business, worse at law, but I believe you can sue anybody for anything these days. The horse farm you now own—and paid a good price. You want Colford? You'll deal with my father and brothers. Again, I'll support you. I doubt you'll want the drafty hall, actually. It's like living in a damn hotel. Maybe Mac can reach some agreement with you instead."

"You'd do that?" He seemed flabbergasted.

"Your family's owed—"

Lashing out, Desmond snarled, "Blood money? I can buy the high and mighty Clan Montgomerie, ten times over."

"I don't doubt that. But does it make you happy, Des? Has it made you laugh as you do with my lads? With me? Held you when you waken from a nightmare? This island's special. Not just to me, to you as well. My grandfather's dead. Destroying Falgannon won't bring you one minute's peace. If I permit you to ruin the isle you'd be sick. *That's* why I'll fight you." She blinked back the tears. "I think you love me, love the island—"

"Love? Spare me," he scoffed, but she saw a tear roll down his cheek. "After my father's death I wore hand-me-downs. Never knew what it was to go to a store and buy new clothes. Afterward, I vowed I'd never accept anything that was secondhand, again. What makes you think I want Evian Deshaunt's hand-me-down love?"

B.A. flinched. "Boy, Des, you play hardball. I owe you another kick in the arse for that. If Evian were here, he's the one who'd feel cheated. I loved him. I'm sorry he died. But what I feel for you is so much . . . *more*. It's the type of emotion that has people saying love is blind. It's not. You just love that person more than anything. I'd watch you turn this paradise into a cesspit of oil leaks, dead seals and ugliness—*if* I thought it'd heal the pain you carry. It won't. But I do love you."

"You use that word to control me. You love this isle, these nutty people. You know what I'm going to do, what I've done. I used you. How can you think you love me?"

She managed a weak laugh. "Men have been using women from the dawn of time, Des."

"My brothers are right now with your sisters," he prodded. "We're taking down everything Sean Montgomerie built, piece by piece. You can't stop us."

B.A. drew in a breath, steeled herself. "My sisters are grown women. They're more than a match for your brothers. Maybe they'll even teach them a thing or two. Let Mac and Cian defend M.E. and Colford. But I shall fight you over Falgannon. This island, these people—you and I—we're more important than events of decades ago. Evian's death taught me one thing: Life's too bloody short to waste. I *love* you, Des. What's more—you love me." She laughed, buoyed by the truth of it. She could see it in his eyes.

"It doesn't matter, B.A."

"Silly man, of course it does."

"Don't you see? I'm trapped. Loving you is a betrayal of everything my mother went through, the pain she suffered in losing my father."

Ignoring tears that clogged her throat, B.A. gave in to her temper. "I can't say I know how she suffered. However, I damn well know something about losing a husband. About surviving. Don't you *dare* tell me I wouldn't understand."

"You didn't have young sons to care for."

"You think that lessened my grief? I wished there'd been a child, something of him to linger in this world to mark his passing. Like a good mother, I'd have done whatever it took to see that child cared for. Yes, you had it hard, but you survived as a family—"

"While you lived in the lap of luxury," he pointed out.

She gasped, jumping to her feet. "Make up your mind, Des. I thought you were fighting my grandfather's ghost, seeking justice for wrongs done to your family. Now I'm hearing you resent *me*."

She picked up the square of plastic, stared at the pretty face that didn't have a care in the world. God, had she been that person? So carefree, not understanding the value of life's precious moments, how they could be stolen so easily? Studying the face, she wondered what her life would've been like had Desmond come for her fifteen years ago. She knew he believed he'd come to Falgannon for vengeance. He could've gone after Colford or Valinor Revisited. He'd chosen Falgannon. Silly man didn't even know why! She did.

"I've learned how precious each day is. So I know damn well how I'd feel if anything happened to you. Knowing that, no way in hell will I believe your mother would look me in the eyes and demand we can't share this. Take me to her. Then stand back. No one dares tell me I can't love you."

"No," came his strangled reply.

"I never thought you . . ." The last puzzle piece suddenly fell into place as she stared at his face. "She's *dead*. November. That's why you came back so haunted."

Reality slammed into her. Bloody hell, he was in shock, denial. The enormity of it nearly made her want to puke. Not only did the ghosts of Michael Mershan and Sean Montgomerie stand between them, now he carried the ghost of his mother. B.A. felt faint.

"I wasted seven years of my life hiding on this island because I was too bloody scared. You stepped into my world and allowed no retreat. You made me love you as I've never loved another soul. I want a life with you, Des. I want to laugh, cry, bear your children, know our love created such special little beings. I'm bloody well not going to toss that away because of people who are dead! You think the knowledge my grandfather destroyed your childhood will be easy for me to live with? That you went"—tears flooded her eyes as she struggled for every word—"hungry because of something my grandfather did? I regret life was rough for your mother, your brothers, you. That's the bloody past. I had no hand in it. What matters to me is the here and now, what we can have together. If you're so blind you can't see that, then maybe you don't love me. You have no concept of the word. And that's so sad. So empty."

"I *promised* her, B.A." His long black lashes batted tears. He glanced to the ceiling. "Hundreds of times I promised. In the hospital watching her die, the last thing she did . . . She begged. I *promised* . . ."

On rubbery legs, B.A. somehow reached the door. She wasn't sure where she was headed, but knew she couldn't stay or she'd be down on her knees begging. Worse, she knew it would make no difference. She feared nothing would.

Two days later, B.A. was going out the door of Lady Cottage when the phone rang. Hearing the voice on the line, she wished she'd ignored the call. The prospect of dealing with another Mershan hardly thrilled her.

"BarbaraAnne, this is Jago Mershan. I'm Desmond's—"

B.A. cut him off. "Mershan? I thought it was Fitzgerald. Yes, we spoke briefly before, you lying bastard."

"I see you share Asha's opinion of me. I'm calling about Des. Look, I'm at an airport waiting connections, but I need to speak with you."

"Since you hurt my sister, I'm so in the mood to listen."

"Asha's capable of extracting her own pound of flesh. And I'll make it up to her if I have to crawl on my belly and beg. Right now, this is urgent. I'm calling about Des. I spoke with him last night. It upset me. Whatever happens, *please* keep him on the island. I'm worried about him. He loves you."

"I know."

"That's a relief. I feared, like your precious sister, you'd pull a tizzy and try to punish Des until he comes around. My brother's erred . . . in many things. We *all* have. Right now, he's in trouble. Our mother died in November and Des hasn't adjusted. It wasn't an easy passing. . . ."

B.A. dropped into a chair. "I figured that out a few days ago."

"Damn," Jago said. "They're paging my flight. I can't afford to miss it and give your sister a head start. His whole life, Des put Mother, Trevelyn and me ahead of what was best for him. He needs someone to put him first. Can you, BarbaraAnne? Please remember that above all he loves you deeply. *Don't* let him off that island."

Rattled, B.A. replied, "I shan't," but it was to a dialing tone.

* * *

Walking through the door at The Hanged Man, B.A. faltered. Her eyes found Desmond at the center of the "Morn, B.A." Club, and like a coward, she almost fled. She bit her lower lip to stop the quivering, not wanting him to see how he still affected her. Dudley sat next to him, scarfing a rasher of bacon.

"Turncoat," she muttered.

"Morn, B.A.," the club chorused in typical fashion.

Desmond's eyes met hers. Damn him. Those beautiful warlock eyes. Guarded, questioning, challenging. She ached so badly to touch him—to kick him in the seat of the pants. Determination etched the curve of his sensual mouth, but that little-boy-lost look still flickered in his eyes.

She knew he was hurting, hadn't even begun to come to grips with his past or losing his mother. She couldn't weaken. For the island's sake, for hers, and for—the stupid blind man—his sake, too. His way, everyone lost.

Tam came over with a platter of scones. He gave her a once-over. "Sit, eat, lass. You look worse than what the moggies drag in."

"Just a sticky bun, Tam." She wanted to run. All those emotions Desmond provoked were careening about, slamming against her heart.

"Take that to the buffet." Tam shoved the platter at her. "I'll bring you a plate of sausage and gravy like your mum taught me to make."

She eyed him suspiciously. Her stomach rumbled, reminding her that she hadn't eaten in twenty-four hours. Putting down her case, she sucked in fortitude.

Setting the platter at the buffet, she asked, "Anyone need anything?"

"We're fine, lass. *The soft* is coming down outside. No one's going to be at the store. Have a seat," Ian encouraged.

"I'll . . . sit over there." She motioned to the windows—away from Desmond.

The twins grabbed her elbows, steering her to a chair next to the bloody warlock. She balked, but the two men wedged her in.

"What? You black-haired men stick together?" she

growled. She glanced about, seeking another path amongst the tables, but chairs shifted and legs stretched, ensuring her only option was to sit. She dropped down in frustration.

"Morning, B.A." Desmond poured her a cup of tea.

She glared at the tea, glared at him, then flashed a scorching look of reproach at her lads. Here was Desmond trying to destroy her isle—*their* isle—and they'd closed ranks with him!

" *'Sigh no more, ladies, sigh no more; Men were deceivers ever,'* " B.A. recited to herself.

"What's she muttering?" Angus squinted, trying to hear.

B.A. sipped her tea, letting her gaze sweep the room so she could casually come around to Des. With his forest green sweater, his eyes appeared even more startling. So handsome, he now appeared every inch the islander.

Tam carried in a plate of sausage, tatties and gravy. "Clean your plate, lass!" he barked.

Concentrating on her food, B.A. attempted to conjure mental blinkers to block Desmond. He wouldn't permit it. When she reached for the salt, he beat her to it. He held out the shaker with that beautiful magician's hand, an arched brow daring her to take it.

"The gravy needs a sprinkle of salt," he agreed.

"Waste of time. Our B.A. won't accept salt from a man," Angus sniffed.

Desmond's brows lifted.

"Blame Maeve. She taught her never to pass a man salt or take it from him. It's one of them witchy things our Maeve insisted she learn."

Des stretched his long legs beneath the table, brushing against B.A.—deliberately. She tried to retract her legs, but he slid one of his behind her calf and the other in front. When she shifted, Desmond clamped his around hers. "Of late, I'm interested in lore of the island. What is it about salt, B.A.?"

" 'Tis how a warlock gains control of a person—asks for salt," Michael the Story supplied. "If you pass it, you give away your free will and are open to his bidding."

"A warlock? Is that how you see me, B.A.?" he asked with a half smile.

"Careful," Ian cautioned. "Remember the rules about Montgomerie women. I'd scoot that knife out of her reach."

"Oh, she's already passed me salt, didn't you, B.A.?" Desmond held the shaker up before her nose and wiggled it.

B.A. glowered as he carefully sprinkled salt over her scones and gravy. Enough! She scooted her chair to get up, but he clasped her leg in a vise. As their struggle escalated, the table rocked. Dudley backed up and hissed.

"Our Desmond's levitating the table, him being a warlock 'n all," Ian joked.

Callum checked under the table. "Not a'tall. Our B.A. is playing footsie with him."

The whole room ducked to peek, leaving B.A. staring at Desmond. Why couldn't he see this was the way life should be? The perpetual joy, the silliness that made Falgannonians' lives so simple, so beautiful.

"You need to watch our B.A. She molests our Desmond in public places. Ashamed you should be, lass." Angus shook his knife at her.

"Och, Angus, I'm a bold sinful lass and a Montgomerie." Deciding to fight fire with fire, she picked up her fork and slid a chunk of scone into her mouth, half-moaning at Tam's culinary skill. She caught Desmond's spellbound stare and ran her tongue over her lower lip to capture a drop of gravy. All smugness vanished from him, replaced by intense longing.

She said with a breathy sigh, "Tongues are useful things, aren't they?"

Michael the Story hissed, "Sic him, lass."

I plan to, B.A. decided. She merely had to plot the finer points of when and where.

Desmond caught her hand as she headed down the pub walkway. "We need to talk," he said.

"About what, Des?"

"I'd like to discuss my plans." He held her hand, anchoring her.

"I'd hoped you might wish to talk about *us*. Trident might succeed in the takeover of M.E., and you can build bloody oil platforms. But guess what? Falgannon is out of the picture. You can't do one thing here until you have something more than that worthless piece of paper."

Triumphant, she started off, but he pulled her around, saying words she dreaded: "Crofters' rights."

"Hmm?" She feigned ignorance.

"You mentioned a provision for the islanders to claim their hereditary lands."

"Only the Frasers have."

He glanced about, clearly wishing for a more private place. "I bought Valinor, paid more than fair market value. Money doesn't mean anything. The islanders can claim Crofter's rights. I'll pay double, triple what they're worth, and give them a relocation fee."

B.A. felt nauseous. "Resettle them where, Des? This island is our home, our way of life. These people stay because they love Falgannon as I do."

"You're sure? My offer would make them rich."

B.A. pressed her lips together, fighting against her pain. "So, only the isle and I shall suffer? How kind, Des. Don't you see? This island exists in a beautiful snowglobe, protected from cruelties of the world. You want to smash that bubble, smash my soul . . . our love."

He blinked but said nothing.

B.A. wanted to kick him. Her eyes went to his hand restraining her. "Let go, Des."

He didn't. He sallied again. "You like Falgannon in that snowglobe, safely tucked up from the ugliness everyone else faces. B.A. Montgomerie, snow princess of Falgannon. You're afraid your lads might want something more than being a feudal vassal to some 'Lady of the Isle.'"

She sneered. "I see how you succeeded in the cutthroat world of international business. I may be a snow princess, but you, Desmond Mershan, are a pit bull. You go for the throat. You play to win, do and say anything to achieve your goals. Well, this snow princess sees nothing wrong with her corner of the world where her people are happy. We don't face drugs, murder, robbery or child molesters. If that's hiding from the real world, most people would pay a fortune to do likewise. You're lucky I'm a smart lassie and see through your viciousness. Suck it up, Des. You're not going to win, no matter how dirty you fight."

He dared her, "Prove it. Call a meeting at the town hall. Let me make my pitch. If the majority goes for it, you deed me the one-third of the isle Sean put up for collateral, stand back and let me go ahead with my plans."

"A bargain with the devil?" She swallowed, scared. "What do I get if you lose?"

"I'll leave Falgannon. I'll give up my plans."

She had to take two breaths to get past her own reaction. The silly nodcock thought he could just walk away? She fought back her anger.

"What's wrong B.A.? Scared your lads will abandon you?"

She laughed, all bluster. "Call your meeting. A week from Friday."

His brows lifted. "Friday the thirteenth? You want to run that risk?"

B.A. was sure her smile looked feline. It *felt* feline. Desmond looked unnerved, but he held his ground. "I'll hazard it, Des."

"The thirteenth it is."

"Now seal the bargain." And B.A. shocked Desmond by leaning into him and opening her mouth against his. She smiled when she felt his thighs stiffen with fear, then she kissed him, fed that intense hunger that gnawed at her day and night; she relished his taste, the scent of his skin. She kissed him with every ounce of her passion, her love. His hands grabbed her, pressing her tighter against him, kissing her back with everything he sought to deny.

She heard the door to The Hanged Man open, aware that the lads filed out to watch. Well, let them! She couldn't care less who saw the love she felt for Desmond. She'd always feel it.

"The lass breaks the kiss first," she heard Jock chime. "Two-to-one"

Michael the Story countered, "Four-to-one says Desmond won't let her go."

"Done," several agreed.

Small feet sounded, then even smaller feet, as Wee Gordie and Dudley approached. "Da, the Viking's pillaging our B.A. again!" Dudley rubbed against Desmond's and B.A.'s legs.

B.A. hated to ruin the lads' betting, but she stepped back. Her heart rolled over in satisfaction when Desmond clung.

"Ha! See, Desmond's not letting go. I win," Michael exclaimed.

Confused, Desmond's eyes searched hers. He wanted to know how she could still care. B.A. reached up and wiped her pink lipstick from his mouth with her thumb.

Almost in desperation, he taunted, "I'll win, B.A. I always do."

"Bite me," she replied. Retrieving her briefcase, B.A. danced down the cobbled road intent on shopping for a Valentine's Day present.

Chapter 29

Sitting behind the table on the town hall stage, Desmond glanced at his watch. B.A. was late. Hairs on his neck warned the witch was plotting a grand entrance. His eyes roved the room and the gathering of men, the few married women, the Marys, Oonanne, Morag and Janet. All were restless and knew their B.A. was up to something. All were aware nothing would happen until the Lady of the Isle showed.

Even Wulf and Dennis were in the audience, wearing the Reborn Falgannonian sweatshirts. At Desmond's raised brows, both smiled and waved.

This past week she'd been everywhere, doing everything. She'd launched her new cologne line for men, Warrior Prince. The image of the warrior on the package gave him pause. He picked up a box and stared at the face—his face, which he shared with Iain Sinclair. B.A. had smiled when he'd joked about royalties. She'd said "Bite me," her new retort to everything.

But she was going to say it once too often.

Outside of her suggestions to bite her, B.A. had stayed polite. Still, he feared she'd kick him in the arse each time he turned his back. In odd moments he caught her looking at him. Those whisky-colored eyes ripped into his soul.

He'd moved back to Rose Cottage. In male sympathy, Dudley took up residence with him. Annie had remained with B.A. Nearing four months old, the gray-striped kitten went everywhere with her. Annie was always thrilled to see Dudley, crawling all over him, driving him nuts, but the instant B.A. left, Annie was on her heels.

Rose Cottage became a bachelor's abode. LynneAnne had returned to New York, accepting a job to restore a turn of the century carrousel. The whole island went to bid her farewell. She'd left Julian with the parting shot, "Bloody pirate, I hope to never see you or your earring again." She'd made it clear she wouldn't forgive Julian for being "Desmond's creature." Personally, Desmond wondered if that was a real warning or female-speak for *"Come and get me."*

Impatient to get this meeting over with, Desmond opened his mouth to start outlining the breakdown of Mershan International's offer, when The Ancients broke into cackles.

"Och, look at that!" Callum the Ancient hooted, nearly choking on his laughter. " 'Tis Mel Gibson!"

"Feeble-minded Mackenzie! Not a'tall, that's William Wallace," Angus corrected, slapping his knee. "Come to battle Desmond Longshanks."

Desmond eyed Callum the Ancient, concerned they'd have to call Lewis for a helicopter to airlift the man to the hospital. Callum the Bicycle went to his great-grandfather and thumped the old man on the back. Desmond shook his head.

Then everyone ran to the doors and windows.

There was a sight to see. B.A. rode a black horse down the hill. Dressed in black leather pants and knee boots, she also wore a leather vest similar to what Gibson wore in *Braveheart*. Silly woman, half her face was painted with blue woad. Slung diagonally across her back was a claymore. Desmond had the feeling it was the sword she'd given him for Christmas. The *plaide* diagonally across her chest was neither Mackenzie nor Montgomerie, but the dark red and black of Sinclair.

Desmond eyed Cam the Tailor. "Your efforts?"

The man beamed. "Aye, unveiling our new William Wallace bridegroom attire for Falgannon Bridal Gallery. It'll be popular online. Already had thirteen orders from Japan."

Desmond offered a hand, but stubborn, the female lifted her right leg over the horse's neck and slid off, landing before him. She stared at him, her mysterious feline smile saying, *Buckle up baby, it's about to get bumpy.* Desmond had never for one minute doubted otherwise.

Lifting his eyebrow, he asked, "May we start, Mel, or do you plan on breaking into your Sons of Scotland speech?"

"Many lesser fields were dismissed after the major finds in the North Sea. . . ."

Desmond had addressed the Falgannonians for the past forty-seven minutes. He feared he was boring them to death. He *knew* he was. He tried to get to the point: the money.

"Due to technological advances, we're now looking at these modest fields once deemed too costly to tap. Smaller companies such as Talisman Energy, Paladin and Trident Ventures are more efficient than the petroleum giants. Already, they're working the East Shetland Basin in the Ninian Field, the Irish Sea, Atlantic Margin and Atlantic Frontier. Trident Ventures has the leases on the Seaforth Field northwest of Falgannon. In a few weeks Mershan International will buy out Trident Ventures. We hope to develop Falgannon as a supply base for the three platforms that will service the Seaforth Field. We plan a heliport, a second commercial harbor on the northwest side and storage facilities. We foresee new housing for families of the rigs' employees and support workers. To this end, Mershan International wishes to purchase your properties—at triple their value. You'd be relocated to another part of the island or to the mainland, if you prefer. Mershan will add 50,000 pounds for each of you to resettle."

He had expected a burst of questions, but they sat smiling. Finally, Angus called from the back, "Fine speech our Desmond gave, eh?"

Murmurs of "Aye" rippled through the room.

Michael the Fiddle yelled out, "Have your hearing aid on?" "Eh?"

Callum the Ancient poked Angus with his cane. "Michael Og wants to ken if you had your trannie on."

"Well, no," Angus replied, "but I'm sure our Desmond did a bang-on job."

"Yes, I did, Angus." Desmond tried to laugh off his unease. "I thought I'd open the floor to questions."

"What if we dunna want to be . . ." Patrick in the front row paused, making a face. "What did our Desmond call it?"

"Relocated," half the room supplied.

"Yeah, what if we dunna want to be relocated?"

Desmond fought his frown. "If you sell your property to Mershan, you'll be rich enough to live anywhere you want."

Ian stood. "You're overlooking the fact if we wanted to live elsewhere, we'd do it. We live on Falgannon because we want to."

Angus waved his cane to emphasize his statement. "I was born on Falgannon. I'll die here, God willin'. B.A., you ain't really going to permit our Desmond to pillage me, are you?"

"Our Desmond wants to kiss Angus?" Wee Gordie gasped.

Frustrated, Desmond sat. They each had to have their say, but he should've seen dealing with these loony Falgannonians wouldn't be a walk in the park. He glanced over at B.A., who was sitting at the other end of the table. Tears of pride moistened her eyes.

Angus pressed, "Tell us, B.A., what you think about the Vikings plundering us."

B.A. stood. "Sons of Falgannon, on our isle, the past matters, our heritage matters, *people* matter. You can travel far and wide, but nowhere will you find the timeless perfection we enjoy here. We have the best of the modern world, yet sleepily cling to our past. In some ways Falgannon exists within a bubble—a snow globe." She glanced at Desmond. "We change little, and in a magical way the island renews itself. I don't own Falgannon but am its keeper, one in a long line reaching back to the dawn of time. I'm charged with nurturing our way of life, with seeing during my stewardship that the island continues as it did before me, as it should after me."

Ian Fraser nodded and called, "You tell 'em, Mel! I mean B.A.!"

"We live in peace, with no fear for our homes, our families. We breathe fresh air and walk on white sand beaches. We're happy. Money can't buy happiness, friendship, peace of mind or love." She flashed Desmond a look. "Our ancestors fought Viking invaders because they believed this isle was worth the struggle. We can't stop oil platforms from being built seventy kilometers offshore, but we dunna have to open Falgannon to the threat of oil spills, dangers of possible terrorism—"

"Oh aye," Innis seconded. "I have a DVD of *Ffolkes—North Sea Hijack* with that laddie Roger Moore. You dunna want Norman Bates to come a-calling on Falgannon!"

"Each of you must decide. Mershan International will give you a period to choose—"

"What's to choose, lass? We ain't going anywhere," Brian voiced.

A chorus of "Ayes" filled the hall.

Desmond sat, defeat pounding in his temples.

Everyone headed to The Hanged Man to toast their victory against the Viking horde. Even Dennis and Wulf went, leaving Desmond alone with B.A.

He packed his papers into his briefcase, glancing at B.A. He wasn't sure how he felt. Not angry. Deep in his heart he'd known the islanders would stand shoulder-to-shoulder with B.A., he supposed. Maybe he felt relief: The matter had been taken from his hands. He might press B.A. to settle Sean's debt, but he could no longer ruin Falgannon. That was good.

"Des, are you all right?" B.A. came over to him.

He exhaled. "Why shouldn't I be, B.A.?"

Her fae eyes roved over his face. "Because this was more than business to you. It's wrapped up with the past and your inability to let go."

"I'm fine, B.A."

She smiled sadly. "I worry about you."

"Enough to come to my bed?" he goaded. "I miss you at night."

"If only it were that simple."

"It is that simple. You make it hard."

They both chuckled at the double-entendre.

She sighed. "The problem of Falgannon is settled. What isn't settled is your past. Until you let go, nothing will work for you, Des."

He sat on the table and eyed her, trying to see what to do next. "I've never kissed a woman with a blue face before." He glanced at her leather pants. "Nor one wearing my clothes."

"They fit rather well." She spun in a circle.

"Oh, aye." He nodded, his mouth quirking up. "You look better in them than I did."

"I wouldn't go that far."

His hands grasped her hips and pulled her between his legs, and he was surprised she came willingly. He studied her half-blue face, those glowing eyes that bored into his soul. Reaching out, he traced the line of her jaw down her graceful neck. Then he kissed her, slow and gentle, ignoring the growling beast within. The kiss brought tears to his eyes. Swallowing, he broke the embrace, feeling as if his insides had shattered.

"What am I to do with you, B.A.?"

"Whatever makes you happy. It's not complicated."

"I . . . can't. It wouldn't work."

"Why? What's so hard about loving me, loving the island?"

He rose, his jaw tight. "It's tearing me apart, B.A. Can't you understand?"

"*Make* me understand."

"I can't sleep. The stress is killing me."

"But you promised this was over. Will leaving Falgannon and me give you peace?"

He threw up his hands. "I can't go on like this. There won't be anything left of me."

"Des, just leave the past in the past. Accept that you're happy here—"

"I can't!" He closed his eyes, trying to control his pain. "Every time I make love to you it's a betrayal."

"Of your mother? Give it up, Des. Vengeance is a cold lover. You're in denial, not facing your grief. You're not stopping to look at your life, what it'll be if you turn your back on me and this island. Envision yourself five years from now. Will you be happy then?"

Staring at Des, B.A. forced herself to say words she'd been holding back. She knew he wasn't ready to hear them. Knew she might lose him if she kept silent.

"I dinna know Katlyn. Because she was your mother she holds a special place of honor for me. She created a beautiful, wonderful being when she gave you life. But instead of adoring that precious child, she twisted you. Don't tell me how she worked hard, she suffered. A lot of people work hard, but they don't lie on their deathbeds begging their son to ruin his life for vengeance. My heart cries for the pain she felt when your father died. I know that pain. I'm sorry for her illness. She was your mother, so you love her—but did she really love you?" She saw his face darken, but wouldn't back down. Too much was at stake. "If you were my son and I was dying, my last thought would be that I love you. I'd consider hardship a small price for having you in my life. I'm sorry, Des, but it seems your mother was a bitter, selfish woman. And you're allowing her to reach from the grave and destroy your life."

"If you were a man I'd ram those words down your throat," he snarled.

His coldness made B.A. flinch. She'd pushed the limits by saying those things about Katlyn, but Desmond needed to stop wrapping himself in the image of his Madonna mother who'd suffered. He'd suffered, too.

He turned and crammed his papers into the attaché. "I'll be leaving come Monday."

B.A.'s legs nearly gave out. She channeled her pain into temper. "You forget, I can stop the ferry if I choose."

"Go ahead. I'll have them fly the chopper in. Might be better that way, anyway." Then Desmond strode down the steps and out the door, never looking back.

"You're a bloody coward, Desmond Mershan!" she called after him, but he didn't slow.

B.A. huffed, leaning against the table. "She was suddenly glad she'd had Skylar finish the Valentine's present. It was going to come in handy later that night.

The clock struck 2:00 A.M. when singing below the castle clued B.A. to their imminent arrival. She hid Desmond's Valentine's present, then paused to fold the duvet down on the bed.

Hurrying to the door, she opened it. The cat came dashing in. Thrilled, Annie gave a squall and charged. Dudley flashed B.A. a disgusted look, which increased when he saw his empty food bowl. Hoping to keep them from being underfoot, B.A. filled both bowls. Annie instantly began chomping—from Dudley's. Dismayed, Kitty sat and sniffed in disdain.

Ian and Brian came through with Desmond slung between them. "Stand aside, lass," Ian laughed. "After eating Tam's cooking for months, he's an armful."

"Me, too," Desmond chirped, lifting his head.

"Go on through." B.A. followed. "He resist you getting him foxed?"

"Not a'tall. Quite willing to drown his sorrows," Brian answered, pouring Desmond into bed. "You won't go thumping our Des again, lass. 'Tis not fair when a man can't defend himself." He tugged off Desmond's boots and handed them to her.

B.A. smiled sadly. "He told me he's leaving Monday."

"Och, hasn't he learned Montgomeries never listen?" Ian patted her on the shoulder. "Happy Valentine's Day. Enjoy your present."

She kissed them both on the cheek. "Thanks. See everyone leaves us alone, please."

Leaning against the bedpost, she stared at Desmond. His long black hair, its waves made her itch to run her fingers through it. With delightful plans in mind, she was eager to have at it, but she could also stand and ogle him all night. Both cats jumped on the bed, headed for Desmond.

"Well, do I start at the top and work down, or begin with the socks and make my way up to that sexy mouth?" B.A. asked herself.

"B.A.?" Desmond mumbled.

"Here, Des." *And ready,* she added silently.

"My head . . ."

She grinned, warming to the task ahead. "You're shitefaced. Let's get you out of your clothes and tucked up."

Annie pounced upon Desmond's foot. Dudley stretched out with a look that said, *Better thee than me*.

"Hey," Desmond complained, as the kitten's play became a little too spirited.

"She's excited to see you." B.A. sat on the bed to pull off his sweater.

His sleepy lids lifted. "Are you?"

"You have no idea."

As she yanked off his sweater, his hands skimmed her ribcage and upward so that his thumbs brushed the tips of her breasts. Back and forth. Back and forth. B.A. nearly lost her train of thought as her body ignited. The damn bustier she had on under her robe pushed her breasts up, so every stroke was like yanking puppet strings.

His white teeth flashed. "Yeah, very excited."

She shuddered, fighting the pull of her need for him. "Hold that delicious thought, Des, and let's get you undressed."

"So you can have your wicked way with me?"

"Precisely." Tugging his t-shirt over his head, she pushed him on the back. "It's after midnight. Valentine's Day."

"Is it?"

She removed his socks, then unbuckled his pants and pulled them off, stopping to laugh at the boxers. He was wearing the pair she'd given him for Christmas, with Bull-winkle the Moose taking a bath on them. Of course, Bull-winkle was slightly distorted by his pulsing erection. Patting it, she said, "Down boy, we've a ways to go."

Despite evidence of his interest, she could tell he was drifting. Fine with her. She had a few tricks up her sleeve and preferred he didn't discover his Valentine's present un-til everything was in place. She wiggled the Bullwinkle shorts off his body, then sighed at the perfection of Desmond Mershan.

"Am I lucky or what?" she said.

Opening the nightstand drawer, she removed Desmond's gift. She uncoiled it slowly so that it didn't jingle. Snapping one end to the ring Skylar had installed at the base of the headboard bedpost, she locked it. On the end of the chain, B.A. slipped the padded leather cuff around Desmond's an-kle, saying a little prayer it'd be as strong as Skylar promised. Somehow, she suspected Desmond would pitch a wee tizzy when he sobered. Then the fun would begin.

The cuff fit like she wanted: not tight. The small lock shut with a satisfying click. The way she looked at it, she was merely continuing an old family tradition.

She set a glass with Morag's goop on the nightstand. She was tempted to let him sleep, but then he'd awaken with a hangover. He'd be cranky enough when he discovered the chain.

Sitting on the bed by his hips, she stroked his beautiful chest. Leaning across him, she put her head against his heart, listening to its slow, strong thudding. His arms came up, clutching her shoulders, cradling her against him. Telling her what she needed to know.

Untangling his arms, she helped him sit. "Des, drink this." He downed half a glass, then pushed it away. She insisted. "The *whole glass*, my braw laddie."

Morag's brew worked without fail, outside of Dennis and Wulf, but she wasn't sure how fast so B.A. pulled the duvet over him. Leaning close, she kissed his forehead. "Happy Valentine's Day, my love," she promised.

* * *

A yanking on the chain brought B.A. awake with a start. It took seconds to get her brain in gear. Desmond was awake, and the sweet man looked perturbed. Good. This wouldn't be fun if he just accepted it.

"B.A., what the hell is this?" He held up the chain attached to his ankle.

"Rather self-evident," she replied, getting up.

He gave several sharp pulls. "Damnit, B.A., this is a lousy joke."

B.A. approached his side of the bed. "Skylar did a bang-on job."

"This isn't funny," he snarled.

She smiled sweetly. "Speak for yourself."

A couple more yanks only increased his temper. "B.A., unlock this bloody thing."

"After I went to all this hard work? I think not."

"You didn't even leave me my shorts!"

She shrugged. "I love Bullwinkle, but dinna think he was conducive to this setting."

He stopped jerking on the chain. "You planned this, had them get me drunk. Why?"

"I'm following the tradition started by our ancestors. I'd think Deporadh and Iain would be proud. Besides"—she held out her arms, showing off her red silk robe—"it's Valentine's Day. That's why I'm in red." She lifted the lapel of her gown an inch so she could peek down at the bustier Oona designed. "Actually, not *all* red. There's a touch of black."

Desmond stared. "You're my present?"

She laughed. "Not quite—you're mine." She touched the cuff, then trailed her hand up the inside of his leg. "The chain's long enough to reach the bathroom, but not to go downstairs. I warned you I'd stop you from leaving the island."

"I never thought you'd chain me to the damn bed!"

Poor Des, his face revealed so many emotions: frustration at finding himself chained, determination . . . Yet his eyes kept going to her cleavage. She had him hooked as well as cuffed.

"Should I consider myself lucky you didn't cuff my wrists, too?"

"Figured your hands might be put to good use."

He glared at her. "What if I *refuse* to put my hands to good use?"

"Your choice." But playing dirty, she slowly pulled on her belt until the sides of her robe parted. "Oona's launching a new line for Falgannon Bridal Gallery."

"Why didn't I know?" Quirking a brow, Desmond sat back and crossed his arms.

"Your first morning on Falgannon, I brought you breakfast and had red roses on the tray? My Lady's Passion always reminded me of red satin and black lace. You echoed my thoughts. Recall?"

"I recollect, B.A." His eyes said he remembered every detail.

"I asked Oona to design something in that shade of red, trimmed with black lace . . . and ta-da." The robe dropped from her shoulders, spilling in a pool of scarlet around her bare feet. The scarlet bustier cinched in her waist and flared over her hips, but she didn't think Desmond noticed; his line of vision didn't get that low. "Will the new Falgannon honeymoon line be a success?" she asked.

His smoldering eyes ruined his air of sangfroid. "It has . . . possibilities."

She turned, lifting her long hair so he could see how the bustier laced up the back. "It also has tiny hooks up the front so a woman can—"

"Or a man," he growled.

She smiled over her shoulder. "Or a man, yes. So the bustier can be undone. Oona said she wants your impressions."

He growled. "I'm not sure I like being Oona's lab rat."

She turned, coming near enough to see the black ring around his pale green eyes. The flare of his nostrils reminded her of a stallion scenting a mare in season. "As I watched you rub those roses against your lips, I wanted to have something like this on. I wanted you so badly, as I'd never wanted any man. Only, you see I'm a coward. I lost everything. I hid on this island, afraid of being hurt again. You wouldn't let me hide. You made me risk all. So I'm taking one final gamble. You've lost your bid for revenge. But can you leave me, Des? Really walk away from me? I won't let you."

B.A. leaned forward, brushing her mouth against his. She savored his taste, which made her dizzy, so she failed to anticipate his spring. Desmond's hands suddenly grabbed her about the waist, lifted her with ease and tossed her diagonally across the bed. On his hands and knees, he loomed over her; his eyes devoured her.

"What am I to do with you, B.A.?"

The woman in her reveled in the pure male power surging through him. She reached up and stroked both his cheeks with her thumbs. "*Love* me, Des, just love me."

He turned to kiss the inside of her left hand, then her right. Closing his eyes, he rubbed his face against her palm. A tear slid across it. She nearly flinched, not wanting to cause Desmond hurt, but she'd be damned if she'd make any escape easy for him.

Then he was kissing her—not a gentle kiss, but one speaking his violent need. It'd been a while since he last shaved, so his whiskers were rough. That didn't stop her from responding in full measure. She held nothing back, pouring her love into her passion, letting her body speak so eloquently those words he didn't want to hear.

Ripping her black thong, he entered her in one hard plunge. It was as though he sought to bring this to a brutal physical level rather than one of love. He stretched her arms over her head, then laced his fingers with hers, and he drove himself into her again and again. Determined not to let him have total control, she arched, meeting each fierce thrust.

A climax came, splintering her into a thousand red-hot shards. But instead of relaxing and allowing himself ecstasy, he increased his pace, driving onward, not giving any retreat.

"Again, B.A."

She purred, "Yes, Des, again." Wrapping her legs about his waist, she increased the angle and let the emotional storm sweep through them.

Desmond held a key between two his fingers: the key to his freedom.

Or was it?

He'd awoken an hour ago, jerked up, covered in sweat,

fighting to escape a nightmare. His heart hurt worse than ever before. It felt as if a fist gripped it, squeezed.

He glanced at B.A., who was sleeping soundly. Small wonder. Saturday and Sunday they'd barely slept. They'd made love with a relentless, lashing passion; B.A. trying to convince him he couldn't leave her, he hungrily soaking up every moment to carry away with him.

His exhaustion had allowed the dream to come. His father's death. Yet, for the first time, instead of seeing it up close, there was an odd distance, as though he looked through the wrong end of a telescope. The heartbreaking memories, the pain he carried, his mother . . . feeling he should've done something *more* to make it easier for her . . . Even the shame, that though he was one of the richest men in the world, he hadn't been able to make her happy. Oddly, he'd viewed it all with detachment. No matter how he tried, he couldn't get closer. Gray mist swirled about him. If he could push his way through the fog, he'd find . . . something. He had to hurry or he'd never unearth the elusive piece.

The key to saving himself.

He stared at the key in his fingers, wondering if he was headed for a heart attack or silently going mad. The answer was just out of reach.

He'd figured out B.A.'s hiding place. She'd taped the key to the bottom of the snow globe LynneAnne gave her for Christmas. The globe had a huge white rose in it, and behind that, a castle. With the snow swirling, the fortress resembled Falgannon. A special gift, it was her sister's promise of what could be. How fitting that B.A. would choose to hide the key there.

Resolute, he knew he couldn't stay. He unlocked the cuff around his ankle, smiling at the lass's audacity. Her imagination. Her love. Few women would go all out to convince a man of their feelings. That B.A. loved him, he had no doubt. Even after all he'd done. And with all the destructive emotions swirling within, that was why he had to go. He feared he might lash out and hurt her.

Desmond stalked to the window, staring into the pale dawn. He tilted his head back against the emotion threatening to swamp him. "I wish you hadn't done this. It's not making it any easier on me, B.A."

Her voice breaking, she replied from the shadows, "I *don't want* to make it easy, Des."

He spun, surprised she was awake. "B.A., don't you see I can't stay? I'll hurt you."

B.A. came up behind him, sliding her arms around his waist, hugging him tightly. "The only way you'll hurt me is if you leave."

B.A. leaned her head against Desmond, fighting tears. She felt his thudding heart. Hard. Too hard. The aftereffects of another nightmare.

If he could only open that heart . . .

He turned, his hands taking hold of her arms. "Come with me," he whispered, a tinge of desperation eking through the words. "Maybe away from Falgannon we could find a life together."

"Maybe?" she echoed hollowly.

Her eyes searched his face, drowned in those beautiful eyes. It'd be so easy to say yes. He was a man she'd follow through hell and back. Only, giving in to him would see a slow death in their relationship take hold. A woman could accept a lot from the man she loves; they had since the dawn of time. But not to watch their love die. No matter how strong a woman was, she couldn't go through that crucible and survive. "I can't."

"Can't or won't?" he growled through gritted teeth.

"Either . . . both." She trembled.

"Damn you." His eyes were full of fury, full of pain. "Damn me . . ."

He pushed her to the bed, his mouth taking hers. He kissed her until reason fled and only the consuming flames of passion remained. He devoured her with the hunger of a man seeking dominance or salvation. He pulled B.A. under him, his weight bearing down to pin her in place as if he feared her resisting him. As if she ever would.

She knew she waged a losing battle, and it'd likely see her gutted in the end. Time was running out. Desmond was too long in planning his revenge, and too wrapped up in grief; he couldn't see anything. He couldn't see what he'd done when he stood before Lady Rock. *Forever.* Worse, he failed to recognize the end result would leave him empty and hating himself.

Yet denying him would never cross her mind.

This was their last battlefield. She *had* to reach him, to cradle his wounded soul with her love and pray it was enough. If not, he'd destroy them both. She poured out every ounce of her love, her need, into her kiss, trying to show him there was something beyond cold vengeance, old promises, childhood pain. She held back nothing, giving everything he demanded, more than he asked. For this was nothing short of war, and she'd fight with every weapon she had, push him as hard as he pushed her. Maybe the conflagration would burn away his hatred, the anguish of the child who never healed inside him, destroy the scar tissue so something wonderful could take seed. They said wildfires that destroyed forests cleansed away decay and choking vines. More importantly, it was only through purging fire that pinecone seeds opened and created seedlings. Witch that she was, B.A. knew this fire would do the same: create a life within her. She prayed with every fiber of her being that love could vanquish the memories strangling Desmond, replace the destructive bent with a bright promise of hope and happiness . . . with her and the child they'd create.

B.A. was betting everything, her entire future, on this final toss of the dice.

Chapter 30

Desmond stood on the pier, staring up the hill at the village. His right arm rested on the edge of the door, the left on top of the Rover. Waiting. His eyes searched for B.A. Hoping she'd . . . what? Drag him back to the castle and keep him prisoner again?

The Cat currently inspected his car's interior as though he was Falgannon's Port Authority and checking that Desmond didn't smuggle any Stop-Breath off the island.

Some of the islanders had come to see him off. They were respectful, but he read in their eyes they thought him a fool for leaving. Maybe he was.

Callum gave him pictures of Dudley, the castle and several of Desmond dancing with B.A. at a *cèilidh*. Souvenirs, he'd said. Desmond swallowed the tightness in his throat, nearly overwhelming when he saw the pictures of B.A., her face bright and shining with love. The same expression was clear upon his countenance.

A ghostly breeze ruffled his hair, which was much longer than when he'd first arrived on Falgannon. B.A. liked the length and it felt natural. He wore boots, black corded riding pants and a knit sweater, clothing now a part of him, who he was, more than any expensive Louis Vuitton had ever been. He'd come as a stranger to the isle, but looked, felt, like he belonged. Gone was the polished businessman. He was an islander to the soul, as though he'd been born of Falgannon. Precisely what B.A. had tried to tell him.

Dudley hopped into the driver's seat, purring loudly, hoping for pets. When none came, he reached up and snagged Des's arm. The daggers of his claws made it through the heavy cable knit.

"Och, you bloody beastie," Des snapped. A burr threaded in his voice.

His hand trembling, he scratched Dudley's chin. Scratching the cat was merely an excuse to linger . . . hoping . . .

He knew B.A. loved him. She'd demonstrated that in every way possible. She just wasn't willing to settle for anything less from him.

Angus the Ferry and Jamie Macleod hurried down the hill, shoulders hunched against the damp. A few more trips and Jamie would take over for Angus, the latter making it clear he wanted rid of the isle—and Janet—as quickly as possible. Soon, the Falgannonians would have a Jamie the Ferry. Desmond wouldn't be around to share that.

"Morn there, Desmond. Be about a half hour before you

can board," Angus called. "We'll lower the gate when we're ready."

So Desmond stood in *the soft,* allowing the mist to hit his face as he glanced up Harbor Hill. He half-expected to see B.A. in her William Wallace gear coming to fetch him. *Praying she'd come.* He imagined she'd pull that sword on him and demand he kneel to her in fealty. Deep in his heart, he wished to see her running down the hill, a suitcase in one hand, the cat carrier with Annie in the other, calling she was going with him.

It wasn't to be, he guessed. The island was more important to her, as it had been to Maeve—likely as it was to every Lady of the Isle.

Angus the Ancient tottered over and held out his autograph book. "Anna Nicole Smith's agent wrote she ain't coming. So if you'd do me the honor, I'd be thanking you."

It felt odd signing an autograph, but on Falgannon out of the ordinary was normal. He signed it carefully with the respect due the dear old man, then passed it back. "The honor was mine, Angus." Reaching into his pocket, he pulled out his wallet and removed his business card, pausing as he saw the plastic covered picture of the young B.A.

Swallowing the tightness, he held out the card. "If need arises . . . you can reach me."

Angus accepted it, his gray eyes incisive. "Need arises? Like, you knocked up our lass and then left her?"

"That's a low blow, Angus." Desmond reeled from the old man's words, reeled from the guilt.

Angus nodded. "Aye, but you deserve it."

Desmond's head dropped. "I'm not a bastard, Angus. My mum died—"

"Why dinna you say?" Angus frowned in exasperation.

"Not recently, in November. I've not worked through the loss . . . It's a long story."

Angus patted his arm. "Open your eyes, lad. The years go too fast and can be damn lonely. I lost my lovely Cammie thirty-three years ago. Don't waste precious time. Stay with B.A. 'Tis the best medicine."

Desmond looked up at the sky. "If I stay, I'll hurt her.

There's so much blackness in my soul. I need to go away and find out how to deal with that."

"Stuff and nonsense. Running away is never the way to deal with a trouble."

The blue Rover topped the crest of the hill, catching Desmond's attention. His heart stuttered, not daring to hope. Pulling perpendicular into a parking space a short distance away, B.A. got out and walked the rest of the way down the steep incline. He saw Annie's small face peeking out the car window.

She'd dressed in jeans and a sweater. No William Wallace blue face, no sword. Her long hair was skimmed back in a ponytail.

"No suitcase," he commented.

With a smile, she shrugged. "Figured I wouldn't need it." She reached into the pocket of her jacket and pulled out a red handkerchief. With trembling fingers, she unfolded it to reveal a small white rose. "It's not very big, and there are only five petals. Already the edges tinge brown, telling how fragile it is, that it needs care. Our rose, from our planting— proof of our love. Falgannon magic. Open your heart, Des. Open your heart and see what you saw when you stood before Lady Stone . . . forever."

She tried to sound confident, but he saw the glistening in her amber eyes, how she pressed her lips together to keep her chin from quivering. Another stake to his heart.

"I *can't*, B.A. I have to get away from who I am, what I am."

"You're Desmond Mershan, the man I love. How much simpler can it be?" Her voice cracked on the question. "What we have is special; this rose tells just how rare. You cannot turn your back on that. You'll come back with me. Won't you, Des?"

He swallowed, then spoke. "Dammit, this . . . this beast inside is eating me alive. I *hate* myself, B.A. I don't want to end up hating you, too."

She reached up and stroked his cheek. "Silly man, you dunna hate yourself, and you'd never hate me. I wouldn't let you use Falgannon to ease the pain of the past. For that you would've hated yourself. The rest . . . Give it time, Des. Time heals. Believe me, I know."

In desperation he pulled her against him, kissing her forehead. "*Please* let me go, B.A. Help me help myself."

"Stay, I'll do everything in my power to make you happy. I love you. God, I love you. Please don't do this."

"I can't see any other way. Maybe if we'd met at another place, another time . . ." He squeezed her tightly against him, whispered, "Good-bye, lass."

Pushing her away, he jumped into his car and locked the doors. B.A. kept talking. When she pounded on the glass and yelled at him, he switched the CD player on high. Iron Butterfly's "*In A Gadda Da Vida*" played, nearly vibrating the car off its tires.

Shutting his eyes, he leaned his head back, shaking so badly he thought he might never stop. He almost laughed, but caught himself, fearing he'd sound like a madman.

Inanely he wondered if anyone had ever figured out what that damn song title meant.

B.A. kicked the door of Des's silver Rover, leaving a dent. "Too bad it isn't his hard head!"

As she stalked off, Ian jogged to intercept her. "You okay, lass?"

She was all right, but getting bloody madder by the minute. "Go tell Angus to cut the engines. Ferry stays in harbor."

Ian smiled. "Done."

Stomping toward the blue Rover, B.A. was unsure what to do next. She *wasn't* letting Desmond off the island. She'd just wasn't.

B.A. tripped, righted herself, then noticed a heavy chain across the road. She'd been too upset to see it before. Skylar had received an order for it to hook boats together when they collected the sheep from an abandoned isle in June. She stared at the metal links, then glanced at Desmond's car, judging it as long as the distance between his car and hers.

"Serendipity," she said. She looked up the hill toward Lady Stone. "Thank you."

Keeping in the blind spots of the mirrors, she approached the vehicle, bending over and crouching low. Peeking over the edge of the back door, she saw Desmond sat with his speakers loud enough to wake the dead, his head leaning back. She couldn't tell, but she thought his eyes were closed.

"All the better to trick you, Desmond Mershan."

Dudley's head popped up in the rear window. He waved a paw at her. She blinked away a tear as she touched the glass. Dudley butted his nose to her finger, then meowed.

"Buckle up, Kitty. I'm hauling his stubborn arse back to the castle."

Kneeling, B.A. carefully fed the chain through the triangle of the trailer hitch, wrapping it around three times. "Three times three, let it be," and she whispered an ancient pagan spell as she set the big hook.

Stalking back to her navy Rover, she got in and slowly backed the car down the hill. Enough to be in range of the chain. She hopped out, wrapped the other end around her car's hitch. Climbing in, she slammed the door hard since the latch was having trouble.

"It's his own bloody fault—he gave me the Rover." Adjusting her rearview mirror, she noticed Annie jumped to the inside wheel well to stare out the back window, watching Dudley in the other auto. "Hang on, Annie, we're taking our men home."

She shifted into drive and hit the gas—maybe a little too hard because the wheels spun on the wet cobbled road. They grabbed, and the sedan jumped forward. As the chain played out, the blue Rover jerked and the silver vehicle bounced.

"Silly man, probably thinks 'In A Gadda Da Vida' is getting wound up." B.A. glanced in the mirror. Desmond's head snapped around. He saw what she was doing. "Got him by the arse, Annie. Next stop, the castle."

Pulling the second car's weight grew difficult. She gunned the gas, only to have the wheels slip again. She muttered under her breath, "Come on, come on . . ."

* * *

Lost in swirling thoughts, his fingers clutched around the snow globe with the rose, Desmond stared at its perfect bloom. The one B.A. had shown him had only five petals, the bush too new to support a flower of this size. But with care and feeding, dozens of blooms such as this would grow on their bush. Or would it die if he left. He shook the globe, watching the snow fall on the rose. B.A. had taped her key to the bottom of this globe. The key to his freedom. But was it? Reaching into the pocket of his jacket, he pulled out the box containing B.A.'s engagement ring.

Desmond felt his car jolt. Jerking around, he saw his Rover crawling away from the pier, moving slowly back up the hill. B.A. had chained their vehicles together and now hauled his up Harbor Road.

"She's a madwoman!" Sliding the ring box in his pants pocket, he turned on the front and rear wipers. The cat immediately swatted at the rear one. "She doesn't play fair, Dudley!"

Switching on the ignition, he pushed the gas. Her car's resistance was strong, the hitch cracking and popping under the torque. He had a slight advantage from being on the flat part of the road curving toward the ferry. Still, he had to be careful and cut the wheel to move parallel along the pier with the steep drop. He didn't have the room to maneuver that she did. His vehicle jump-bucked, but then the witch hit her gas and his wheels spun. He applied pressure to the pedal, the engine revving higher. The wet pavement prevented either of them from gaining the advantage.

A bloody tug of war! He blinked, fighting the emotions threatening to swamp him. Tears blurring his vision, his hesitation caused him to let up on the gas. Instantly, B.A. dragged him to the edge of the hill and gained speed. He glanced in the rearview mirror. If she crested the hill and reached the flat area in front of the store, control would shift to her.

Despite the rain, clusters of Falgannonians came to watch this new source of entertainment. Another time he'd delight in this quirkiness, their pleasure in every moment of life. Right now, he was shattered inside and didn't know how much longer he could hold together. Pressure built inside him to a dangerous level. Without meaning to, he floored the gas.

An odd ripping echoed inside him, then a noise like grinding metal, followed by a *ping-pong-ping*. It took a moment to comprehend it was the sedan, not him, creating that bizarre sound. Dudley went flying through the air as Desmond felt the hitch break free from the Rover. No time to look back; the Rover shot forward, up and over the pier. For a second he was weightless, sailing crosswise through the air toward the ferry, then crashing through the gate rail. The sedan dropped, leaving the back wheels hanging over, spinning uselessly in the air. Cutting the motor, he stared into Angus and Jamie's horrified faces.

Not pausing to consider his predicament, his head whipped around and he spotted villagers running toward the bottom of the hill. He searched frantically for B.A.'s Rover. His heart nearly stopped when he spotted it, half on the pier, half off.

He forced the door open and crawled out. Jumping from the ferry, he landed hard on the steep concrete incline, jarring his teeth. Leaning on his fingertips, he scaled the ramp. Wulf and Julian appeared, waiting to grab his wrists to pull him up.

"Come on—your lady's in a mess!" Julian's eyes met Desmond's, full of fear, turning his blood to ice.

They ran to where the crowd gathered. Desmond shoved people aside until he reached B.A.'s sedan. Dennis, the Michaels, the Frasers and Callum were spread around the vehicle. Balanced on the knife-edge of the pier, it rocked like a bizarre seesaw. Up against the pylon on the passenger side, the glass from that window was shattered. The hitch from his car hung outside, swinging like an obscene pendulum.

Brian yelled up the hill to Jock, "Hurry, man!"

Ian yanked Desmond's arm as he started forward. "Steady, lad. Time for cool heads. Jock's fetching a rope. We'll tie it off. You forgot rule number one—never let a Montgomerie female behind the wheel of a car when she has a mad on."

"Can you lean on the car's front until I get her out?" Desmond asked.

Brian nodded. "Maybe . . . but what if it starts rocking worse before we have it secured? The passenger door is smashed. B.A.'s out cold. We can't tell how badly. Pull yourself together man; her life depends upon it. Let's look in the passenger side."

Desmond forced back panic and followed the Frasers. Most of the broken glass wasn't inside the car, but had been knocked out by the hitch.

"Guardian Angels are working overtime today. She had the wheel cut sharply to turn into the store when the hitch gave. The hitch's path curved at the last minute, whiplashing through the window instead of into her," Ian explained.

"It didn't hit her?" Desmond choked.

"No, the bloody car stalled. No power steering, no power brakes. With the wheel locked, she nearly flipped. Hamish said he saw her head slam into the side window. But I don't think she hit it too hard, since the glass isn't cracked. She'll be coming to any sec. We need to present a calm front."

The buzzing inside Desmond's head was so loud it took a minute for him to hear Annie crying. It broke his heart. She was hanging from the last bench. If she let go, she'd drop into the water thirty feet below, possibly hit one of the boats there. It twisted in Desmond, but he couldn't do anything. If he called to Annie to come, her frail weight might be the straw that toppled B.A. and her over the edge.

"Got it!" Jock ran up panting, looping the rope around the front bumper.

"No!" Wulf growled and shoved Jock aside. Carefully, the Norwegian pulled the rope back. "That bumper will give away at first tug."

The big man scooted forward, glided the rope around the wheel. Men at the other end quickly dragged it up the hill and tied it off around an old bulldozer.

Desmond offered Wulf a hand. "Can we use the 'dozer to pull her onto the pier?"

Wulf's head gave a small shake. "Motor's out. I'm waiting for parts."

Desmond moved with Wulf, Julian and Ian to the driver side. Desmond wanted to howl; instead he said determinedly, "Let's get that door open and her out."

"Careful, Des," Julian warned. "That rope might not hold the car if it goes over."

B.A. stirred, jerking around in her seat.

Desmond risked tapping on the window. "Dammit, B.A., look at me."

She glanced up, puzzled. "What . . ."

"The hitch on my car gave. Your sedan stalled. You couldn't control it without power brakes and steering. Damn, a man barely could. You slammed up against the pylon, but your rear wheels are over the edge."

"Desmond! Annie's about to fall." She panicked and reached between the seats, setting the car to rocking again.

Five men screamed, "Whoa!" and threw their weight on the hood to counter her.

"Dammit, B.A.! Stop! Listen to me! You *can't* move!" Desmond stressed frantically.

B.A. cried, "She's going to fall."

"She's not," he lied without hesitation. "Do what I say. Annie and you'll be fine. B.A., are you listening?"

"Yes, Des," she said weakly.

"Can you unlock the door?"

"Not sure." Her voice quavered. "The lock has been catching. Remember?"

"Stay still. Don't move, B.A.," he instructed.

She nodded, then immediately turned to look at Annie. "Here, Annie, kitty, kitty . . ."

Annie took to screaming twice as loud. The tiny cat dragged herself to the back of the seat, but fear kept her from moving farther. B.A. kept calling, and Annie howled piteously.

Desmond carefully tried the door handle. It didn't work.

Julian came up close, leaning close to Desmond so his words didn't carry. "Wait, Des. Open the door with that odd incline, the weight will shut on B.A. Get her to roll down the window. Once it's down, pull her out the opening. That'll be less tricky."

Men shouted and rushed to the other side. Desmond panicked, thinking she was going over, that his precious B.A. would slip off the pier's edge. In that instant he knew that nothing in his life mattered more, nothing ever would. Without B.A., he wouldn't want to live.

He exhaled in relief when the car didn't shift. Dudley had jumped up on the pylon. Callum made to grab him, but Dudley growled. Giving his nemesis a dirty look, The Cat Dudley launched himself in a graceful arc through the open passenger window and scurried over the two seats to the rear.

"Grab the front," Desmond yelled. Julian and he threw their bodies onto the warm hood, trying to balance the weight of the fat feline moving inside.

Dudley approached Annie, and like a mama cat he grabbed the small gray kitten by the scruff of her neck. He jumped from the last bench to the second one, then into the passenger seat and finally out to the pylon, dragging terrified Annie with him.

Julian laughed. "If that doesn't beat all. Reckon you could do that with B.A.?" he joked, trying to ease the tension.

"Would if I could." Desmond eased off the hood cautiously and stepped to the window. "B.A., can you switch the ignition to accessory, then roll down the glass? Slowly."

B.A. nodded and did so. "Did you see? Dudley's a hero."

"Yes, he is." Desmond blinked away tears. "Now let me be one, too, B.A."

"Des, I love you." She trembled, tears streaming down her pale cheeks. The way she spoke made it seem like a goodbye. His eyes darted to the boats bobbing below, fear a razor to his soul.

"Bloody hell, B.A., don't go all female on me now. I need my warrior woman."

"Des . . . *hurry,*" Julian pressed.

Desmond saw the rope holding the car beginning to fray, filaments unwinding strand by strand. "B.A., you need to carefully rotate in the seat so you can snake your arms out the door."

"Des!" Julian, Dennis and Ian pressed.

He ignored them. More lads rushed up, word having spread to the rest of the villagers, but he only peripherally noticed. "Come on, B.A. It's bloody wet out here. We need to go in and congratulate Dudley on being a hero. Worm your arms out the window."

"Yes, Des."

Slowly, she shifted. Immediately the car seesawed. The lads shouted, but Desmond blocked everything, focusing on her whisky-colored eyes. His breath held as both arms poked out. Desmond didn't hesitate. He grabbed them and pulled.

The Rover shifted, screeching and popping, wood splintering as the rope snapped and whiplashed into the car's front. With superhuman effort he held on to her, dragging her body, then her legs from the sedan, the car sucking at her as though determined not to let go. With a grinding noise it finally went over the edge, crashing onto Phelan's lobster boat moored below.

For an instant Desmond teetered on the pier's edge, B.A. in his arms. He had her. With a spinning vertigo, he saw the wreckage of the boat and car beneath them, his feet barely touching the wooden pier, his body and B.A.'s hanging out over it.

In that bizarre instant of time, his life flashed before him. His father's death, the agonizing years of his mother's illness, his brothers crying in hunger, his shame at wearing hand-me-downs. He saw himself cutting B.A.'s picture from the magazine and putting it into his wallet. For a shard in time he vividly saw Sean Montgomerie's funeral, was back in the pew. B.A. sat with her sisters. Never had he seen seven more beautiful women. Only an indefinable air about BarbaraAnne drew his attention. Her chin tilted against grief, she'd sat in the pew, all prim and proper, that mass of long blonde hair in a French braid. Though her sisters were equally stunning, he was unable to take his eyes from B.A. She turned and looked directly at him, making eye contact. Time suspended and the world held its breath as they stared at each other. Odd, disturbing—never in his whole life had he felt so connected to anyone.

Everything telescoped, granting realization that the pain, sorrow and anger was part of the trail leading him to B.A., the one shining certainty in his whole life who loved him with her whole heart.

He swallowed regret that he'd not taken B.A. with him to Ireland, let his mother see the beauty of their love before she died. Maybe she would have changed her mind, understood there was something more important that getting revenge for the past.

He didn't blame his mother. She'd been ill and hadn't gotten treatment for her condition until too late. Over years, she'd worked herself to the bone to keep them together. She'd loved him as much as she could, but too much of her had died when his father did. As he might die if he lost B.A.

B.A. was love, laughter and happiness. She'd save him if he gave her the chance.

She clung to him, shuddering, though not as tightly as he clutched her or trembling as hard. Slowly, the pieces of his life faded and he stood poised on the pier, mystified by why they hadn't fallen. Had the magic of Falgannon reached out to protect them?

His belt jerked. Desmond felt himself pulled back until he was on solid footing. Only then did he risk looking behind him.

Julian grasped Desmond's belt, holding on for dear life. Behind him, Dennis held Julian's belt, then Ian clutched Dennis, Brian held Ian, Wulf, Callum, the Michael's—a chain of dozens of B.A.'s lads. Each was risking harm to save the people they loved.

Yes, the magic of Falgannon had stopped B.A. and him from falling.

"Helluva way to start the morning, Boss. Two cars wrecked, and Ferry isn't too happy," Wulf called out in his booming Viking voice.

Setting a shaky B.A. onto her feet, Desmond squeezed her. "Small price. I was saved."

"Everyone to The Hanged Man to warm up." Shaking his cane, Angus barked, "Either of you do something like this again and *I'll* beat you regularly! I'm too old for nonsense like this."

"Go on, Angus. We need a moment."

"Cedric is waiting to check you over, come on," Angus insisted.

Shaking like a leaf, B.A. stared. "You won't leave, will you, Des?"

He kissed her forehead, afraid he might never let her go. "B.A., I'll never leave you."

He finally started them toward the pub. "It won't be easy." His steps halted and he turned to face her. "You understand I need professional help? The terror this morning burned through some of the nonsense that's screwed me up, but I'm not healed. I still have problems I have to face, find a way to work through them. Can you handle that?"

"Des, I can deal with *anything* as long as you love me."

He pulled her close, laughing and crying at the same time. Reaching into his pocket, he took out the small box and slid the diamond on her finger, "I love you, BarbaraAnne Montgomerie. You're the air that I breathe, the blood in my veins. You're my heart, my soul."

She hardly looked at the ring. "It's about time you told me that, Desmond Mershan."

"I love you, B.A.," he repeated over and over.

"Of course you do, you silly man."

Epilogue

Late March, the following year

"Look out below!" B.A. called, then tossed the scuba tanks over.

Desmond watched them fly from the crenellation, hit and bounce when they landed. "Did you see that?" he asked. "She's a madwoman, I tell you."

Julian arched a black brow. "What set her off this time?"

Desmond shifted the bundle in his arms, rocking it. "She doesn't want me diving again."

"You'd think she'd find a cheaper way to express her feelings," Julian said drolly.

"I'm glad she's giving them the heave-ho when they're empty instead of full." He shifted his tiny black-haired baby to his shoulder to burp her. "Your mum is in a dither, Katlyn, because she's pregnant again. Hormones have been flying warrior's banners the past few days."

"Congratulations." Julian smiled. "Fast work. Katlyn's only three months old."

"Thanks. Happens after a 'dry spell,' Morag tells me."

Desmond eyed his beautiful wife glaring at them. "Speaking of which—have you heard from LynneAnne?"

"She gave me a birthday present."

Baby Katlyn burped, so Desmond went back to rocking her. "What?"

Julian tugged on his diamond earring and pretended to study the renovations to the castle. He exhaled. "If you must know, it was a pair of boxer shorts."

Desmond laughed. "I have a few of those. Got Woody Woodpecker last month."

Julian choked. "Woody Woodpecker? B.A. is a hoot. LynneAnne has the same sense of humor. I got a pirate's skull and crossbones."

"Desmond Mershan, bring that baby up here this instant!" B.A. yelled from the castle roof.

"So it looks like the castle's coming along, B.A. is pregnant again, and I saw your paintings in a New York gallery last month . . ." Julian cut himself off.

"New York?"

"I popped over to confer with the Trident exploration team."

Desmond harped, "New York? And you got a birthday present?"

"Okay. I took the redheaded witch out to supper."

"And?"

"And nothing. I took her to eat. It was my birthday."

"And you only got a pair of shorts?"

Julian switched subjects. "Your design for the oil platforms is gaining worldwide attention, Desmond. Less costly, yet you have so many safeguards built into them."

"I'm proud of the design. Anything to lessen dependency upon the Middle East. Only, I don't want oil from our platforms to end up hurting Falgannon. That's why I've focused on this."

Three couples went riding by on bicycles, laughing and waving. Julian waved back, since Desmond's arms were full.

"How's B.A.'s matchmaking efforts?" he asked.

"She's averaged about one marriage for her lads every

couple months. Not counting Janet and Wulf. And by the way, Janet's expecting."

"Wulf, a papa? Cool, a baby Viking! I loved the house you designed for those two. Energy efficient, yet so in keeping with the isle, warm and full of heart."

B.A. marched down the stairs. Dudley and Annie trailed after her. Three kittens tried their best to follow. Two were gray; one was pudgy, golden and had a little white bib of fur on his chest.

"The island holds its breath, thinking The Cat Nigel will soon be the new terror of the isle," Desmond said to his tiny daughter. "Uh-oh, looks like we're in trouble now, Katlyn. Lucky I cut her a rose from our bush, eh?"

B.A. opened her mouth to fuss, but stopped when he handed her the rose. She smiled at it, then him, love in her eyes. "I told you to put the baby to bed." She leaned over and kissed Julian on the cheek. "Welcome home, *Jules.*"

"You've talked with your sister."

She smirked. "LynneAnne said I should ask how high the skull and crossbones fly these days."

"Your sister's nuts." Julian turned away, looking at the castle. He inquired, closing the topic of LynneAnne, "When will you be able to move in?"

"Maybe for Christmas," she said hopefully.

Desmond shook his head. "Valentine's Day."

She smiled. "Valentine's Days are special on Falgannon. After all, we are the Isle of Love."

Des leaned toward B.A. to kiss her, but paused. Blinking, he saw two figures atop the castle. Iain and Deporadh? A ghostly breeze ruffled his hair, and suddenly he knew B.A. carried twins—a girl and a boy—and what they would name them.

He smiled and kissed her softly. Leaning his forehead against hers, he agreed, "Yes, we are, my love. Yes we are."

DIVINE
MADNESS
MELANIE JACKSON

Down a dirt road, Seraphina Sandoval fled her past. Someone in her position could trust no one—not even the sublime stranger she met on her way.

No, Seraphina could ill afford to trust. When the Dark Man had found her, she'd been someone else, and she had bartered her soul. All good things come to an end, and she had spent centuries on the run. She had ended here: Mexico—an arid land of ancient rites and vampires; and in the arms of a man with a past more bizarre than her own, a man whose eyes vowed joyous oblivion. It would be madness to trust, to believe in a union for the ages, but she had only moments to decide: leave, or take the ride Fate offered. She'd always been one for a ride.

THE SAINT

MELANIE JACKSON

One hundred and sixty years ago Kris Kringle walked the earth spreading the message of love and peace. Then he was kidnapped and given a drug that wiped out his memory, while the goblins hijacked Christmas.

Kris has been found. But he's not what you think. He dislikes the fat caricature the goblins stuck him with. He's the most powerful death fey living, who gave up mortal women because none could complete him. That's why he needs Adora Navarra. Only she can help take back his image and punish the wicked. And only she can complete him....

ATTENTION
BOOK LOVERS!

Can't get enough of your favorite **ROMANCE**?

Call **1-800-481-9191** to:

We accept Visa, MasterCard or Discover®.

LEISURE BOOKS ❤ LOVE SPELL